50

DANGEROUS PASSION

"It's all right, Rachel," Alexandre said softly. "Nothing is going to harm you."

His soothing drawl touched her overwrought nerves and proved an instant salve of comfort.

"Alexandre?"

She was lifted upward until she was once again standing on her own feet, but not released from the circle of his steel strong arms. He held her to him, gently cradled against his chest.

She could feel the warmth of him penetrating through the thin fabric of her robe and gown. His head lowered toward hers. She closed her eyes and felt the soft, trembling touch of his lips brush lightly over her own. The blood within her veins turned suddenly to hot spiraling waves.

Then his lips left hers and slipped to the curve of her jaw, the sensitive flesh just below her ear, and the long, ivory-hued column of her neck. Rachel leaned into him, her head thrown back as his lips moved steadily downward, caressing, until finally they found the small hollow at the base of her throat, and the thin vein that pulsated wildly just below the skin's surface . . .

Praise for Cheryln Jac's NIGHT'S IMMORTAL KISS:

"Lovers of the vampire romance will thoroughly enjoy this latest offering by talented newcomer Cheryln Jac."—*Affaire de Coeur*

"NIGHT'S IMMORTAL KISS is a mesmerizing tale of supernatural love that has a fairy tale ending."—*The Talisman*

"A moody, haunting novel that will grip you to the very last page."—Patricia Simpson, author of *Raven in Amber* and *The Haunting of Brier Rose*

". . . an evocative read in which sultry Southern nights hold the promise of forbidden love and the threat of mind-chilling danger."—author Lynn Turner

PUT SOME FANTASY IN YOUR LIFE –
FANTASTIC ROMANCES FROM PINNACLE

TIME STORM (728, $4.99)
by Rosalyn Alsobrook
Modern-day Pennsylvanian physician JoAnn Griffin only believed what she could feel with her five senses. But when, during a freak storm, a blinding flash of lightning sent her back in time to 1889, JoAnn realized she had somehow crossed the threshold into another century and was now gazing into the smoldering eyes of a startlingly handsome stranger. JoAnn had stumbled through a rip in time . . . and into a love affair so intense, it carried her to a point of no return!

SEA TREASURE (790, $4.50)
by Johanna Hailey
When Michael, a dashing sea captain, is rescued from drowning by a beautiful sea siren – he does not know yet that she's actually a mermaid. But her breathtaking beauty stirred irresistible yearnings in Michael. And soon fate would drive them across the treacherous Caribbean, tossing them on surging tides of passion that transcended two worlds!

ONCE UPON FOREVER (883, $4.99)
by Becky Lee Weyrich
A moonstone necklace and a mysterious diary written over a century ago were Clair Summerland's only clues to her true identity. Two men loved her – one, a dashing civil war hero . . . the other, a daring jet pilot. Now Clair must risk her past and future for a passion that spans two worlds – and a love that is stronger than time itself.

SHADOWS IN TIME (892, $4.50)
by Cherlyn Jac
Driving through the sultry New Orleans night, one moment Tori's car spins out of control; the next she is in a horse-drawn carriage with the handsomest man she has ever seen – who calls her wife -- but whose eyes blaze with fury. Sent back in time one hundred years, Tori is falling in love with the man she is apparently trying to kill. Now she must race against time to change the tragic past and claim her future with the man she will love through all eternity!

Available wherever paperbacks are sold, or order direct from the Publisher. Send cover price plus 50¢ per copy for mailing and handling to Penguin USA, P.O. Box 999, c/o Dept. 17109, Bergenfield, NJ 07621. Residents of New York and Tennessee must include sales tax. DO NOT SEND CASH.

D0424568

DISCARD

PINNACLE BOOKS
WINDSOR PUBLISHING CORP.

PINNACLE BOOKS are published by

Windsor Publishing Corp.
850 Third Avenue
New York, NY 10022

Copyright © 1992 by Cheryl Biggs

All rights reserved. No part of this book may be reproduced in any form or by any means without the prior written consent of the Publisher, excepting brief quotes used in reviews.

If you purchased this book without a cover, you should be aware that this book is stolen property. It was reported as "unsold and destroyed" to the Publisher and neither the Author nor the Publisher has received any payment for this "stripped book."

The P logo Reg U.S. Pat & TM off. Pinnacle is a trademark of Windsor Publishing Corp.

First Printing: August, 1994

Printed in the United States of America

Dedication

This book is dedicated to everyone who has helped and encouraged me along the way,

To the ladies of the group who let me spout off once a week,

And as always, to Jack, who gives me all the inspiration I need to write romance.

NIGHT'S IMMORTAL KISS

by Cheryln Jac

When the soft rays of the moon
envelop the earth
Strange things are said to happen;
Werewolves howl, witches cast spells,
vampires rise from their crypts,
leprechauns dance, and love blooms.
Myths? Legends? Fairy Tales?
Perhaps.
Then again . . . perhaps not.

Prologue

Alexandre tasted the acrid tang of the liquid as it filled his mouth and slid easily down his throat. He dropped his head back to let it rest against the leather covering of the tall wing chair in which he sat. Fire danced within the grate of the fireplace only inches from his outstretched feet and moonlight, soft and golden, shone through the tall windows of the small parlor. The glow of each, fire and moonlight, was the only illumination in the high-ceilinged room.

Alexandre savored the warmth that the liquid created within him, the nightly nourishment settling comfortably in the pit of his stomach, and felt a tickle upon his skin as a thin rivulet of crimson escaped the corner of his lips. Renewed strength swept over him, flowed into every vein and muscle, sparked life into every cell and fiber of his body. Yet even as the juice of life warmed his insides and filled him with renewed vigor, he cursed himself for his weakness, for lacking the courage to end it all. He had tried, time after time, he had tried, but in the end he was never able to do it, and had found no foe who could stand to the task. At the same time that he cursed himself, he also, as he had done hundreds of times, denounced the gods who had created his kind, the hunters of the world, *Les Chasseurs.*

Alexandre closed his eyes and let the silver chalice drop from his fingers to the floor. Only when he felt the soft touch of moonlight on his face, the wind rifling through his dark hair, and the cool mist of the clouds against his flesh, was he happy and truly free of the horror that made up every moment of his existence.

Chapter 1

New Orleans, Louisiana
June, 1994

The cab stopped at the entrance of the long drive that led to *Sans Souci* Plantation and Rachel felt her first shudder of apprehension. The tall iron entry gates that led to the ancient old mansion, almost hidden from view by the drive's curves and overgrowth of brush, hung slightly askew on their hinges. It was obvious with only a glance that the bottoms of the spear-topped bars had long ago sunk into the ground and become firmly implanted in the earth, leaving the gates permanently open. Vines of wild, brilliantly green kudzu ivy wrapped around each of the thin wrought iron rods, and every curve and angle of metal was covered by a thick coat of flaking rust.

Rachel's gaze moved slowly over the scene as her apprehension grew.

A tangle of weeds hugged the bases of the timeworn brick pillars which supported the gates. The white paint that had covered the posts' wooden caps, and the spheres topping them, was gray with age and neglect, the wood cracked and splintered from its long exposure to the elements.

Rachel glanced at the cab driver as he stared at the house and felt her heart miss a beat at the sickly expression that came to his face. He clutched the steering wheel tightly; his knuckles white from the pressure of his grip. Rachel felt another shiver of trepidation and tried to shrug it away. There was nothing to fear. Marc would be only a call away, waiting to help her, to come to her rescue if she needed him.

Unconsciously she slipped a hand beneath the flap of her purse and let her fingers touch the cool metal of the transmitter he had given her. Resnapping the flap, she turned and glanced over her shoulder. Her eyes skimmed the landscape but there was no sign of his car, no hint of his presence.

He's there, she told herself silently. Stop worrying. He's there.

She turned back to look at the curving entry drive. Ancient live oaks framed each side, and their sprawling branches entwined gracefully overhead to form a canopy of green. The awning of leaves blocked out the sun and allowed only a few rays of light to penetrate the tunnel which man had obviously designed, but nature had ultimately created. Trailing shrouds of prickly Spanish moss hung from the gnarled branches, curtains of sheer gray that, from a distance, reminded Rachel of delicately woven lace panels. The drive itself was a patchwork of sunlight and shadow covered by a layer of moss, its surface broken only by the wheel markings of the vehicles which had passed over it. In those areas the crushed white oyster shell that had once been the drive's only pavements, shone through, glowing a brilliant white wherever they were touched by the sun's rays.

Rachel rolled down her window and was instantly assailed by the musky odor that hung in the air, heavy and dank, belying the brightness of the afternoon sun that broke through the thick trees in spots. Suddenly, at the same time, she was assailed by the urge to order the cabbie to turn the car around and take her back to New Orleans. Back to the airport. Back to the jet that had brought her from Baton Rouge.

Stop this, Rachel! she silently admonished herself. You're being silly. The place is neglected and run down. That's all. You've seen dozens like it before. And you've got back-up. Remember that.

She looked back toward the house. A shiver, as light as quicksilver, tripped up her spine and a knot of unreasonable fear coiled tight and burned in her stomach. Something about the place, about the lack of information she'd encountered when trying to research its mysterious and reclusive residents, and the cabbie's obvious fear at even approaching the house, instilled Rachel with the desire to run. To turn around and run from *Sans Souci* as fast as she could. But she couldn't. Rachel's fingernails dug into the car seat. She had to go through with this. She had to find out what had happened to her twin brother, Steven, and this was the last place she knew, anyone knew, that he'd been. And it was this place which, whenever she thought of Steven, pulled at her.

Rachel closed her eyes. The psychic bond between her and her brother, the bond that had always allowed them to communicate without words, albeit in a limited way, had grown stronger with the passing of each mile she'd traveled toward New Orleans.

As an ex-cop, Rachel knew the procedure that followed a missing person report. She'd waited the obligatory time, and the New Orleans police had come up with nothing. She had made her own phone calls, her own inquiries, and had come up with nothing. And then Steven began to call to her. At first she thought it was just because she'd been thinking of him. But then his silent calls for help had become more constant and desperate within her mind. It was then that Rachel had known she had to act, had to do something herself. She'd contacted Marc Dellos, her old partner on the Baton Rouge Police Force, and now a detective with the New Orleans Police Department. After a few minutes of good-natured insistence that she hadn't changed her mind about returning to the force, and reminding him of the two bullets she'd taken in the back, Marc had agreed to help. But then she'd known he would. They'd always been close, and Rachel knew if she ever gave the slightest hint of acceptance, Marc would make a move to turn their friendship into something much more.

Inhaling deeply, and forcing herself to at least appear calm, Rachel tapped the cabbie's shoulder. "Sir, could you please continue on to the house now?"

The driver looked back at her. An uneasy fear glistened in his blue eyes.

"Sir?"

The man turned back toward the steering wheel, took a deep breath, and straightened his shoulders. "Yes, ma'am," he croaked huskily. "To the house." He pushed down on the accelerator and the cab rolled forward.

Rachel felt a sensation of unreality come over her as the car moved into the tunnel of trees. The hot summer air, heavy with humidity, suddenly seemed to turn still. The very quiet was almost spellbinding in its intense lack of sound. No birds chirped or flew between the immense trees. There was no soft buzzing of insects, and no evidence of animals hiding in the foliage. The soft crunch of the car wheels on the moss-covered shells was the only sound that splintered the unearthly calm. Gloom enveloped them.

"You sure you want to go to *Sans Souci*, miss?" the driver asked. He looked at her in the rearview mirror. His tone, as well as his eyes sparked with hope that she would say she'd changed her mind.

Rachel ignored him and, with every nerve in her body suddenly alert, every muscle tensed and taut, leaned toward the window. Steven had been here, was possibly still here. She sensed him, could feel him. That invisible, unexplainable bond tugged at her. Steven had been here. Now she had to find out if he'd ever left.

She peered around the cab driver toward the house, which was slowly growing nearer, since the cabbie was hesitant to drive above crawling speed. At first glance, from just inside of the entry gates, the house, shadowed at each end by ancient live oak trees, had looked white. Now, as they approached Rachel saw that its walls were actually gray, its whitewash having long ago faded and no effort made to refinish it. The mansion was two stories in height, with four dormer windows breaking the sloping line of the roof and attesting to a third floor or attic. Six Corinthian pillars graced the front of the house. These, too, were gray with age, and in some places huge chunks of stucco had fallen away from the colonnades to leave exposed patches of the clay bricks beneath. A boxwood hedge hugged the base of the first floor gallery, but where it wasn't overgrown and straggly, it was dead . . . nothing but a maze of brittle twigs. Cypress shutters adorned each ceiling-high window, eight to each floor. Traces of forest green paint were still visible on some of the shutters' louvered slats, and a delicate wrought iron balustrade wrapped around the second floor gallery, though even at a distance Rachel could detect patches of rust within its curling bars.

"Don't get too many fares want to come here," the cabbie grumbled.

"Oh?" Rachel said.

He nodded. "They practice voodoo here, way I hear it. Real secretive, them Beaumondiers. Curious, you know?" He tapped a finger to his head. "Some say people come here, they don't always leave."

A chill tripped up Rachel's spine.

"If you don't mind my asking, what's a pretty young thing like you doing coming to this place?"

"I'm the Director of the Louisiana Antebellum Preservation Society," Rachel said, and handed him a card. At least that much was the truth. "We like to take an interest in preserving the old homes in the state and this looked like a good prospect." Well, that was the truth, too, it just wasn't the real reason she was at *Sans Souci*.

The man nodded and she turned her attention back to the house. The plantation appeared deserted, but then, from what little she had been able to ascertain about the Beaumondier family in preparation for this *visit*, she wasn't surprised. They were extremely reclusive, with several of their members shunning society completely. But why? she wondered. The Beaumondiers were quite wealthy, at least, they were rumored to be. So, if true, why would they not only live in near total seclusion, but so blatantly neglect their home?

Rachel. Rachel.

"Steven?" she whispered, and cocked her head to one side in an effort to better discern the call that only she could hear. Her fingers curled into fists and her entire body stiffened as she waited. "Steven?" she whispered again.

"We're here," the cabbie said needlessly, as if to reassure himself they'd actually made it.

The taxi stopped before the mansion. Rachel returned her attention to the house. A worn and badly cracked slate path led from the drive to the house and ended at a set of stairs which curved outward on each side to create a fan effect. She could see where mortar had chipped and disappeared from between several of the brick risers, leaving gaping holes in the stairs that led to the first floor gallery. The driver hurried around the car to open her door. Rachel stepped from the cab and brushed a hand over the front of her apricot linen slacks. She knew she should have worn a suit rather than the slacks and matching silk blouse, but the thought of nylons clinging to her legs in this heat and humidity was more than she'd been prepared to bear. She'd been born and raised in Louisiana, but the humidity in Baton Rouge never seemed as thick as that in New Orleans.

She looked back at the cabbie. "Would you wait, please?" she asked. "I understand there's no phone here to call a cab back out when I want to leave."

The man shook his head vehemently and backed away. "No, ma'am. Not here. I ain't waiting here. No, siree. You pay me now, and I'll . . . I'll wait out there." He pointed toward the gates.

"But . . ."

"Out there, lady." He pointed again, jabbing his finger toward the opposite end of the tunnel of trees. "I'll wait for you out there. Not here."

Rachel sighed in frustration and didn't try to hide the frown that marred her forehead. She pulled two twenty dollar bills from her purse. What was it about the Beaumondiers that caused such nervousness in people? She'd had to approach three different cabbies before one had finally consented to drive her here. When she'd mentioned her destination to the first three they'd each practically thrown her back out of their cabs. And this one had only complied reluctantly. Why had they refused? Fear? Rachel mulled that thought over. But if so, of what? Rachel handed the twenties to the cabbie. "I'll give you two more of these if you wait for me."

The man quickly pocketed the money and nodded. "I'll wait." His head jerked toward the gate. "Out there." He bolted back into the cab and slammed the gearshift knob into drive. Bits of shell and moss spewed into the air from beneath the whirling tires as the taxi shot down the shadowed entry drive.

Rachel turned toward the house. She hoped he was telling the truth, but from the look of fear that had been on his face each time he looked at the house, she sincerely doubted he'd be at the gate when she was prepared to leave. Oh, well, it wasn't as if she'd have to walk all the way back to town. Marc would be out there somewhere.

She moved slowly up the walkway and immediately began to feel as if she were being watched, yet when she glanced around she saw no one. Not a curtain moved behind the dust-covered windows, nor did a leaf in the gardens stir or a shadow shift. She climbed the stairs and approached the front door. It was dark oak and heavily carved with the likenesses of fruits, vines and flowers, and here and there the small leering face of an elf or gremlin peered out of the sculptured surface. Rachel tried not to grimace. The door would have been much more appropriate on some old dilapidated castle in the moors, or even gracing a regal English Tudor. She tried to ignore the tiny leering wooden faces that stared at her. A huge fanlight window spread above the door and peer windows framed the massive entry. Rachel, nearly cringing, reached to lift the heavy knocker that was nestled in the center of the door. The once sleek, but now tarnished brass face of a cat, its eyes of glittering onyx, stared back at her as she raised the lever. She rapped it against the mottled plate and heard the sound echo within the house.

The feeling that she was closer to her brother Steven than she had been in weeks grew stronger as she waited.

Several minutes later, having received no response to her knock, she rapped the brass lever again. The door swung open before Rachel had even released the lever and she stepped back, startled.

The man who had answered her knock appeared older than anyone she'd ever seen, and was dressed in a black suit that looked even older than he was. He held the edge of the opened door secure in the grip of one gnarled and bony hand while he stared at her in open appraisal, one white brow cocked haughtily. His gaze traveled over her quickly. "Yes?"

"I'm . . ." She was forced to clear her throat, a bit taken back at his cool and somewhat arrogant manner. "I'm Rachel Domecq," she said. "I have an appointment with Mrs. Yvette Beaumondier."

Understanding flashed into the aged blue eyes that looked down at her. "Ah, yes, the lady from the Preservation Society." He moved back and swung the door open wider in invitation for her to enter.

Rachel stepped into the dimly lit foyer and paused. She found herself forced to blink several times in an effort to accustom her eyes to the intense gloom. A candelabra sat on a marble-topped table to one side of the entry; its tiny flames were the only light in the room. A huge, dramatically curving staircase hugged one wall, but its steps disappeared from sight within the darkness that hung over the outer reaches of the foyer long before the landing was visible.

Instinctively Rachel held her purse a little tighter. The weight of her gun, nestled within the leather folds of her bag, reassured her, even though she hadn't used it since she'd left the police department, and wasn't sure how good her aim would be. She made a mental note to find the time, every week, to get to the practice range after she got back home.

"Please, you will wait in the parlor." The servant indicated a room to her right, its tall double doors of dark and, surprisingly, considering the outside of the house, *polished* oak standing open. "I will inform the madames Beaumondier of your arrival."

Rachel entered the room he indicated and found it not much better illuminated than the foyer. The heavy burgundy-colored damask drapes that adorned each of four ceiling-high windows, were drawn. The only other light came from six etched and frosted crystal sconces of an antique brass chandelier that hung from the ceiling.

A black cat suddenly appeared from beneath one of the drapes. It walked toward Rachel, its head held high, eyes gleaming a brilliant yellowy green, and diamonds embedded within its yellow leather collar sparkling brilliantly as they picked up the light of the flames in the fireplace.

Rachel bent down. "Hi, kitty," she said softly, and extended her hand toward the animal.

It stopped, lips curled back, short hair instantly bristled, and hissed.

Rachel stood. "Well, hello to you, too." She took a seat on a velvet settee, its cloth the same dark hue as the draperies and other furnishings in the room, its trim and legs of intricately carved rosewood. The cat sat primly, and stiffly, just to one side of the fireplace grate and focused its eyes upon her.

She stared at the fire that crackled in the grate of a fireplace made of Italian black marble which seemed only to add to the room's gloominess. Why in the world would anyone want a fire on a day that was at least ninety degrees outside? Not to mention the near-suffocating blanket of humidity that wafted through the air. Rachel moved to a seat farther from the flames and pulled a tissue from her purse to pat at her cheeks.

"Ms. Domecq. It is so good to meet you at last."

Rachel stashed the tissue in her pocket and turned to see a woman enter the room who looked to be in her late thirties. She was dressed in white form-fitting slacks and a white silk blouse. A red scarf was draped around her neck and pinned to one shoulder with an ornate gold and diamond brooch. Rachel felt a sense of mild surprise. The woman, if this was Yvette Beaumondier, was not the tanned blonde bombshell type that Steven normally fell for. California beach bunnies is how Rachel usually referred to his affairs. This woman was no beach bunny, California or elsewhere. She was beautiful, there was no doubt, and sophisticated, but there was a definite air of fragility about her which was intensified by the pale, almost translucent quality of her skin. In contrast, her dark ebony hair was rich and lustrous, falling freely over her shoulders in cascading waves to create a silken shawl of blackness, and her almond-shaped gray eyes, framed by a lush ruche of dark lashes, held slivers of blue that seemed to pick up the light and reflect it a thousand times. Exquisitely painted red lips parted in a smile and she held out a hand.

The cat rose regally to its feet and curled itself affectionately around the woman's ankles.

Rachel saw instantly why her romantic and impulsive twin brother would be captivated by this woman. Her beauty was almost ethereal.

"I am Yvette Beaumondier." She held a hand out toward Rachel. "Welcome to *Sans Souci,* Ms. Domecq. I hope you encountered no trouble finding our home."

Yvette's handshake was firm and strong, belying the aura of delicateness that surrounded her, but her flesh was cold to the touch, the slim fingers that gripped Rachel's like bands of ice pressed to her skin. She looked into Yvette Beaumondier's eyes and found they also held no warmth, in spite of the curved lips and welcoming words.

"Thank you for allowing my visit, Miss Beaumondier." Rachel withdrew her hand from the other woman's grasp. "And for consenting to consider the Preservation Society's proposal about the plantation."

Yvette waved a dismissing hand through the air and moved to stand before the fireplace. "It is time the Beaumondiers joined the twentieth century. We have been stuck in our old ways much too long." She laughed softly. "Of course, we have yet to convince my *grandmere* or brother that designating *Sans Souci* a historic landmark will not bring a herd of tourists with their clicking cameras and curiosity clammering to our door."

The cat meowed.

Yvette bent to pick it up. "And I see you have met Apollyon."

"Yes, she's quite beautiful," Rachel said. Though about as friendly as a statue of marble, she added silently.

"Oh, Ms. Domecq, you've arrived."

Rachel turned to see another woman walk into the room. She had the same fragile air and pale appearance about her as Yvette Beaumondier. Physically the two women looked extremely alike, though Rachel judged Yvette to be at least fifteen to twenty years younger. The older woman swept into the room in a blur of swirling chiffon, midnight blue wisps of fabric that draped from her arms and billowed about her legs as she walked. Her dark hair was piled in a profusion of curls atop her

crown, and wings of silver gray strands swept upward from each temple.

"Welcome to our home, Ms. Domecq. I hope my daughter has been making you comfortable." She clasped Rachel's hand in hers. "I am Marguerite Beaumondier."

Though the words of welcome were warm, Rachel felt a chill in this woman's tone as well. Her fingers also emanated the same iciness that Yvette's had.

Since there was no telephone at *Sans Souci,* Rachel had been forced to communicate with the Beaumondiers by letter and their written words had not only welcomed her visit, but had made them seem eager to receive her. So why did they seem so aloof? The Beaumondiers were one of New Orleans' oldest families and, from what she had learned, nearly its wealthiest. Yet Rachel had discovered that very few people seemed to know them personally. . . . Except for Yvette, who it was rumored, loved to party, especially in some of the city's worst dives.

Rachel chanced a quick glance toward Yvette Beaumondier. Her beauty was stunning and Rachel found it hard to believe the rumors she'd heard about Yvette's choice of entertainment locales. She smiled at Marguerite. "It is a pleasure to meet you, Mrs. Beaumondier. Your home is quite . . ." she searched for an accurate way to put her impressions of *Sans Souci* into vocal description "authentic."

"Yes, there has been little change here over the years, but please, Ms. Domecq, call me Marguerite, and . . ." she nodded toward her daughter, "Yvette. We do not stand on formality here."

"And you should call me Rachel."

Marguerite smiled. "Now, come, you must meet my mother, Catherine. Nothing can be done about *Sans*

Souci without her approval, you understand, and I am forced to confess, she is not in favor of your proposal."

"What proposal?"

All eyes turned toward the entry from the foyer where a woman who looked very much like Yvette Beaumondier, though younger, stood lazing against the doorjamb.

"Suzanne," Marguerite said, "please, come in, dear, and meet our guest."

Suzanne Beaumondier walked into the room, her head held high, shoulders back, an air of great pride fairly emanating from her. [illegible] eyes, darker and more striking than those of the other two women, moved over Rachel in quick assessment, and then returned to stare at Marguerite. Her mane of dark hair had been allowed to flow freely down her back, long strands of blackness that caught the glow of the chandelier's candles and reflected it in a rich lustre of ebony, and served to accentuate both the tiny breadth of her waist and the diaphanous pallor of her skin.

"What proposal, Marguerite?" Suzanne repeated, without looking at Rachel.

"Designating *Sans Souci* a historic landmark," Yvette said. "I told you, remember?"

One dark brow arched upward. "Does Alexandre know what you're doing?" Suzanne asked. She stared pointedly at Marguerite. "Or did you . . ."

"Suzanne, this is our guest, Ms. Rachel Domecq, from the Preservation Society," Marguerite cut in. "Rachel, may I present my other daughter, Suzanne."

Rachel smiled and held out her hand. "I'm pleased to meet you," she said.

Suzanne looked at Rachel's extended hand but did not accept it, or offer her own. "I'm sorry, Ms. Domecq, but I do not agree with my *mother* and *sister* that *Sans Souci* be designated a historic landmark. This," she

waved a hand around to indicate the house, "is our home, not a monument to the ages. And certainly not a tourist attraction, which is exactly what it would become if we accept your proposal." Her gray blue eyes turned glacial.

A deep, raspy meow drew everyone's attention toward the door to the foyer.

"Asmodeus, where have you been?" Suzanne said.

The cat, almost identical to Apollyon, though much bigger and with eyes that sparkled green rather than yellow, pranced toward her merrily. Suzanne scooped him into her arms and then glanced at the others. "If you will all excuse me, I have other things to attend to." She turned without waiting for a reply and left the room. Her hushed footsteps could be heard seconds later as she mounted the wide, curving staircase in the foyer.

"Please, excuse Suzanne," Yvette said. "My sister is young and can be quite rude at times."

Rachel smiled. Suzanne Beaumondier had appeared to be about the same age as she was, twenty-seven, and she felt certain age had nothing to do with either her coolness, or her stance against the Preservation Society's supposed proposal.

Marguerite motioned for Rachel and Yvette to follow her into the foyer.

Rachel looked up at the massive, three-tiered crystal chandelier that hung from the second floor ceiling above and dominated the foyer. "It is a beautiful old house." Or could be, Rachel thought, if someone took some interest in keeping it up. They climbed the same wide staircase Suzanne had just ascended and, at its landing, turned down a hallway lit only by a lone candle set on a side table. Heavy draperies of dark blue velvet trimmed with gold silk fringe had been pulled across a tall window at the opposite end of the hall.

"It's a dump," Yvette said bluntly.

Rachel glanced at the woman in surprise.

"What Yvette means, Rachel," Marguerite said, "is that she and I would much rather live in France, where our family originated, than remain here in New Orleans, but, unfortunately, my mother will not hear of it."

They paused before a tall door. "This is my mother's room. She rarely leaves it anymore so we must come to her. We'll leave you alone to visit with her."

Rachel opened her mouth to object, not certain she wanted her first encounter with Catherine Beaumondier to be just the two of them, but Marguerite continued.

"She's expecting you. Tea will be served in the parlor when you are finished talking with *Maman.*"

"Thank you." Resigned, Rachel stepped over the threshold as Marguerite opened the door for her. She hadn't really come here to meet an aging matriarch who hibernated in her room. Then again she didn't know where she might find a clue as to what had happened to Steven, and this was as good a place to start looking as any.

She heard the door close softly behind her.

"Come in, come in," someone barked from across the room. "Don't just stand there hugging the door like some frightened little mouse." The voice was high-pitched and ragged, with a definite trace of impatience in the tone. An old woman who looked to be in her eighties, but held herself as regal as a queen, shuffled out from behind a tall pink dressing screen that stood in one corner. She moved toward Rachel, immediately linked arms with her and urged her toward one of the white wicker chairs that encircled a glass-topped table near a tall window. Beneath voluminous folds of sheer, pink lace panels, heavy draperies had been pulled across the window to block out the sun. The only light came from several oil lanterns, their shades of pink crystal producing a rosy hue over the room which, combined with the curtains and other frills of embellishment, created an atmosphere of cotton candy fluff.

Rachel was amazed. The old woman's room was a drastic contrast to the decor in the rest of the house, at least what she'd seen of it.

"Sit down, young woman. Sit down," the old lady ordered.

Rachel sat in one of the wicker chairs and got her first really good look at Catherine Beaumondier. She had calculated the matriarch of the Beaumondiers to be in her eighties. She'd been wrong. A hundred or even a hundred and twenty would be a more accurate guess.

Catherine Beaumondier was reed thin, almost skeletal. Her thick white hair, pulled into a chignon at her nape, formed a halo around a face that, even weathered and extremely creased with age, showed signs of a former beauty that Rachel sensed must have been breathtaking.

Catherine wrapped a gnarled hand around a tapestry cord that hung from the ceiling in a corner of the room, gave it a few tugs, and then shuffled over to the table and sat down. Her gray blue eyes bore into Rachel's. "I'm Catherine Beaumondier," she said needlessly, though quite proudly. "Catherine Ann Mornay Beaumondier. My husband's name was Deneuxe, but I don't use it. Never did. We keep the Beaumondier name." She laughed, the sound seeming at once older than time itself, and touched with youth and energy. "I understand that's the fashion now, for young ladies to keep their own family's name." She shook her head. "Guess we were a bit ahead of our time."

"Mrs. Beaumondier, about the house . . ." Rachel began.

"Yes, the house. You want to call it a historic landmark. Fix it up. That right?"

Rachel nodded. That's what she had wired them. A lie, but the only way, she knew, that she could gain access to *Sans Souci* and find out what had happened to her brother. Steven had told her during the last phone call that he had fallen in love with Yvette Beaumondier, yet when the police questioned her, Yvette claimed never to have heard of Steven Ligere. Then when confronted with the bartender's statement that she had flirted with Steven in his bar, Yvette claimed to remember him, but said she'd never seen him again after that night.

Utilizing some of the contacts she'd made while on the force in Baton Rouge, Rachel had managed to discover that several other men had disappeared from New Orleans without a trace in the last few years. They had all been tourists traveling alone, just like her brother, though Steven had actually been working, taking the last few shots for his new travelog book. All of the missing men had last been seen in a Bourbon Street bar, although not necessarily the same one that Steven had been in. Rachel found the series of disappearances strange and intriguing, even if the New Orleans Police did not.

"Call it a historic landmark if you want," Catherine said, and shrugged, "but fix it up . . . no." She shook her head and her eyes turned dark and hard. She leaned forward across the table, toward Rachel. "I want this house to rot, Ms. Domecq. I want it to fall to the ground and decay until there is nothing left of it. Maybe then, when that happens, the Beaumondiers will have finally found a way to be free." She sat back and crossed thin, bony arms across her waist. "Maybe."

Rachel felt a moment of disquiet. "But, Mrs. Beaumondier . . ."

Just then the same gangly, white-haired man who had opened the front door to her knock appeared beside them. Startled, Rachel jumped in her seat. His entry had been so quiet she had not heard him approach, let alone enter the room. He set a silver serving tray onto the table, placed a cup before each woman and poured tea into each one. When finished he looked at Catherine and, at a nod from her, he turned and walked back toward the door.

"Hanson, find my grandson and tell him to come in here, would you please?" She turned back to Rachel and smiled. "You'll like Alexandre."

Before Rachel could respond, the door opened again and she heard heavy footsteps move from the hardwood floor of the hallway to the thickly woven floral carpet that covered the floor of Catherine's bedchamber. Rachel peered over her shoulder and felt her heart practically thud to a stop.

"You wanted me, *grandmere?*" Alexandre Beaumondier paused a mere few yards from the table and stared at Rachel. "Danielle?" he murmured, the word little more than a soft gasp. His face, tanned to a burnished bronze, seemed to momentarily lose some of its rich color and his brows, like the elegantly arched wings of a raven, nettled together in a frown over eyes that had turned as dark as a winter's midnight storm.

"I want you to meet Ms. Rachel Domecq, Alexandre," Catherine said. While she stared at him, assessing his reaction, the fingers of one hand held the thin string of a teabag and steadily lowered and raised it within her cup. "She's the one from the Preservation Society I told you about."

He nodded at his grandmother's words, but his gaze continued to bore into Rachel, as if in an attempt to delve past the physical plane of her existence and uncover the spirit that made up her being, the essence of her life and emotions.

"She'll need a tour of the house and grounds, Alexandre." Catherine's tone was one of definite dismissal, which Alexandre ignored.

Gathering his composure, he reached out and took one of Rachel's hands in his. "The pleasure is all mine, Ms. Domecq." The deep timber of his voice was like a caress of satin to her flesh. His eyes, the inky color of polished gun metal, splintered with shafts of blue, held her gaze pinioned as he lifted her hand to his lips.

Rachel felt mesmerized, unable to breathe or look away, to formulate thought or reply. All she could do was stare into his eyes—eyes embedded within a face of aristocratic curves and ridges of strength, eyes so fathomless, so dark, that they seemed able to bare her soul to his scrutiny and leave her with no will of her own. The fingers that held hers tightened their clasp slightly, his eyes held hers pinioned, his captive, his prisoner, and Rachel felt the world slowly slip away. Reality abruptly spun away in a blur, dissipating into a mist of gray fog.

Suddenly she saw a castle, its tall turrets spiraling into the clouds, its rock walls blending with the craggy mountainside upon which it was built. Before the tall oak doors that made up the citadel's entry, hundreds of people were gathered, jeering, the torches they held high over their heads casting an eerie glow into the black night. The gleam of the flames grew to turn the surrounding fog orange and the sky a bright yellow, and high above the screaming mob, in a small window of the turret, she saw his face, etched with sorrow and some anger, as he looked down on the crowd.

Then he was gone and the castle gave way to an open sea, miles and miles of endless blue that blended earth with sky, a rolling horizon that slowly evolved into a lush tropical paradise. An infinite stretch of bayou spread out before her, a dark green richness of ferns and ancient oaks, of majestic pines and giant cypress with their bulbous trunks submerged in black, motionless waters. Then the thick swampland slowly faded, and a city emerged in its place, stuccoed walls of pastel, tiled roofs, arched doorways and shuttered windows. A man in thigh-high black boots and a hip-length brocade vest swaggered into view, a bejeweled dagger tucked into his sashed waistband, a wide-brimmed hat adorned with the colorful plumage of exotic birds set jauntily on his head, and curls of long, dark hair draped across his broad shoulders. He turned, and she saw that it was again Alexandre Beaumondier.

Rachel reached out toward him, and as she did, his image began to fade. The city disappeared. In its place, a wide field of golden grass took shape, a thick copse of trees at its every border. A dozen men ran from the shadowy depths of the foliage into the open meadow, their gray uniforms with butternut cord trim, threadbare and ragged. They held their sabres and muskets at the ready, racing toward their enemy with pride and determination. A death-defying yell rang in her ears as it burst from their lips. Men in dark blue uniforms emerged from the opposite grove of trees, their swords drawn and raised. The morning sun glistened off the upheld blades to create a radiant arc of color. She saw Alexandre's hat fly from his head, saw him raise his sword high and race toward the enemy, toward certain death.

A scream split through Rachel, bloodchilling, tearing at her nerves as, without warning, the picture began to swirl madly and turned into a blaze of light that gave way instantly to a depthless void of blackness, an abyss

of cimmerian darkness without end. She felt herself falling, spiraling into that bottomless pit, and reached out
to anyone who could save her.

Chapter 2

Alexandre caught Rachel in his arms as she slid from the chair.

"How?" he asked, staring at his grandmother. "How can she look so much like Danielle?"

Catherine shrugged and continued to steadily dunk and lift the teabag. "Coincidence," she said softly. A twinkle of slyness sparked in her old eyes. "Or perhaps fate."

Alexandre ignored his grandmother's statement as he lifted Rachel to his chest and rose to his feet. "I'll take care of her, *grandmere.*"

"I thought you would." She hurriedly erased the smile that had curved her lips and allowed her eyelids to flutter closed in order to conceal the satisfaction she knew lit her eyes at the caring she'd heard in his tone. Perhaps, she thought, there was still hope for Alexandre, but she must not let on to the others what she sensed, or even to Alexandre himself.

Turning on his heel, Alexandre carried Rachel from his grandmother's room. As she lay against him, her head settled upon his shoulder, the clean, sweet smell of her hair and the jasmine essence of her perfume teased his senses. Stolidly he gathered the edges of the emotional shroud he had wrapped around himself so long ago, in defense of both the world and his own feelings, and pulled them tighter together. She wasn't Danielle, he told himself. She was a stranger, a woman who had come to *Sans Souci* merely to convince them their home had historic value. He didn't know her, wouldn't know her, and didn't feel anything for her. Nothing.

Halfway down the hall he paused, then, with an almost indiscernible squaring of his shoulders, he continued toward the tall, draped window. At the last door on the left he stopped and with a forceful swing of his foot, kicked it open. Alexandre looked into the room, every muscle in his body taut with tension, every nerve cell charged with anxiety and dread. The mustiness of the long-closed room wafted out to assail and engulf him in even more unwanted memories, reviving the pain and anguish he had tried so desperately to put behind him, the feeling of loss he had lived with for so long.

Ages ago he had sworn never again to step foot in this room . . . yet here he was, once more. But then he'd had no choice but to bring her here. The other bedchambers were those of the family, and this one belonged to her. It always had. Alexandre looked down at her face, a face he had thought never to see again. Taking a deep breath he stepped over the threshold and pushed the door shut with the wedged heel of his boot. He walked across the room and, pulling back the dusty bedspread, laid Rachel down in the center of the huge, ornately carved canopy bed, then sat on the edge of the mattress and looked idly about at their surroundings. Every piece of furniture in the room, from the tall, scallop-topped armoire set against one wall, the twin settees that were set before the fireplace, the huge poster bed with its velvet and lace coverlet and canopy, to the elegantly carved writing desk by the windows, were of delicate cherrywood, their paddings covered with tapestry of pale blue and ivory. The draperies, drawn closed across the tall jib-doored windows, were of the same color and damask fabric, and the ivory rug that covered the floor had a bouquet of large pink and blue cabbage roses amid a blanket of green vines woven into its center.

Alexandre sighed. Not one detail of this bedchamber had left his memory in all the years since she'd been gone.

He rose and moved to the window, grabbed a panel of drapery in each hand, and pulled the curtains aside. Bright rays of afternoon sunlight streamed through the dust-covered windows, bathed Alexandre in their warmth, and caressed the flesh that once had shriveled and burned at their touch. Sunbeams spread throughout the interior of the room for the first time in over two centuries, glistening off the dusty furniture and reflecting from the cheval mirror that stood in one corner. Alexandre looked back at her. Over two hundred years, and yet it was as if the last time he had seen her had been only yesterday.

No, not her, he reminded himself sternly. Danielle. He looked back at Rachel. Danielle, not her.

Rachel moaned and Alexandre returned to the side of the bed to stare down at her. Thick waves of auburn hair framed her face and spread across the snow white pillow case, the lustrous strands were a brilliant accent to the apricot hue of her blouse and slacks and a soft compliment to the magnolia cast of her skin. Her lips were full, her nose delicate and slightly upturned. Beneath finely arched brows her eyelids were closed over blue eyes that reminded Alexandre of the endless sea his family had traveled across so many years before when forced from their home in France.

Alexandre sighed and closed his own eyes in an effort

to block out the image he had thought never again to see. He knew Rachel was in no danger, not like Danielle had been. She had merely fainted, yet even knowing this, he couldn't bring himself to leave her. Not just yet, he thought. Reason and logic told him she was not Danielle, but reason and logic were having a hard time overruling the conflicting emotions her appearance had ignited within him.

He'd thought the pain of Danielle's rejection long-healed, memory of her faded and near forgotten, but now . . . he felt a knot of emotion catch in his throat and opened his eyes to look down at Rachel . . . he knew he'd been wrong.

Rachel stirred, rolling onto her side, and her eyes fluttered open. She took a deep breath and choked on the mustiness that clung to the air in the room. Memory of where she was and what had happened momentarily escaped her. She rolled onto her back again and pushed herself onto her elbows, then, squinting into the bright sunlight, saw the tall silhouette of a man standing nearby. Fear seized her abruptly. Her first impulse was to scream and fling herself to the opposite side of the bed from which he stood. Instead, her body froze and her fingers clutched at the sheet beneath her.

Seeing her alarm, Alexandre moved to sit on the edge of the mattress. "You're all right," he said softly. "There's nothing to fear." His hand reached toward her and, with a touch so gentle as to be nearly nonexistent, traced the curve of her cheeks with the tips of his fingers.

Rachel stared up at him and a small moan, unexpected and unbidden, escaped her lips. Waves of desire swept through her body as her flesh burned at his touch and her passions erupted in a swirl of need. Suddenly all she wanted was to feel his arms around her, to know the crushing strength of his embrace and the ravishing sweet torture of his lips on hers. She leaned toward him, seeking his touch, needing his warmth.

Alexandre saw what was happening to her and steeled himself against it. Though everything in him hungered to pull her up against his chest, to take what she was so mindlessly offering, he remained still, fighting his desires. He did not want this. He would not go through that torment again. In sudden anger, he grasped Rachel's arms and his fingers wrapped around her slender wrists in a crushing, cruel grip.

"Stop this! Rachel, do you hear me?" he growled harshly. "Rachel Domecq. Stop this . . . now!"

His hard voice jerked her from the languid haze that had encompassed her mind and instantly cooled the unexplainable ardor that had overwhelmed her. She pulled away from him and pressed herself against the bed's headboard. An unreasonable fear lodged in the back of her throat, impeding her voice. "What . . . what happened?"

Alexandre stood and softened his tone. "You fainted. I carried you here and remained so that you would not wake up alone in a strange room."

Rachel felt slightly nauseous and overly warm, as if the desires that had so unreasonably fired her blood at his touch were not yet completely extinguished. She couldn't bring herself to look at him. "Could . . . could I have some water, please?" Pushing up, she leaned her back against the headboard and, closing her eyes, dropped her head into her cupped hands. Every cell in her body felt drained of its energy; her strength unexplainably expended.

"Certainly," Alexandre said. "I'll return in a moment." He walked from the room.

Rachel heard the click of the latch as the door closed

behind him and looked up. What in God's name was the matter with her? She'd been about to seduce him.

Her mind reeled in wonder and confusion as her skin warmed with embarrassment. And she had never fainted before. Had never even come close. Her purse! She grappled about the bed and then spotted it lying beside her. Unzipping the large bag, she reached inside and immediately breathed a sigh of relief as her fingers curled around the smooth wooden handle of the gun. Moving her hand to another pocket she located the tiny radio transmitter Marc had given her in case she needed to get in touch with him.

She held it before her lips. "Marc?" she whispered. "Marc, are you there?"

The transmitter exuded a second of static and then she heard his voice. "Yeah, Rae, I'm here. Are you all right?"

She sighed in relief. All right? Only if having delusions was considered all right. "I'm fine," she fibbed, in direct contrast to her thoughts. "Just checking in."

Rachel turned off the transmitter, dropped it back into its pocket, rezipped the bag and lay back against the pillow. Memory of what had happened before she fainted filled her mind. She'd looked into Alexandre Beaumondier's eyes and saw . . . what? Rachel felt a surge of impatience with herself. Visions? she thought with disgust. Other times? Other places?

That was ridiculous. Anger with herself overrode the fear that had left her feeling helpless, an emotion she was unused to experiencing. She had never been a weak woman, had never before given in to uncertainty. Of her and Steven, she was the strong one, the one who always knew what to do, the one who always challenged, fought, and rescued. Steven was the bonvivant, the devil-may-care wanderer, the impulsive one.

Rachel smiled wistfully. Wasn't it the man who was supposed to be Sir Gallahad? Somehow, between her and her brother, the roles were reversed. She was usually the one charging to his rescue, bailing him out of trouble, financially, emotionally, and now maybe even physically.

Visions? she thought again. How could she have looked into Alexandre's eyes and seen other times? People had tried to convince her that the silent communication that she shared with Steven was a psychic one, but Rachel had always denied that. She didn't believe in the supernatural, the paranormal, or any other kind of abnormal. What she and Steven shared was a biological linking because they were twins. They'd shared the same seed and the same womb. There was a physical bond between them. Special, yes, but that was all. Period.

She swung her legs to the edge of the high bed and slipped to the floor. The heels of her pumps made no sound on the carpet as she slowly made her way around the room, looking at each piece of furniture, running her fingers over the mantel of the fireplace, looking at herself in the tall cheval mirror that stood near the armoire. On the top tier of an etagere set in one corner of the room was the white porcelain figurine of a horse and foal lying in a field of golden grass. Rachel felt a surge of warmth sweep over her as she stared at the delicate statuette. Without hesitation she lifted it, knowing exactly what to do, turned the little knob that was disguised as a porcelain flower and set just behind the horse. A soft, chiming melody instantly began to echo from within the delicate figurine. Rachel set it back on the shelf, turned toward a rose and lemonwood desk nearby, and paused. She looked back at the statuette and her heart suddenly began to pound against her breast in crashing, frantic thumps. How had she known that it was a music box? And how had she known the flower was its key?

Rachel stared at the statuette as if it should provide her the answer. "Oh, this is silly. I saw the knob, that's all," she mumbled. But the words rang hollow. Somehow, unconsciously, she'd known the flower was the key even before she had lifted the statuette from the shelf. And what's more she'd known exactly what tune it would play. Her hands began to tremble and her legs felt suddenly weak. She settled into one of the blue settees before the fireplace and sank back against its soft cushion.

"I have your water," Alexandre said.

Rachel jumped and barely managed to arrest the scream that threatened to rip from her throat at his sudden appearance. She hadn't heard him enter, hadn't heard him walk across the room to where she sat, yet he stood only inches from the side of her chair. Taking a moment to settle her shattered nerves and quiet the trembling in her fingers, she merely stared up at the glass he held in his hand.

"Your water," he said again.

She took the glass from his hand. "Thank you."

Alexandre moved to stand at the fireplace, resting one arm along its mantelpiece and propping a foot atop the copper hearth rail. "If you feel up to it in a while, I'll show you around the house and grounds, as my grandmother requested."

Rachel nodded and took a sip of the cool water. She looked around the room, in every direction, at every piece of furniture, but not at Alexandre. She wasn't ready to peer into those night dark eyes again. Not yet. His words had been cool, his posture stiff, but there was something about him, some undefinable intensity, that unnerved her. Her gaze paused at the silver glimmer of mirror that was set into the tall door of the armoire. It sat against the opposite wall and gave a clear reflection of the entire room, including Rachel on the settee . . . but not of Alexandre standing at the fireplace.

Where had he gone? She whirled around. He was still there, standing just as he had a few seconds before—one arm resting on the mantel, his foot propped on the fireplace fender.

Rachel trembled in confusion. Why couldn't she see his reflection in the mirror? She glanced back at the silver glass. Again she saw the room, saw herself, and no trace of Alexandre.

She turned back to him, but he had moved slightly, toward one end of the mantel. She breathed a sigh of relief and admonished herself for being so silly. He had moved, that was all. Obviously before she'd even looked in the mirror the first time, she just hadn't realized it.

Her eyes raked over him now, taking in the way his broad shoulders were like two mountainous planes, the wall of chest only barely concealed by the sheer white threads of his silk shirt, and the long, obviously well-honed arms that were hidden beneath voluminous sleeves. Her gaze dropped lower. Slim hips and lean legs were encased within black slacks that hugged his form. Embarrassed by her blatant assessment of him, Rachel forced her eyes upward, but he wasn't looking at her. Instead, he seemed to be staring at a small, framed petit-point on the mantel.

Alexandre's face was in profile to her, his expression one of deep thought and, relaxing somewhat, Rachel continued her observation of him. The soft, blue black strands of his hair glistened in the spray of sunlight that teemed into the room, a blanket of velvet awaiting a caressing touch. She forced herself to turn away at the disturbing thought, but within seconds lost the struggle to keep her eyes averted and looked back. His features were aristocratic and strong, accentuating the sense of masculine virility and raw power that seemed to emanate from and around him. He reminded her at once of the noble elegance of an ancient Greek God, the rugged savageness of a Plains Indian, the exotic splendor of an Inca ruler, and the conquering darkness of the Spanish conquistadors.

She glanced back toward the mirror, again seeing her own reflection, but not his. She saw the fireplace, the mantel, even the small petit-point he stared at . . . but not Alexandre. A shiver of fear, of trepidation of the unreasonable, the impossible, snaked its way up her spine.

As if he felt her eyes upon him, Alexandre turned. Their gazes met, midnight gray fusing with ocean blue, holding, conveying a message, establishing a link, structuring a bond that neither was able to deny, nor willing to admit.

Rachel started and tried to look away, but it was too late, and impossible. His gaze held hers unmercilessly, and again she felt the magnetic pull she had experienced upon their first meeting, and the sense of timelessness that had come with it. She tried to fight against it, tried to turn away from him, and found herself powerless to do so.

"Are you ready now?" Alexandre asked. His gaze dropped away from hers.

The spell shattered and Rachel rose hastily, if unsteadily, to her feet, both embarrassed to have been caught watching him, and confused at the captivation that engulfed her every time she looked into his eyes. He was a stranger, she told herself. A stranger. And yet, even when she said the words in her mind, they felt wrong. What was there about Alexandre Beaumondier that drew her so? That made her feel as if she already knew him. Really knew him.

"Yes, of course," she said, struggling to maintain her composure. She straightened the collar of her tailored blouse, slipped the strap of the eelskin handbag over her shoulder, and moved to precede Alexandre from the room as he held the door open for her.

She brushed past him, wanting to reach out and touch him, yet forcing her hands to remain at her sides. The scent of dogwood, mingled with a hint of muskiness, emanated from him and conjured images of dark forests and rich earth in Rachel's mind. It was an alluring, yet strange fragrance and one she knew she had never experienced before, nor would ever forget.

"Most of the rooms on this floor are used by the family," Alexandre said as they walked down the long hallway toward the stairs. "And one is Hanson's, of course."

Rachel nodded. "Was that the guest room you carried me to?" The moment the words passed her lips she knew, unexplainably, the answer to her own question.

"No, that was . . . that room hasn't been used in years. It used to be considered a guest room, but we have not had guests at *Sans Souci* in a very long time."

Rachel quickly glanced at Alexandre but the dim light of the expansive hallway left his face in shadow, a mask of darkness that hid any emotion which might be in his eyes. If the thick layer of dust she'd noticed in the room was any indication, she could believe his statement. "I understand, Mr. Beaumondier, that your family lives a rather . . ." she searched for a delicate way to voice what she had heard, "*quiet* life."

They stopped at the landing. He stared down at her for several long seconds and Rachel was of the distinct impression he was trying to make up his mind about her. "Call me Alexandre," he said, finally. "And if you do not mind, I will call you Rachel. Formality is not required here."

She nodded and he continued.

"As to our lifestyle, yes, we do live what you would refer to as a quiet life. Most would call it reclusive."

Rachel's left brow soared slightly at his use of the description she had tried to avoid.

"Occasionally Yvette feels the need to socialize, but the rest of us choose to remain apart from such things."

"Such social isolation is a rare thing today," Rachel said. "Especially for a man such as yourself, and a woman as beautiful as your sister, Suzanne."

Again Alexandre paused and looked down at her for several long seconds before answering. His gaze raked over her blatantly, scrutinizing, assessing, measuring.

Rachel felt a cold chill sweep across her skin.

When he finally spoke, there was the slightest hint of a hard edge to his tone. "We prefer seclusion and privacy. In truth, it has been a way of life in our family for generations, and most likely will continue to be."

His last comment startled and puzzled her, but Rachel refrained from questioning him further about it. The pitch of his voice left no doubt in her mind that the subject was not open for discussion or explanation. She decided to try another topic. "There must be many fascinating and unusual stories surrounding this old house."

"Such as voodoo gatherings? Sacrifices being conducted in the bayous?" He moved to stand at the railing that bordered the landing and looked down into the foyer.

Rachel laughed lightly to cover the nervousness his words had instilled within her. "I'm sorry, Alexandre, those are two rumors I *hadn't* heard. But they do sound fascinating."

He turned toward the stairs, looked back at Rachel, and extended his arm to her. "Yes, I guess I can see how if you're not the one embroiled within the center of the rumors, they could sound fascinating."

She slipped her hand around his bent elbow, laid it on his forearm, and instantly wished she hadn't. The heat of his flesh seared through the delicate silk weave of his shirtsleeve to hold her fingers, wrap around them, and penetrate, turning her blood to a fervent conflagration that left her weak from its severity. Rachel gripped the mahogany banister with her other hand, both to conceal her hand's trembling and to steady herself.

Alexandre looked down at Rachel, his features drawn in concern. "Are you all right?"

She took a deep breath in an effort to regain her poise. It helped, but did not entirely eradicate the churnings of emotion that were playing havoc within her body. Rachel closed her eyes. What was it about Alexandre that sent her into a physical tailspin every time he came near? This had never happened before with any of the men she had dated, or even the few she'd been involved with. And she didn't want it to happen with Alexandre Beaumondier.

"Rachel? Perhaps you should lie down a while longer."

"No, I . . ." She tightened her grip on the banister and looked up at him. The last thing she wanted was to spend her time at *Sans Souci* lazing about. She needed to see the plantation and get some answers. Whatever had happened to Steven, it had something to do with this place, she felt certain of that. "No, thank you, I'm fine. Just a little weak, I guess, from my fainting." She laughed nervously. "I really don't know what's wrong with me. I've never fainted before. Ever."

For the next half hour, Alexandre escorted Rachel through the old house, showing her the double parlors, half of which she'd already seen, the music room, his study, the dining room, ballroom and warming kitchen. Nowhere did she feel a sense of Steven. If he was still at *Sans Souci,* he was not in the house, and if her impressions were right, he never had been.

Her mind was spinning with questions as to what to do next when her attention was pulled back to Alexandre.

"We still follow the antebellum custom of meals being prepared in the cookhouse. Ours is a few dozen yards to the rear of the main house. As I'm sure you're aware, because of your job, in times' past the prepared food was brought in and kept in the warming kitchen until it was time to serve."

Rachel nodded.

"Hanson rarely uses the warming kitchen, what with only the family here to feed."

"I've approved the restoration of several plantations in the state whose cookhouses were still standing, though far from functionable," Rachel said. "Could I see yours?" She wanted, needed, to see everything on the plantation.

"If you wish." Alexandre led her through the warming kitchen and out onto the wide first floor gallery. Several dozen yards from the gallery steps a small brick cottage stood between two giant live oak trees, its roof covered by shingles, its window shutters secured open and badly in need of paint.

Though it was in no better repair than the other buildings of the plantation, time and neglect had helped the small brick building appear quaint, rather than turning it into a picture of cold decay, as it had done to the main house. Anxious to see inside, Rachel crossed the broad expanse of weed-choked lawn that grew before the cottage. She paused at the building's closed door, its plank surface having long ago lost whatever finish had covered it. Gripping the simple wrought iron latch that was the door's handle, she pushed it open and stepped inside just as Alexandre moved toward her. "I hope you don't mind?" She knew she should have waited for him, should have asked his permission before entering, but for some reason she'd been afraid he'd say no, and she wanted to see inside, *had* to see inside.

He shook his head and followed her into the small building. The interior was one large room, its only light was that from the two small windows that framed the door. Since Alexandre had stated that the cookhouse was in use Rachel had expected the interior to be a modern kitchen, a utilitarian room designed for the efficiency of preparing meals. What she saw was practically archaic. Antique, at best. Instead of a refrigerator, there was a pine ice chest, the type she'd seen in museums. There was no stove, only a huge kettle hanging from a hook within the fireplace, and the sink actually had a pump rather than handles and faucets. She moved toward a drysink set against one wall and stopped. Her nose wrinkled in distaste. The carcasses of two white rabbits lay on the drainboard, their heads hanging over the ledge. Rachel saw that their throats had been slit, and a small lake of blood now filled the shallow copper drysink.

She turned to Alexandre and asked in a tone of disbelief, "Someone really still cooks in here?"

For the first time since she'd met him, Rachel saw Alexandre smile. It transformed him, banished the dark brooding aura that he seemed shrouded within, and dissolved the edge of anger that he carried like a defensive weapon. For just the briefest of seconds the somber eyes glowed with warmth and life, and Rachel saw a suggestion of the real man who dwelt beneath the cool facade. "Yes, Hanson prepares all our meals here," he said, pulling her from her reverie.

"But, it's so . . ."

"Old?" Alexandre provided teasingly.

Rachel didn't answer, suddenly embarrassed at her criticism.

"Hanson likes it this way," Alexandre said. "The cookhouse has been his own private domain for many years, and I'm sure if he wanted it changed or modernized he would say so and it would be done."

"Oh, of course." Rachel felt as if she had just been politely reprimanded for sticking her nose where it didn't belong. She stepped from the cookhouse and back into the bright sunlight of the late afternoon. Its warmth washed over her, and the heavy moisture that hung in the air touched her skin and left it feeling as if she'd just rubbed a coating of hand cream over it.

Behind her Alexandre closed the door to the cookhouse.

"What are those?" she asked, pointing toward several other buildings.

They began to walk toward them. "The building that looks like a miniature of the main house is the *garconniere,*" Alexandre said. "As I'm sure you know, the *garconniere* was a suite of rooms once used for male guests. It's my home now."

"Your home?" His comment had surprised her. "But I thought, I mean . . . I'm sorry, it's really none of my business. I just assumed you lived in the main house."

"I live my life somewhat differently from the others of my family."

The comment brought forth a thought Rachel had yet to ponder—the stark differences between Alexandre and the Beaumondier women. While his flesh was bronzed and golden, theirs was pale, almost colorless in its whiteness. Alexandre exuded an aura of strength, power and virility. The Beaumondier women appeared fragile and delicate, though only physically. Their strong personalities, evident the moment they spoke, left little doubt that they were anything but fragile and delicate. She looked at Alexandre again. He seemed comfortable in the sunlight, as he should, she thought, but the others, the women, kept the drapes drawn. She remembered Marguerite, while in the parlor, giving a wide berth to one of the tall windows whose draperies had slipped apart slightly and allowed a pencil thin beam of light to penetrate the room. Rachel frowned. And, now that she thought of it, in the little time she had been around them, all of the women seemed to have made a point of staying well away from the windows.

She frowned. Did the Beaumondier women suffer from some type of disease that denied them sunlight? She had heard of people like that, but had never met any.

With a hand at her elbow, Alexandre steered her along a narrow path, away from the *garconniere.* "That small structure over there," he pointed to what looked like a Victorian gazebo which was in the process of falling down, "was once the *pigionniere,* and beyond it is the carriage house."

"Are any of your slave cabins still standing?" Rachel asked, not certain why she'd voiced the question. It was one she usually asked when considering one of the plantations for a grant toward restoration, but no one was truly considering *Sans Souci* for refurbishing. Though a slave cabin might be a perfect place to keep someone prisoner.

The thought startled her. Prisoner. Why had she thought that? What earthly reason would anyone have for keeping her brother prisoner? It wasn't as if they could demand a huge ransom from Rachel for his safe return. She didn't have that kind of money, or anything else a kidnapper might want. A car, several years old, a condo, nice but not luxurious, a few stocks and bonds, a comfortable investment, and her job. That's all she had.

"A few," Alexandre said, breaking into her thoughts. "When my family kept slaves," he said, "in the old days, the house servants had cabins made of brick. Those remain intact, though crumbling. The wooden ones that were home to the field hands have long since fallen or been torn down. There is a mill on the plantation, a pumphouse, and a few barns and storage sheds here and there, but most are near collapse."

"That's too bad." Rachel glanced at him from the corner of her eye. "Perhaps some could be saved and restored."

"We have no use of them. They've outlived their time as it is, like so many other things around here." A shadow passed over his eyes, turning the gray blue to dark, and he looked away, staring out at the landscape, as if searching for something on the horizon only he could see.

They approached the carriage house.

"Could we look inside?" Rachel asked, but she wasn't sure whether the question came from the analytical part of her thoughts that always had the Preservation Society and its interests in mind, or the frantic part of her brain that sensed that somewhere on this plantation, and within the secrets of this reclusive family, lay a clue as to what had happened to her brother.

Alexandre pulled one of the tall doors of the carriage house open. Once they had been painted a dark forest green. Now they were so faded and dull they appeared nearly brown. A cloud of grit swirled up from the ground and blended with the stale air that escaped the building's dark interior as the door swung open and a shaft of sunlight pierced the shadows.

Rachel coughed and put a hand over her mouth.

"Sorry," Alexandre mumbled, waving a hand at the dust-filled air. "I should have warned you, we don't use the carriage house for anything."

She nodded and stepped forward toward the door. Suddenly, without warning, she felt Steven, felt his shock and confusion, and . . . his terror. She grabbed hold of the doorjamb to steady herself. Her limbs began to shake so badly she thought her legs would fold beneath her. Fighting the gripping sensation, her fingers tightened their grasp on the doorjamb and the feeling disappeared as quickly as it had come. She glanced at Alexandre, but he was staring into the old carriage house and hadn't noticed her near-faint. Rachel rolled her head, shook her shoulders and forced a calm over herself she was truly far from feeling.

The disturbed dust of the interior settled, and she peered into the vast cavern. The outline of several antique buggies could be discerned in the shadows, their cracked and, in some cases ragged, canvas hoods heavy with years of dust, the spokes of their huge wooden wheels laced with cobwebs.

"Obviously you haven't opened this place in a long time either," Rachel said.

"No." Alexandre held out his arm for her.

She accepted it and walked beside him into the lofty

interior of the carriage house. The soft sole of her pump suddenly came down on something small and hard. Thrown off balance, she fell against Alexandre.

Caught in his arms, she felt him stiffen. Then he gently, but firmly set her away from him. "Are you all right?" he asked.

Rachel heard his question and nodded in response as she looked into the swirl of dust at her feet. A circle of cracked glass, lying in the dirt, caught the light that streamed in through the open doorway at their backs and reflected it in a rainbow of color. She bent down for a better look and gasped.

It was a detachable camera lens.

Chapter 3

Rachel picked the lens up and slowly turned it over and over in her hand forgetting, for the moment, Alexandre's presence. The impression of Steven almost overwhelmed her. The lens was his, she felt certain. A rush of excitement filled her. He always carried a half dozen or more lens on every shoot, and if he'd come to *Sans Souci*, no matter what the reason, he wouldn't have missed the opportunity to photograph the historic old house.

But why was this inside the old carriage house? She pressed her fingers around the small cylinder, but it offered no answers. Steven was very careful with his equipment. He bought only the best. If he had merely dropped the lens and noticed its absence later and was able to return, he would have spent hours searching for it, retracing every step he'd taken until he found it. That meant either one of two things to Rachel; he didn't know he'd lost it or, what she felt was more likely, he wasn't able to come back to search for it.

She started to slip the lens into the pocket of her slacks, looked up, and found Alexandre watching her. "Oh, I'm sorry." She pulled her hand from her pocket and held the lens out. "Is this yours?"

"A camera lens, isn't it?"

She nodded. "Yes, I believe so."

He shook his head. "I have never liked cameras, nor they me. But it might belong to one of Yvette's friends. She does occasionally . . ." he looked suddenly uncomfortable, "entertain at home."

Rachel dropped the lens back into her pocket. "I'll ask her when we get back to the house. These things can be very expensive."

After a brief examination of the ancient, dust-covered carriages, they walked back out into the sunlight. "Those buggies are absolutely fabulous, Alexandre. They'd be a wonderful addition to a museum." She was babbling, she knew, but she needed to get him talking. Not only because his nearness seemed, for some reason, to almost completely unnerve her, but also to detect if he knew anything, or was hiding anything, about Steven. "Am I the first visitor you've had here recently?"

A muscle twitched in his neck and Rachel noticed his jaw tighten before he answered. "As I said before, my sister entertains occasionally, but as far as I know, you are the first to come to *Sans Souci* in a very long time."

"*Sans Souci.* Without care," Rachel said. "Do you know what prompted your ancestors to give the plantation such a sad appellation?"

"It's a long and unpleasant story, Rachel, and one I'm sure my *grandmere* would rather was not made public."

His answer served only to pique Rachel's curiosity, but she did not persist.

Yvette and Marguerite were waiting for them in the parlor when they returned. A silver serving set was in the center of a small table near the fireplace and the spicy aroma of orange flavored tea filled the room. Marguerite poured a cup for Rachel and handed it to her, but she noticed that the woman took none herself, and neither did Yvette or Alexandre.

Conversation for the next hour was casual, yet cautious. Settled comfortably in one of the ladies' chairs near the fireplace, Rachel crossed her legs and felt the camera lens in her pocket press against her thigh. She slipped a hand into her pocket and pulled it out. "Oh, I nearly forgot. I found something in the carriage house that Alexandre thought might belong to one of your friends, Yvette." She pulled her clenched hand from her pocket and held the lens out in her palm.

Rachel heard Yvette's sudden intake of breath and saw her eyes widen. She lifted up a pale hand, its long nails painted blood red, to push nervously at a wisp of hair that had fallen onto her temple. Then the woman's gaze met Rachel's and she quickly caught herself. "No, it isn't mine. And I haven't entertained at the house in ages, as Alexandre could also have told you." She stared at Rachel's outstretched hand, the lens picking up the glow of the oil lamp on a nearby table and reflecting it softly. The faint shadow of a frown pulled at Yvette's brow. "I'm not even sure what it is. Some sort of mirror?"

"I think it's a lens to a camera," Rachel said calmly, feigning a degree of ignorance.

"Well, I can't imagine what it was doing in the carriage house, or anywhere else on *Sans Souci* for that matter." Yvette turned to Alexandre. "Alex, why on earth would you think it belonged to me?"

"I thought perhaps you had taken up a new hobby, sister dear," he said pleasantly. "Maybe something quiet and peaceful, for a change."

Rachel heard the venom in his tone and felt the tension that suddenly hung in the air between sister and brother. She looked at Alexandre and saw the taunting gleam in his eyes as he stared at Yvette, saw the challenge in the uplifted corner of his lips, but did not understand it.

Something was going on. Something was very definitely happening. But what? Unspoken words were being flung back and forth, and Rachel sensed with a dreaded certainty that they concerned her, and possibly Steven.

"Alexandre," Marguerite interrupted, her voice sugar sweet, "since Ms. Domecq must have many more questions to ask about this drafty old barn we call home, perhaps we should invite her to dine at *Sans Souci* tonight."

Rachel turned to Alexandre and saw the scowl that darkened his brow at his mother's suggestion. She looked back at Marguerite. The gray hair at her temples caught the glow of the fire in the grate and shimmered silver, accentuating the paleness of her eyes. "Thank you, Mrs. Beaumondier, really, but I have a cab waiting at the gates. I can return tomorrow afternoon, when it might be more convenient and we could talk then."

"Oh, I sent your cab back to town hours ago," Yvette said.

Rachel gawked at the woman in disbelief. "You what?"

"I saw that horrid little man pacing back and forth in front of the entry drive." Yvette chuckled softly. "I ordered Hanson to pay him whatever his fee was and send him away. I'm sure Alex can see you back to the city whenever you leave."

"That was not your place," Alexandre said in a voice of stern reprimand.

Her dark brows lifted haughtily as her gaze met his, but Yvette did not answer.

Rachel fought to control her anger, and her tongue.

She wanted to agree with Alexandre, it had not been the woman's place to send her cab away. On the other hand, perhaps Yvette had done her a favor. Now she had the perfect excuse to accept Marguerite's dinner invitation and prolong her visit to *Sans Souci.* And she had more questions now than ever.

"Well, now that the matter is settled, I'll inform Hanson that Ms. Domecq will be joining you for dinner, Alexandre," Marguerite said cheerily.

Rachel looked from the woman to Alexandre and back again. "Won't you be dining?"

Marguerite smiled, a gesture that, once again, did not reach her pale eyes. "No. Because of the schedule we keep Yvette, Suzanne and I always dine quite late. But we'll see you again later." Without another word, the older woman left the room.

Yvette stood. "Perhaps, Alexandre, since you two did quite a bit of walking around this afternoon, Rachel would like to freshen up or rest a bit before you dine. Since Danielle's room has already been opened, I had Hanson dust and tidy it."

"Oh, thank you," Rachel said, "but that wasn't really necessary." The deepening scowl on Alexandre's face was making her nervous.

"Nonsense, Rachel. Alexandre can show you to the room in case you've forgotten where it is. I'll look forward to seeing you later this evening. Perhaps you might even care to spend the night. You're quite welcome to."

Before Rachel could respond, Yvette slipped from the room and disappeared into the dimness of the foyer.

"Would you like me to show you upstairs?" Alexandre asked.

She saw the fury in his eyes, heard it in his voice, and knew he was not happy that she was staying, even if only for a little while longer. Rachel smiled. "No, thank you. I really feel fine. Not the least bit tired. But I would like to browse through some of the books in your library, if you don't mind? Many of them look fascinating, and quite old."

"They are." The words snapped off of his tongue, sharp and curt. Alexandre caught himself, suddenly aware of his tone, and the frown that pulled at his forehead smoothed. "I'll see you to the library. You are welcome to peruse whatever books in there you like."

"Oh, please, Alexandre," she touched his arm with her hand and he paused, his eyes darting from her hand to her eyes. "I can find my way. I don't want to bother you."

His lips turned up in a smile and Rachel again marveled at the change that came over him with the simple gesture. "You are not bothering me, Rachel. It is my pleasure."

They walked side by side across the foyer, his fingers cupped about her elbow. Though the touch was light as a sparrow's feather, Rachel felt it as a scalding fire on her flesh that made her heart race and her breath catch in her throat.

"I'll leave you now," Alexandre said at the door to the library. "There are some matters I must attend to that cannot wait."

"Of course."

He began to turn away, stopped, and slowly turned back, his eyes a bland of puzzlement, suspicion and wariness. Though against what, Rachel couldn't fathom. She stared up at him.

In direct contrast to what blazed in his eyes, Alexandre took her hand in his and, lifting it to his lips, grazed them sensuously across the top of her fingers. "Until later, Rachel," he said softly.

Shivers of blazing heat rippled through her fingers

and raced up her arm to meld with the maddening beat of her heart. He continued to hold her hand and look at her thoughtfully, his dark, penetrating gaze boring into her. Rachel felt a wave of weakness assail her and grasped the doorjamb in an effort to steady herself. Night suddenly surrounded her, a stygian black sky that spread to the ends of the earth, a sable landscape sprinkled with a thousand stars that glimmered like brilliant diamonds set upon a blanket of velvet. The moon, a distant golden orb, shone pale yellow, its image marred only by the filmy gray shadow of a cloud wafting past on the night breeze.

"Rachel?" Alexandre held her arms and shook her gently. "Rachel, can you hear me?"

His face loomed up before her and she blinked rapidly, trying to orient herself to what was real and what was not. She leaned against him for just a moment, borrowing his strength until her own returned. "I . . . I'm fine," she said, the sound of her voice little more than the soft fluttering of a butterfly's wings on the wind. "I think."

"Maybe Yvette was right. Perhaps you do need to rest a while. Let me see you upstairs where you can lie down."

"No." She pushed away from him and held to the doorjamb again, her fingers pressing tightly to the carved wood. "I'm fine, really." She smiled to emphasize her words. "I'll just get a book and sit down for a while."

He nodded and turned away, walking toward the rear of the house. Rachel watched him go and found herself wondering why a man as handsome and wealthy as Alexandre, a man who most likely could have any woman he chose, go anywhere in the world, do anything he wanted, would so thoroughly sequester himself on a rundown old plantation.

She turned and looked into the room, but suddenly she knew that this was not the room she wanted to see. She walked back into the foyer, turned to her left, and entered the next room. Everything about the study decreed it as Alexandre's. Cherrywood panels covered the walls, two of which were floor to ceiling bookshelves. Burgundy drapes framed the two tall windows and the same hue of dark color was woven into the ivory rug that spread across the center of the hardwood floor. She walked slowly past the bookshelves, letting her fingers skip lightly over the ancient leather bindings as she quickly read the goldleaf-embossed titles.

She paused abruptly, her attention caught by the faded lettering on one of the books.

Two hours later Rachel was deeply engrossed in the same book.She sat in a tall wing chair, her elbows resting upon its dark leather upholstered arms, and stared down at a photograph of Alexandre Beaumondier. His Confederate uniform had been sharply pressed. The stars of a general shone from his butternut collar, and a gleaming sword was attached to his sash waistband. Under the picture a handwritten date labeled it as having been taken in 1863. Rachel flipped back several dozen pages to another picture of Alexandre. It wasn't really a photograph but rather a picture of an oil painting. In it he was dressed in buckskin from head to toe, moccasins on his feet, one arm draped over an old musket. She turned back another fifty pages and stared at yet another picture.

"My God," Rachel whispered, her gaze riveted on the old portrait. It was another depiction of Alexandre, but this time he was dressed in the exact costume in which she'd seen him when she'd looked into his eyes earlier. Thigh high black boots covered his legs, and a bejeweled dagger was tucked into a silk sash at his waist.

Long black curls spilled from his head and cascaded over his shoulders, and he held a wide-brimmed, plume-adorned hat in the fingers of a hand propped upon his hip.

With trembling fingers she rifled to an earlier page in the book and stared again at the face of Alexandre Beaumondier. This time the picture was a pencil drawing, but very detailed, and unmistakable. With a group of men, standing on the shore of a primitive bayou, Alexandre Beaumondier stood next to Bienville, the man who had discovered New Orleans.

"This is impossible," Rachel murmured. "These have to be pictures of his ancestors." She flipped the pages back and forth, looking from one picture to the other. "But how can all the Beaumondier men look so much alike? So identical?" There were some differences, to be sure, but they were almost minute. Long hair, a beard, or a mustache, but nothing major. Physically, the men were the same. It was impossible, yet obviously it had happened, and more than once. Alexandre's great grandfather, great great grandfather, and those before him, were all depicted in the book she held in her hands. Only his grandfather and father seemed to be missing.

"I thought I left you in the library."

The smooth drawl of his voice cut into her thoughts and startled her. Rachel's heart skipped a beat. For the second time that day Alexandre had been able to approach her so quietly she had not heard him. A rush of guilt swept over her. "I'm sorry. I just wandered in here and became enthralled by this book. I hope you don't mind?"

"No."

But he looked like he did mind.

"Hanson is almost ready to serve dinner," Alexandre said.

She set the book aside and looked up at him. "Of course. I was just going through this book and came across several pictures of Beaumondier family members." She walked toward him. "The men of your family seemed to have played some very important roles in New Orleans' history."

"Yes, but that is in the past." He offered her his arm. "Shall we?"

They entered the dining room and, though she'd seen it briefly on the tour of the house with Alexandre earlier, Rachel marveled at its distinct differences from those of other plantations she'd seen. Most antebellum homes contained the lighter designs of Duncan Phyfe, or the delicate lines of French provincial. However, the furnishings of *Sans Souci*'s dining room were massive and heavy, more the type suited to a rambling old castle than a southern plantation.

Alexandre pulled out her chair.

A castle. She remembered a castle, perched high atop a mountainside, its turrets locked in the misty gray of passing clouds.

Alexandre assumed his seat at the head of the table, the opposite end from where she sat, and a good distance away. Too far for intimate conversation, she thought. But then, maybe that was his intent. A rather large white china plate, its edge trimmed in gleaming gold, sat before her on a delicate lace placemat, and next to it lay her utensils, their silver handles heavily scrolled. Beside her place setting was a silver chalice, its face embedded with what looked like a ruby surrounded by a dozen tiny emeralds. The stones glistened beneath the glow of the brass and crystal chandelier overhead, as did the wine within the chalice.

She glanced toward Alexandre. A chalice, identical to the one before her, sat on his placement, but it was devoid of anything else. He had no plate or utensils before him. She frowned. "Aren't you eating?" she asked.

"I have found my appetite somewhat lacking this evening," he answered. "But please, enjoy your meal. I will have my . . . wine, and keep you company."

Hanson appeared at her side and slid another plate atop the one before her. The succulent aroma of roasted rarebit, baked potato, and cheese-covered broccoli met her nose. "It looks delicious, Hanson, thank you."

The old man bowed slightly and left the room without a word.

She turned back to Alexandre. "I don't think I've ever met a genuine butler before. He seems very good. Efficient. Has he always worked for your family?"

Alexandre, who had been drinking from his chalice, lowered it from his lips. "Hanson is much more than a butler, and performs his duties quite well. And yes, he's been with my family for many, many years."

"That's unusual."

Alexandre's eyes narrowed, only slightly, but enough so that Rachel noticed and hurried to define her statement.

"In today's world, I mean. Most people don't stay at their jobs too long, not like they used to. A couple of years and then they usually begin to look for something better or different. You know, the grass is always greener type of thing."

"Yes. I suppose you're right. But I don't know what I'd do without Hanson."

"My brother, Steven, has a great job. Actually, he works for himself." Rachel watched Alexandre for some type of reaction, any kind of reaction, and saw none.

"He freelances for magazines and is in the process of putting together a book."

Alexandre set the chalice down. "What type of writing does your brother do?"

"Oh, he's not a writer. He's a photographer."

The comment hung in the air like a black cloud in the center of a pale blue summer sky. She saw a shadow pass over Alexandre's eyes, knew he was remembering the lens she'd found earlier in the carriage house, and felt a surge of both excitement and fear. Had she been right in suspecting that Steven's disappearance had something to do with the Beaumondiers and their unusual home? Had she given too much away? But she really had no choice, not if she was going to find out where he was. She had to get someone in this family talking, so she hurried to continue.

"Steven was in New Orleans a while back photographing some of the old antebellum homes in the area for a portrait book he's putting together. From what little I know of the project, *Sans Souci* would be a perfect addition."

Alexandre's expression remained stoic. "Perhaps, but Catherine would never approve." He drained the last of the liquid from his chalice and set it down on the table. The goblet was whisked away almost immediately by Hanson who had reentered the dining room to retrieve Rachel's plate.

Rachel had the sinking feeling that Alexandre was right, in which case the camera lens they'd found in the carriage house probably did belong to one of Yvette's infrequent guests rather than Steven. Perhaps she hadn't wanted to say anything in front of her mother for fear she'd disapprove.

Marguerite swept into the room. "Alexandre, good, you're finished." She paused near him. "Yvette and Suzanne and I are going to have tea in the parlor. We thought you two could join us, if you were finished in here."

Rachel placed her napkin on the table and rose. "Oh, thank you, but I really should be getting back to my hotel room in town. I don't want to impose on your hospitality any longer this evening."

"Nonsense." Marguerite swept up beside Rachel and linked arms with her. "We get such few visitors to *Sans Souci*. We'd just be crushed if you didn't spend a little time with us. At least stay the night. I'm sure Alexandre won't mind seeing you back to town in the morning."

Rachel glanced uneasily at Alexandre, and just as quickly looked away. Black fire burned in his eyes, reflecting his disapproval. She didn't know why, but for some reason Alexandre didn't want her to stay at *Sans Souci*, and because of that, she wanted to.

Rachel stood at the window in her room, the same room Alexandre had carried her to earlier when she'd fainted. The visit with Marguerite, Yvette and Suzanne had been—she searched for a word to describe the ordeal—forced cheerfulness. In contrast Alexandre had seemed to retreat further and further into a bout of brooding as the evening progressed.

She held the transmitter to her mouth and pushed down on its button."Marc? Marc, can you hear me?" she whispered.

"Where the hell are you?" he thundered back

She slapped a hand over the transmitter's small speaker grid and glanced over her shoulder, fearful the sound of his voice had been loud enough for the others to hear, even through her closed door. Several seconds passed, but no one came to the door of her room or pounded on one of the walls. She inhaled deeply and pressed the button again. "They want me to spend the night. Everything's fine. You can go on home now."

"Not on your life," Marc answered. "If you're staying, I'm staying."

Rachel smiled. Marc had always tried to protect her, even when they'd been partners on the force. She closed her eyes and an image of Marc Dellos drifted into her mind's eye. Not handsome in the classical sense. Not like Alexandre. Marc was rugged. Rugged and sexy, with a hard, well-developed athlete's body, sandy blonde hair, pale blue eyes, and a face whose curves and angles were more hacked than carved.

She pulled the sheer lace curtains away from the window. The ancient ivory threads were so timeworn and fragile that several broke apart at her touch. "I didn't know you were so fond of sleeping alone in your car."

"I'm not," he answered. "But I am fond of you, and keeping you alive."

"Sweet dreams." Rachel clicked off the transmitter and dropped it back into her purse.

Every time she'd closed her eyes she had seen Alexandre Beaumondier, his sinewy length wrapping around hers, pulling her to him, his dark eyes drawing her into other worlds, other places, other times. What was the matter with her? She should be thinking about Steven, trying to get answers to the questions that would lead her to him. She shouldn't be lusting after a man she hardly knew. But her mind wasn't cooperating. Thoughts of Alexandre continually invaded, took over, and wiped out all other images from her mind. She could feel him, the warm touch of his fingers as they'd enveloped hers, his lips pressed to the back of her hand. The sound of his voice echoed in her memory's ear, rich, deep, and hypnotic. She recalled the unusual aroma that clung to him, the muskiness that reminded her of ancient forests and rich earth, and she remembered the dark, burning intensity of his eyes, steel gray pools sparked with blue that drew and mesmerized her.

She peered through the window into the night. What was it about Alexandre Beaumondier that intrigued her so? That had so immediately sparked her desires and, at the same time, chilled her blood?

Suddenly a spot of white moved across the weed choked grounds and caught Rachel's attention. In order to get a batter look, she pressed closer to the glass pane to block out the reflection of the light behind her.

Yvette hurried toward the sprawling oaks that bordered the edge of what long ago had obviously been a formal garden, but was now nothing more than a broken brick path that wove through dried shrubs and dead, gnarled stumps of old rose bushes. Wings of sheer white fabric, turned nearly pellucid beneath the moon's light, billowed out around her as she ran, and her long, dark hair, loose and unpinned, cascaded down her back.

Rachel glanced at the watch on her wrist. It was well after midnight. Looking back through the window, she saw Yvette disappear into the moss shrouded shadows beneath the huge trees. What was she doing outside so late at night?

Chapter 4

Rachel turned from the window and hurried across the room. She grabbed her purse from the night table where she'd set it earlier, flipped open its stiff flap and angled its interior toward the lamp. The black metal of her snub-nosed .38 millimeter handgun gleamed wickedly in the candlelight. Not exactly a cannon, she thought, but efficient. And deadly, when needed. She pulled the weapon out and held it cradled in the palm of her hand. Her index finger slipped naturally and comfortably within the circle of the trigger guard. How long had it been since she'd used a gun?

Five years, her mind answered instantly. Five years since she'd left the police force, returned to school, and then, with the help of connections she'd made while on the force, taken up a new profession. Being shot in the back by a teenage punk and left for dead in a dark alley had awakened her to the fact that she did not want to die. Especially that way. After a few months' recuperation she'd been back on the streets, but she hadn't been able to shake the feeling that her uniform made her a target for every lunatic and crazy in the city with a gun, a knife or even just a pair of deadly fists. That's when she'd known she had to get out, that she couldn't be a cop anymore.

Rachel's gaze moved back to her purse, to the small transmitter Marc had given her. Should she call him again? She glanced out the window. No, not yet. What could she say? Yvette is running around in the gardens in her nightgown?

Rachel dropped the gun into the deep pocket of the cotton robe Marguerite had given her to use and secured the belt at her waist, then slipped her feet into the pumps she'd worn that day. They weren't exactly made for walking around dark grounds in the middle of the night, but she had no choice. She turned toward the door. The voluminous folds of the gown's pale blue skirt rustled softly about her legs.

She would have to hurry if she were to discover where Yvette was going so late at night. Even now the woman might be too far from the house for Rachel to follow successfully. She slipped from the room, closed the door softly behind her, and stood still for a moment, allowing her eyes to get accustomed to the sudden darkness of the hallway.

A soft flutter to her left caught her attention and she jerked around to face a tall window at the end of the hall. Its drapes were drawn. She thought she saw a shadow flit across the moonlit glass, but it was there and gone so quickly she couldn't be sure.

The silence that filled the house was almost deafening, an abyss of calm that sent an unreasonable chill of apprehension snaking its way up her spine. She stood still and listened, her senses attuned to the slightest sound or movement. Her cop instincts and reactions had obviously returned two-fold since her arrival at the plantation, and for that she was grateful.

The house seemed more than quiet. . . . It felt empty and desolate, as if there was not another living soul within its ancient walls.

Rachel shrugged away the thought. It was ridiculous. Yvette may be out and about, and Alexandre was probably in the *garconniere* where he'd said his apartment was located, but Marguerite, Catherine, and Suzanne, were most likely in their rooms and asleep for the night. Especially Catherine. She was too old and frail to be anywhere else. And Hanson, too. Rachel moved cautiously down the dark hallway, feeling her way along the wall, moving in the direction of the staircase landing and away from the tall window. She descended the stairs hastily, though carefully, and ran across the spacious foyer. At the large front door she paused again and looked back over her shoulder at the landing.

A shiver of chills skittered up her spine. She hadn't been able to shake the feeling of being watched since the moment she had arrived at *Sans Souci.* The sensation had been constant, even while she'd been in the guest room. Her eyes strained to pierce the darkness, but if there was anyone there, watching her, she couldn't see them.

Rachel pulled open the entry door and moved past it onto the wide gallery. She hadn't realized how dry it had been inside the old mansion until the warm, moist night air surrounded her. Stepping lightly to avoid making any sound, she hurried around to the rear of the house where she'd seen Yvette. There was no one in sight. She looked up at the tall window that marked the hallway at the end of the second floor, but beyond its glass, which had turned a brilliant silver beneath the moon's faint light, she could detect nothing. Every window in the house was dark except her own room. But the feeling of being watched persisted.

She ran across the weed-choked expanse of ground that led to what was left of the formal gardens. Suddenly a scream pierced the still night, a rising cresendo of fear that echoed on the dark, undetectable waves of humidity that hovered over the earth. The sound filled the shadows, and brought a semblance of life to the hulking black trees and draping veils of gray moss.

Rachel stopped abruptly. Fear hammered in her breast and she fought to control it. A certain amount of fear, she'd learned while being a cop, kept you alert and cautious. Too much fear paralyzed you, and sometimes caused your death. Her right hand slipped into the pocket of her robe and her fingers curled around the handle of her gun.

The scream stopped as abruptly as it had started and the silence that followed seemed more eerie and threatening than the bloodchilling cry. The night held a deathly calm, a calm without sound or movement.

And then she felt it. Steven! Suddenly his presence was all around her and stronger than it had been all day. "Oh, my God," Rachel murmured, looking around frantically. He was here. She knew it. He was at *Sans Souci*, or at least he had been. And he was in trouble.

The thought instilled her with new courage. Grabbing a handful of gown in her free hand, Rachel ran toward the trees. She pulled the gun from her pocket and held it at the ready. Beneath the gnarled branches of the ancient live oaks was only blackness; the weak rays of the moon blocked by the thickly leaved limbs.

With her arms outstretched before her, Rachel moved through the grove almost blindly, her eyes able to discern little more than black shadows against a slightly paler night. Her fingers encountered a long, draping curtain of moss and she pushed it out of her way. Suddenly she found herself engulfed within a blanket of the barbed growth as it fell from a tree limb overhead. Stiff little needles pricked at her flesh and snagged in both her long, free-flowing hair and the delicate silk threads of the robe she'd borrowed from Marguerite. A startled shriek escaped Rachel's lips. Her arms flailed the air while she kicked out and whirled around in an effort to escape the enveloping foliage. Tiny thorns scratched her unprotected hands, breaking the skin and leaving behind thin trails of exposed flesh and blood. Finally the offending cloak of growth slid from her shoulders to fall to the ground. Dozens of small, brittle quills were left behind, snared within the fabric of her gown, and the long, tangled waves of her hair.

"Damned stuff. Might as well be alive," Rachel mumbled, her tone laced with the disgust she felt at herself for being careless enough to run into the moss in the first place.

A few yards ahead, moonlight shone onto a small area that was devoid of trees. Rachel hurried toward it, uncertain if it was the direction Yvette had taken or from where the scream had originated.

Long since having given up an occupation that required physical exertion and stamina, Rachel was forced to pause and bend over. Cupping her hands to her knees, and leaning on them, she gasped for air. Her forehead was covered with perspiration and the thin robe clung to her.

Damn. Why hadn't she called Marc?

After regaining her composure and her breath, she straightened and peered at her surroundings. The night had turned still again. Not even the chirping of a bird or the nightsong of the ever-present cicada broke the unearthly silence. Nothing moved. Nothing sounded.

A chill swept over her warm skin. Rachel's fingers tightened around the gun, the cold metal like a caress of security to her nerves. She turned to look back in the direction from which she'd come, back at the house, and gave a start of alarm at seeing only blackness; an endless chasm of ebony that seemed to wrap around her like the folds of an all consuming cloak.

From the star sprinkled sky above a thin, spine wrenching screech cut through the air and echoed endlessly within the dusky boughs of the huge trees. Rachel looked up just as the cloud that had drifted before the moon and obscured it from sight, passed on. Black wings cut across the face of the golden orb, flapped wildly, and plummetted toward her. For one brief second she watched the hawk-sized bird in wonder, assuming it was diving toward the earth in pursuit of prey for its meal. Suddenly, the realization that it was a bat descending directly toward her brought instant shock and panic. Forgetting the gun in her hand Rachel threw her arms up before her face in an effort to ward off the attack. Long claws scraped at her arms while leathery wings beat at her hands and head. Over and over the battering appendages thrashed at her, the tips of the bat's wings snagging in her hair, and all the while the thing screeched loudly as if in fury.

Sharp teeth bit into one of her fingers. She cried out, jerked her hand away and dropped the gun. Screaming and swinging her arms, Rachel tried to evade the creature. It swooped wildly before her. She stumbled back away from it and screamed at the hideous little face that flew toward her again. Huge pointed ears, tiny, glowing red eyes, and lips bared back from long, pointed fangs.

Rachel threw herself to the ground in an effort to avoid the animal's dive. It swished overhead and arched up toward the sky in preparation, she feared, for another attack. Rachel staggered to her feet and took several steps to her left.

The thing swooped down. Its bloodcurdling cry and the sound of its wings beating against the night air, sent another wave of terror through Rachel. Why was it attacking her? She looked around frantically for her gun, but the light moonlight was too dim and the weeds were too tall and thick.

Keeping her hands raised to prevent the bat from getting at her face, Rachel lunged to her right. The thing disappeared into the shadows of the trees. Rachel grabbed up the folds of her robe and gown and bunched them into a wad in her arms. Don't panic, she told herself. Don't panic. Get to the house. Don't panic. She turned and ran in the direction she thought led to the house.

The toe of her left pump struck against the protruding root of an oak tree. Rachel lurched forward. She threw her hands out in front of her and landed on her knees. Bolts of lightning-sharp pain spiraled up each limb at the impact and nearly stunned her into unconsciousness. She shook her head and ignored the pain in order to glance quickly over her shoulder, fearful of seeing the horrid little creature plunging down at her again. But the night was still, and the bat nowhere in sight.

Rachel pushed herself back to her feet and moved on. The broken brick path of the decaying formal gardens came into view, and she hastened her pace. The house was just beyond. She tore across the weed-choked lawn. Gasping, her lungs screaming for air and rest, she grappled her way up the stairs. The old boards creaked beneath her weight. Her hands found one of the supporting pillars, and she used it to steady herself as she tried to straighten. The door to the house was only a few feet away. Rachel released her hold on the pillar, reeled weakly, and stumbled across the gallery. She'd barely made it halfway to the door when the heel of her pump sunk into a crack in the boards of the floor, and wedged tightly. With a soft shriek, Rachel pitched forward, arms outstretched in search of a wall, a door, anything to break her fall. Her fingers skimmed across something silky, smooth and hard.

Suddenly she was no longer falling. Strong hands clasped her waist, then slipped around to her back, enveloping her within an embrace of warm, velvet clad arms. She screamed, still too emeshed in fear and panic for reason, and pushed away, twisting, hitting out at whatever, or whomever held her.

"It's all right, Rachel," Alexandre said softly. "It's all right. Nothing is going to harm you." The soothing drawl of his voice touched her overwrought nerves and proved an instant salve of comfort.

"Alexandre?"

She was lifted upward, the imprisoned shoe left behind, until she was once again standing on her own feet, but not released from the circle of his steel strong arms. He held her to him, gently cradled against a wall of silk-sheathed chest, one strong hand pressed to her back, the fingers of the other skimming lightly over her tousled hair. She could feel the warmth of him penetrating through the thin fabric of her robe and gown, his strength giving her the power of command over her own body. The piquant and distinct scent of his cologne invaded her senses and blended with the heavy fragrance of jasmine that filled the air near the house. The hard hammering of her heart and the ragged struggle of her lungs for breath did not cease with the comfort his arms offered. Instead it persisted, though the cause was no longer fear. She pushed away from his chest and looked up at him, her eyes coming to meet his, the blue of a mediterannean sea melding with the dark sultry gray of a fog swept and moonless night.

A sweep of darkness emanated from those depthless

eyes and reached out to surround her, to enshroud her within its warm mantle and entice her into its endless core. It offered her no time or opportunity for reaction, whether acquiescence or resistance.

Shivers of both delicious anticipation and fearful apprehension danced atop her skin. Memory of the terror filled events of only moments before faded from her mind as if they'd never happened. And with them, her worry over Stephen vanished as well.

Alexandre's embrace tightened around her, crushing her against him, pinning her arms between them, her hands pressed flat atop the lapels of his silk lounging jacket. His head lowered toward hers. She closed her eyes and felt the soft, trembling touch of his lips brush lightly over her own, felt the heat of his breath waft across her cheek. The blood within her veins turned suddenly to hot spiraling waves that rushed along winding trails and curves, melded with the accelerated beat of her heart, and flowed outward again in fiery abandon. As the tip of his tongue caressed her lips, following their curve, she opened for him, hungrily inviting his seduction of her senses. The world slipped away, time and reality lost their meaning as his tongue explored the deep caverns of her mouth, flicking against her own tongue, caressing, teasing.

His lips left hers and slipped to the curve of her jaw, the sensitive flesh just below her ear, and the long, ivory-hued column of her neck. Each kiss pressed to her skin was like the touch of a searing flame, stoking the fires that simmered deep within the pith of her body, igniting the sparks of desire that ached for release.

Rachel leaned into him, her head thrown back, reveling in the rapturous pleasure his touch invoked. His lips moved steadily downward, caressing, burning, inciting, until finally they found the small hollow at the base of her throat, and the thin vein that pulsated wildly just below the skin's surface.

Chapter 5

Alexandre's lips pressed against Rachel's throat and slid slowly, softly, toward the small hollow at its base. He had not kissed a woman since Danielle, had experienced no desire, no need to be close to a woman, to feel her arms around him, her lips beneath his, her breasts crushed to his chest. But suddenly, with Rachel, all of the old emotions he'd thought long dead, all of the passion and longing he had believed he could no longer feel, were rapidly and unexplainably returning. Alexandre tightened his arms around her, his splayed hands pressed against her back and held her to him.

Danielle. He had held Danielle this way. Loved her. Needed her, and then he'd . . .

Alexandre stopped and his mind flew back to the present as he felt a faint scratch of broken skin beneath his lips. The distinctive scent of blood emanated from the barely noticeable abrasion and ignited the age old hunger within him, stoking the fires of savagery he struggled every hour of his existence to repress. Heart, mind, and baser instincts raged against one another. Alexandre stiffened even as he felt his jaws part and his mouth open. His hands held steady against her back, holding her crushed to his tall length, blending the pliant, subtle curves of her body with the taut, hard planes of his until there was no space left between them.

No, he screamed silently. No. Not her. He stiffened slightly and snapped his eyes closed as the struggle within him waged fierce, good fighting evil, right staving off wrong, desire overcoming the natural instincts of his hunger and need. The natural composition of his being, of what he was, told him to take her, to drain the life force from her and absorb it into his own veins. His mind argued that he hadn't taken a human's life, or drank of their blood for years . . . ever since Danielle had turned away from him, and then disappeared.

A shudder wracked Alexandre's body as he fought for control. His chalice had been full at dinner. And refilled. His thirst should have been satiated. But the potency of the animal blood was so much weaker than that of humans, and the fulfillment it brought him was always so brief, so fleeting.

Alexandre tore himself away from Rachel, practically pushing her back into the pillar that edged the gallery.

"What . . . what's the matter?" she mumbled, dazed with the passion that his kiss had aroused within her. She stumbled over the shoe that was still wedged in the gallery's floor and wrapped trembling fingers around the iron balustrade that stretched between each pillar in order to regain her balance.

"I'm . . . I'm sorry," Alexandre muttered, and turned away from her. He stood with his shoulders stiff, hands clenched at his sides, his gaze studiously averted from hers. "I shouldn't have done that, Rachel. I had no right, and it was wrong. I'm sorry."

Rachel stared at him in silence. His face was in profile to her, each curve an inky shadow, each line a faint stroke of moonlit flesh. Wrong? she thought, confused. She pulled the robe tighter about her breasts. The haze of passion began to pass and cold reality return. She had been kissed by her share of suitors, but none had ever apologized for it, or said that it was wrong. Yet instead of anger, an insane urge, an almost irresistible urge, to reach out and touch him, to wrap her arms around his neck and again pull his lips down to hers, swept over her and she fought to control it, to thwart it. She crossed her arms beneath her breasts, holding to herself tightly in order to maintain control over her actions. What did he mean, wrong? Wrong to have kissed her? Wrong to have made her feel so passionate?

But before she could even think of voicing her thoughts and questions, he turned without another word to her and stalked from the gallery. She watched him move determinedly across the lawn, past the skeletal remains of *Sans Souci*'s once formal garden, and disappear into the darkness.

"Rachel, is something wrong?"

She jerked around, unaware that anyone else was about. Rachel looked at Yvette, who stood framed within the doorway to the house, the soft glow of an oil lamp at her back turning her gown into a frothy veil of whiteness that seemed to both cling to her body, and gracefully drape it.

"Oh, I, uh . . . ' Rachel paused, unsure of what to say. She had seen Yvette earlier in the garden. The woman had obviously been going somewhere. But where? And how had she gotten back so quickly? And into the house before Rachel? She hadn't been standing on the gallery that long with Alexandre. An uneasiness crept over her. Or had she?

"Rachel, is everything all right?" Yvette repeated. She stepped from the doorway onto the gallery.

Rachel took a step back and felt the smooth, cool surface of a pillar behind her. "Yes, yes, I'm fine," she said hurriedly, unsure of the reason for her nervousness. "I'm fine, really. Fine," she repeated inanely. "I just, uh, got my shoe caught in the floor here." She bent down to yank the shoe from the crevice which held the heel. "I nearly broke my neck, that's all. Luckily Alexandre was here to catch me or I guess I would have."

"Luckily," Yvette said, and smiled. She looked around quickly. "So, where is my *brother?*"

Yvette's slight change of tone on the word brother was not lost on Rachel, but if there was a meaning behind it, that was lost. "Oh," Rachel glanced over her shoulder in the direction he'd disappeared. "I think he went for a walk."

"And he didn't invite you?" Yvette said coyly. "How thoughtless of him. Moonlight walks on the grounds *Sans Souci* can be very relaxing, and romantic."

"Oh, it's all right," Rachel hurried to say. "I mean, I really didn't care to go for another walk. I just returned from one and, well, maybe he wanted to be alone, you know? He seemed in a quiet mood. I get that way sometimes, too, when I want to think." She was babbling, and knew it, but it's what she did when she got nervous. And she *was* nervous. Too many strange things were happening, and she wasn't sure how to interpret Yvette's comment about "romantic."

"Really?" Yvette smiled and sauntered to the gallery's edge. Apollyon suddenly appeared at the door and followed her. "And what do you think of my brother, Rachel?" Yvette continued before Rachel could answer, "Sometimes I worry about him." She slung a slender hip onto the railing of the wrought iron fence that spanned the space between two of the gallery's pillars and looked up at Rachel. "I mean, Alexandre needs to get out more. To socialize, you know? But . . ." She shook her head, as if remembering something sad.

Rachel waited, suddenly feeling breathless, afraid to speak or move for fear Yvette wouldn't go on.

"Ever since *she* left him," Yvette said, "he's been such a recluse. Isn't that right, Apollyon?" She rubbed her dangling foot affectionately along the cat's jawline.

"She?" Rachel echoed.

Yvette smiled, rose to her feet and moved to stand before the steps that led into the garden, her back to Rachel. Apollyon threw a cold glare at Rachel and moved to follow Yvette. "Yes. Didn't you know?" She looked back at Rachel and chuckled softly. "Oh, but then, why should you?" She shrugged. "Alexandre was engaged to be married. Of course it was a long time ago, but he's never forgotten her, even though the rest of us agree he's better off without her."

"What . . . what happened?" Rachel asked, feeling as if she were being too inquisitive, yet unable to help herself.

Yvette shrugged again. "Oh, she broke it off. I don't remember exactly why, really. And it doesn't matter. She's gone, thank the stars, and that's all there is to it. I didn't really care for the girl, but that's not important. What does matter is that Alexandre gets on with his life." She smiled slyly and looked back at Rachel. "And I believe he's thinking the same thing, if that kiss he gave you is any indication."

Rachel felt her cheeks suddenly burn with the heat of embarrassment. So, someone had been watching.

She opened her mouth to retort but the voice that spoke wasn't hers.

"Yvette, what are you doing out there?"

Rachel turned toward the door to see Suzanne step across its threshold. Why was everyone up so late? She'd thought everyone had retired hours ago but neither Yvette or Suzanne were dressed for bed. Then she remembered Marguerite's comment that the women kept unusual hours.

"Oh, just having a nice girl to girl talk with Rachel," Yvette cooed. "About Alexandre."

Suzanne looked at Rachel. "Oh?" She turned her gaze back to Yvette. "You wouldn't be trying to play cupid again, now would you?"

"Excuse me, but I think I'll retire now," Rachel said. She tugged on the tie of her robe and moved toward the door. "I only came out for a breath of fresh air. My room felt a little stuffy, but I'm tired now."

Suzanne frowned, and with a look of anger in her eyes glanced hurriedly toward Yvette and then back at Rachel, but didn't move from the doorway when Rachel approached. Her eyes narrowed as they focused on Rachel's neck. "You seem to have gotten a few scratches since I last saw you, Rachel," she said. "Did you have some sort of accident?"

Rachel's hand rose to touch her throat. She felt the shallow roughness of torn flesh and suddenly remembered that horrible creature's unprovoked attack and the stinging sensation on her neck and cheek when it scratched her. But in lieu of what had happened after that, on the gallery with Alexandre, the injuries, as well as the incident itself, had been nearly forgotten.

"Oh, I went for a walk a little while ago and . . ." she paused. For reasons she didn't understand, Rachel felt suddenly that she shouldn't tell them what had happened. "And I accidentally walked into some moss from one of the trees." She forced a light laugh from her lips. "It fell on me and, well, I'm embarrassed to say I panicked and while thrashing about in an effort to get it off I guess it scratched me."

Yvette chuckled. "Dangerous thing, our moss."

Suzanne threw a glaring glance toward Yvette and

then, turning back to Rachel, smiled, though her eyes remained cool. "Well, you should be more careful when you go out at night, Rachel." She stepped from the doorway. "One never knows what one might encounter in the darkness."

Marc Dellos lay the back of his head against the car seat, crossed muscular arms over his chest, and stared through the windshield at the dark sky. The moon was barely a sliver of gold in the sky, surrounded by a light sprinkling of stars and several sprawling lengths of black clouds. His gun, a .45 Luger, lay on the seat beside him, ready if he should need it. A transmitter, the mate to the one he'd given Rachel, lay next to the gun. Cajun jazz hummed softly from the car's radio and his windows were rolled down, just a little, to allow some circulation of air and to prevent the glass from fogging over. Marc sighed. He shouldn't have let Rachel go in there alone. He'd heard too many weird tales about *Sans Souci*. Or more accurately, about its residents. Nothing that could be proven, of course, they were just tales, and most sounded like nonsense. But then, since moving to New Orleans, Marc had heard a lot of weird tales, and many, he'd been told, nonsensical sounding or not, were most likely true.

Rachel had been in touch with him from the moment she'd lost contact with her brother, and though it wasn't Marc's case, he'd kept an eye on what was going on. Which he'd had to agree with her, was very little. But then, there was very little to go on. Steven had been seen in several bars, both alone and with various women, including one whose description matched both Yvette and Suzanne Beaumondier. Both women claimed, when questioned by officers, to have no knowledge of a Steven Ligere.

Marc settled deeper into the seat.

Interesting people, these Beaumondier sisters. They were the only ones of the family known to visit the town, but only the worst bars, the dank dives that even some of the lowest of the city's low wouldn't patronize. Alexandre Beaumondier handled the family's financial transactions, but all by written correspondence. As far as anyone could say, he, like his mother Marguerite, never left the plantation. And old Catherine, the family matriarch, hadn't been seen in so many years that most people believed she was dead.

Flapping wings flit before the moon, a black silhouette only momentarily in sight. The movement pulled at Marc's attention and broke into his thoughts.

Dawn crept over the horizon slowly, the night's mist clinging to the earth as if in refusal of being vanquished. It stubbornly huddled over the dew-kissed grasses, lurked within the tree spotted landscape, and finally, in surrender to the day's approaching warmth, began to dissipate.

Rachel stood at the window of her room, the curtains drawn. She'd been standing there for well over an hour, watching for something, and nothing. Her sleep had been restless, comprised mainly of a series of short naps between endless tossing and turning. Twenty minutes ago she had heard a door shut downstairs, and though she'd love nothing better at the moment than a cup of coffee—a very strong cup of coffee, preferably chicory coffee, she hadn't made a move to leave her room. It had probably been Hanson, the butler, going out to the cookhouse to prepare the morning meal, and she didn't want to bother him.

She remembered the old man and shuddered. No, if she were truthful with herself her hesitation in going downstairs had nothing to do with not wanting to bother Hanson, but rather that she just didn't want to be in his company. At least not alone. The man was . . . eerie. Macabre. Spooky. Yes, she thought. Apt descriptions, all of them. Hanson was nothing more than skin and bones, and obviously quite old, but that didn't bother her. It was . . . she shuddered again. She didn't know what it was that bothered her about the old man. A look about him, or a sense of something just not right. His skin was pale and white, but it wasn't quite the translucent paleness that the Beaumondier women's held, it was more a deathly sort of white . . . colorless, like his eyes.

Rachel turned from the window and retrieved the transmitter from her purse. "Marc?" she whispered, holding it close to her lips so that she didn't have to speak too loud.

Static was her only answer.

"Marc?" she repeated.

Again the transmitter bristled with nothing more than static, loud and screeching, which only sharpened the jagged edges of her already-taut nerves.

She waited a few minutes and tried again. "Marc? Marc, are you there? Can you hear me?"

Nothing.

An uneasiness moved over Rachel. Turning hurriedly from the window she dropped the transmitter on the bed and, throwing open the large armoire where she had hung her slacks and blouse, retrieved them and quickly dressed. Something was wrong, otherwise Marc would have answered. She quickly ran a brush through her hair, more out of habit than the need to primp, and reached for her purse. It felt light and empty. She snapped back one of its leather pockets.

The gun wasn't there. Rachel started and looked around the room. Where was her gun? Her heart hammered against her breast. And then she remembered. She'd dropped it last night when that thing had attacked her. A string of unladylike curses danced through her mind. She scooped the transmitter up from the bed and dropped it into the pocket of her slacks. She would have to go back to that meadow later, if she could find it, and look for the gun. But first she had to find out why Marc wasn't answering her call.

"God, let him be all right," she mumbled aloud, and opened the door to the hallway.

The house was quiet. Deathly quiet. Draperies had been pulled across the window at the end of the hall. Rachel stared, puzzled. Last night they'd been open. She remembered seeing the moonlight streaming in through the big square panes. With a shrug, Rachel turned away and walked toward the landing. Obviously someone had closed them after she'd retired and they just hadn't been reopened yet.

A lone taper, burned nearly to the rim of the brass candlestick in which it sat, flickered feebly on a small petticoat table near the staircase landing and cast a sickly yellow glow over the hallway.

Rachel walked briskly toward the landing, descended the stairs and exited the house. No one had seen her, she felt certain, and for that she was grateful. She didn't need to try and come up with a reason why she was going out at dawn. Of course she could claim it as merely a morning walk, but that excuse sounded feeble even to her mind, especially as she was dressed in silk slacks and blouse, and expensive Antonio pumps with two-inch heels.

She ran down the drive, careful to stay off the road itself and keep within the shadows of the oaks that bordered it. Her heels, she discovered quickly, sunk into the soft ground if she put too much weight on them, so she didn't, which caused her to move slower than she wanted to.

Why hadn't Marc answered? Where was he? Had something happened to him? Had he left? She banished that thought immediately. Marc wouldn't leave, that was certain. He wouldn't leave until she came out. So, where was he then? Why hadn't he answered her?

By the time she got to the main gate and stepped out onto the river road, she was nearly breathless from the combination of her hurried pace, careful steps and mounting fear.

She looked around frantically. Where had he hidden the car? Blue. It was light blue. Her eyes searched the landscape. Finally, she saw a small swatch of light blue within a copse of trees and bushes across and just down the road. She began to walk toward it and, as she neared, the shape of the car became more well-defined.

She broke into a run. "Marc? Marc?" She veered from the road onto the small dirt path that led to the copse and the car, whose hood was half-camouflaged with bramble. "Marc?"

"Rachel?" Marc leaned out of the driver's side window. "What the hell are you doing out here?" He pushed open the car door and stepped out of the vehicle, straightening to his full height as she neared and paused before him. Alarm suddenly pulled at his features. "Are you all right?" He grabbed her forearms. "What's wrong? What's happened?"

"Me?" Rachel asked, gasping for breath. Relief

flowed through her at finding him safe and in one piece. "Are *you* all right?" She twisted away from him, slapped a hand to her breast and leaned the other on the car door as she fought to slow both her pulse and breathing.

"Sure, I'm fine, but you don't look so good. A little out of shape there, kiddo? I think your face has a bit of a greenish tint to it." He laughed.

Rachel slammed a curled fist into his heavily muscled upper arm. "It's not funny, dammit. I thought something had happened to you."

He looked perplexed, his rugged features sobering at her words and screwing into a frown of puzzlement. "Why?"

Rachel straightened and whirled to face him. "Why? Why?" she snapped, her temper flaring. "Because I called you, dammit. I called you several times on that stupid little transmitter and you didn't answer me, that's why."

Marc smiled. "Well, the only time I've left this car, as my cramped body can attest, is when I woke up this morning, walked over into those trees and watered them. And I'm sorry, but I didn't think to take the transmitter."

"Watered . . . ?" Rachel's cheeks flushed with warmth. "And here I was worried that you were . . ." She shook her head and laughed.

"Well, since you came out you could have at least brought me some coffee," Marc said. "I kind of drained my thermos last night, which is probably why I woke up this morning feeling like Lake Ponchartrain." He laughed easily, a rumbling baritone of sound that served to chase away the last of Rachel's pique.

"Bring you coffee, right," she said. "I should have just sashayed my way into that creepy little butler's kitchen, told him I needed a cup of coffee for the cop who was sitting in his car just beyond the plantation's gates and sashayed my way back out again."

"Creepy butler?"

"Well," Rachel looked thoughtful, "maybe not creepy really, just kind of . . . strange. Sickly looking. Like he belongs in a horror movie, or something."

"What about the others?" Marc said, suddenly serious. "What's with them?"

Rachel shrugged. "I haven't found out a whole lot, really. The women are all pleasant enough, and Alexandre is a true southern gentleman, though I get the impression that he wasn't all that thrilled that his mother invited me to spend the night."

"Umm, probably more miffed at the fact that she hadn't put you in his room."

Rachel sent him her best reprimanding glare.

"What else?" Marc demanded.

"Oh, this. I almost forgot." She pulled the camera lens from the pocket of her slacks and, holding it flat in her palm, held it out to him.

"What is it?" Marc picked up the lens by its black edge, careful not to touch the glass itself, and held it up to look through it. "Some kind of lens?"

"A camera lens to be exact," Rachel said. "I think it might be one of Steven's."

"Any way to be sure? I mean if there's no fingerprints on it."

"No."

"Where'd you find it?"

"Alexandre was showing me around the place and I found it in the old carriage house." Rachel crossed her arms and leaned a hip against the front fender of Marc's Thunderbird. "Actually I stepped on it."

"Did he see you pick it up?"

She nodded. "Yes, but he acted surprised. He said

Yvette entertains at the house every once in a while and thought it might belong to one of her friends. I asked her, but she said no. She claimed not to have had anyone to *Sans Souci* in a long time and this," Rachel nodded toward the lens Marc was in the process of slipping into a plastic bag he'd pulled from his shirt pocket, "is not that old."

"How do you know?"

"When you have a brother who is a photographer you learn those things, whether you want to or not."

Marc reached into the car and, flipping up the glove box between the two front seats, deposited the lens and plastic bag into it. "I'll have the forensic guys do a job on it. Maybe they can find a fingerprint."

"I'd better get back before everyone gets up and I have to come up with a reason I'm wandering around outside so early," Rachel said. "Why don't you run that into the lab and get yourself a bite to eat." She turned away and then paused. "Oh, and while you're at it, change your clothes." She laughed as her eyes raked over him. "You look like you slept in those."

"I thought that was the new look." He laughed, then turned serious. "You going to be okay?"

"Yes. Alexandre is supposed to drive me into town after breakfast, but . . ." She smiled slyly. "If I can find a way to postpone that, I will. I haven't found out enough about the Beaumondiers yet, or really looked around. But I know Steven was here."

"How?"

"I just do. I can . . ." she shrugged "feel him."

Marc nodded. He was well aware of the bond between Rachel and Steven. He didn't understand it, but the time he'd spent as her partner had given him reason to accept it as fact. "If I don't hear from you by the time I've finished up in town, I'll figure you're still here and drive back out. If you need me, this," he jabbed a finger toward the car, "is where I'll be."

"You're not going to get in trouble for this, Marc, are you?" Rachel asked, for what must be the hundredth time since he'd picked her up at the airport the day before.

"Nah. I'm on vacation, remember?"

"Yeah, some vacation."

"Hey, I can think of better places to go, but I always told you, Rae, if you needed me, for anything, all you had to do was call. And I meant it. Anyway, it's kinda nice having you around again, even if it is only for a few minutes at a time."

Rachel smiled. He had always been there for her, and most likely always would be. A feeling of melancholy came over her. Why couldn't she feel more than deep friendship for him?

On impulse she closed the distance between them, stood on tiptoe, and give him a quick kiss on the cheek. "I'll talk to you later." She crossed the road and hurried along the drive. As she neared the house Rachel was surprised to see Hanson shuffling along the garden's crumbling brick walkway and carrying an ornate silver serving tray.

"Good morning," she said.

Hanson's head jerked in her direction and she could have sworn that the expression on that otherwise lifeless-looking face was one of definite disdain.

Rachel stopped, startled at the impression.

One of his gnarled, spindly hands moved to drape a linen napkin over a large, chalice type of glass that sat on the tray, but not before Rachel's keen eyes saw the film of redness left within the chalice's bowl.

"I've never been able to acquire a taste for tomato juice myself," she said, glancing again toward the linen-covered chalice. Maybe if she tried to start a conversation with him he might not seem so odd, and maybe, if she was lucky, she might learn something that would help her in her search for Steven.

But Hanson didn't answer, and when she glanced at him, she saw that his old eyes, those seemingly lifeless, near colorless blue orbs, were blazing with malevolence.

"There is coffee on the sideboard in the dining room, Ms. Domecq," Hanson said. Both his tone and his posture were very proper and calm, in spite of the fire she'd seen simmering in his eyes.

Rachel nodded. "Thank you, Hanson. Is Mrs. Beaumondier up yet? Marguerite, I mean."

"The ladies do not partake of breakfast, Ms. Domecq, therefore they do not rise in the morning."

Startled, Rachel could utter little more than, "Oh."

"*Monsieur* Beaumondier requested that I also give you his regrets but he will not be able to see you until later today. He has some . . . business matters to attend to."

"Oh, but I thought . . ." She clamped her mouth closed. This was the perfect opportunity to snoop, and they'd handed it to her on a silver platter. "Well, that's fine, Hanson. I'll just have some coffee and . . ."

"There is also toast and a trencher of scrambled eggs. I'm sorry," he sniffed, "but since the Beaumondiers do not eat a morning meal I usually do not have many breakfast type foods in the pantry."

"No problem," Rachel said cheerfully, "scrambled eggs and toast sound delicious." Though she wasn't exactly sure what a trencher was.

They were at the rear of the house and as they neared the steps leading to the gallery, Hanson veered onto the narrow path that led to the cottage that was his kitchen.

"Do you think the Beaumondiers would mind if I just

wandered around the grounds for a while after breakfast?" she called to him.

Hanson stopped and looked back at her. "Stay within view of the house, Ms. Domecq," he said, then turned and disappeared into the cookhouse.

Chapter 6

Rachel stepped through the rear door and into the warming kitchen. It was empty and the house silent. She walked to the door that led into the foyer and paused to listen again. Not the slightest sound met her ears. Returning to the opposite side of the room, near the back door, she quickly pulled the transmitter from her pocket. Rachel threw one more furtive glance toward the foyer door before flipping on the radio and speaking. Hopefully no one was up yet. "Marc?" she whispered. "Marc, can you hear me?"

As before, her answer was a buzz of static.

"Damn." He was already out of range. She slipped the tiny radio back into the pocket of her slacks and walked into the dining room. True to his word, Hanson had placed a full pot of coffee and a platter of toast and scrambled eggs on the sideboard.

"So, a trencher is a platter," she said to herself. "Must be an old-fashioned word." Her brows rose. "Could be archaic, judging from how old he looks."

Pouring herself a mug of coffee, and delighting in the fact that it was indeed chicory coffee, Rachel inhaled deeply of its tangy aroma. Most visitors to the south found the natives' choice of the strong chicory coffee appalling. Rachel loved it, the stronger the better, and she usually preferred it *cafe noir,* undoctored by either cream or sugar. She spooned a mountain of eggs onto her plate, took two pieces of toast and settled into a chair at the long table.

Stay within view of the house, Ms. Domecq. Stay within view of the house. She wondered at the old butler's words as she started her search outside for clues to Steven's disappearance. Were they meant to protect her, or warn her? Was he afraid she might get lost if she wandered too far, or that she might stumble across something the Beaumondiers, or the old butler himself, didn't want found?

Rachel stepped onto the rickety porch of a slave cabin, placed a hand on the plank door, and pushed. The door swung open easily, though its hinges creaked loudly and momentarily shattered the silence. She entered. Sunlight shone through a lone, dirt covered window on the opposite side of the room to create a haze of weak light. Something scurried across the wooden floor and disappeared into the shadows of a far corner. She took a step forward and felt an invisible veil fall across her face. Rachel jumped back, slapping a hand at the cobweb she hadn't seen and trying to brush it from her face and hair.

Afraid the web's creator might be clinging to her, Rachel hurriedly brushed herself off and vigorously shook her head. Her gaze moved over the room slowly, appreciating its history, its significance to the past, its connection to a way of life long gone. Once, she thought, a family had lived here, this one room serving as their kitchen, living room, and bedroom. Her gaze moved to a rock fireplace that took up at least half of the wall opposite the door. She remembered Alexandre having said that the brick slave cabins, the only ones left standing on *Sans Souci*, had been for the house servants. She looked around in curiosity. The wooden floor was a rarity in slave cabins. Most she came across were merely hard-packed earth.

The song of a cardinal suddenly broke through her reverie and Rachel returned to the porch of the tiny cottage. The bird's song was a lilting melody on the still afternoon air, happy and full of life, yet considering her surroundings and situation, haunting.

Rachel sighed. She had looked through every slave shack that was still standing, at least the ones she'd come across. She had searched the carriage house again, the old stables and barn, even the ruins of the *pigionniere*, and found nothing. She'd discovered no trace of Steven, and felt no sense of his presence again, either past or current.

Rachel abruptly changed her direction of thought. She didn't want to consider what the absence of her former feelings about Steven could mean, what the lack of hearing him, sensing him, might imply.

"If he was dead, wouldn't I know?" she murmured to herself. Tears filled her eyes at the thought of never seeing her brother again. No, he wasn't dead. He was her twin. A part of her. She'd know if he was dead, just like she always knew when he needed her. "I'd know if he was . . . I'd know, dammit," Rachel swore, and slapped a hand against one of the crudely cut support pillars. "I'd know because a part of me would be dead, too."

She glanced at her wristwatch, then, stepping from the porch, at the horizon. It was getting late, and the afternoon sun was waning. Surprisingly the day had passed quickly. Too quickly. She was no closer to finding out where her brother was, or what had happened to him, than she had been when she'd arrived yesterday. The plantation, according to all accounts, was over six thousand acres in size, and she'd only managed to search a few of the outbuildings around the house. She remembered the layouts of some of the other plantations she had both accepted and rejected for preservation grants over the past few years. Given the size of *Sans Souci,* it, like the others, probably had dozens of other buildings dotting its vast acreage, if they hadn't deteriorated into nothingness from years of neglect and decay. And what about the Beaumondier house itself? She hadn't felt Steven's presence there, but she could be wrong. There were two main floors, an attic, and maybe even a root cellar. And there were so many rooms.

No, she thought, and began to wander in the direction of the house. She'd received no sense of Steven in the house. If he had come to *Sans Souci,* he hadn't entered the main house, at least not for any length of time. She would have been able to feel something of him, in spite of the size of the house. Yet that puzzled her. If he had come here, and she felt certain he had especially considering the camera lens she'd found, then why would he not have gone into the main house? Steven loved the south's old antebellum houses, and the Beaumondier mansion was a natural for inclusion in the book he'd been putting together on Louisiana's historic plantations. She couldn't take the chance she was wrong. Somehow she'd have to find a way to search the main house.

As she stepped onto the gallery Rachel sensed instantly that she was not alone. She glanced in both directions but saw no one. And then, as if drawn, she turned to look at the *garconniere.* Alexandre had just exited its front door and was approaching the house along the crumbling brick pathway that meandered through the once-formal garden. Without giving thought to her action, she moved to stand beside one of the pillars, stepping into its shadow, out of the light of the sinking sun, and watched him come near.

The softness of the sunset transformed the dead and overgrown garden to a place of almost mystical enchantment, a vista of disguised colors. Dried brown leaves shone golden, brittle branches were touched with pink sunbeams and given the deceptive glow of life, gray veils of Spanish moss turned to filmy curtains of lace, while the dark forest green leaves of the tall, gnarled and sprawling live oaks glimmered emerald green and silver.

And through all of this, Alexandre Beaumondier passed like a burnished bronze god. The curls of his hair turned a glistening blue black beneath the soft rays, while here and there the brilliance of the waning sunbeams caught within the strands and gleamed like a cache of precious stones hidden among the silken tresses.

Seemingly oblivious to her presence, he strode toward her with all the grace and fluidity of a large jungle cat. Each swing of his legs, each sweep of his arms were more that of a great lion or a panther's symmetrical, smooth and effortless execution of muscle than the unconsciously mechanical movements of a mere mortal man.

Rachel felt the slight acceleration of her pulses that seemed to occur whenever he was around, felt her heart begin to flutter within her breast as she watched him. He was one of the most handsome men she had ever seen, and one of the most mysterious. She could not deny she was attracted to him, any more than she could deny that she was unexplainably and unreasonably afraid of him.

After Steven had called and announced that he'd

fallen madly in love, at first sight, with a woman named Yvette Beaumondier, and before Rachel had come to New Orleans, she had done a little checking on the Beaumondier family. She'd found little concrete information.

Rachel momentarily lost sight of Alexandre as he passed beneath the shadows of a huge live oak.

What she had discovered was that rumormongers labeled Alexandre a recluse. A man who protected his seclusion from the world to near eccentricity. Newspaper gossips described him as a man of powerful wealth and old family lines who shunned everyone, including women. Local politicians and business people disliked him for his refusals to help them financially, and the police . . . a shiver curled up Rachel's spine . . . the police, according to Marc, suspected there was more to Alexandre Beaumondier, and the rest of his family, than met the eye. They just didn't know what it was.

Why? Rachel wondered, her mind going back to Alexandre's reclusiveness. Why had Alexandre shut himself away from the world for so long? And so completely? Merely because, as Yvette had said, he'd once loved and been spurned?

Alexandre continued to follow the path as it curved toward the house and as he neared Rachel, he looked in her direction and their eyes met.

Suddenly, without warning blue fused with gray and Rachel felt herself spiraling out of control. She no longer stood on the time worn gallery of *Sans Souci,* was no longer surrounded by dying and dead foliage, blue skies and sprawling moss laden oak trees. Walls of rock encompassed her, huge square carved blocks of rock. Her gaze rose to meet a turreted roof. A castle. She looked around. A huge tapestry hung from one wall, the arched curve of a doorway split another. Golden light, mingled with gray black shadows, flickered a reflection upon the wall and tapestry. Rachel turned to look behind her. A massive fireplace made up the bottom half of the far wall. Flames danced within its monstrous grate.

Shock and pleasure rippled through her, for standing before the raised rock hearth was Alexandre. His dark hair glistened in the reflection of the flames that cast his face in a contrast of light and shadows, transforming his cheekbones to cliffs of saffron, the sweeping hollows beneath to valleys of inky darkness. He was dressed in the attire of seventeenth-century French nobility—a white shirt, both its collar and the cuffs of its billowing sleeves of ruffled lace, a thigh length vest of embroidered tapestry, tight black breeches, and a flowing, floor length cape was draped over his shoulders.

As Rachel watched, Alexandre swept the cape from his shoulders, let it fall onto one of the tall wing chairs that stood before the fireplace, and turned to a young woman with flowing blonde curls who stood several feet away. She seemed frightened of him, her large brown eyes brimming with tears of fear, and her hands trembled. Smiling seductively Alexandre moved toward her and drew her easily into his arms. He whispered something in her ear, smiled, and brushed his lips across hers. The girl moaned softly, her fear gone now, and clung to him, wrapping her slender arms around his shoulders as she pressed her lithe body to his. Alexandre touched a trail of kisses down the long, bare column of her neck.

Rachel felt a swell of tears fill her eyes and her vision blurred. She shook her head and everything turned to a murky panorama of green and black. Suddenly light broke through the darkness, golden and blinding. She looked up to find herself surrounded by trees, thick growing, sprawling trees, and through their heavy limbs, in one spot, shone a brilliant beam of sunshine. Birds chirped merrily from within the foliage covered boughs and squirrels chattered and rustled across the dried leaves on the ground. She heard laughter, deep and drawling, and turned. Alexandre stood only a few feet away, his arms outstretched toward her, love shining in his eyes. Rachel reached a hand toward him, wanting nothing more than to move into the circle of his embrace.

"Rachel, are you all right?" Alexandre said.

She frowned and stared up at him as if through a dense fog. He wasn't smiling anymore. And the light of love that had been in his eyes, that sensuous glimmer that had made her feel so warm and loved, so complete, was gone.

"Rachel?"

She closed her own eyes and shook her head, then looked back at him again.

"Damn, Rachel, answer me. Are you all right?" Alexandre asked again, his tone harsh.

Tears blurred his image. She wanted to see that warm glow in his eyes again, yearned to feel his love reach out to her again, needed to . . .

"Rachel?" Alexandre tugged at her arm gently. "Rachel, answer me."

"I . . . I'm fine," she managed, and shook her head again. "I . . . I just felt faint for a minute, that's all." She laughed weakly.

His eyes bore into hers, delving past the lie in search of the truth. "What happened?" he asked softly.

That was a good question, Rachel thought as the fog of her vision seemed to lift from her brain and reality returned; what had happened? She and Steven shared a physical bond, that had always been how she'd always explained their ability to communicate with just thoughts. But visions? She'd never experienced anything like that before. And she'd never believed in them.

She looked up at Alexandre, but his eyes held nothing more than a beautiful swirl of gray blue color. "I just felt a little weak, that's all."

"Weak?" His glare turned calculating and dropped to her throat. "Did you sleep all right last night? You didn't go out again after . . . ?"

"No, no. I was fine."

Alexandre felt a rush of relief. He didn't trust them, any of them. Not around her. He couldn't. Not after . . . He forced the thought from his mind. And he didn't trust himself either. "Have you eaten anything today?"

"Hanson made me some toast and eggs this morning."

His eyebrows rose, arcs of black that soared upward like the spreading of a raven's wings. "That's all? You haven't eaten anything since?"

She shook her head. "No, I was wandering the grounds, just taking a walk. I guess I lost track of the time, but I wasn't really hungry anyway."

He took her arm and steered her toward the door. "Hanson probably has your dinner ready now."

Rachel looked up at him as he led her into the dining room. "*My* dinner? You're not eating again?"

He pulled her chair from the table, waited for her to slide onto it, and then took his own seat. "I had a rather large lunch. But I will enjoy a drink while you dine." He retrieved a bell that sat near his place setting and shook it slightly.

Its musical tinkle echoed throughout the large room. The door that led from the warming kitchen swung open and Hanson appeared with a serving tray. He paused beside Alexandre, removed a large swatch of white linen that covered the tray, and placed a silver chalice before him. The old butler set an identical one before Rachel, along with a plate laden with steaming chicken stew, rice and crawfish, fried okra and yellow squash.

The delicious aromas of the food filled the air and teased her already watering taste buds. Her stomach did a little flip flop and growled. She quickly looked at Alexandre to see if he'd noticed, but if he had he was pretending otherwise. She felt her face flush. Obviously she *was* hungry.

"Good evening, Alexandre." Yvette swept into the room. "Oh, Rachel, you're still here." She smiled. "Good. I took the liberty of assuming you'd stay tonight so I sent Hanson into town today to retrieve your things from the hotel. Perhaps later we can visit a while in the parlor."

Rachel stared at her, dumbstruck.

"Yvette, you shouldn't have done that," Alexandre said. His tone was as harsh as the coldness that immediately filled his eyes. "Perhaps Rachel has other plans and prefers not to stay here again tonight."

"Oh, no, that's fine," Rachel hurried to say, having collected herself and overcome her surprise at Yvette's audacity. Actually, this was better than she'd hoped for. Even so, there was something about Yvette that just didn't set well with Rachel. It was almost as if the woman didn't want her to leave, yet she made little effort at visiting with Rachel. And then there was the camera lens. She'd denied knowing anything about it, but if it didn't belong to one of her friends, and if Alexandre was telling the truth and he knew nothing about it, then whose was it? And how had it gotten to *Sans Souci?* Unless . . . Rachel hadn't considered Suzanne before, since Yvette had been the one Steven had mentioned. Was it possible the lens was connected somehow with Suzanne, and didn't belong to Steven?

"See, Alexandre, I knew it would be all right." She smiled smugly. "Have you seen Marguer . . . mother, this evening, Alexandre?"

"No."

Rachel couldn't help but note the curtness in his abrupt answer.

"Oh, well, I'm going out for a while." She swept toward the entry door. "I'll see you two later."

"Yvette," Alexandre said, a definite warning tone to his voice.

She laughed. "Oh, don't worry darling, I'm not going into town. Just down the road a bit."

Rachel picked at her food and pretended not to notice the scathing glance Alexandre threw after his sister. Why was he so angry that she was going out? Did he expect them all to remain in seclusion just because he chose to?

"So, did you find anything interesting in your wanderings today, Rachel?"

She glanced up to find him looking directly at her. The anger that had been etched on his face only a few short seconds ago, during his conversation with Yvette, was now completely gone. He smiled as her gaze met his. Rachel felt the instant pull his gray eyes seemed to invoke over her, drawing her toward him, infusing her with the desire to be held by him. She jerked her eyes away from his, breaking the mesmerizing spell he had so easily cast over her.

"Well, I looked through some of those old brick slave cabins you'd mentioned," she said, hearing the quaking in her voice and straining to subdue it. "They're in remarkably good condition, actually. They'd make a wonderful exhibit."

He sipped from his chalice, his gaze never veering from hers. "What else did you look through, Rachel?"

She suddenly found the room extremely warm.

Rachel! Help me!

Rachel sat bolt upright in her chair. The fork she held slipped from her fingers and clattered noisily to her plate.

Oh, God, Rachel! Please.

"Steven," she whispered. Fear for him coursed through her veins. Her body turned to angles of stiff tension and her fingers curled into fists.

Rachel!

She squeezed her eyes shut and dropped her head forward slightly. Where are you, Steven? she screamed silently. Where are you?

Help me! Oh, God, Rachel! Help. . . .

"Steven!" She shot to her feet. Her legs knocked into the chair she'd just vacated causing it to scrape across the hardwood planked floor in a grinding skid. She clenched trembling fingers into fists at her sides. His cries echoed in her mind, tormenting her. Railing at her helplessness. Her ineffectiveness. Her eyes glistened as she stared across the room and looked past Alexandre, past the brick and plaster walls, past the overgrown gardens beyond the house.

Alexandre, alarmed at her sudden outburst, rose to his feet. He didn't know what was happening, but he knew he didn't like it. "Rachel, what is it?" He walked around the table to stand at her side. "What's wrong?"

She saw him! Her heart pounded wildly. Steven was lying on some sort of high bed or table, its surface draped with an old gray sheet or cloth. Rachel closed her eyes. A tall floor candelabrum stood beside the bed, black, wrought iron, its tapers having burned down long ago. Dried wax drippings hung from each ruffle-lipped sconce.

"Steven," Rachel whispered. She squeezed her eyelids tighter together and tried to concentrate, to ignore Alexandre and call to her brother. "Steven," she whispered again. "Steven, where are you?"

He turned to face her, his face ashen and gaunt. His lips formed her name.

"Steven?" she murmured louder.

His image faded.

"No."

"Rachel." Alexandre grabbed her shoulders and forced her around to face him. "What's the matter? What did you see? Who's Steven?"

She swallowed hard and refused to let the threatening tears come to her eyes. "My brother."

He looked at her in puzzlement. "You have visions? Of your brother? Why? What does it mean?"

"Nothing." She shrugged and forced herself to smile. "Nothing, really." Rachel suddenly felt as if she had no strength, as if her legs were, any second, going to refuse to hold her weight any longer and buckle beneath her. She lay a hand on Alexandre's forearm to steady herself.

"You need some air." Slipping an arm around her waist, Alexandre led her through the foyer and out onto the front gallery. At the top of the steps that fanned down to the entry walk, they paused. To the right the moon hung just above the horizon and turned the treetops to a ragged silhouette of blackness.

"What happened in there?" Alexandre asked. His arm remained wrapped securely around her waist. He looked down at her as he waited for her to answer, breathing deeply of the sweet scent of jasmine that seemed to cling to her. He wanted to slip his fingers through the long wavy strands of her hair, feel the auburn gold threads slide over his flesh. He wanted to press his lips to hers, cup her breasts within the palms of his hands. He wanted to . . .

Rachel closed her eyes and let the warm night air caress her frazzled senses. He was holding her. She wanted to turn in his arms and move deeper into their embrace. Nothing mattered anymore, nothing but Alexandre.

Alexandre saw what was happening and released his hold on her. He moved to stand beside one of the pillars, leaning a shoulder against it lazily. "What's going on, Rachel?" he asked. "What happened to your brother?"

Rachel inhaled a deep, shuddering breath and moved to sit on one of the wooden chairs that graced the front gallery. Her reeling senses quieted and thoughts of Steven returned. He was alive. She knew that now for certain. He was alive. But he was in trouble. She forced a composure to herself that she was far from feeling.

Her gaze rose to meet Alexandre's again and, like the surge of a wave washing away the old sand, his eyes, and what emanated from their misty gray depths, washed all thought of anything but him for her mind.

Alexandre asserted a steely control over himself. He wanted her, more than he had wanted anything in a long time, but he also wanted the truth of what had happened just a few minutes ago, what she'd seen, what was happening. He turned away from her. "Tell me what's wrong, Rachel," he said, his voice low and commanding.

Again reality surged forth as his eyes released their hold on hers. Rachel stared at his back, wanting to reach out and touch him, yet forcing her hands to remain still. She couldn't give herself away now. Steven was somewhere nearby. If not on *Sans Souci*, then somewhere closely adjacent to it, and in spite of Yvette's denials to the police, Rachel felt certain the woman knew more than she was telling. Perhaps she was even behind whatever was happening to Steven.

Alexandre fought the urge to turn back to her, to draw her body against his and cover her lips with his own. It was more than the fact that she looked so much like Danielle. At first he felt sure, it had been nothing more than that. But no longer. In the few short hours he had been in her company, he had begun to feel a strength within Rachel Domecq that he admired, and which drew him. He had begun to find her curiosity enchanting, her intelligence enticing, her company more than just pleasurable.

"My twin brother, Steven and I share a sort of psychic bond. We always have," Rachel said. She turned to look out upon the dark landscape as she spoke. "He was calling to me a few minutes ago, while we were dining, and I became scared. I thought he was in trouble."

"But he wasn't?"

"No," Rachel lied, wishing it was the truth. She forced herself to laugh and rose from her seat. "He likes to play little tricks on me. See how much he can rile me. He's always done that. You know, the usual rotten type of things brothers do to sisters?"

One corner of Alexandre's mouth curved upward and he turned to find her standing beside him. "No, sorry, I don't," he said, his voice edged with desire. "Being the youngest, I never really got to do anything like that."

Rachel laughed. "Really? I would have thought with two sisters you'd have had plenty of opportunity for pranks."

"Perhaps once or twice, I don't remember. It's been too long."

"Too long?" She forced a gaiety to her voice she wished she could really feel, but her mind was still too preoccupied with worry over Steven while her body was responding to Alexandre's nearness like a moth to flame. "Really, Alexandre, you make yourself sound absolutely ancient."

An almost sad smile curved his lips.

Chapter 7

"Perhaps we'd best join the others in the parlor now." Alexandre drew the shroud of emotional protection around him that he had woven so long ago and reminded himself, perhaps cruelly, that the feelings burgeoning to life within him toward her had to be denied at all costs. He cupped her bent elbow with his hand, though even that innocent physical contact cost him, and urged her toward the door.

"Just a few more minutes, Alexandre, please," Rachel said. "It's so peaceful here, and so beautiful."

Alexandre, slightly unnerved by her words, turned his head to follow her gaze. It had been a long time since he'd thought of his home as peaceful or beautiful.

Rachel moved down the stairway. "In the twilight," she said, her voice floating to him over her shoulder, "the gardens, even overgrown as they are, seem sort of mystical, don't you think?" She was trying to be tactful. She could have said dead, which would have been a more appropriate description of them, but overgrown sounded a bit nicer. She was also trying to distance herself from him. Keep him at arm's length. Whatever there was about Alexandre Beaumondier, whatever physical allure he possessed, it worked on her extremely well, and now, when she should be thinking of nothing except Steven, just wasn't the time for her to respond to it. "It really is beautiful. Their leaves reflect the golden glow of the moon in a myriad of colors." She turned to look back at him. "As if the night brings them the life that the daylight denies them."

"Perhaps that is true of many things." The deep, honey smooth drawl of his voice reached out to touch her. It slid over her arms, snaked its way up her spine, and skipped along the curves of her legs until Rachel felt as if she were aching with the need to feel his arms around her, his mouth on hers.

She pulled her gaze from his, embarrassed, and looked out at the hulking dark forms of the trees that dotted the landscape of *Sans Souci.* "Night has always been my favorite time," she said softly.

"I always prefer the daylight myself," Alexandre said.

She turned, startled at how close he was. Her heartbeat accelerated and she felt her fingers tremble. The now familiar scent of dark forests and fresh earth surrounded him, emanated from him, a strange yet sensuously enticing fragrance. Rachel felt it engulf her. "But the night can mask the harshness of the world," Rachel said, her voice little more than a ragged whisper now. "It can soften the sometimes cruel touches of reality, disguise the ugliness that the light of day so uncharitably reveals to all, and transform some place such as a dead garden, that might in the sunlight scare us, into a place of shimmering elegant beauty."

"Sometimes," Alexandre said, so close to her that the warmth of his breath wafted over her temple and stirred the tiny wisp of a curl that lay there, "it is better to see things as they truly are, Rachel, than merely as you want them to be."

She looked up at him then, sensing he was trying to

tell her something without actually saying it. "Is it?" She leaned toward him, unable to help herself, unwilling to help herself. "Is it always, Alexandre?" she whispered.

He looked down into her eyes. It was like being swept back in time, back to over a hundred years ago, to a woman he had thought long dead, long banished from his thoughts. It was as if he were looking into the same eyes, at the same face, hearing the same voice. He had loved Danielle with all of his heart, and he had thought she loved him as much. But he'd been wrong.

He felt the will to resist her leaving him.

"Is it, Alexandre?" Rachel repeated.

His arms slipped around her waist and he dragged her against him. "Sometimes, Rachel," he whispered, his voice husky with emotion, "sometimes." His hands pressed against her back and crushed her breasts to his chest, her hips to his thighs.

Her head tilted back as she looked up at him. Her hands moved slowly atop his chest, sliding over the lapels of his jacket until her arms encircled his neck.

A battle waged within him even yet, right against wrong, mind against heart, logic against passion. He wanted her, more desperately than he had wanted anything in years, but knew he shouldn't take her. In the end it would be no different than before. His head lowered.

Rachel struggled to defy the lure of his lips, to foil the sensuous enchantment that came with being held in his arms, but it was a battle, even before she began the fight, that she knew she could not win. Once in his arms wanting him was an irresistible obsession, succumbing to him a fate she had no control over. She felt his mouth cover hers, his lips gentle and yet hard, hungry and yet caressing, threatening to devour her, and promising to love her. His tongue moved between her lips, an emissary of desire, reaching out to awake the passions that lay asleep within her and incite the fervor of her own needs.

All thought of resistance, of defiance and distance, fled her mind. Rachel let her eyelids flutter closed. It was a strangely tender kiss, yet threaded with an aura of demand. His arms crushed her to him. She felt his heartbeat resound against her breast, her own racing as rapidly as Alexandre's, the two beats coming together in rhythmic cadence and melding as if one.

Rachel signed at the ecstasy his kiss invoked. Her arms tightened around him, one hand slipping within the curls of hair at the nape of his neck, her fingers burying themselves within the silken blackness.

His tongue thrust deeper into her mouth, a searching vanguard of flame, each stroke igniting yet another burst of fire within her, each caress stoking the coiled passion his touch had aroused. She felt the agony of his self-imposed loneliness in the urgency of his kiss, sensed the magnitude of love he had to give in the ravishment of his touch to her senses. A trembling weakness spread through her body, a languor that left her nearly helpless in his arms and filled her with an aching need for him to continue the sweet torment of his assault.

Never before had she been kissed like this. Not by the man she'd dated for two years before joining the police force, and not even by the man she had married and believed would love her forever.

Alexandre's hands pressed against her back, a gentle grasp, a resolute demand, bringing her closer to his tall length, curves filling planes, lithe softness drawn against hard muscle, fitting, melding, fusing. His lips caressed hers, cajoled her senses, demanded her surrender. They trailed a path along the curve of her jaw, leaving behind flesh tingling with pinpoints of flame. They searched the shape and texture of her ear, the tip of his tongue moving along the shell-like curve and sending a shiver of delicious tremors racing up her spine.

His arms crushed her tightly, their secure clasp nearly robbing her of the ability to breathe, but she didn't care. For the first time in her life Rachel was lost in a haze of passion, in a swirl of sheer pleasure and want. Hot, hungry emotions engulfed her, leaving her limbs languid, her thoughts delirious, her desires clawing through her body, through her veins and overriding every thought except those of the man who held her. His tongue plunged into her mouth again to duel with her own as one of his hands slid through the long tangles of her hair and cupped the back of her head.

She felt his other hand slip around her waist and move upward until his fingers encircled and cupped her breast.

Lost in a swirl of rapture, Rachel moaned softly, the faint, almost imperceptible sound swallowed immediately as it left her lips and passed between his.

"Well, Alexandre, I do believe you've taken a liking to our little guest."

Through her haze of passion Rachel felt Alexandre stiffen in her arms at the sound of his sister's taunting remark. He tore his lips from hers and spun around.

Rachel stumbled at his sudden desertion. She hurriedly reached toward a nearby pillar to steady herself while she fought to get her disordered senses under control. Her cheeks burned with embarrassment.

"Do you have no sense of privacy, Yvette?" Alexandre sneered. He made no effort to conceal the rancor he felt at her tactless intrusion.

Yvette laughed and sidled up the walkway toward them. "Well, of course I do, Alexandre. I guess I was just so happy to see you finally coming out of that shell you've been living in for so long that I couldn't resist commenting."

"I didn't know you ever made an effort to resist doing anything you wanted to do, *Yvette.*" He put a deriding emphasis on her name.

"Oh, Alexandre," she cooed, batting her long lashes and feigning a pout, "you make me sound absolutely horrible."

"Not horrible, Yvette," he stood with his gaze pinioned on her, "just avaricious, and a bit vexing."

"Self-indulgent? Me?" she scoffed merrily. "Why, Alexandre, you know very well that all I ever wanted, and still want, is for you to be happy."

Alexandre glanced over his shoulder at Rachel and quickly turned his attention back to Yvette. "The subject is closed, Yvette."

"But Alexandre, whatever I've done, you know I did it for you."

Rachel saw Alexandre's shoulders stiffen further.

"For me, Yvette?" His tone was one of scathing derision. "Or for the illustrious Beaumondier name?"

Her eyes narrowed and all pretense of good humor disappeared from her face. "Both, Alexandre, whether you choose to believe it or not." She turned suddenly to Rachel and smiled. "Rachel, dear, I wanted to tell you; I was in town last night and heard something very disturbing."

Rachel felt a sense of uneasiness. "What, Yvette?"

She smiled and the gesture, rather than give comfort, sent a ripple of apprehensive shivers over Rachel's flesh. "Well, you're the sister of that man who is missing, aren't you? That photographer, Steven Ligere." She glanced at Alexandre. "You remember, Alexandre, the police came here because they thought the man had come here to *Sans Souci?*"

Alexandre turned and looked at Rachel, suspicion blazing in his eyes, but that wasn't what made her heart feel as if it had just shattered into a million pieces. Past the suspicion and surprise, she saw the hurt his sister's words of Rachel's deceit had brought to him.

"Alexandre," Rachel said, "I can explain."

"There's no need."

"Yes, there is." She put a hand on his arm. "Please."

He didn't answer, but he didn't turn away either.

"The society does want to look into preserving *Sans Souci*, and yes, Steven is my brother and he is missing, but that's not why I came here," she lied. "The police are doing everything they can to find Steven, and . . ." well, she'd told one lie, she might as well tell another, "and anyway, I'm not that worried about my brother. He's always going off on some unannounced trip or impulsive jaunt without telling anyone, including me. I'm used to it."

"Then why did the police come here?" Alexandre asked. "Why are they even looking for him if, as you say, this is a common thing with him?"

Rachel sighed. "Because Steven never went back to his hotel and all, or most, of his clothes are still there. But really," she hurried to add, "that doesn't mean a thing, and you'd agree, if you knew Steven." She forced herself to laugh. "He's probably scooting around the bayous or something, taking pictures to his heart's content, and I doubt the thought that anyone would be worried over his abrupt departure has even entered his mind. It never does."

"He did seem a rather impulsive sort," Yvette said.

Rachel whirled to look at her. "The police told me that you claimed never to have met Steven."

Alexandre glared at Yvette.

She laughed lightly, the soft, musical sound wafting

across the night air. "Oh, no, Rachel, you must be mistaken, or they didn't relate the right information. I told them I'd met Steven, in a bar on Magazine Street. He bought me a drink and we chatted for quite a while. Then he invited me to a late dinner, but I declined. We danced a few times and . . ." she laughed again, "well, he said he thought he was falling in love with me." She shook her head as if in disbelief. "Men. I've never met one before who believed in love at first sight. It was kind of refreshing, actually. Rather cute. But," she shrugged, "I left a short time later."

"And you never invited him here?" Rachel asked.

"I don't mean to insult, Rachel, but, well, to be honest, your brother just wasn't my type." She laughed softly. "I'm sure you know how that is. I prefer tall and dark. Your brother was, if I remember correctly, sort of fair, and well under six feet." She brushed past them. "I'll leave you two alone now. Sorry for the interruption."

Rachel stared after Yvette, not because she had anything more to say to the woman, but because she was afraid to look at Alexandre, reluctant to face the disillusionment she knew was in his eyes.

"Shall we go in?" he said brusquely, his tone causing her apprehension to deepen.

Why did it seem to matter so much to her what he thought? She'd just met him. It wasn't as if she was in love with him. He was a man who lived his life in total seclusion, shunning everyone and everything. She could never live like that. Never love anyone who lived like that. She looked up at him as his hand moved to cup her elbow. No, she wasn't in love with him . . . was she?

They walked into the parlor together, neither speaking to the other, yet each intensely, almost painfully, aware of the other's closeness.

"Oh, there you two are," Marguerite said. "Suzanne and I were just wondering where you'd gotten to."

"We were just on the gallery enjoying a breath of air," Alexandre said. He moved away from Rachel to take up a position by the fireplace.

Marguerite poured tea and handed a cup to Rachel who sat on the settee opposite her.

Asmodeus jumped onto the settee and, with no hesitation whatsoever, slid his sleek black body past Rachel's arm and settled in a tight, curled ball on her lap. Rachel set the cup of tea onto a nearby table and absently stroked the animal's back. Black lids slowly closed over brilliant green eyes and the cat began to purr.

"It looks like you have definitely made a friend of Asmodeus," Marguerite said.

Alexandre watched her silently, shaking his head at Marguerite's silent offering of tea.

Rachel looked up. "He's such a sweetheart, he really doesn't deserve a name that means Devil."

"I'm not sure Apollyon would agree with you," Yvette said, and stooped to pick up Asmodeus's female counterpart who, with her nose held regally in the air, had been in the process of wrapping herself around Yvette's ankles. "He's always giving my little Apollyon a bad time." She began to pet the animal's head. Apollyon didn't close her eyes, but merely stared down at Rachel with disdain.

Rachel averted her gaze. Temptress, she sneered silently. Apollyon was about as tempting as a dragon. She glanced back at the cat. A shiver of unease snaked its way up her back. It was ridiculous, she told herself for the umpteenth time. Impossible. Apollyon was just a cat. A plain, ordinary cat. She wouldn't, couldn't, be looking at her with contempt.

Marguerite laughed lightly. "I'm not so sure I would

agree either, Rachel," she said. "Asmodeus is sometimes a little too independent for his own good, and ours."

"And loyalty is a trait the Beaumondiers have always valued above almost all others," Yvette said. She looked at Alexandre. "Isn't it, Alexandre?"

Chapter 8

"Miss Catherine sends her regrets," Hanson said, standing in the doorway of the parlor, "but she will not be coming downstairs this evening. She is not feeling well."

Rachel's hand paused atop Asmodeus's back. "Oh, I'm sorry," she said to the old butler. "Is there anything I can do?"

The old butler looked at Rachel and she shivered, experiencing the sensation that rather than looking *at* her, he was actually looking *through* her. "I have taken care of Miss Catherine," he said coldly. He turned toward the others. "Will there be anything else this evening, Miss Marguerite?"

"No, Hanson, thank you."

"Mr. Alexandre?"

Alexandre shook his head.

Hanson nodded and, backing away from the doorway, disappeared.

"I'm sorry, Rachel," Marguerite said. "I know you wanted to talk to her about the house and such, but . . ." she shrugged. "Perhaps *Grandmere* will be up to talking with you tomorrow. You will be able to stay, won't you?"

"Well, I will have to be getting back to my office soon, but . . ." she paused, "another day or two should be all right."

"Good."

Rachel glanced up at Alexandre, but if she was hoping to see pleasure on his face at the prospect of her visit being prolonged, she was disappointed.

Alexandre let his arm slide from where he'd rested it on the mantel and moved to stand before one of the tall windows that looked out onto the front landscape of *Sans Souci.* He wanted her to stay, and he knew he should want her to leave. Though it had been obvious to him almost from the start that her personality was nothing like Danielle's, Rachel's physical resemblance to the woman whom he had loved so long ago was uncanny, so much so that he found it hard to believe her visit to *Sans Souci* was one of mere happenchance. He glanced over his shoulder to where Rachel sat talking with Marguerite.

He wanted her to stay, and he knew he should do everything in his power to entice her to go. Her continued presence at *Sans Souci* was dangerous for both of them, but especially for her.

Rachel! Rachel, help me!

Rachel shot up from her pillow, her hands clenched into fists, every muscle in her body taut with tension. "Steven?" she mumbled into the darkness of her room. "For God's sake, Steven, where are you? What's wrong?"

Rachel! Rachel!

Tears filled her eyes, hot and stinging. He was terrified and in trouble, and for the first time in her life, she didn't know how to help him.

Rachel threw back the coverlet, slid from the bed and hurried across the room to the window. She slapped back the heavy draperies and stared through her tears at the moonlit night. "Steven?" she said again, trying hard to concentrate, to make him hear her. "Steven, where are you?" She crossed her arms and held them tightly to her ribs. "Where are you?"

Oh, God, Rachel, help me. Help me. . . .

The hot moisture of her tears fell over her lids and streamed down her cheeks in snaking, silver trails as the feeling of helplessness engulfed her. He was somewhere near, she felt certain of that. But where? "Where are you, dammit?" she swore, and choked back a sob. "Steven, answer me!" Why was it she could always hear him so clearly, but he could not always receive her messages. She closed her eyes and cut off the flow of tears. Steven, where are you? Please, tell me where you are.

No further messages came through. No more cries for help, no pleas for her to hear him, no screams for her to come to his aid.

Silence engulfed her, overwhelming her overly alert senses, thundering in her ears louder than any storm, any scream could. Rachel pushed the window up, unlatched the jib door and walked out on the wide gallery. She stared into the darkness, trying to penetrate the inky blackness that dwelt beneath the tall, moss draped live oaks, to pierce the shadowy landscape of the overgrown brambles and weeds that had once been a formal garden . . . to find Steven.

Last night Yvette had disappeared into those dank shadows, but tonight there was no movement in the murkiness, no . . . her gun! She hadn't gone back for her gun. Returning hastily to the bedchamber, Rachel slipped on a baptiste wrapper that matched the yoke embroidered white gown she wore. Neither belonged to her. She had found both placed neatly across the foot of her bed when she'd returned to the room that evening and, in spite of the fact that Hanson had retrieved her own things from the hotel, Rachel had found the beautifully delicate ensemble too tempting to resist wearing. The gown flowed about her like whispering threads of the sheerest of silk, rustling softly whenever she moved, billowing about her feet like wisps of ivory fog. The neckline, embroided with tiny orange flowers and brilliant emerald green leaves and vines, plunged deeply between her breasts, while her arms remained bare, until she slipped into the voluminous sleeves of the wrapper.

Quietly exiting her room she hurried to the landing down the stairs and out the front door. At the edge of the gallery she paused and looked around, hoping no one was up and about. She had to get her gun. The heels of her shoes sank partially into the earth as she moved across the grounds. Stopping at the place where she thought the attack from the bat had occurred, Rachel looked around. Moonlight glistened on the blades of wild grass that covered the ground, but nowhere did she see the gleam of a gun's polished steel barrel.

"Damn, it has to be here." She began to kick at the tall blades of grass with her foot, swishing them back and forth.

"Looking for something, Rachel?"

Rachel gasped and whirled around. "Yvette."

Yvette smiled and walked closer.

"I . . . I couldn't sleep and thought I'd . . . I was just out walking," Rachel lied, "and dropped my . . ." Dropped her what? Her mind spun in search of an answer, in search of a plausible lie. "Dropped my bracelet. I was, ah, twisting it about my fingers and I dropped it."

"Perhaps you'd have better luck finding it in the morning. When it's light."

"Yes," Rachel turned back toward the house. "You're probably right."

She hurried across the weed-choked landscape, up the gallery steps, and through the foyer without looking back. But she knew Yvette was still standing there, watching her. She could almost feel the woman's stare on her back. The entry door clicked shut behind her. She didn't pause until she had ascended the wide staircase, dashed down the hallway, and closed the door to her bedroom behind her. Her hands were trembling violently. Rachel was ashamed to admit that there was something about Yvette Beaumondier that made her uneasy, and it had nothing to do with Steven. Yvette was beautiful, there was no denying that, and she had been nothing less than gracious, if somewhat cool, to Rachel the entire time she'd been at *Sans Souci*. But there was something about the woman's eyes, a coldness, that was unnerving.

Rachel shivered. How could Steven have thought he'd fallen in love with Yvette?

She crossed the room to stand at the window again. "Where are you, Steven?" she murmured. "If it really was Yvette, and you came here, then where are you?"

Alexandre stared at the chalice that sat on the table beside him. It had sat beside him for the past several hours, and all during that time he had fought the urge to reach for it. He felt the thirst within him, the growing need, and struggled to contain it. To deny it. His mouth watered, while at the same time his throat felt parched. Every instinct within him told him, beseeched him, to lift the chalice to his lips, to drink the animal blood Hanson had brought him. It was the only thing that gave him strength, that let him get through each day and night, and continued the cursed existence he had tried so many times to end.

His hand, resting atop the curved arm of the leather wing chair, curled into a tight fist. He had tried so many times since Danielle left him to end his existence. At first he had merely walked out into the light of day. But the scorching rays had not killed him as he'd hoped. The burnt flesh had brought him excruciating pain, but he hadn't ceased to be and eventually, as he tried again and again, he had built up a tolerance for the sun's bright rays. He had entered churches and plunged his hands into their holy water—only to find himself writhing in agony, but far from ending his existence. And then he'd remembered his grandmother's words; only the touch of steel can truly end our existence before its rightful time. And so he had fought in the world's wars, hoping for the blade of a bayonet or the fragment of a bomb to pierce his heart.

A whispered oath escaped his dry lips, but his eyes never left the thick, red liquid that glowed a deep crimson beneath the flickering flame of the candle that sat near the chalice.

"Why can't I do it?" Alexandre asked aloud.

Before Danielle had come into his life, before he had experienced love, and warmth and tenderness, he had existed exactly as the others; caring only about himself, satisfying his needs and desires. But knowing Danielle, being the recipient of her love, even if only for a while, and finding that he could give love, that he not only wanted her, but loved her, had altered his thoughts and feelings, and he couldn't go back to the old ways. He was changed, and yet he wasn't changed. His heart knew love, had felt compassion and warmth, and liked it, but his body still felt the need to kill, to drink the blood of others. It was the main force of his existence, an existence he damned with the passing of each new day, and yet he couldn't bring himself to end it with his own hand.

After Danielle had turned from him, and then disappeared, he had tried to go on as he had before, but it had proven impossible. She had touched him where no other woman ever had, leaving a mark of humanity burned onto his heart, and a self-hatred that was almost all consuming. But starvation was a termination of existence Alexandre could not force himself to endure. Soon he had found himself preying on only the dying, stealing the last vestiges of life from their ancient veins, robbing them of their final few precious moments of life.

And so he had gone on. Yet, even now, more than two hundred years since the day she walked out of his life, each time he lifted the chalice to his lips and drank, he heard Danielle's rejection echo within his mind. As the rich crimson liquid flowed down through his throat and warmed his veins, he saw the horror of realization shining from her eyes, and perceived, like a tangible force, the revulsion and disgust she'd felt at having to acknowledge the truth to herself about the man she loved.

Alexandre stared at the chalice, the tangy scent of the animal blood that filled it wafting up to tease his senses. He had not tasted human blood for over two hundred years, surviving on the life force of the animals Hanson slaughtered.

He closed his eyes and lay his head back against the chair. Hanson. One of them, yet not one of them. He sighed and finally giving into the craving that burned his throat, he reached a trembling hand toward the chalice. His fingers came in contact with the long silver stem. He opened his eyes just in time to see the chalice tip at his touch.

It fell on its side with a clatter. The gleaming metal smashed against the marble top of the table, the liquid poured forth, spread across the table and, flowing over the carved mahogany edges, dripped to the floor.

Alexandre sighed and, feeling weaker than he had only seconds before, lay his head back against the chair. Maybe this was it at last . . . the end.

Chapter 9

Hanson, carrying a small silver serving tray, hurried along the crumbling brick path that led to the *garconniere.* If Asmodeus hadn't alerted him when he did, it might have been too late. He slipped past the entry door, closed it quietly behind him, and shuffled hastily across the wide parlor to where Alexandre sat in a tall wing chair facing the fireplace. The logs in the grate smoldered, but their flames had long ago died down.

Hanson cast a worried glance toward Alexandre. He was nearly unconscious now. He placed the tray on the table beside Alexandre's chair and knelt down.

"Why, Mr. Alexandre?" the old man asked, his ragged voice barely audible. "You haven't refused your repast for so long." He shook his head and raised the linen napkin that covered the tray. "Why, sir? Why did you refuse it now?"

Asmodeus jumped onto Alexandre's lap and meowed, his long tail swishing at the still air.

"Come on, Mr. Alexandre," Hanson said. He positioned a gnarled old hand behind Alexandre's head to help support him and, lifting the refilled chalice to his lips, tipped it slightly. "Drink up now, sir. Drink up."

Alexandre felt the chilled liquid slide over his tongue

and slowly ooze down his throat. His body reacted almost instantly. Within seconds fire flowed through his veins, and his heart, having nearly stopped, began a steady beat beneath the wall of his chest. Strength surged through every fiber of his being, invading each tissue and muscle, instilling virility and vigor.

"There, sir, that's good." Hanson pulled the chalice from Alexandre's lips, withdrew his hand from behind his neck, and straightened.

Asmodeus, having settled on Alexandre's lap, watched silently.

Beneath the arched curves of his dark brows, Alexandre's eyelids opened, his eyes once again the deep swirling gray of a midnight fog. He looked first at the cat on his lap, who had begun purring, and then up at Hanson. "You should have let me go, old man," he said softly, his tone edged with both affection and regret.

The butler shook his head. "I couldn't do that, Mr. Alexandre, even if you meant it. You know I couldn't do that. Not ever."

Alexandre nodded, ran a gentle hand over the cat's sleek black back and, sending Asmodeus jumping gracefully to the floor, pushed himself up from the chair. "Yes, I know. We'd best get to the house then," he said. "I suppose our guest is already up and about?"

"I'm afraid I don't know, sir," Hanson said. "I was in the cookhouse when . . ." he glanced as Asmodeus, "he came and got me. But I will tend to Ms. Domecq immediately."

"Good. I'll come over to the house in a while. I want to change."

"Very good, sir," Hanson said, and retrieving both the chalice from the floor and the one from the table, quietly left the *garconniere*.

Alexandre climbed the stairs to his bedchamber, Asmodeus in hot pursuit. He swung open the doors of a large, heavily carved armoire that dominated one entire wall of the bedroom and pulled a clean shirt from one of its hooks.

The cat jumped onto the huge four poster bed that dominated one wall of the room and settled comfortably within the folds of the deep blue velvet coverlet.

Alexandre shrugged out of the wrinkled shirt he had been wearing, dropped it onto a nearby chair, and pulled on the clean one. He glanced at Asmodeus who had lain his head on his front paws and was watching Alexandre. "Well, mister, are you proud of yourself? Calling in the troops to rescue me?"

Asmodeus meowed.

Alexandre chuckled in spite of himself. "You're not a Saint Bernard, Asmo, you're a cat. How come you can't seem to remember that?"

Asmodeus meowed, rose, stretched, his short hair standing on end like a bristled brush, turned in a circle, and then settled down again in exactly the same spot. He curled his body tightly around itself and closed his eyes, as if to say the conversation, and his self-appointed rescue duties were over.

Alexandre ran a brush through his thick black hair and slipped into a black jacket. He left the door to his bedchamber open so that Asmodeus could leave when he wanted to, then proceeded from the *garconniere* to the main house. The thought of seeing Rachel was all that dwelt within his mind. It was wrong, he knew, to even go near her, yet he couldn't seem to help himself. A flash of anger fired his mind. That was untrue. He *could* help himself, *could* force himself to stay away from her, but if truth be told, he didn't want to.

He paused at the door to the dining room. She was already there, seated at the long table. Her auburn hair hung loose, a waterfall of red-brown waves that spread over her shoulders like a delicate shawl, the silken tresses a rich compliment to the white silk blouse that draped her lithe form. Memory of her in his arms, of the feel of her body pressed to his, of his lips drinking in the sweetness of hers, swept over him. The sight of her instantly stirred a hunger within him that had nothing to do with food.

She set her coffee cup onto its saucer and the soft, tinkling sound broke the reverie Alexandre had found himself plunged into.

He walked into the room. "Good morning, Rachel," he said, his voice stiff, his words formal.

She smiled up at him. "Good morning."

Alexandre slid into his usual chair at the head of the table just as Hanson entered the room from the warming kitchen. He carried a covered tray toward Rachel. "Good morning, sir. Ms. Domecq."

"Good morning, Hanson. How are you?"

"Fine, thank you, ma'am." He placed a chalice before Alexandre and, moving to stand beside Rachel, set a plate laden with scrambled eggs, a slice of ham, a mound of fried potatoes and peppers, and toast before her.

"Oh, my, this looks delicious. But," she laughed, "about five thousand calories."

Alexandre nodded to Hanson but kept his gaze on Rachel.

The butler left the room.

Rachel felt Alexandre's eyes on her, but forced herself to keep her attention on her food. She was afraid of what might happen if she didn't. One good, long look into those eyes of his and she knew, as before, she would forget about everything else, and she couldn't let that happen. Not now. Now she had to concentrate on the reason she was at *Sans Souci.* Steven. She had to concentrate on finding Steven.

Alexandre watched her steadily. He had tried to tell himself that he felt nothing for her. That what she had stirred within him was nothing more than memories, good memories, but just that, memories. Except now that he was once again in her company, he knew that he had lied to himself. She looked uncannily like Danielle, but that was where the resemblance ended. She was not Danielle, this was not 1793, and what he felt for her was not love. He would not let it be love. Not this time. Love might bring happiness to others, but to him, and to those like him, it brought only pain, anguish, and years of bad memories. No, he would not go through that again.

Alexandre turned to look out one of the tall windows that graced one wall of the dining room. Sunlight streamed through the small glass panes, casting the room with a cheery brightness, from the polished dark oak furnishings, and a rainbow of color from the twin brass and crystal chandeliers that hung overhead.

He had never found out what had happened to Danielle after that night she'd turned away from him. Painful memories filled his mind. Her family had been due to arrive in New Orleans the next day. He had warred with himself all day, anguishing over confessing the truth to her and loathing himself for having not told her sooner. And then there had been no more time, and he could put it off no longer. They had all been there, his great grandmother, Catherine, his grandmother, Marguerite, his mother, Yvette, and his sister, Suzanne, all gathered in the parlor, surrounding him and Danielle, waiting patiently, almost knowingly.

He'd sat with her on the settee, held her hands in his, and explained the truth to Danielle in halting words, the difference in their worlds, of themselves. And he had watched, helpless, as first disbelief, then shock, and finally repugnance etched themselves on her beautiful face. A scream had ripped from her throat. She'd torn herself away from him, cringing in terror, and bolted from her chair. The others had remained silent. Alexandre had risen from his own seat and reached out to comfort her, but she'd recoiled away from him in both fear and disgust. Her words of rejection, of damnation, had cut him deeply, piercing his heart as deftly, as thoroughly, as any steel blade could have. Yet a steel blade would have been kinder for it would have ended his misery. Danielle had run from the house that night. Run from them, from him. And he'd never seen her again. He had searched for days, for months, wanting nothing more than to apologize, and assure her that she had nothing to fear from him, that he would never harm her. Her family, who had sailed over from France for the wedding, also searched, as did the authorities, but there was no trace of Danielle to be found. It was as if she had simply run out into the night and disappeared.

Alexandre turned back to look at Rachel. He had his suspicions of what had happened to Danielle, and they were not that her family had merely stolen her out of Louisiana in a hush of secrecy so that he would never again attempt to contact her. But he had never been able to confirm his own suspicions. Fear of what he would discover had kept him from really trying.

Now Rachel was here, and it was as if it were starting all over again.

She lifted a forkful of egg to her mouth.

Alexandre watched her slip the fork from between her lips and felt a stab of passion fill his chest that was so abrupt, so intense, he nearly groaned with the effort to stifle it. He couldn't let anything more happen between them. Alexandre closed his eyes. He couldn't risk her life. Memory of Danielle blended with the reality of Rachel. He couldn't face going through that again. He couldn't love her, and lose her. A long sigh escaped his lips. He wouldn't go through that again.

"I thought, if you have the time, you might show me around some more of the outbuildings today," Rachel said, and smiled at him.

Alexandre rose hastily to his feet, the abruptness of the movement and the collision of his calves against the chair's front padding causing it to reel backward and scrape noisily across the floor. The napkin he'd laid on his lap fell to the floor. "I'm sorry, Rachel, but I have some things I must attend to this morning. If you'll excuse me?" He turned without waiting for her answer and strode from the room.

Rachel stared after him, totally shocked. "What the hell did I do?" she mumbled. "Suddenly turn into Attila the Hun?" Rising from her seat Rachel walked into the foyer. She realized she had been avoiding meeting his gaze, but that didn't warrant such an abrupt and cool departure from him. Through one of the small windows beside the foyer's rear door she spotted Alexandre as he stalked away from the house.

Walking softly, almost on tiptoe, Rachel moved to the door that led to the warming kitchen and slowly pushed it open. The room was empty, the old butler nowhere in sight. She checked the ovens, just to make sure he wasn't preparing something and would return momentarily. They were cold and empty. Rachel hurried back into the dining room and, as a last minute thought, ran to the door that led to the foyer and looked out. No one was there. A glance up the stairs assured her no one was approaching from the second floor. She turned and moved to the stand beside one of the tall windows within the opposite wall, slipped a hand into the pocket of the black slacks she'd chosen to wear and pulled out the transmitter.

"Marc? Marc, can you hear me? Are you there?"

"Do I have someplace else to be?" his voice came back. He chuckled, then his voice sobered. "Are you all right, Rae? Anything happening in there?"

"I'm fine, just checking in. Alexandre's gone out to his office. He keeps it in one of the small buildings behind the house. The others are still in their rooms, I think. Except for the butler. Heaven only knows where he's at. Lurking, probably. I'm going to look around."

"Okay, but be careful."

"No, I think I'll be as careless as I most possibly can," she sniped back. A wave of guilt immediately washed over her. Now why had she snipped at Marc like that? He'd only told her to be careful.

Rachel heard a soft sound behind her, like a rustling, or the slide of a foot across a carpeted floor, and stiffened. She hurriedly slid the transmitter into her pocket and glanced over her shoulder. A sigh of relief blew from her lips.

"Apollyon, you really shouldn't sneak up on people like that. You nearly gave me a heart attack."

The cat, ignoring Rachel to the point of not even looking in her direction, jumped onto the table with a swish of her tail and, crouching before Rachel's plate, began to lap up what was left of her eggs.

"What?" Marc radioed.

Rachel jammed her hand into her pocket and retrieved the transmitter. Pulling it out she held it to her lips. "Nothing," she whispered. "It's just a cat."

"Did you get back what you lost the other night?"

Rachel frowned, then realized what he was referring

to. She felt another surge of guilt. Cops didn't lose their guns. But then, she wasn't a cop anymore, and she was out of practice. "No," she said. "I looked for it, but it wasn't there."

"You mean someone else found it?"

"Either that or it sprouted wings." It had been the wrong thing to say, and she knew it instantly. The word wings immediately brought back memory of the thing that had attacked her and made her drop the gun in the first place. She shivered as its image formed in her mind.

"Get out of there, Rachel," Marc said. "Something's going on in there that's not right."

"I can't, Marc, not yet. Steven's here. Or at least he was. I've felt his presence several times, and heard him calling to me. I have to find out what's going on."

"Rachel."

"No, Marc." She glanced over her shoulder to make sure she was still alone. Or at least, that it was still just she and Apollyon in the room. "I can't leave here until I know about Steven. You promised you'd help me, so either help me, or leave me alone."

Silence met her stoney request.

"All right." His voice was sullen.

Rachel said a silent prayer of thanks. She hadn't wanted to talk to him like that, but she had to stay. And she didn't relish remaining at *Sans Souci* without anyone waiting out there to lend her back-up if she needed it. But she would have, if he'd decided to leave.

"Just make sure you don't do anything foolhardy, Rae," Marc said.

Rachel decided not to comment on his warning. "Did you find out anything on the lens?"

"Joe at the lab said it didn't have any prints on it, and one of my guys checked out a couple of stores. It's a common lens. Sold just about everywhere to both amateur photographers and professionals alike. We're not going to get a break from that."

Rachel didn't know whether she should be relieved or disappointed that they hadn't found Steven's prints on the lens. She heard a clatter of sound from the warming kitchen. "I've got to go, Marc. Call you later." She snapped off the transmitter and slipped it back into her pocket just as Hanson stepped past the swinging door and into the dining room.

"Will you be wanting anything more, Ms. Domecq?" the old man inquired.

"No, thank you, Hanson, I'm fine. I think I'll just go in the study and read for a bit while I wait for Miss Catherine to come down."

He nodded. "As you wish."

Rachel walked into Alexandre's study and went immediately to the wall of shelves where she'd found the journal on her first night at *Sans Souci.* She searched the line of books on each shelf, but the journal wasn't there. She frowned. Had she left it on one of the tables? Turning, she looked about the room, but the book was nowhere in sight. Rachel walked to stand behind the huge dark oak desk that dominated one side of the spacious room. Its design was macabre to say the least. Its sides, rather than flat, were bowed outward and resembled the barely folded wings of a huge bird. The feet of the desk were intricately carved claws wrapped around smooth balls of black marble. She opened the top drawer but there was nothing inside other than a few old-fashioned writing quills, a cut crystal ink well, and some loose sheets of paper. The next drawer yielded a leather bound journal which proved to be an accounting of household expenses for the past year, which, as Rachel's gaze zipped over them, appeared to be almost nonexistent. The third drawer she opened provided the journal, slipped beneath a leather bound, and seemingly ancient, book of poems by Poe.

Had Alexandre, perhaps in the middle of doing something else, absently placed the journal in the drawer of the desk? Or, her mind spun with a suspicion she did not want to harbor, had he purposely put it there . . . hidden away, out of sight, so that she could not look through it again?

Lifting it from the drawer, Rachel replaced the book of poems and carried the journal across the room. She pushed open the heavy burgundy drapes that had been drawn across the twin windows set into the room's outer wall. With the bright rays of sunlight streaming into every corner of the study and chasing away its gloominess, Rachel settled onto one of the big wing chairs that faced the cold, unlit fireplace.

An hour later she moved to sit at the desk. She flipped back to one of the first pages of the journal and stared down at the picture depicted there. It was a castle, set high on the side of a mountain, half of the structure appearing to meld with the sheer cliff that bordered one of its sheer rock walls. Far below, in a valley beneath the mountain, was a small village. Its buildings appeared to be little more than crudely built cottages with shuttered windows and thatched roofs. She noticed her fingers begin to tremble. It was the same castle she'd seen when she'd . . .

Rachel closed her eyes and shook her head, then stared down at the page again. She couldn't deny it. It was the same castle she'd seen that first time she'd looked into Alexandre's eyes. She sat back against the chair and released a long sigh. What did it mean? Was she having some sort of psychic experience? Receiving a psychic impression from him? Was her mind picking up images that dwelt in his mind?

She flipped several pages, stared at another picture, read paragraphs of flowing script, and thumbed through several more pages. The journal spanned decades of time. Centuries, really. But it was all too much to remember. Sliding open the top drawer of the desk she searched for a pen or pencil. There were none. "Damn," Rachel swore softly and gathered up a quill and inkwell. She stared at the archaic writing instruments. "Isn't this taking this reclusive thing a bit far?" Laying a piece of paper before her, and, flipping from one page to the next, she began taking notes.

The date printed in flowing script under a drawing of the castle was 1575. And its name, as best she could decipher the French wording, was *Laire des Chasseurs*. Rachel frowned. French had not been spoken in her home, and she'd taken only one year of it in school. "Hunter's Lair?" she mumbled, not at all certain she'd deciphered the words correctly. "What kind of name is that for someone's home?" She flipped the page. The next picture was of an old painting and one every school child in Louisisana was familiar with, but paid little attention to. It was dated 1593, and its caption pronounced it the arrival of Bienville to the shores of Louisiana. Rachel stared at the picture. She had seen it a hundred times, but now would always view it differently for beside Bienville, among others in the group, stood Alexandre Beaumondier.

Rachel flipped several more pages until coming to another picture. It was dated 1696 and was a portrait of a man dressed in what appeared to be trappers' garments. Fringe hung from both his arm sleeves and leggings, and a fur cap covered his head. Even though he had long hair and a heavy beard and mustache that covered the bottom half of his lean face, it was unmistakably Alexandre.

The next picture was dated 1775. Alexandre Beaumondier was elegantly dressed in a gold-trimmed thigh-length blue jacket, tight gray trousers, and boots that reached to above his knees. His hair was combed smoothly back away from his face and arranged in several rows of tight sausage curls at his nape, along with one before each ear and at each temple. He was standing in a receiving line of what was obviously a soiree, and next to him stood George Washington.

"I don't believe this," Rachel muttered to herself. "This just obviously can't be."

Several pages further into the journal revealed a picture labeled 1815, and a notation below the date claimed it was just after the Battle of New Orleans. Alexandre was pictured sitting at a table with the country's future President, and New Orleans hero, Andrew Jackson. And beside him was the city's most famous pirate, and Jackson's ally during the battle, Jean Lafitte. Before them, his hands shackled behind him, stood a young English officer, obviously a prisoner taken during the battle.

She flipped from the 1815 picture back to the one dated 1775. Only thirty-seven years. Could it be father and son?

Rachel scribbled several notes to herself on the paper, then flipped through several more pages of the journal. 1865. Alexandre stood, dressed in the uniform of a Confederate cavalry officer, next to his commander, Robert E Lee, in what was unmistakably the scene of surrender at Appomattox Courthouse, and the end of the War Between the States.

Rachel made some notes and turned the pages.

1910. Alexandre as a soldier during World War I.
She flipped another page of the journal.
1944. Alexandre as a soldier during World War II.
She thumbed past several more pages.
1953. Alexandre as a soldier during the Korean War.
And still more.
1972. Alexandre as a soldier during the Vietnam War.

Rachel let the pages slowly fall from her fingers, staring again at each picture as it passed. Every Alexandre Beaumondier throughout the years, nearly four hundred years, looked identical. There was no physical difference in any of them that she could discern, at least not the way the artists had captured the men on canvas or pad. Nor were there any disimiliarities in the dagguereotypes, or the more modern day photographs.

Was it possible for each generation of males in a family to look identical to those who had gone before him? Rachel stared at the pictures. She'd never heard of such a thing, and felt certain the odds against it were astronomical, yet there was no other explanation.

Chapter 10

An hour later, after mulling through the journal several more times, and staring at every picture, portrait and drawing until she felt certain they were memorized within her mind for all time, Rachel returned the book to the drawer of Alexandre's desk and stood. She stretched her stiff body and, folding the paper and stuffing it into the pocket of her slacks, walked to the foyer. The house was still silent. She glanced at her watch. It was after noon.

She stepped into the foyer, frowned, and looked up the wide staircase toward the dimly lit landing. Did the Beaumondier women always sleep all day? Her cop thinking suddenly kicked in. Or, were they doing something during the daylight hours that they didn't want anyone to know of? Marc had said the police was suspicious of the Beaumondiers, even though they had nothing concrete to be suspicious about.

Moving to the entry door Rachel opened it and stepped out onto the gallery. Hot, humid air enveloped her instantly, along with the soft, humming sounds of the life that came from the surrounding trees and brush. She closed her eyes. Steven? She filled her mind with his name. Steven, can you hear me? Answer me, Steven. Answer me.

Long seconds later, filled with disappointment at feeling nothing from him, and struggling to stave off her fear, she opened her eyes. She remained still for a while longer, waiting. Finally, Rachel walked back into the house, welcoming the coolness its thick walls and dank shadows offered. She paused just inside the foyer, her ear cocked for any sound. None came. On impulse she moved back to the door and pulled the transmitter from her pocket again.

"Marc?" she whispered into it.

"Yeah?" he bellowed back.

She slapped the transmitter against her breast and looked around hurriedly, then lifted it back to her mouth once assured she was still alone.

"Don't talk so loud, dammit."

"Sorry," he whispered.

"I'm going to search the house."

"In the daytime? Don't you think that's a little dangerous?"

"No one's up yet except the old butler and Alexandre, and neither of them are around."

"You mean the women are all still asleep? It's almost two o'clock in the afternoon."

"I know. They don't like the daytime."

"Sounds weird to me. You sure you haven't seen any voodoo stuff going on in there?"

"Positive. I think they've got some kind of disease. You know, that one where you can't go out in the sun."

"You mean like an immune deficiency? Like the bubble boy, or something?"

"Something like that. Anyway, I think that's one reason they stay in seclusion a lot. Except for Alexandre. He doesn't have it, so I'm not sure why he's a recluse."

"Maybe he's just weird."

"I'm going now," Rachel said curtly. She clicked off

the transmitter and dropped it back into her pocket. His reference to Alexandre had caused her temper to flare, yet she knew it shouldn't have. Alexandre was as much a suspect in this thing as the rest of his family, whether she liked it or not. She moved a hand to her pocket. The tiny radio nestled there gave her some sense of security, though she would have felt safer if she had her gun.

The thought only served to increase her uneasiness. She was nervous enough without the weapon, but knowing that someone else was now in possession of it only made her apprehension all the worse.

Rachel turned and looked around the elegant room. She had already searched the study. Other than the journal, which served to thoroughly confuse her about the family and its ancestry, specifically its male ancestry, and told her nothing of her brother, there wasn't anything in the room to help her. She walked into the dining room. Her gaze swept over the long Phyfe table and chairs and the ancient English sideboard with its mirrored center behind curving shelves, but sensed nothing out of the ordinary. The parlor, with its array of bric-a-brac, statuettes, and vases, also revealed no secrets. The warming kitchen offered even less. It was so starkly bare that Rachel was sure it hadn't been used for over a century, if even then. She stepped out onto the gallery, in need of a breath of air and a moment to try and decide what to do next.

Rachel sighed, feeling a definite sense of defeat. She couldn't very well search the bedchambers with the Beaumondier women still in them. "But they never seem to leave them," she muttered to herself in complaint. Turning, she walked back into the warming kitchen. It looked the same as she imagined it had one hundred years ago—crude if you had to use it, quaint if you didn't. She needed a cup of coffee. Rachel crossed the kitchen and opened the pantry door, cringing as it creaked loudly on its dry hinges. Well, if anyone was awake in the house they certainly knew what she was up to now. She reached toward the wall to flick on the light switch and then remembered that *Sans Souci* had never been wired for electricity.

"Authenticity is great," Rachel mumbled, "but this is a little too much." Somehow though, she sensed, in spite of her words, that authenticity, or even reclusivity, had nothing to do with why the Beaumondiers had never had electricity put into the house. Or running water for that matter. Or modern plumbing or air-conditioning. They were used to living like this, as odd as that seemed.

Opening the door wider to allow in what little sunlight could pierce the shadows of the pantry from the kitchen, she browsed the shelves. It didn't take long; there wasn't much to browse. A few dried "things" and several jars of pickled something or other. Rachel turned one of the jars in an effort to see if it was labeled. It wasn't, but judging from the layer of dust that came away from the lid onto her fingertips, the small cache of jars had been there for quite some times. "Maybe the Yankees passed them up," she mumbled. She stood on tiptoe to look at the top shelf, sighed in defeat, then bent low to scan the bottom one. A box of teabags sat on the bottom shelf, along with a can of coffee.

"Thank heavens," Rachel muttered. She reached for the can. As she did, the door behind her started to close.

Rachel spun around and made a grab for it. Her fingers reached for the narrowing shaft of light between door and jamb. Pain shot through her hand and up her arm as the heavy planked beams nearly crushed her fingers against the doorframe.

"Damn," Rachel swore, and pulled the door open

again, but stopped halfway as something else caught her attention. She stared at the shadowed stairwell behind the door which, only seconds before, she had not even been aware existed. Hurrying back into the kitchen, she grabbed one of the old oil lamps that sat on the dry sink and a box of matches. Removing the glass chimney from the lamp she touched a match to its wick, replaced the chimney, and re-entered the pantry. She held the light high over the staircase. It was extremely narrow and steep, climbing upward at a dramatic angle, then curving and disappearing behind the wall.

Rachel bent to get a better look at the stairs themselves. They were covered with dust, and between their balustrades were thick layers of cobwebs. She shuddered. It was obvious no one had traversed these stairs in a very long time. Rachel didn't want to be the first, but something, some unexplainable urge, prompted her to climb them.

She held the light high in one hand, gripped the rough banister with the other, and set one foot tentatively upon the first stair, afraid to place her weight on it lest it cave in. It didn't. She mounted another, and then another. The staircase seemed to go on forever, climbing high up into the house, with no doors or windows on either side. She was forced to slap cobwebs from her path several times, hoping their creators were nowhere around.

After several minutes she paused and looked back in the direction she'd come. There was nothing behind her, she hoped, but inky blackness. She turned and looked up. The same inky blackness met her from that direction. She began to climb the stairs again.

"God, don't let me run into something I don't want to run into," Rachel mumbled, and slapped at another cobweb as it attached itself to her face. Every terrifying creature from every horror movie she'd ever seen seemed to threaten her from the darkness beyond the lamp's glow, and Marc's comment about voodoo now echoed in her mind.

Suddenly a door loomed up in front of her. "If there's a monster or something locked up in here, I'm done for." Taking a deep breath, and summoning all of her courage, Rachel reached out, turned the old porcelain knob, and pushed. At first nothing happened. "Dammit, open," she said. She pushed again, this time putting her weight into it. The door shot open with a loud groan.

Rachel flinched at the noise. "Boy, it was a good thing I was a cop because I'd never have made a very successful cat burglar." She stepped into the room beyond the door and nearly gasped at its size. It seemed to go on forever. As her gaze took in everything, including the sloped roofline and open beams she realized why the room seemed so immense. . . . she was in the attic. "Oh, good," Rachel mumbled, "isn't the attic where old southerners always keep their crazies locked up?"

Sunlight streamed in through the dormer windows that broke each wall of the roof, three to a side, though the rooflines were all so far apart that the center of the cavernous attic remained steeped in darkness. Old trunks, large crates, and discarded furniture was piled everywhere, along with dress forms, an old rocking horse, a scattering of toys, a baby carriage, and several rolled carpets. It was a treasure trove of antiques that Rachel knew, because of her job, were probably worth a small, perhaps even a large, fortune. Curiosity overrode her hesitation and sense of propriety. Setting the oil lamp on one of the dust covered bureaus in the center of the attic, Rachel began to explore. She opened several trunks, muttering exclamations of delight and awe at the pristine condition of the ancient clothes packed within, the exquisite tailoring of the men's suits, and the magnificent elegance of the swirling folds of fabric that made up the hoopskirts and ballgowns of an earlier time.

In another trunk she found ladies' shoes that laced up high over the ankle, satin slippers, and men's riding boots. There were kid gloves, cravats, brocaded vests and ruffled shirts, bulging crinolines, lacy pantaloons, beribboned camisoles and bonnets adorned with feathers and tulle. Everything the proper couple of the 1800s might need. Turning, Rachel flipped open another trunk. Again the clothes were neatly folded, but these were of another era, an earlier era. The men's jackets were longer, their trousers shorter. Rachel lifted a ladies' gown from the top of the pile. Its short bodice was of fluffed muslin and pleated. Its sleeves were cap style. A satin ribbon trimmed the gown just below the bodice and from it the skirt flowed out in billowing waves. Empress style, she noted, before hoopcages. The 1700s.

Rachel refolded the gown and carefully placed it back in the trunk, then closed its lid. Standing, she looked around the attic again and then began to wonder about the piles of age old belongings. "This stuff belongs in a museum. It's fantastic." She stopped in front of an old armoire whose design was one of elegant simplicity. The mirror on its left door was cracked. She reached out and ran a finger absently along the jagged line that broke the smooth silver surface.

She looked over her shoulder at the spacious cavern that loomed behind her. It had nothing to say, nothing to tell her. Steven had never been up here, of that she was certain, and that was her only reason for being at *Sans Souci*. Not history, or collecting artifacts for a museum, or even noting the eccentricities of the Beaumondiers. Finding Steven, that was what was important. That was why she was here.

Rachel turned away from the mirror. She'd best get back downstairs before anyone missed her. Or found her. Brushing off her slacks she began to reach for the lamp. A flash of gold caught the corner of her eye, and she turned, curious. Sticking out from between the armoire and the wall was the corner of a gilt frame. It had momentarily caught the reflection of the afternoon sun as it moved before a dormer window on its slow descent from the sky and sent a stream of hazy yellow light through the room. Rachel reached out and pulled the frame from its wedged position.

As rotting burlap fell to the floor, Rachel froze in place. Her fingers gripped the edge of the frame, and turned white from the pressure of her hold as she stared down unbelievingly at the portrait within the gold frame.

"This is impossible," she murmured. She felt her heartbeat accelerate until it felt like the crashing beat of a rock drummer gone out of control. Her pulse raced and her hands had begun to tremble. She jerked her hand away from the gilt frame and took a ragged breath. "This isn't possible," she repeated, staring at the image of the woman painted on the canvas. "It just isn't." Her gaze moved from the face of the woman to a small brass plaque affixed to the bottom of the frame. She knelt and brushed a jagged shred of burlap from the brass plaque, then tipped the frame back slightly so as to catch the feeble sunlight.

Her heart thudded madly. "Danielle Toutant," she whispered, "1793."

Rachel released the frame instantly allowing it to crash against the wall. She stared at the face of the woman in the portrait, a face that was identical to her own. "No, this is impossible." But even as she said the words, even as she tried to believe them, she couldn't deny the proof that was before her. The painting was over two hundred years old. Two hundred years, her mind repeated needlessly. It had been wrapped in burlap and stored up here for heaven only knew how many years. It wasn't a painting of her. And yet it was.

Chapter 11

Rachel couldn't seem to take her eyes off the portrait. Numerous things she had encountered since coming to the Beaumondier plantation had left her filled with questions and doubts and pondering her own sanity, but this had to be the ultimate puzzle. It was as if she were looking into a mirror, but a magical one, a mirror that showed her the past, and somehow, unexplainably, put her in it.

Rachel almost laughed through her shock. The woman looked like her, exactly like her, but it wasn't her. It was Danielle Toutant, and this was no mirror, magic or otherwise. This was real. Rachel's gaze moved over the rest of the painting. Danielle wore an empress style gown, similar to the dress Rachel had pulled from one of the trunks. Its bodice was a gathered network of sheer pale yellow lace over white muslin. The sleeves were short and puffed, leaving her arms bare. The neckline was deep and square, revealing only a hint of subtle cleavage, while a white ribbon encircled her ribs, just beneath her bosom and above the folds of her gown. Her auburn hair, the exact shade as Rachel's, was pulled up to her crown in a cascading avalanche of curls that fell on one side to drape her bare shoulder.

A dozen questions assaulted her mind, but one overrode all the others—could they be related? Rachel's mind churned over the possibility. That had to be the answer. Somehow she and Danielle must have been related. It stood to reason, if they looked this much alike, that Rachel was a descendant of Danielle's. That had to be it. It was the only sane, logical explanation.

The thought stopped her. The portrait was here in the Beaumondier attic, which led one to believe that Danielle was a member of the Beaumondier family. So . . . Rachel felt a chill sweep over her . . . wouldn't that mean if she were related to Danielle Toutant, even distantly, she was also related to the Beaumondiers?

She searched her mind for memory of the name. Toutant. The woman's name had been Toutant. Danielle Toutant. Rachel closed her eyes and tried to remember the names of her French ancestors. She couldn't remember a Toutant. Her mother's maiden name had been Marcel. Her grandmother's Aneneuve. Her mind skipped over the past. There'd been a Devereaux, several Reichellards, Pellichouts, DeMoynes, a Landreaux, and of course Ligere, but no Toutant. She would remember if Toutant had been one of her ancestor's names, wouldn't she?

Rachel opened her eyes and looked back at the woman who smiled at her from the portrait. "Give me some answers, dammit," she swore softly.

Pushing herself upright, she let the portrait fall back against the wall and retrieved the oil lamp. She had climbed the stairs and entered the attic on the hope that she might find something. Well, she stared back at the portrait, though it had nothing to do with Steven, she'd found something. She just didn't know what to make of it.

Rachel walked across the room and stepped back into

the narrow stairwell. She paused and looked down at the steep, curving steps. Going down was going to be a lot more harrowing than coming up had been. Hopefully, she wouldn't fall and break her neck.

Reaching the bottom of the stairs without incident, she crept quietly into the pantry and retrieved the can of coffee before opening the door to the kitchen, just in case anyone else was about. At least she'd have an excuse for being in there. She pushed open the door to the warming kitchen. It was empty. She let out a sigh of relief, put the oil lamp back on the dry sink and turned down its wick until its flame went out. The can of coffee she discarded on the table. She'd lost her desire for caffeine, at least for the moment.

Rachel peeked into the foyer, feeling a rush of relief that it, too, was empty and the house was still silent. She let the door close and walked across the warming kitchen. The heels of her pumps clicked dully on the old plank floor. She had to radio Marc. Had to tell him what she'd found. Stepping out onto the gallery she slipped a hand into the pocket of her slacks and, as her fingers wrapped around the small transmitter, paused. She glanced back over her shoulder into the warming kitchen. No, she should get farther away from the house, just in case. The last thing she wanted was to be overheard. Especially with what she had to say.

From one of the upper floor windows of the *garconniere* Alexandre watched Rachel walk across the overgrown gardens of *Sans Souci*. As his gaze followed her, his mind whirled with memories he had kept long buried, back to a period in his life he tried never to think of, but which had haunted him ever since, and which, with Rachel's arrival, refused to be silent any longer.

It had ended in tragedy then, and it would end in tragedy this time . . . if he let it.

His hand closed around a porcelain figurine that sat on a table to one side of the window. The delicate face of the tiny mountain maiden disappeared beneath the flesh of his fingers as they curled tightly around the statuette. He could not deny the astounding physical resemblance Rachel had to Danielle, even so, the longer Rachel remained at *Sans Souci*, the more he found the two women acutely different. One's personality was no more like the other's than the night is like the day. He had loved Danielle for her gentle nature and sweet innocence. She had been a delicate soul wanting nothing more, it had seemed, than to please Alexandre and be his wife.

Of course that had all changed the night he had confessed the truth to her.

Alexandre's fingers tightened further around the porcelain statuette, knuckles turning white from the pressure, the tips of his fingers turning red. He could still hear her voice, ragged and choked with fear as she backed away from him, away from his touch, his love.

The statuette shattered within his grip, the delicate figurine breaking into a dozen jagged pieces. Alexandre absently let the broken shards of china fall from his fingers onto the table, not even noticing that his hand had been cut, and a small rivulet of blood snaked down the side of his thumb.

His gaze followed Rachel as she moved toward one of the huge live oaks and disappeared into the inky shadows created by its wide-spreading and moss-laden limbs.

He was falling in love with Rachel, swiftly, almost uncontrollably, and for the first time in his long life, he was scared. Not for himself, but for her. His love had brought tragedy to one woman. He didn't want that to happen again. Not to Rachel.

In the beginning, that day when he had carried her into Danielle's room, when he had held her to his breast and looked down into her face, he had felt passion stir within him, and convinced himself it was only because she looked like Danielle. Then later, after he'd kissed her, he knew it was not because she looked like Danielle. They were identical in appearance, but that was where the similarities ended, and with each passing hour that he spent in her company, he noticed more and more differences. In Rachel he saw strength as well as tenderness, life as well as spirit, sensuality as well as innocence. And all combined to stir his senses, to arouse his passions and stoke his hunger for her.

"But who are you really, Rachel Domecq?" he whispered into the darkness. "Who are you really, and why have you really come to *Sans Souci?*"

She had telegraphed Yvette that she was a representative of the state's Preservation Society, explained that they were interested in helping to preserve the Beaumondier plantation, and requested an audience. He knew that, Yvette had shown him the letter. But why? That's what he wanted to know. There was something else behind her visit, of that he felt certain.

He frowned, the slight shadow of creased flesh that was always between his brows deepened to a ragged crevice. But why had his family allowed the visit? That was the question that haunted him. The one that worried him. Visitors were always discouraged from coming to *Sans Souci*. Always. So why had Rachel's request been acknowledged? Rage at his ignorance of their intentions filled him. His hand swung out and, in a gesture of helpless fury, swept the fragments of the porcelain statuette from the marble-topped table and onto the floor.

"Damn," he whispered harshly. "Damn them for whatever it is they're up to this time."

It was no coincidence that she was here. He felt certain of that. But, other than the desires she aroused within him, that was all he felt certain about. His mind whirred with more questions than answers.

He had tried to stay away from her ever since that first night. Alexandre sighed. And he'd failed. Miserably. He had pulled her into his arms as memories of Danielle, of what she'd made him feel so long ago, filled his mind. He had kissed Rachel while Danielle's name echoed in his mind, but all too soon, as his lips had caressed hers, all thoughts of Danielle had fled him. It was Rachel who stirred his passions now. Rachel whose lips he longed to kiss. Rachel whose body he ached to hold within his embrace.

Alexandre swore softly. But was it true feeling that stirred him . . . or the old hungers struggling to overpower him. Did he want to love her? Or kill her?

It had been so long since he'd loved and equally long since he had killed.

A wash of agony swept over him as heart and mind battled for control, as old instincts fought to overwhelm his tautly controlled resolve. It was no coincidence that Rachel Domecq, who looked so much like Danielle Toutant, the only woman he had ever loved, had come to *Sans Souci,* and that meant Rachel was in danger. He didn't know how he knew that, or even why he thought it, but he had no doubt it was true. He would try to protect her from the others, and from himself, but Alexandre knew, with a dread that nearly tore a groan from his throat, that if they rose up against him, if they united and turned their will as one against him, she would be lost.

The only alternative was to find a way to make her leave . . . before it was too late.

His gaze pierced the shadows within which she'd enveloped herself, seeing through them as if they were not even there, as if the light of day still shone brightly upon the earth. She stood still, in profile to him, partially turned toward the road that bordered the front acreage and which gave entrance to *Sans Souci*. The black of her slacks melded with the deepening shadows, while the white of her silk blouse did little to illuminate her. Alexandre smiled. He didn't need the sunlight to see into the shadows. He had no problem seeing her . . . now . . . or when she was in the house, closeted in her bedchamber, in Danielle's bedchamber.

He turned from the window, walked across the room and sank into a brocade-covered chair. Even though it had been nearly ninety degrees that day and, with the sun sinking from the sky, was still most likely in the low eighties or high seventies, a fire blazed in the grate before him. Its flames danced wildly, licking at the grate's top, leaping for the chimney flute. The room was dark except for the faint stream of sunlight that seeped in through the window, the rays filtered by the heavy lace panel that hung between the drawn back draperies, and the orange cast of light given off by the fire.

"Damn you, Yvette," Alexandre whispered fiercely. All the old suspicions he'd held against his mother loomed forth anew. "Damn you. And damn them."

"Marc, can you hear me?" Rachel said into the transmitter.

"Loud and clear, beautiful," he came back.

Rachel smiled. It really was a pity she couldn't feel anything more toward Marc than friendship. He would make someone a terrific husband. She pushed the sentimental thoughts away.

"I found something else I need you to check out," she said, her tone all business.

"Go."

Rachel swallowed hard, anticipating his reaction. "A picture."

"A picture?" Marc shot back, the tone of his voice one of incredulity. "That's it? A picture? How am I supposed to check out a picture when I haven't seen it?"

"You have, in a way," Rachel retorted.

"What the hell is that supposed to mean? I'm psychic, too?"

"It's a portrait of a woman who looked exactly like me."

"Someone did your portrait without you knowing it? And it's at *Sans Souci*?"

"No." She took a deep breath in an attempt to steady her nerves which, remembering the portrait and thinking about its implications, had shaken her up again. "It's a portrait of Danielle Toutant."

"Who's that?"

"A woman who lived around here over two hundred years ago. She was most likely married to one of the Alexandres of the Beaumondier family."

"One of the Alexandres?"

She could tell from his voice that his patience with her explanation was wearing thin.

"Rae, do you think you could stop talking in riddles and just tell me what the hell's going on?"

She sighed. "It seems, according to a family journal I found in the study, that every male member of the Beaumondier family has been named Alexandre."

"Cute," Marc said.

"Yes, well, anyway, I found a portrait of her, dated 1793, in the attic and I want you to . . ."

"1793? And she looked *exactly* like you?" he cut in.

"Yes, exactly, mirror image. That's why I want you to find out everything you can about her. Who was she? Where'd she come from? What happened to her family? Does she have any descendants around here? And was her husband actually a member of the Beaumondier family."

"I get the picture." He chuckled. "Pardon the pun."

"You're pardoned." She smiled. "But listen, this is really uncanny. There has to be a connection between us, Marc, for me to look so much like her, and I want to know what it is."

"Find out anything on Steven?" he asked.

She felt a clog of despair wedge itself in her throat. "No, but hopefully finding out more about this family will help. I still feel his presence here, but mostly at night. It seems to leave me once the sun comes out."

"Oh, great. You sure you haven't seen any little dolls with pins sticking out of them anywhere in there? Or maybe a chicken's foot wrapped in wax and feathers?"

"I'll radio you tomorrow and see if you've come up with anything on Danielle Toutant."

"You don't want me to stick around tonight?"

Rachel hesitated. She didn't like the idea of being at the Beaumondier plantation with no back-up nearby. Marc was her life preserver, her security . . . but there was no time to waste. She had the distinct impression, especially after his last calls to her, that if she didn't find Steven soon it would be too late. But there was something about that portrait, something that niggled at the back of he mind. She had a feeling, a hunch, that somehow that portrait could be connected with Steven's disappearance. She flipped on the transmitter. "No, I'll be fine. Get that information for me, as much as you can, and I'll talk to you tomorrow."

"I don't like this, Rae, leaving you out here alone. It's not what we agreed on."

"I know, but I'll be fine, I promise." She prayed that was true. "Do this for me, Marc. Please?"

"Goodnight, love," Marc said. "Talk to ya in the morning. and you'd better answer."

She heard the transmitter click off, and slipped her own into the pocket of her slacks.

Alexandre left by the back door of the *garconniere*. It was at times like this, when he felt as if the world that he existed in and hated was tearing him apart inside, that he needed the solitude of the night skies, the peace that the wind, the clouds, and the brilliance of the stars gave him.

He walked easily amongst the dense copse of pine and live oaks that grew at the rear of the *garconniere,* and skirted the cypress bayous that meandered beyond the oaks. Finally he came to a small clearing deep in the bowels of *Sans Souci*'s vast acreage, where no one came, where no one could see him. Alexandre lifted his face to the sky, stretched his arms outright and, his transformation quicker than the mortal eye could see, he took to the skies.

Rachel leaned against the trunk of an old live oak. Darkness surrounded her, the sun having sunk beyond the ragged line of the horizon over half an hour ago. The long draping strands of Spanish moss that hung from the tree's limbs swayed slightly, stirred by a soft, almost unnoticeable breeze that rifled over the land.

Moonlight filtered down through the outer boughs, creating a checkerboard pattern of light and darkness around the trees' perimeter but leaving the area directly beneath it in near total blackness. She knew she should return to the house. Hanson had probably already prepared her dinner and stored it in one of the ovens in the warming kitchen to keep it from cooling. And Alexandre, if he was at the house, might be wondering where she was. But she remained still, listening to the sound of the night creatures all around her, feeling the peacefulness of the night.

Rachel! Rachel, help me!

Rachel bolted away from the tree trunk, suddenly alert and anxious. "Steven?"

Oh, God, Rachel, please! Help me!

Rachel closed her eyes. Steven, for God's sake, tell me where you are.

She waited for his response, or another cry, her body stiff, every muscle taut with tension, but nothing more came. It was as if his mind had been abruptly shut off, his consciousness obliterated.

Steven! Rachel screamed silently. Steven!

Silence was her only response.

She sighed and began to walk back toward the house. "Please, God, let him be all right," she mumbled softly in prayer. "Please, he's all I've got. He has to be okay. He has to be."

Their parents had been gone for almost five years now, killed instantly when a drunk driver had sped through a red light and plowed into the elder Ligeres' tiny compact. Tears filled Rachel's eyes at the memory. Even now, after all this time, she still missed them terribly. She quickly blinked the tears away. Crying had never been an emotion she allowed herself to indulge in. It accomplished nothing, except to make her feel worse, turn both her eyes and nose tomato red, and leave her with a headache the size of Mt. Vesuvius.

She stepped onto the crumbling brick path. Moonlight lit her way, softening the harsh decay of the red clay bricks. A shadow moved across her path. Startled and suddenly fearful, Rachel glanced up.

High overhead, just passing before the moon, she caught a glimpse of outstretched wings.

Before coming to *Sans Souci*, before her harrowing experience of the other night, she would have assumed it to be nothing more than a large hawk, and marveled at the sight as one of beauty and mysticism. But no longer. Not after that thing had attacked her. Rachel shuddered and hurried toward the house, but before taking more than a few steps, she paused. A light was on in the *garconniere*. Perhaps Alexandre hadn't gone to the house yet. Not knowing why she did it, and unwilling to examine her motives, Rachel turned to see if Alexandre was there.

Chapter 12

Alexandre watched Rachel as she hurried toward the house. She seemed frightened and nervous, as if she expected something to pounce on her at any moment. Memory of the other night, when Yvette had assaulted her, came to his mind and with it a rush of anger. He had confronted his mother, demanded to know why she had attacked Rachel, but she had offered him no explanation, saying only that he had nothing to worry about because she wouldn't have really hurt Rachel. That comment in itself had aroused Alexandre's curiosity, but she refused to explain further, laughing off his questions and concern. Yvette, he knew, was not one to care if she hurt someone, physically or otherwise, so his conversation with her, and her assurances, did nothing to alleviate his worry.

Turning his attention back to Rachel, he saw her look up at him, saw the momentary terror in her eyes as she, too, remembered the other night.

Alexandre arced his body and soared away from the moon and toward a cool, wispy veil of black cloud that hung just below the glowing golden orb. Within seconds he felt the chilling cloak of the black cloud envelope him, obscuring him from her sight, but not her from his.

He watched her hesitate at the juncture of the path, turn away from the house, and head for the *garconniere.*

Rachel approached Alexandre's apartment quietly, unaware that she was literally holding her breath. The old building Alexandre had made into his home was built in much the same style as the main house, but on a smaller scale. A white portico hovered above the entry, a once-glistening white adornment that was now gray with age, its paint worn and peeling from want of care. The red bricks of the structure had a weathered look, years of exposure to the elements having left their mark upon each dull red square of earth and gray line of mortar. The draperies of each window were drawn, and even in the moonlight she could see that the glass panes had accumulated years of dust. Cobwebs, lacy and glistening silver beneath the night's glow, edged the corner of each pane.

She stepped into the shadow of the portico and approached the entrance. Unlike the entry door of the main house, this one was plain and uncarved. The tall, narrow peer windows on either side of it were dark, as was the fanlight window overhead. The door itself, minus a knocker, had once been white, but its paint was nearly gone now, leaving its smooth panels of cypress wood raw and exposed.

Silence hung over the *garconniere* like a winter cloak, seeming to shroud the beautiful structure in a macabre sense of neglect and unearthliness.

Rachel inhaled deeply in an unconscious effort to heighten her courage and lessen her anxiety. She knocked lightly on the door of Alexandre's quarters and waited. Long minutes later, she knocked again, but still there was no response. She didn't know whether his lack of answer filled her with relief or dread. Her gaze darted to the doorknob and she clasped it within her fingers before she could change her mind. It turned easily in her hand. Rachel refused to acknowledge the guilt she felt at what she was about to do and, with a hurried glance over her shoulder to make sure no one was behind her, or watching, pushed the door open and stepped into the *garconniere.*

The light she had seen earlier had been turned off and now she was immediately swathed in a darkness that was so complete, so intense, it took her breath away and nearly stilled her heart.

Slowly, as she stood frozen to the spot, afraid to move, her eyes accustomed themselves to the complete lack of light and shapes began to take form around her. Within seconds she could make out the general arrangement of the room and the furniture set around it. She walked cautiously across the small foyer and peeked through the first doorway she came to. It was the parlor, furnished and arranged much the same as that at the main house, though this one was much smaller. The next room on the ground floor seemed to be a study or library. The next was a music room, judging from the harp that stood silhouetted before one window and the piano next to it. The last room on the ground floor looked to be a small dining room. Rachel re-entered the foyer, lit only by the glow of the moon filtering in through the fanlight window, and looked around. A staircase, set against one wall, curved its way to the second floor.

"Well, I've come this far," she murmured to herself. "I guess I might as well keep going."

She took each step cautiously, not sure whether she was more afraid of merely tripping in the dark, or meeting something or someone on her ascent. By the time she reached the landing her heart was hammering so loudly Rachel felt sure it could be heard for miles. The landing gave way to a hallway that led to both the right and left, spacious though not nearly as wide, nor as high-ceilinged, as that in the main house. Windows at each end, tall and rectangular, were uncurtained and allowed in what light there was from the night outside. The one facing north streamed with moonlight, the one to the south illuminated by only a soft reflection of the stars.

Rachel, suddenly needing all the reassurance she could find, turned left and walked toward the moonlight. There were only two doors to each hallway, one on each side. Moving without hesitation, lest she lose her nerve, Rachel turned the knob and quickly pushed open the door to her left. The room was musty. Stale air spewed out immediately to surround her. She coughed. Obviously no one had been in this room for years. She closed the door, turned, and opened the other. The same smell of neglect met her nostrils.

Rachel walked past the staircase landing to the opposite hallway. She opened the door to the left. The room was only dimly illuminated by the faint streams of light that shone through the floor to ceiling windows set in the wall opposite the door. A tall four poster bed, its deep blue canopy and coverlet both trimmed with the twisted gold threads of torsage fringe, dominated the left wall. Against the right stood a huge, heavily carved armoire, its intermingling cherry and lemonwood surfaces gleaming. The wardrobe's top piece was an intricately carved crown of rose vines and blossoms, while its doors both held an inlaid sheet of mirror. Rachel walked toward it, mesmerized by its beauty.

"This has to be at least four, maybe five hundred years old," she murmured, and touched her fingers lightly, almost worshipfully, to the surface of the smooth wood.

"Try six," Alexandre said.

Rachel froze. The mirrors showed a near complete reflection of the room behind her, yet did not reveal Alexandre's presence. She turned to find him standing directly behind her.

He reached out and touched the back of his fingers to her cheek, moving them slowly over her flesh in a sensuous caress. Alexandre knew what he was about to do was wrong, that he would regret it for the remainder of his existence, but he also knew it was too late to stop, too late to turn back the passion her mere presence aroused in him. His gaze moved over her face, pausing to linger upon each feature, each plane and curve, committing them to memory. Long after she was gone he would remember her like this—her eyes a deep, vibrant green accentuated by tiny flecks of gold. Emotion caught in his chest as the swirling colors drew him in and reminded him of another place, another time; the green of the forests that had surrounded his home in France, the gold of the flames that had devoured each leaf and limb as the villagers rioted in anger and panic and set their torches to the foliage surrounding *Laire des Chasseurs*.

Her nose did not have the aristocratic plane so many of the Beaumondier women had, nor the aquilline slant of nobility, but rather a pert, almost defiant upturn, and her lips. . . . Alexandre felt the passion that had simmered within him ever since her arrival begin to consume his body. Her lips, so full and sensuous, so inviting as she stared up at him and he saw them tremble slightly, were more temptation than any mortal man could resist, let alone Alexandre Beaumondier.

"You shouldn't have come here, Rachel," he said huskily. But whether he was more afraid for her, or for himself, he wasn't sure.

Rachel remained silent, her throat, her entire body, suddenly paralyzed by the need to be held by him, the need to be loved by him.

Alexandre's gaze slipped lower, to the shadowed flesh where the tailored collar of her blouse came together just above the sloping valley of her breasts, to the enticing pink-tipped and pebbled nipples covered only by the sheer lace of her bra and the delicate threads of her silk blouse, to the narrow breadth of her waist, the slim curve of her hips, the long line of her legs. Alexandre felt himself tremble. He would not be able to turn away from her now. If there had been any doubt in his mind of that moments before, there was none now. He was lost to her, just as he had been lost to Danielle.

Rachel's eyes met his again, and unconsciously, she leaned into this touch.

Her slight acquiescence toward him, the barely perceptible moan that slipped from her lips, banished what little self-control, what little restraint Alexandre still held over himself. He pulled her into his arms almost savagely, and an agonized growl of need erupted from his throat. She was soft and warm in his arms, her body pliant and supple against his, her curves filling his planes, melding with his length until there was no space, no light, no air left to separate them.

Her hands slid up over his shoulders and Rachel wrapped her arms around his neck and held him to her. "Oh, Alexandre," she whispered softly, pressing her length to his, *"Je t'aime, mon, beaux chère."*

For the brief flash of a millisecond Alexandre wondered at the French words she'd spoken and a troubling memory that Rachel had mentioned she spoke very little French. And then the thought left his mind as quickly as it had invaded it. His mouth closed over hers, hard and hot, a demanding caress of flame that had set out to conquer her hesitations and command her surrender. His lips twisted hungrily atop hers. All the loneliness, the need, the urgency of his long pent-up emotions swept over him like a tidal wave of desire and pulled her into its void.

Rachel parted her lips in invitation to his kiss and his tongue thrust deeply into her mouth, seeking the inner caverns of sweetness he knew lay hidden there in the moist darkness. He kissed her with a firm mastery born of years of expertise, his tongue curling around her own, teasing her senses, his arms crushing her to him, her breasts to his chest, her hips to his upper thighs, the hardness of his arousal to the bottom of her stomach.

A yearning ache invaded her body, and as it spread, pervading and conquering, all thought or consideration of anything other than Alexandre Beaumondier was swept from Rachel's mind. Fiery heat moved rapidly through every cell, every muscle, every fiber. It spread through her limbs, turned her languid in his arms, and filled both her mind and heart with only one thought, one need—to be one with him . . . forever.

She held him, nearly helpless, both her body and senses overwhelmingly aware of him; of the faint scent of dark forests and rich earth that clung to him, an enticing fragrance that, like an exotic potion, stroked her desires; of the ragged sound of his breathing as it intermingled with her own, so foreign and yet so familiar; and of the sense of timelessness his touch invoked within her, a sense that this was her home, this was where she belonged, where she had always belonged.

As his mouth ravaged hers, pulling her, inviting her, taking her to an isle of ecstasy she had never known existed, a world of passion she had only dreamt of, her hands slid from around his neck. As if they had a mind of their own, her fingers moved to the open collar of his shirt, released the small pearl buttons that secured its front, and slipped beneath the silk sheath. With a touch as light and gentle as the caress of a feather, as burning and indelible as that of smoldering steel, her fingers moved sensuously, seductively, over his flesh, teasing, tantalizing, inciting his passion. And, as he had tainted others with his mark centuries before, she branded his soul with hers.

His lips left hers and traveled in tender, nipping forays down the long column of her neck, stoking the fires that already burned within himself and igniting the ones that had lain asleep within her. With all the grace of a swooping eagle in pursuit of its prey, Alexandre bent slightly, swung an arm around the back of Rachel's legs, and swept her into his arms. Cradling her against his chest, and refusing to think of the inevitable heartache he would be forced to face, Alexandre's lips once again captured hers and he carried her to the huge bed that dominated the room.

"Love me, *je t'aime, mon beau coeur,*" Rachel whispered against his lips. "Love me."

In spite of the urgency he felt gnawing at his own body, the need to lose himself within her, Alexandre moved slowly, savoring each slip of his hand over the smooth curve of her length. Aching to rip the thin, frail barriers of her clothes away, to reveal her naked flesh to his hungry desires, Alexandre forced himself instead to move with infinite tenderness. As his mouth worked its mystical magic upon hers, and she writhed beneath him, her body responding to his every touch and begging for more, his fingers deftly released the buttons of her blouse, brushed the silky fabric aside, and unhooked the front clasp of her lacy brassiere. One hand moved to cup her breast, his thumb roaming in a circle around the taut, rosy nipple now exposed to his touch. Alexandre's body felt as if it were about to explode from need. He slipped his mouth away from hers.

Rachel felt suddenly deserted. She reached for him, and then she felt his lips upon her breast, and her arms dropped, hands clutched the silken sheet as the feel of his mouth covering her nipple, his tongue laving it, sent a shudder of pleasure through her that left her trembling weakly. His name slipped from her lips, over and over, in gasps of rapture and pleading; rapture like none she had ever known, pleading for him not to stop.

His fingers deftly unfastened the thin silver buckle at her waist, the small button of her slacks, and slid the hidden zipper downward. A fiery path of burning flesh was left behind as he pressed a trail of kisses down the curve of her rib cage, into the turn of her waist, and across the slight swell of her stomach. She felt the soft fabric of her thin linen slacks move away from her hips, to be replaced by the sweet torturous touch of his lips.

"Alexandre," Rachel breathed, writhing beneath him. And then suddenly he was gone. Her eyes shot open to find him standing beside the bed, bathed in the light of the moon which, had moved before the window and was now shining through it in a filtered stream of amber haze.

Meeting her gaze, the steely gray depths of his eyes immediately seizing and holding the gold-flecked forest green of hers his prisoner, Alexandre began to deftly remove his own clothing.

Rachel felt a flush spread over her face and invade her entire body as he shrugged out of his shirt, and then, with a quick flick of his fingers at the waistband, let his snug-fitting black slacks fall to the floor. It wasn't that she had never witnessed a man undress before, or had never seen a man naked, but she had never settled her eyes upon one so indifferent to her gaze on his disrobing form, or one with a body of such delicious magnificence.

His shoulders were broad, like the sprawling crest of a mountain range while his arms were well-honed lengths of muscle that could be at once coils of strength and embracing bands of tenderness. His chest was a hard-packed wall of sinew, the distended pectorals a smooth plane of vigor and power. He looked away from her as he picked up and threw his slacks toward a nearby chair and Rachel's gaze dropped to the lean, taut line of his stomach. At its base a thin line of silken black hairs trailed downward and spread into a small, dense forest.

Rachel felt a thrill of excitement course through her body, and a flash of apprehension fill her mind, as her eyes came to rest on the rigid evidence of his arousal.

Sliding back down beside her on the bed, Alexandre silently pulled her into his arms again, his limbs entwining about hers, holding her. His lips descended on hers once more, a sweet ravishment that took everything she had to offer, and sought more.

Rachel trembled in response as shivers of pleasure rippled over the surface of her skin. His touch awakened passions within her she had never known existed, aroused desires she had been unaware she possessed. She fairly held her breath, afraid to move, afraid to do anything lest she break the spell within which he had enveloped her, lest she destroy the exquisite torture of lying beside his naked form, of being caressed by his hands, kissed by his lips, held in his arms. She felt a swelling wave of hunger begin within her, a glorious ache of need that she new, instinctively, only Alexandre could assuage. At the touch of his tongue on her breast, like the lick of fire to her flesh, she arched her body toward him, pressing against his mouth, against his length, silently asking, pleading, begging for more of the sweet torture his caresses wrought.

His hand moved downward, slipped between her thighs, and nudging gently, urged them apart. A conflagration of hunger, deep and gnawing, delicious and volcanic, erupted within her as his thumb moved in a rythmic circle atop the tiny nub of flesh that was the sensual core of her being. Two of his fingers slipped inside of her, caressing, massaging, stroking, destroying whatever rational thought still lingered within her senses and bringing her need of him to near unbearable depths.

"Alexandre," she moaned, begging him to both release her from and give her more of the pleasure-filled torment his touch aroused within her.

His lips claimed hers again and she felt her body fill with him, felt the hard shaft of his hunger, his need, satiate the delicate softness of hers. She trembled with the force of ecstasy their union brought.

They moved together, almost as one, her hips rising to meet his, aching to give him the same rapturous pleasure his lovemaking was instilling in her. She raked his back lightly with her fingernails, slid the tip of her tongue within the shelllike curve of his ear, and moved her mouth down further to pull the taut button of his nipple into her mouth. She had no inhibitions, no hesitations now. Her only emotion was desire, consuming, overwhelming, and all for Alexandre.

"Yes, Alexandre. Yes, *mon beau coeur,*" Rachel whispered, her voice deep and throaty with the emotions filling her.

An intense rending suddenly filled her body, shattering

the trembling waves of pleasure she had been experiencing and turning them to violent, delicious currents of euphoria. Like a volcano overflowing, Rachel felt rumbling wave after wave of rapture erupt from the depths of her torso and move outward, like searing, burning bolts of electricity. She clung to him then, tears filling her eyes, his name on her lips.

Alexandre, lost in the world of passion, of love and feeling that he had forsaken over two hundred years ago, released the tight rein he held over his own emotions and let his seed finally spill into her.

He stood at the window and looked out at the night. "Damn you, Rachel," Alexandre whispered softly. "Damn you." He didn't know which he feared more, her or himself. She had the power to stir things within him that were better left alone, left dead and buried where they had lain since 1793, and that was dangerous, for both of them. The hunger hadn't come over him this time, but that was only because he had just feasted before he'd come to her in his room.

His hand closed into a fist at this side. But what if he hadn't? What would have happened then? Would hunger have been stronger than passion?

Alexandre nearly groaned in anguish. He still tried to convince himself that Danielle had just left. Had been so disgusted with what he'd told her that, after her rejection of him, she had merely run away. He turned to look through the rippled glass panes of his window upon the grounds of *Sans Souci*, to the outline of the trees beyond the garden, to the soft rays of the morning sun just beginning to peek over the ragged tips of those tall green sentinels.

His hands clenched and unclenched at his sides. That

Danielle had run away was merely what he preferred to believe, not what, in his heart, he knew to be the truth, which tonight he must face, lest he put Rachel in farther danger. He felt a rending ache within his heart just thinking about it.

He still found it difficult to believe, but hadn't his own mother been witness to it? He had successfully blocked it from his memory, but Yvette had not.

Alexandre inhaled deeply and released the breath in a long sigh of resignation. The thought of what she'd said, the reality of it, was still extremely painful to accept, but he no longer had a choice. He could not let history repeat itself.

His mind spun back to that day, long ago, when Yvette had declared he must know the truth. He had refused to stop looking for Danielle, had maintained that he must apologize to her and assure her she had nothing to fear from him. Yvette, angry at his insistence to continue the search, had felt forced to tell him the truth—Danielle was dead.

Alexandre's fingers clenched and unclenched. And she was dead because Alexandre, upon her rejection of him, had plunged into a frenzy of momentary madness and jealousy and killed her.

He felt the familiar thirst of hunger niggle at the base of his throat as the sun began to warm the earth outside. Unlike the others, who merely had to feast once a day, Alexandre's diet demanded he feast several times within that same period. It had been more than twelve hours since his last repast. He turned away from the window, glanced at Rachel asleep in the bed and began to walk out of the room. If he ignored the mild craving, he knew it would grow stronger, until he was unable to control it.

Chapter 13

When Rachel awoke, the bright rays of the sun were streaming into the room through the bedroom windows. She glanced up at the canopy, seeing deep, midnight blue instead of pale ice blue she was used to. Momentarily disoriented, Rachel sat up quickly clutching the sheet to her naked breasts, and with the movement, remembered where she was—in Alexandre's bedchamber, in the *garconniere*. She turned to look down at the space beside her, but she was the only occupant of the high-sitting, wide bed. Even his pillow held no indentation where his head had lain. There was no telltale twisting of the sheets on his side, no stray strand of black hair glistening atop the pristine white pillowcase to attest to the fact that he had been there, that she had not dreamt what had transpired between them only hours before.

Rachel threw back the covers and swung her legs over the edge of the mattress. Wondering where Alexandre had gone, Rachel wrapped the bedsheet around her naked form and shuffled into the adjoining dressing room. Tepid water sat in a pitcher on a dressing table. She poured it into the large bowl sitting next to the pitcher, doused a towel in it and slapped it to her face. It didn't have the refreshing reaction it would have brought had the water been ice cold, but it helped. She washed quickly, ran a brush through her hair, then hurried back into the bedroom. Her clothes were neatly draped across a settee. Obviously Alexandre had done that. Last night, she remembered, they had been hastily discarded to the floor.

Suddenly a static sound broke the silence.

Rachel nearly jumped from her skin, then realized it was the transmitter in the pocket of the slacks she held in her hand. She pulled the radio out and held it to her lips. "Marc? Are you trying to reach me?"

"No, I'm trying to reach Mars," he quipped. "Are you all right? You're late calling in."

Rachel glanced at her watch. It was nearing ten, almost a hour beyond their usual check-in time. "I'm fine. Sorry, I just overslept. Exhausted I guess." She blushed at the blatant lie.

"Anything new on your end?"

"No." Chalk up another lie.

"So why're you so tired? Up snooping all night?"

She ignored his sarcasm. She'd learned long ago, when they had shared a patrol car, that Marc wasn't a morning person. "You haven't found out anything on . . ." she glanced over her shoulder, "you know, what I asked you to look into yesterday. That, uh, woman?"

"No. Got a couple of guys checking things out for me, but nothing yet."

She took a deep breath. "Nothing on Steven?" It wasn't a question she wanted to ask, because she was damned scared of the answer, but she had to do it.

"No."

"Okay. I'm going to do a little more looking around today. Check in with you later." She had to get back on track and stop herself from being detoured and derailed.

Steven was all that mattered. She had to concentrate on finding him.

"Make sure you do," he answered. "It's boring as hell out here and I get real antsy when you don't call."

"Yes, sir," Rachel said, and chuckled. She slipped the transmitter back into her pocket and, leaving the room, descended the stairs and left the *garconniere.*

"I will not do it, and that's final," Alexandre said.

"Do you know what you're saying?" Yvette fairly shrieked. "Do you have any idea of what you're truly saying?"

"Yes."

"No, I don't think you do," she retorted curtly. "I truly don't think you do, Alexandre."

Rachel tiptoed across the foyer and crept up the wide staircase. This was the perfect, and might be the only, time she could search Yvette's room. Obviously Alexandre and his sister were in the midst of an argument, and though she'd love to eavesdrop, she forced herself to go upstairs. Finding Steven was why she'd come to *Sans Souci,* or at least finding out what had happened to him or where he'd gone, not settling domestic disputes in the Beaumondier family, or . . . she experienced a flash of guilt . . . losing her senses over one of them.

She crept up to Yvette's door, still nervous that she might be seen or interrupted by Catherine or Suzanne, or Lord help her, Hanson. The knob turned easily in her hand and the door swung open quietly.

"Thank heavens," Rachel muttered. She slipped into the room. It was dark, but then she was getting used to that. It seemed darkness was the norm in *Sans Souci.* And there was no time to light a lamp. She hurried to the window and slapped open one of the draperies. The room was a landscape of peach and ivory hues, the bed coverlet a maze of ivory lace, the canopy dripping ruffles of peach silk. Two small rosewood ladies' chairs sat before an oak-faced fireplace, their cushions covered with burnt orange velvet. Rachel looked around. The room held much the same type of furniture as the one she was staying in, but she had not expected the warm tones. In her mind's eye she had pictured Yvette's room as white. Stark, cold, white . . . like the woman who inhabited it.

Her gaze scanned the room and caught on a writing desk. She hurried to it and began to search its shallow drawers.

Pens, odd pieces of jewelry, paper, quills, a map of the city of New Orleans, another of Algiers across the river and . . . Rachel's fingers froze on the corner of a plane of smooth leather. She pulled it from beneath a pile of writing paper and held it up to the light. STL was engraved on the front in gold script. Her heart nearly thudded to a stop. She had seen it a hundred times. She didn't need to open it to verify who it belonged to. It was Steven's wallet. She flipped it open anyway. On the left flap, encased behind plastic, was Steven's drivers license. He smiled out at her from his picture.

Rachel fought to control the surge of tears that threatened to engulf her. "Not now," she mumbled. Two hundred dollars in cash was still neatly tucked in the billfold, along with several of Steven's business cards and a half-dozen more for people he worked with and called on to assist him on various projects. Slipped within the plastic cases on the right side of the wallet were several charge cards, his social security card, a library card, and a picture of Rachel.

He was here. This proved it. He had come to *Sans Souci.* If nothing else, this proved that Yvette had lied.

Rachel placed the wallet back in Yvette's drawer. She quickly went through the rest of the room, looking in the armoire, beneath the bed, in the dressing room, everywhere she could think of, but found nothing else, except Apollyon. When Rachel reached under the bed and, feeling fur, tried to pull out whatever it was, the cat had let out a low growl and nearly clawed Rachel's hand off.

"You know, Miss Pris," Rachel whispered to the sleek black feline, "your brother is a lot friendlier than you are."

Apollyon, who had come hissing and skulking out from under the bed, glared up at Rachel as if to say "Who cares? Drop dead."

"You could take some lessons in niceness from him. It might win you a few friends."

Apollyon turned her back to Rachel and began to lick the paw Rachel had grabbed.

After closing the draperies she had pulled open, Rachel tiptoed to the door, opened it and peeked out. The hallway was empty, and still dimly lit. She hurried from Yvette's room and down the hall to her own door. Opening it, she began to step inside and then hesitated. Memory of Yvette and Alexandre arguing flashed into her mind. She closed the door softly and walked back to the stairs, then stood still at the landing.

The murmur of voices rose to meet her. They were still quarreling. Rachel crept quietly down the wide staircase, her curiosity too piqued to ignore, her guilt at eavesdropping not strong enough to prevent it.

"This family needs you to fulfill your obligations, Alexandre," Yvette said. "There's no one to carry on the name if you don't."

"Is that really so bad?" he sneered. "You know damned well if the world knew the truth about us they'd be more than glad to see the illustrious Beaumondiers die out." He laughed, but the sound held no humor or warmth. "Hell, I have no doubt they'd most certainly be more than willing to help us on our way, just like before."

"That was a long time ago."

"And things haven't changed," Alexandre said. "Neither have people."

"But we have," Yvette countered.

"No, we haven't, and that's the problem. We're still the same, and there's no help for it."

Rachel heard footsteps move across the room.

"Alexandre, you must understand, this has to be done, it's your . . ."

"No, I won't do it. Not now, not ever."

"Alexandre," Yvette said, a pleading tone in her voice now. "Please, you've got to think of . . ."

"No."

"You can't do this to us, Alexandre."

"It's late," he said coldly. "Don't you think you'd best retire to your bedchamber?"

Yvette suddenly appeared at the open door. Rachel pressed herself hurriedly against the curved wall of the staircase in an attempt to disappear within the shadows.

"Think about it, Alexandre," she said, her voice hard and demanding.

Yvette took a step into the foyer, paused, and slammed a curled fist against the doorjamb. "Damn you, Francois," she said, her tone one of loathing and disgust. "He's inherited your cursed morality, and that damned vein of goodness that ran through you, which I discovered too late." Yvette paced the length of the foyer, spun, and walked back toward the door she'd just exited. "You lived too long, Francois," she said harshly. "Too damned long. I should have known better. Should have seen what you were. And now my mistake in allowing you those extra years may cost us everything."

Rachel stared down at Yvette's back. She felt the breath catch in her throat and horror clasp her heart at the woman's words. What did Yvette's words mean? Was Francois their father? And had she killed him? Is that what she meant by her mistake in allowing him to live longer?

Yvette whirled around and took a step toward the stairs. As she did, her gaze rose and met Rachel's. A cold smile curved her lips. "Well, Rachel, my dear, we had begun to wonder where you had gotten yourself off to."

Rachel felt like cowering away from her, but with the wall at her back, there was nowhere to go. She forced herself to straighten to her full height and smile. "Hello, Yvette, how are you this morning?"

Yvette sighed. "Not well, I'm afraid. I was just on my way upstairs to lie down. I have a horrible headache."

"Oh, I'm sorry to hear that." Rachel hurried past Yvette. "Perhaps we can talk a bit later," she said.

Yvette looked at her coldly. "Yes, dear, I'm sure we will, later." Yvette's features broke into a cold smile. "Alexandre's in the study," she said casually, then turned her back on Rachel and continued up the staircase.

Rachel watched Yvette until she was out of sight. She didn't want to talk to Alexandre at the moment, didn't want to see him. What she wanted, desperately, was to radio Marc, to tell him that she'd found definite proof that Yvette had been lying, that Steven had come to *Sans Souci.*

"Rachel, are you all right?" Alexandre asked.

She turned to see him standing in the doorway of his study, the glow of an oil lamp at his back.

Their eyes met and she felt herself immediately being drawn into the vortex of timelessness his gaze could create. She fought the pull, struggled to maintain a grasp on her dwindling shred of reality. As before, the effort was in vain, yet this time instead of complete pictures, Rachel found herself emeshed within a kaleidoscope of blurring colors and impressions. She was surrounded by gray mist, an impenetrable cold, swirling fog that touched her skin and left her chilled. Fire suddenly burst out all around her, hot, consuming, robbing her of air. And then the blue of the sea engulfed her. She felt a rocking motion, water splashing up to spray lightly against her face. Then the heavy, humid air of the bayou, its strong scent of wild grasses and rich earth reached out to envelope her.

"Rachel?" Alexandre touched her arm.

In spite of the rush of tingling warmth the contact of his flesh with hers instantly aroused within her, Rachel tore herself away from him. "How . . . how do you do that?" she whispered, her mind and heart in a turmoil of fear, confusion, and anger. Her eyes darted to and from his, afraid to look directly at him, yet unable to help herself.

"Do what?" he asked. But he knew. She could see his past. Not too many mortals could. Only one other ever had—Danielle. He had explained it to her, and her love had turned to hate. And now there was Rachel, touching him where he didn't want to be touched, making him feel things he didn't want to feel, awakening emotions in him he didn't want awakened. And yet, for all his self-denial, he did want those things, desperately. He just knew, now more than ever before, that it wasn't meant to be. Not for him. Not for his kind. He had made love to her, and it had been wonderful. Glorious. But it had been wrong. He couldn't deceive her further, and yet he couldn't tell her the truth, couldn't bear to see that same spark of loathing and disdain burn within her eyes.

Rachel took a step back from him, aching to be in his arms, yet suddenly afraid of him. "How do you make me see other things, Alexandre?" Her eyes narrowed in suspicion. "How do you do that?"

A deep frown pulled his brow together. "See other things?" he repeated, his voice deep and hard as he feigned confusion at her words. "What other things, Rachel? What did you see?"

She shook her head. "I . . . I don't know really. Colors mostly. And images. Fleeting images."

"Colors." He nodded. "Fleeting images." He smiled compassionately. "Perhaps you should lie down for a while, Rachel." He reached past her and pulled a tapestry cord she had not noticed hanging against the wall at the bottom of the staircase. She heard nothing, but within seconds Hanson appeared.

"Hanson," Alexandre said, "I'm afraid Rachel is not feeling well."

The old man nodded, almost knowingly. "I shall make her some tea, sir," he said, and promptly disappeared.

"Would you like me to help you to your room, Rachel?" Alexandre asked.

She shook her head. "No, I . . . no, I'm okay." Rachel turned and, gripping the banister securely, hurried upstairs. Something was wrong. Her hands trembled violently. Something was terribly wrong. She closed the door of her bedchamber behind her and leaned against it, letting her head drop back to rest against the smoothly paneled wood. But what? What was it that she felt certain was so terribly, terribly wrong?

Chapter 14

Rachel drank the tea Hanson brought and almost instantly felt herself begin to relax. She lay down on the bed, her thoughts a jumble of fragmented pieces—Alexandre and the feelings he aroused within her, their lovemaking, his seeming coolness toward her this morning; Steven, his sudden and mysterious disappearance, finding first his lens and then his wallet; and Yvette's attitude, cold, at times almost spiteful, yet solicitous, as if for some reason, in spite of her feelings, she wanted Rachel to stay at *Sans Souci.*

Her mind struggled with the maelstrom of questions that each new moment at *Sans Souci* seemed to bring, but found no answers. Finally, feeling drained, Rachel ordered her mind to cease, at least for a while, its relentless pursuit of explanations and rest. She snuggled into the softness of the pillow. Within minutes she was asleep.

The door to her room opened slowly, almost tentatively. Alexandre stood quietly in the doorway and looked across the room at her. Why had fate done this to him again? He had destroyed the woman he loved once. Was he destined to do it again? Was that his only reason for existing? To destroy?

His fingers tightened around the doorknob. "If the

God your kind pray to truly exists," Alexandre whispered hoarsely, "then I pray that he will protect you from us, Rachel Domecq." Tears filled his eyes. "But mostly from me."

Asmodeus slipped between Alexandre's legs and sauntered into Rachel's room, his sleek black coat making him almost invisible in the darkness. He jumped up onto the bed and, curling his body into a tight little ball, settled down atop the folds of the pale blue coverlet that was rumpled about Rachel's feet.

"Watch over her, Asmo," Alexandre said softly. "Watch over her."

Taking the one step that removed him from her room, Alexandre quietly closed the door and retreated toward the stairs.

When Rachel finally woke it was night. Startled at the intensity of the darkness in her room, she walked to the window and drew the drapes. Asmodeus, nestled within a mount of coverlet, raised his head to throw her a glance, then settled back upon his curled paws. Black lids dropped to cover green eyes and he began to purr.

A crescent moon, and a widespread sprinkling of glistening stars across a vista of velvety black sky met Rachel's gaze as she stared through the window.

"My God, I must have slept the entire day away," she mumbled in disbelief. She turned back toward the room. "I've never done that before." She shook her head to rid it of the drowsiness of sleep and as she did her gaze come in contact with the empty cup in which Hanson had brought her tea. She approached the small table that stood beside the bed, picked up the cup and held it to her nose. There was no unusual smell. Rachel peered into the bottom of the delicate china cup. There was a slight, almost imperciptible residue of powder there. She dipped a finger into it. A few gritty white particles clung to her fingertip. "That old creep gave me some kind of sleeping potion." Anger churned within her breast. "But why?" Why would they want her to sleep through the day? It didn't make any sense.

She slammed the cup back down on its saucer. "I could have had an allergic reaction to whatever that stuff was and gone into convulsions. Or died." The last thought sent a shiver of apprehension rippling over her skin. "Died," she repeated. Is that what one of them wanted. To kill her? She frowned. But why? Was there something about her and Steven that threatened them somehow? Memory of the portrait of Danielle suddenly flashed into her mind, and along with it, the question that had nagged at her ever since—were they related? Was the connection, in spite of it being so removed, and in the distant past, somehow a threat to the Beaumondiers today?

She looked back at the cup. "I ought to arrest that old coot and make him talk." Then she remembered she wasn't a cop anymore. "Well, I ought to have Marc arrest him." She discarded the idea immediately. Hanson would never reveal anything, regardless of what kind of penalty he was looking at. And it wasn't the old man she was after. All she wanted was to find her brother.

She was suddenly alert. "Marc." She hadn't called him since that morning. She needed to tell him about discovering Steven's wallet and find out if he'd turned up anything on a link between Danielle Toutant and the Ligeres. Rachel retrieved the transmittor from her pocket and turned back to the window. With a flip of her finger she unlatched the lock and threw the window upward. Warm night air, carrying with it the heady fragrances of jasmine, dogwood, magnolias and wild grasses drifted in to encompass her. Rachel inhaled deeply then turned on the transmitter and held it to her mouth. "Marc?" she said softly. "Marc, are you there?"

"Damned right I'm here," he snapped back. "Where the hell are you?"

"Just waking up from a nap."

"A nap? Didn't you oversleep this morning?"

"Yes . . ."

"And you needed a nap? Dammit, Rachel, are you sure you're okay? Are you sick? Maybe you should get out of there."

"No, I'm fine." As long as I'm not fed crushed sleeping pills in my tea, she thought and fought to stifle a yawn. Or fighting off vicious bats in the middle of the night. "Have you found out anything more on, uh . . ." she glanced toward the door to reassure herself no one was standing there and decided to be cautious in her choice of words anyway, ". . . that other woman we were talking about?"

"Other woman? You mean Da . . . the dead one?"

"Yes."

"No. My guys are still checking but so far they haven't come up with anything. Of course, that was a long time ago, so it might take a while."

"Well, I came up with something else."

"Yeah, what?"

"Steven's wallet."

"Shit."

"And it was intact, complete with driver's license, cards, money, charge cards, and a picture of me."

"Oh, hell. A picture of you? Now I really don't like this. They knew who you were, Rae, before you even got there."

"Maybe not all of them." She hoped not all of them.

"Rae, this is a set-up. I don't know what for, or why,

but it's a set-up. Come out of there. I'll get the Captain to order a search for Steven. We'll find him."

"No."

"Rae."

"Marc, I'm staying. There's no telling what they've done with Steven. If he's . . ." her voice cracked. She took a deep breath and forced herself to go on. "If he's still alive, there's no telling where they have him, and I believe, because of our bond, that I have the best chance of finding him. And also of discovering what the hell is going on out here."

"Where'd you find the wallet?"

"In the drawer of Yvette's desk." She breathed a sigh of relief that he evidently wasn't going to argue further. At least not right now. But she knew he wouldn't give up, and his next words proved it.

"I don't like this, Rae. The Beaumondiers claim Steven never came out here. If that's true, what the hell is Yvette doing with his wallet in her desk? That would mean she lied, Rae. It would also mean that she knew who you were before you even wired them about the proposal from the Preservation Society."

"Right."

"So why'd they let you come?"

"Someone evidently wanted me here."

"Why? For what?"

Rachel shrugged. "I don't know. But I think finding out about Danielle Toutant, and if the Beaumondiers and I are related to her might give us some answers."

"That's a long shot, Rae."

"I know, but I have a feeling. Call it a hunch, if you want. I just feel that there's something there, Marc."

She heard him curse softly.

"This thing is beginning to smell nasty, Rae. Real nasty. Something's wrong."

"Obviously something's wrong," Rachel snapped. "My brother is missing."

"I'm sorry. I didn't mean that. But . . . Rae, the cops down here have always thought there was something peculiar about the Beaumondiers. Strange, you know? They've suspected them of a lot of things over the years, and I do mean years. Going way back. But they could never get enough evidence to prove anything. Hell, they can't even give any logical reason why they suspect them of half the stuff they suspect them of doing. But you name it, and they suspect them of it."

"Suspicion isn't proof," Rachel said, not sure why she was defending the Beaumondiers.

"Right, so no charges have ever been filed. There aren't even any casebooks on them. But that's beside the point, Rae. The point right now is that I don't like you in there alone. I want you to come out before something happens to you. We'll hire some professionals to look into this."

"I can't, Marc, don't you understand?" She felt her temper flaring again. "My brother's in trouble and I may be his only hope. Anyway, don't forget, I am a professional." She remembered the fact that she'd lost her own gun and felt a sinking feeling in the pit of her stomach. "At least I used to be. And you still are."

"Rae . . ."

"Marc, Yvette Beaumondier has something to do with my brother being missing, and I've got to find out what."

"We can get a warrant. You bring that wallet out here and any judge in the parish will issue us a warrant. We could arrest her. Take her into the station for questioning. Confront her with this whole mess."

Rachel shook her head. "That might jeopardize whatever chances Steven has." She sighed, glanced over her shoulder, and turned back to the window. "He's still alive, Marc, that much I'm sure of, at least I was a few hours ago when he called to me, and I won't do anything to jeopardize that situation. Yvette being in possession of Steven's wallet doesn't prove a damned thing really, not as far as the police are concerned, and you know it. She could say she found it. Or she accidentally picked it up when she left the bar and was going to mail it back to him but hasn't gotten around to it."

"Yeah, true."

"But what really scares me is that Steven's calls to me seem to be getting less frequent, and weaker."

"Rae, you've got to come out of there."

"Will you stop saying that?" she snapped. "I'm not coming out yet. I'm not giving up on my brother." She tried to soften her tone, feeling a flash of guilt at taking her edginess out on him. He was worried about her and she should be grateful. "Just give me a few more days, Marc, please. He's the only brother I have. The only family. I can't just . . ." She felt the tears well up in her eyes and her voice broke. Inhaling deeply and blinking the tears away she continued. "I have to keep trying, Marc."

"Then you radio in on time like we agreed, Rachel, or goddamn it, I'll call the Seventh Cavalry and we'll come in there and get you."

Rachel smiled. "I will, Marc. I promise." She clicked off the transmitter and slipped it back into her pocket. Think, Rachel, she ordered herself. Stop fooling around. Stop letting yourself get detoured. Think.

Not bothering to light a lamp, she began to pace the room, passing within the faint stream of moonlight that shone through the open window, into the darkness, then back and forth again. This thing was a puzzle and, unfortunately, rather than putting the pieces together, she just seemed to keep accumulating new ones that didn't fit with the others. "But they have to," she mumbled. "Somehow they have to all fit together."

Asmodeus watched her from his curled position on the bed, his large green eyes barely moving as his gaze followed her from one end of the room to the other.

"I need to get into Yvette's room again." Rachel turned from the fireplace and began to pace toward the bed. "Maybe there's something else in there, something that will tell me more about what's going on."

Asmodeus yawned, lifted his rear end and, extending his front legs to their full length, stretched lazily.

Reaching the bed, Rachel whirled around absently and began her return trek toward the fireplace. "She knows something, I'm certain. Yvette knows something. But how do I get her to open up to me? How do I find out what the hell she knows? Or what she did." The last thought send a cavalcade of chills racing up Rachel's back.

Asmodeus jumped down from the bed and pranced gracefully across the room.

Rachel, in midstride, felt something furry move between her legs. She hesitated in her step and felt herself suddenly thrown off balance. "Oh." Her weight fell forward and her left ankle twisted, hurling her foot out from under her. She threw out her arms.

Asmodeus emitted an abrupt and startled screech, as his body was momentarily squashed between Rachel's ankles. He scrambled to escape and shot under the bed.

Rachel's threw out her arms to break her fall. The heel of her left hand crashed down atop a black wrought iron flower-shaped medallion that was one of a pair, which adorned each upper corner of the fireplace. Her knees thudded into the area rug set before the hearth, its

The Publishers of Zebra Books
Make This Special Offer
to Zebra Romance Readers...

AFTER YOU HAVE READ THIS
BOOK WE'D LIKE TO SEND YOU
4 MORE FOR *FREE*
AN $18.00 VALUE

NO OBLIGATION!

ONLY ZEBRA HISTORICAL ROMANCES
"BURN WITH THE FIRE OF HISTORY"
(SEE INSIDE FOR MONEY SAVING DETAILS.)

MORE PASSION AND ADVENTURE AWAIT... YOUR TRIP TO A BIG ADVENTUROUS WORLD BEGINS WHEN YOU ACCEPT YOUR FIRST 4 NOVELS ABSOLUTELY *FREE*

(AN $18.00 VALUE)

**Accept your Free gift and start to experience more of the pas-
sion and adventure you like in a historical romance novel. Each
Zebra novel is filled with proud men, spirited women and tempes
tuous love that you'll remember long after you turn the last page.**

Zebra Historical Romances are the finest novels of their kind. They are written by authors who really know how to weave tales of romance and adventure in the historical settings you love. You'll feel like you've actually gone back in time with the thrilling stories that each Zebra novel offers.

GET YOUR FREE GIFT WITH THE START OF YOUR HOME SUBSCRIPTION

Our readers tell us that these books sell out very fast in book stores and often they miss the newest titles. So Zebra has made arrangements for you to receive the four newest novels published each month.

You'll be guaranteed that you'll never miss a title, and home delivery is so convenient. And to show you just how easy it is to get Zebra Historical Romances, we'll send you your first 4 books absolutely FREE! Our gift to you just for trying our home subscription service.

BIG SAVINGS AND FREE HOME DELIVERY

Each month, you'll receive the four newest titles as soon as they are published. You'll probably receive them even before the bookstores do. What's more, you may preview these exciting novels free for 10 days. If you like them as much as we think you will, just pay the low preferred subscriber's price of just $3.75 each. *You'll save $3.00 each month off the publisher's price.* AND, your savings are even greater because there are never any shipping, handling or other hidden charges—FREE Home Delivery. Of course you can return any shipment within 10 days for full credit, no questions asked. There is no minimum number of books you must buy.

4 FREE BOOKS

TO GET YOUR 4 FREE BOOKS WORTH $18.00 —MAIL IN THE FREE BOOK CERTIFICATE T O D A Y

Fill in the Free Book Certificate below, and we'll send your FREE BOOKS to you as soon as we receive it.

If the certificate is missing below, write to: Zebra Home Subscription Service, Inc., P.O. Box 5214, 120 Brighton Road, Clifton, New Jersey 07015-5214.

FREE BOOK CERTIFICATE

4 FREE BOOKS

ZEBRA HOME SUBSCRIPTION SERVICE, INC.

YES! Please start my subscription to Zebra Historical Romances and send me my first 4 books absolutely FREE. I understand that each month I may preview four new Zebra Historical Romances free for 10 days. If I'm not satisfied with them, I may return the four books within 10 days and owe nothing. Otherwise, I will pay the low preferred subscriber's price of just $3.75 each; a total of $15.00, *a savings off the publisher's price of $3.00.* I may return any shipment and I may cancel this subscription at any time. There is no obligation to buy any shipment and there are no shipping, handling or other hidden charges. Regardless of what I decide, the four free books are mine to keep.

NAME

ADDRESS APT

CITY STATE ZIP

( )

TELEPHONE

SIGNATURE (if under 18, parent or guardian must sign)

Terms, offer and prices subject to change without notice. Subscription subject to acceptance by Zebra Books. Zebra Books reserves the right to reject any order or cancel any subscription.

ZB0894

GET
FOUR
FREE
BOOKS
(AN $18.00 VALUE)

AFFIX
STAMP
HERE

ZEBRA HOME SUBSCRIPTION
SERVICE, INC.
120 BRIGHTON ROAD
P.O. BOX 5214
CLIFTON, NEW JERSEY 07015-5214

thick weave the only thing that saved her kneecaps from major bruising.

A creaking noise, combined with that of rock sliding across rock, sounded as Rachel collapsed onto the floor and began to gasp, her fright and the fall having knocked the air from her lungs.

Asmodeus, fully-collected and feeling brave again, crept out from under the bed and approached Rachel. He rubbed his body against the arm she was leaning on to support her weight.

"Asmodeus, for heaven's sake," Rachel said, finally gaining some sense of composure, "you nearly killed me." She patted his head. "I thought I was at least safe around you." She rose shakily to her feet and turned toward the bed. Her entire body was trembling, and her legs felt like two wobbly sticks of rubber about to collapse. She needed to sit down again for a few minutes.

The cat meowed and pranced toward the fireplace.

"Yeah, right, you're sorry," Rachel quipped. She struck a match and held it to the wick of the lamp set on the night table, then looked back at Asmodeus as he began to sniff around the grate. "Don't tell me you smell a mouse," she warned. "I don't think I could take that right now." Rachel felt her skin crawl. "Not a mouse."

Asmodeus's head suddenly disappeared behind the ornately carved cherrywood panel that framed the outer edges of the fireplace.

Rachel frowned. "Asmodeus?"

The cat pulled his head back into view and looked at Rachel. He meowed.

"How'd you do that?" She rose from the bed and slowly walked toward him. "What's there?"

The cat meowed again and stuck his head back into the space between fireplace and wall.

Rachel stared at the thin cavity and felt her heartbeat

speed to a maddening pace. Every nerve in her body began to tingle in a combination of fear and excitement. Was this some sort of secret passageway that had opened when she'd fallen against the fireplace. She looked at the marble and wood front. Her gaze caught the wrought iron medallion as her mind registered the dull pain that throbbed in her hand. Was that it? Had her hand hit that medallion when she'd fallen? And in just the right way to open this secret door?

She looked down as Asmodeus. He was sitting patiently, looking up at her, the top of his head covered with dust and tangled cobwebs.

She turned her attention back to the fissure behind the fireplace. A door. But to where? The cellar? A secret room? She put her hand out toward the dark space. Cool air met her fingers. Rachel gripped the edge of the fireplace and, pushing against the wall with one hand, pulled it toward her. It moved slowly, rock grating against rock slab, old hinges creaking in protest of being forced to move again after only Lord knew how many years.

"A hidden staircase," Rachel murmured. Her first thought was that the stairs led to the attic, as had the others she'd come across in the pantry. But these led down, so that wasn't right.

Asmodeus sidled past her and promptly disappeared down the stairs.

"Curiosity killed the cat," Rachel called after him. But, ignoring her own warning to Asmodeus, Rachel hurried to pick up the oil lamp from the table beside the bed and, holding it high, stepped onto the small landing behind the fireplace.

The air smelled stale, the wood rotten, cobwebs hung from the ceiling, the walls, and filled every corner and crevice. A thick layer of dust covered the stairs. Rachel placed a tentative foot on the first step and tested her weight against it. The stair creaked but appeared solid. She put her full weight on it and swung her other foot warily down onto the next step. Ten minutes later, her heart nearly in her throat, her pulse racing so fast she felt certain her veins were going to burst at any second, Rachel had descended twenty steps and reached another landing.

Asmodeus meowed from the dark somewhere beyond where she stood, as if beckoning her, or warning her away. She wasn't sure which.

Rachel lifted the lantern higher. There were no more stairs in front of her. Instead the enclosed staircase turned into a slightly declining tunnel. "I must be below the first story of the house now," she mumbled. The smell of her surroundings had changed along with the terrain. Now there was the odor of old earth and moist rock, of long closed off air and rotting roots. She moved into the tunnel. Cobwebs turned the squared ceiling corners where rock walls met bricked ceiling to lace archs, moisture glistened off of the rocks, and here and there, protruding through cracks in the ceiling, plant roots hung down resembling long spindly fingers. Rachel took a step forward, and felt something hard beneath her foot. She immediately stopped and cringed with dread. Had she stepped on some sort of tiny animal? Or maybe a huge spider? Nausea filled her breast as she felt the lump beneath the sole of her shoe. She forced herself to raise her foot and take a hurried step back. With a deep breath she bent forward and shone the light on the dirt floor. There was nothing there except a tiny jagged rock.

Relief washed over her like a tidal wave. If there was one thing she hated it was stepping on bugs—snails, spiders, worms, whatever. Once, while playing with Steven in the bayous of Shadows Teche near their grandmother's house, Rachel had almost stepped on a baby snake who had been curled up on a rock warming itself. Only Steven's scream and shove had saved her and the snake, but she'd been sick the remainder of the day just thinking about it.

She sighed and moved forward.

The tunnel continued to descend in a straight path. "Is this thing ever going to end?" she wondered aloud, mentally cowering as her voice echoed back to her.

Asmodeus meowed from somewhere ahead of her as if in answer to her question.

Several minutes and a lot of cautious steps later, Rachel concluded that the tunnel was most likely an old escape route for slaves during the Civil War and would probably end in either a collapsed pile of dirt or beneath the floor of an old cabin in the bayou. She was about to turn back when she noticed the light from her lamp suddenly shone dully on a wall of dirt and rock directly in front of her. "A pile of dirt, just as I thought," she mumbled. But rather than turn back, she approached the dirt wall slowly and, as she neared, realized it wasn't a dead end at all. The tunnel cut abruptly to the right. One leg of it had caved in, but the other leg was still passable.

Her curiosity renewed, Rachel turned the corner. The flame burning the lamp's wick danced steadily within its glass chimney, its weak yellow-orange glow reflecting off the rock walls on either side of her and turning them to glistening angles of silver and shadow.

Asmodeus wrapped himself around Rachel's legs, rubbing her calves with the back of his head.

She glanced down and then held the lamp up higher. "Don't trip me down here," she warned, and looked around. Five feet beyond where she stood, and almost beyond the light cast by the lamp, a wide, squat door, its rough planked planes softened by the golden light, its black wrought iron handle and hinge guards too old and unpolished to gleam, served to abruptly end the tunnel.

Chapter 15

Rachel stared at the door but didn't move toward it.

Asmodeus purred contentedly and swished against her legs.

The silence of the tunnel was almost overbearing, pressing down on her like a great weight. She swallowed hard. The door didn't look like it had been opened in ages. For that matter, neither the tunnel nor the stairs had appeared as if they had been disturbed by footsteps either. But then why should they? The Civil War had been over for almost one hundred and thirty years. The last slaves who had escaped from *Sans Souci* had most likely passed through this door months before Lee surrendered at Appomattox.

Rachel took a step toward the door and stopped, her brow furrowing into a deep frown. An underground slave railroad in New Orleans? No, that was wrong. Most of them were farther north. She looked at the door more carefully. It was possible this was an escape tunnel for slaves, but . . . She glanced back at the caved-in juncture of the tunnel. So where had this tunnel led? A shiver of apprehension tripped up her spine. Her gaze returned to the sealed door.

Rachel inhaled deeply, trying to summon the courage

to turn the old wrought iron handle, and then wished she hadn't taken the deep breath. The air was stagnant and near foul. She coughed softly.

"Well, that was stupid," she said, looking down at Asmodeus and coughing again in an effort to clear her lungs.

He meowed, as if agreeing.

"Thanks, *friend,*" she said, and then chuckled. "But you got me down here so don't run off and leave me alone when I open this door, okay?"

The cat rubbed against her calf in answer.

"Okay, Mr. Brave, let's do it." Rachel approached the door and, grasping the iron handle which was shaped like a horizontal S, she pushed on it. It refused to move. She pushed again. Nothing.

Rachel took a step back. "It's locked. So, now what?" She looked the door over and as her gaze moved to its top corner she noticed an old black key hanging from a cobweb-covered hook. Rachel, her nose wrinkled in disgust at having to slip her fingers within the flimsy spider's lair, reached up and retrieved the key. She hurriedly brushed her fingers against her slacks. "Yuck!"

"Meow."

"Thanks for your understanding," Rachel said. She stuck the key into the small hole below the door latch and turned it, then, still holding the lamp in one hand, grasped the handle with the other and pushed down. It was tight. She repositioned her grip on the handle and, practically using the full weight of her body, pushed down on it. The latch finally slipped downward and she felt the door give.

Suddenly Rachel wasn't so sure she wanted to find out what was behind the slab of heavy planks. A plethora of horror movie scenes began to trip through her mind—a pit filled with writhing, poisonous snakes; a sadistic crazy with steel claws on each finger ready to slice her into shreds; an unkillable giant wearing a hockey mask and ready to murder everything and everyone in its path.

Rachel snatched her hand away from the door. "Maybe this wasn't such a great idea, Asmodeus."

The cat sat down beside her and, as if their surroundings were the most natural of any he'd ever been in, began to clean his paws.

"Well, okay, smarty. If you're not nervous I guess I'm not either." She reached for the door latch again, her fingers curling around the cool metal. "Not much anyway." She stepped back and pulled the door toward her. The hinges creaked loudly as they strained against the years of unuse and the rust that had invaded their shafts, a spine-tingling sound that echoed eerily in the dank tunnel. Rachel held the lamp before her and, skirting the door, stepped past it.

She'd been wrong. It wasn't an escape route. It was a room. Its walls were made of the same rock as the tunnels, its ceiling and floor both of crude brick and mortar. To one side of the room were several rows of huge wine racks that reached nearly to the ceiling. Each held a scattering of dust-covered bottles. Another wall had crates and bulging burlap sacks stacked against it. A crudely fashioned table and two chairs sat in the middle of the room, an old brass candle holder stood in the center of the table, its taper having long ago burned into a puddle of wax that half-covered the holder and part of the table. Rachel took another step into the room and held the lamp high. She turned to look into one near corner and a scream instantly ripped itself from her throat as she jumped several inches off of the floor. The lamp wavered in her shaking hands but she managed not to drop it in her shock. She stared at the sight before her.

In sitting positions, their backs against the walls leading to the corner, and looking as if they were smiling up at her, were a row of bodies, though they were mostly skeletons. There were five of them, sitting side by side on the floor, heads upright against the wall, hands lying limp at their sides, legs outstretched before them, and sparsely covering each were the ragged remnants of the clothes they had died in. As her shock subsided, Rachel took a step toward them. Her gaze swept slowly over each man, over the garments and accessories that still clung to their bones. The style of clothing on or around each was ancient. She frowned and looked closer. One man had worn pantaloons to just below his knees. The cloth, though intact, was little more than rotting grayish yellow threads that lay atop his thigh bones. The man's stockings had evidently rotted away as there was no trace of them. Her gaze moved to his shoes. Leather, with a fancy silver ornament attached to its top. She looked up. Several long, dried curls of hair hung down over one side of his skull. Her gaze moved to the next skeleton. What was left of his shirt showed ruffles on both chestfront and sleeve cuffs. A tri-cornered hat lay discarded on the floor next to another skeleton. Its brim was adorned with black cord, though in places it still shone gold, attesting to its original color. A profusion of feather spines dangled from one side of the hat, the plumes having long ago disintegrated.

Rachel studied the various ragged garments. The styles seemed to be late 1600s to mid-1800s she calculated. But what were these men doing down here? Had they been trapped in this underground room somehow? Perhaps accidentally locked themselves in? She glanced back at the door. It only locked from the outside. Had they been held prisoner in here, and then left to die? Or was there some more macabre explanation? One no one wanted to acknowledge? She looked back at the skeletons. No, that explanation didn't work. Though the clothes were nothing more than a few ragged pieces of cloth, there was enough left so that it was discernible these men had not all died in here at the same time. The fashions differed too much. She looked from one skeleton, the last on the left, to the one sitting farthest from it. The design of their clothes seemed to suggest a difference of at least fifty years. Maybe more. She turned away from the grisly scene and walked toward the table in the center of the room. As she did, the lamp she held cast its light across the far end of the room, illuminating its corners and the cot that was pushed up against its rock wall.

Rachel stopped abruptly, her heart once again jumping to lodge in her throat. "Oh, my God." Wanting nothing more than to turn and flee, she forced herself to walk slowly toward the lone figure lying on the bed. It was the body of a woman, and much better preserved than those of the men, suggesting they had been here considerably longer, though not too much Rachel realized as she drew nearer.

She paused beside the cot. Once, long ago, when the woman had been alive, she had most likely been quite lovely. That was evident from the long ruche of dark lashes that lay fanned across high delicately arched cheekbones. Dark curls of hair, though dry and brittle in appearance now, cascaded from the crown of her head, and spread over her shoulders. One long curl lay haphazardly atop her shrunken breast. Rachel's gaze traveled over the woman's form. She was posed as if in funereal mode, her hands crossed one over the other atop her breasts, the folds of her once beautiful ivory gown spread out about her legs like an unfurled fan. "Who were you?" Rachel whispered. She looked back toward the woman's face but a brooch, pinned to the gathered lace neckline of the dress caught her attention. Rachel's heart nearly stopped its beating altogether, and the breath caught in her lungs. She shook her head in disbelief. "Oh, no, this can't be."

Rachel took a step closer to the corpse and, holding the lamp directly over her, bent down to get a closer look at the brooch. It was the same one. There was no doubt in her mind at all. It was the same brooch Danielle Toutant had worn when she'd posed for the painting Rachel had found in the attic. She was sure of it. Rachel straightened quickly and took a step back. Fear, dread, confusion, and horror fought for control within her breast. It wasn't possible. She blinked rapidly but nothing about the room, or its occupants, changed. Danielle Toutant. What was she doing here? Rachel glanced at the men and then back at Danielle. Had someone killed her, killed them, and then placed each body down here in this dank, underground tomb or . . . She shuddered. Had someone lured or forced each of these poor souls down to this room, and then left them to die?

Rachel turned and looked at the men who had also suffered the same fate as Danielle Toutant. But why? What had any of them done to deserve this horrid death?

Asmodeus jumped onto the table. The rattling sound it made beneath his weight as the rickety wooden legs scraped the floor cut into Rachel's thoughts and drew her attention. She turned and looked at the cat. He meowed.

"You're right. It's time to get out of here," she said. "Come on." Rachel hurried toward the door and, stepping past it and waiting for Asmodeus to pass, pulled it shut behind her. The sound echoed loudly within the narrow tunnel. "Good, Rachel, tell everyone in the house what you're doing."

She walked as rapidly as she could back up the tunnel, climbed the narrow stairs, and squeezed out through the space between the wall and the fireplace front. She set the lamp down on a table and brushed herself off, feeling as if she was covered by cobwebs and dust.

A loud knock sounded at her door.

Rachel jumped and clamped a hand quickly over her lips to stifle the scream that burst from her throat. She whirled around to stare at the door.

The knock came again. "Rachel? Rachel, are you all right?"

Alexandre. She breathed a sigh of relief, and then suddenly wondered if that was the right reaction. She wanted it to be. God, how she wanted it to be. But could she really trust him? Could she trust any of them? Someone at *Sans Souci* had committed murder. Several murders and . . . She nearly laughed aloud. What was she thinking? The bodies were what? Two, three hundred years old? Whoever had killed those people was long dead.

Except for the person who kidnapped Steven, she reminded herself.

She walked toward the door and, reaching toward the knob, paused, and threw a quick glance down at her clothes. Both her blouse and slacks were dingy. She couldn't let Alexandre in. He'd want to know what had happened to her. She looked toward the fireplace. It still stood open, its face standing away from the wall. He'd see the fireplace. She grasped the doorknob and leaned against the paneled wood.

"Alexandre, I was just changing clothes," she said through the door.

"We were getting worried," he answered. "It's late, and you didn't come downstairs for dinner."

"I'm sorry. I fell asleep. Let me dress and I'll be down in just a few minutes."

Silence was her only answer.

Rachel opened the armoire where she'd hung her clothes. She didn't have too much choice. Her trip to New Orleans had been a hurried one and she hadn't packed a lot. Pulling an emerald green silk blouse and matching slacks from the armoire she undressed quickly and, retrieving the transmitter from the pocket of her black slacks, threw the white blouse back into her suitcase. She held the transmitter in the palm of her hand and stared at it. She should call Marc. Tell him about what she'd found. Later, she decided. Anyway, discovering two-hundred-year-old bodies had absolutely nothing to do with why she was here, and it was a mystery that could wait until later. She ran a brush through her hair. The long red-brown strands fanned across her shoulders. A touch of blush to her cheeks and a swathe of lipstick put a little color back into her face. Rachel slipped into the green outfit and, stepping before the tall cheval mirror that stood in one corner of the room, gave herself an assessing once-over.

Satisfied, she turned back to the bed, picked up the transmitter and flipped it on. She'd better check in with him. It wouldn't be wise to cause him worry and have him try to radio her while she was downstairs with the Beaumondiers. "Marc?"

A knock sounded behind her.

Rachel turned to face the door.

"Good girl, Rae," Marc said just then, "you didn't fall asleep again."

"Later," she whispered into the transmitter and quickly turned it off. She slipped it into her pocket, walked to the door and opened it.

Yvette stood in the hallway, smiling. "Rachel, Catherine wanted me to tell you that she plans to come downstairs this evening, and would like to talk with you."

Rachel nodded and returned the smile, but her heart felt as if it were sinking. If Catherine came downstairs, if she talked to her, there would most likely be no further reason for Rachel to stay at *Sans Souci.* But she couldn't leave. Not yet. Not without discovering more information about Steven. She ordered herself to remain calm. "I'll be right down," Rachel said. "I just have one little thing to do."

"I'll wait for you." Yvette put a hand on the edge of the door and, pushing it back open, walked into the bedchamber. She paused in the center of the room and turned to look back expectantly at Rachel.

"Oh, well, I just wanted to open the window a little before I left," Rachel lied. "Sometimes it gets a little stuffy in here and I thought a bit of night air might help."

Yvette chuckled. "You should be careful, Rachel," she said, and threw her a sly gaze. "Things other than air have been known to find their way through open windows."

"Well, I'm sure you don't have burglars at *Sans Souci,*" Rachel said, and laughed.

"No. No burglars."

Alexandre stood before the fireplace, one booted foot raised and resting on the edge of the brass fender that skirted the hearth, one arm, bent, lying atop the mantle. He stared at Rachel, trying to look interested in what she was saying to Catherine, and all the while wondering why she was really at *Sans Souci.* He felt desire coil tightly within him as memory of her naked body pressed to his own, joining and moving in unison with his, arousing emotions and pleasures he had thought never to feel again, suddenly invaded his more cool and logical thoughts.

Yvette glanced at her son and then back at Rachel Domecq and a shrewd little smile curved her lips.

"And we've sponsored several other estates in this area," Rachel said. "I assume you've heard of *Magnolia Woods? Cherry Blossom?* And *The Oaks?*"

It had been over two hundred years since he'd made love to a woman, since he had dared to let himself even get close to a woman. And then *she* had come to *Sans Souci,* literally and unconsciously smashing through the taut control he had held over himself for so long, destroying his resolve, making him feel things he had never wanted to feel again.

Rage and desire burned within him, each emotion fighting to overwhelm the other. He should have left *Sans Souci* the moment he saw her, but even then it had been too late. When she'd looked into his eyes, he knew she had seen his soul, just as he had seen hers, and even though he'd tried, he had known at that very moment there was no turning back, no denying the inevitable.

Rachel glanced toward him. His eyes caught hers and Alexandre felt the need to reach out to her, to touch the ivory flesh he knew was hidden behind the soft folds of silk. His fingers flexed involuntarily.

"Hi, everyone."

The conversation came to an abrupt halt as all eyes turned toward the door.

"Well," Suzanne laughed, and sauntered into the room, "don't let me kill all this friendly little chatter."

Catherine turned back to Rachel. "Yes, please, dear, go on."

Suzanne seated herself at one end of a velvet-covered tete-a-tete across the room and turned her gaze toward the window, and the night beyond it.

Alexandre returned his attention to Rachel. Several women had come to the house in the past years since Danielle, invited by Yvette or Marguerite in the hopes he would be attracted to one of them. His mother and grandmother didn't understand why he resisted their efforts, why he rarely left the plantation, seldom associated with people, and he guessed they had long since given up trying to understand why he wouldn't kill or drink the life force of humans.

Only his great grandmother, Catherine, seemed able to understand that after loving Danielle and experiencing her disdain at learning the truth about him, Alexandre could no longer go on as he had before. He could no longer bear to rob a human being of life, or turn them to the type of existence he was forced to endure and had come to loath.

"The Preservation Society is very interested in *Sans Souci,* Mrs. Beaumondier. As one of the oldest estates in the New Orleans area, it is very significant historically," Rachel said. She glanced quickly at Alexandre and smiled, but took care not to look directly into his eyes.

The shadow of a frown tugged at Alexandre's brow as he continued to watch Rachel. Yes, it was too much of a coincidence. She looked almost exactly like Danielle, the same shade of hair, like rich earth touched with the brilliant redness of the sun, the same svelte figure, each curve and plane designed to fit snugly into his, and the same forest green eyes sparking with fire.

Almost identical and yet they were so different. He nearly scoffed at his own ridiculous thoughts. Of course they were different. Rachel was vibrant, smiling, and alive. Danielle was dead. He nearly groaned at the reminder. Dead. All these years. Dead. And all because of him.

"Sometimes the monies are appropriated through various grants, both State and Federal, while other times repairs are paid for with grants from the Society itself," Rachel said.

"Money is of no concern to the Beaumondiers," Catherine said. "It never has been, and I'm sure," she glanced fondly toward Alexandre, "it never will be."

Alexandre continued on with his own thoughts, though he looked at the others in the room as if he were deeply absorbed in the conversation between Rachel and Catherine. Her brother was missing, at least according to the police. Alexandre remembered the two officers who had come to the door. It had been morning and they'd been quite agitated when he'd informed them that they would have to return that evening if they wanted to speak with Yvette. They had been even more agitated that evening when, upon their return, Yvette vehemently insisted that she had not accompanied the young man they were seeking, Steven Ligere, from the bar where she'd met him the night of his disappearance. Obviously they'd thought Yvette would provide a break in the case, and were not pleased to find otherwise.

Alexandre moved his gaze toward Yvette. By the time the police had left, they'd acted as if they'd believed her. Alexandre wasn't so sure he did. His mother lied. He'd never caught her at it, of course, at least not directly, but his suspicions ran deep, and not without cause.

"But *Sans Souci* should be preserved for its historical value, I'm sure you can see that. It's one of the oldest plantations in the state, and it would be a shame to lose it," Rachel said.

Alexandre's gaze returned to Rachel. She had said that she wasn't worried about her brother, that he frequently went off without telling anyone, including her. But it was too much of a coincidence, he thought again. Yvette meets Steven Ligere in a bar in the *Vieux Carre,* and Steven Ligere disappears without a trace.

That in itself could be explained away. But then a few days later the Beaumondiers receive a wire from the missing man's sister stating that her employer, the state's Preservation Society, would like to sponsor historical monument status to *Sans Souci,* and his family invites her to the plantation to discuss the matter.

No, he decided. There is more to this visit than an inquiry from the Preservation Society. And more to his family member's sudden interest in history. Much more. And he was damned well going to find out what it was.

Chapter 16

"You seem to have convinced my grandmother to consider your plan," Alexandre said.

Rachel, seated on a wicker lounge chair, looked across the gallery at him. Before leaving the house he had discarded his jacket and now stood a few feet away, clad only in a silk shirt, its snowy white threads a stark contrast to the bronzed planes of his face, and black slacks that suggestively hugged his lean thighs. Alexandre leaned one muscular shoulder against the massive bulk of a pillar and turned his back to the shadowed landscape beyond the house. From the windows of the parlor, beyond which burned several oil lamps, soft yellow light poured out onto the gallery to touch the burnished flesh of his face and create shadows within each hollow, turned the curls of his hair to glistening waves of ebony, and the grayness of his eyes to dark, swirling pools of midnight mist.

Rachel wanted to reach out to him, to run her fingers through the thick tendrils of his hair, over the taut curves of his body, down the long length of his arms. She wanted to lose herself within his embrace, feel his arms around her, crushing her to him. She wanted to taste his lips ravaging hers, experience once again the glorious sensation of his need filling her, pleasuring her, taking her to heights of desire she had never been aware even existed.

Her body fairly ached with need of him.

Asmodeus jumped into her lap. The sudden and surprising interruption jerked Rachel's thoughts back to the moment at hand. Alexandre had made love to her, and then turned cool, as if he regretted their brief closeness. His eyes, whenever she happened to look at him, seemed distant and shadowed with something close to suspicion. Did he know? she suddenly wondered. Had he discovered her true reason for being at *Sans Souci?*

Rachel felt an urge to cry. The passionate lover of the night before who had swept her into his arms and seduced her with sweet words and even sweeter kisses and caresses, was gone. He had left her bed in the middle of the night, and disappeared. Rachel felt a surge of desire fire her blood. She wanted him back, that warm, passionate Alexandre of the night before. She ached for him. And she didn't know how to call to him. How to reach out to him.

"Asmodeus, I swear," Suzanne said, walking out onto the gallery, "you don't seem to want to be around me at all lately, you finicky little devil." She laughed, the sound, like the merry tinkle of chimes, echoing on the still night. "Maybe I should just give him to you, Rachel."

Asmodeus began to purr loudly and nestled himself deeper into Rachel's lap.

"See, Rachel, what'd I say? The little traitor has fallen in love with you."

Rachel smiled, wishing they were talking about Alexandre rather than Asmodeus. The thought surprised her. She hadn't really thought of love. After her last romantic experience she had decided she wasn't cut out for love. At least not the kind that resulted in marriage, kids, the white-picket-fence-surrounded house and meatloaf on the table at five o'clock. She was too independent for all that domesticity. Too stubborn. Sometimes too selfish. Isn't that what John had said when he'd suggested divorce? And he was right. She'd finally admitted that, after her fury had cooled down. Though she'd realized later that she was more angry at having been dumped than at losing John. She glanced back at Alexandre. So why did she want so desperately for him to love her?

"Well, I think I'll run out and get myself a little nightcap."

"Be careful, Suzanne," Alexandre said.

She laughed lightly and stood on tiptoe to kiss his cheek. "I'm always careful big brother, but thanks for worrying about me." She turned and waved toward Rachel. "Ta-ta."

Rachel watched her disappear into the darkness of the walkway that led to the drive. She looked back at Alexandre. "She's not walking somewhere, is she?"

He frowned. "No."

Rachel looked back toward the drive. She heard no car motor start, saw no headlights. So if Suzanne wasn't walking, what was she doing? Tiptoeing down the drive? She decided not to pursue the subject as Alexandre's answer, short as it was, did not invite further questions.

Alexandre turned and looked out at the night sky. "Sometimes I wish the sun would never go down," he said softly.

Rachel rose and walked to stand beside him. She shook her head. "I know what you mean," she said, "except I usually wish it would never come up."

"Daylight is a warm kiss to an otherwise cold world,"

Alexandre said. "It brightens and feeds the flowers and wildlife. It's a time of renewal and continual birth."

"And it forces us to look at ourselves for what we really are," Rachel countered. "It shows us the harshness of life."

"And night hides our secrets, allows us to disguise our realities in cloaked splendor. We can move about in the shadows, never acknowledging what we are, what we are capable of, until it's too late." He sighed softly. "The great masquerade."

Rachel turned to him, a slight frown tugging at her brow. "I think we see what we want to see of the world," she said softly. "Whether night or day."

"If that were true, Rachel, we'd have a perfect world. And we don't." With sudden swiftness, Alexandre pushed away from the pillar and descended the stairs. Before she knew what he was doing, he was gone.

"Well, he obviously isn't enamored of my company anymore," she mumbled.

Asmodeus meowed.

She smiled down at the cat. "Well, at least you're still infatuated with me."

Rachel! Rachel, help me!

The cry nearly shattered her nerves. It had exploded in her head, like the sudden crashing of cymbals—loud, abrupt, deafening. And intense. The feeling she got from the tone, from the aura surrounding them, was profound. Steven was frightened beyond all control. She could feel his panic.

Rachel grasped her arms about one another, her fingers encircling her upper arms tightly. Steven, Steven, where are you? She closed her eyes to heighten her concentration. Steven, listen to me. Answer me. Where are you? You've got to tell me where you are.

Oh, God, Rachel, help me!

His voice echoed through her mind, his words, his terror invading her body, filling her, causing her hands to tremble violently.

Rachel!

A sudden stabbing pain pierced her neck, dug at her, and burned her flesh. "Steven?"

She felt him, so clearly that it was as if he were inside of her body. Her heart lurched and slammed into a frantic, thudding beat, and her pulse began to race madly. Steven, she cried silently. Steven.

She ran out onto the walkway that led to the drive. Her limbs were shaking. Steven? "Oh, God, where are you?" She ran to the center of the drive. Steven?

A shadow passed before the moon. Rachel looked up quickly. A sense of dread swept over her, but she saw nothing. She ran toward the old formal gardens. Steven?

Aghhhhhh!

Rachel stopped, frozen in her tracks, every nerve in her body trembling, every fiber chilled, every muscle tense. Steven? Steven, for God's sake answer me. She closed her eyes, her hands clenched into fists and held tight to her breast. Steven, please, answer me. Steven?

But the only sounds that met her ears, and her mind, were the soft chirping of birds in the surrounding trees, the faint rustling of leaves and foliage as squirrels, rabbits and other small creatures wandering freely about the darkened garden. Steven did not call again.

Rachel felt tears well up within her eyes, felt desolation and defeat fill her breast. "Steven," she murmured, sobbing on his name, "help me find you." The tears slipped over her cheeks. "Where are you? My God, what's happening?"

* * *

Suzanne emerged from the shadows of the alley and into the bright lights of Bourbon Street. She reached up to wipe a drop of moisture from the corner of her mouth. It came away red on the tip of her finger. She looked about. The colorful neon glow of light on the fronts of the bars that lined the streets was like a rainbow of dazzling, blinding color—red, blue, pink, yellow, orange, green. She remembered when the street had been nothing more than a quiet residential neighborhood. But that had been years ago, when she'd gone to the saloons that lined Magazine Street. Before that she had haunted the wharves. And before that she had preyed on runaway slaves.

"Hi, beautiful."

She turned. A man stood in front of her, his hair golden and glowing like flaxen strands of silk beneath the bright lights. He was handsome. Almost too handsome, and he knew it. The sly little smirk on his face told her that. She hated men whose arrogance and self-conceit were so obvious. It was always interesting to watch them realize how truly vulnerable and weak they really were.

Suzanne smiled. "Hello, handsome," she drawled.

Rachel closed the door to her bedchamber and, walking to stand beside the window, pulled the transmitter from her pocket. "Marc? Marc, are you there?"

"As always," he quipped back.

"Anything new?"

"Nope. How about you?"

She closed her eyes. The image of Danielle Toutant and five men who had also died in that long secret room under *Sans Souci* turned vivid in her mind. It had always been there, hovering, since the moment she'd discovered them, but as a shadow, a foggy picture. Now, as she purposely summoned it back, it returned in full force and she felt her stomach turn. "I found something," she said into the transmitter, her voice weak and barely audible.

"What? You found something else? Is that what you said?"

"Yes," she hissed, "and don't talk so damned loud. I'm in a house remember, though at times it feels more like a mausoleum."

"Sorry," he whispered. "What'd you find?"

"Bodies."

"Bodies?" He practically screamed the word.

Rachel slapped the transmitter against her breast. Lord, if he didn't get her caught, nothing would.

"Yes, bodies," she whispered.

"Shit."

She waited for him to calm.

"How many?" he asked a second later, his tone one of business. "No, it doesn't matter. I'll get a warrant."

"No."

"No? Whatdya mean *no?*"

"They're old, Marc. Over two hundred years. Some maybe three hundred."

"You broke into a crypt?"

"I wish. Then it wouldn't have been such a grisly shock. No. I was frustrated and began pacing in my room. I tripped over the cat and my hand slammed against a medallion on the fireplace and the damn thing swung open."

"The fireplace opened?"

"Yes, only a little, but enough so that I could see it was a secret door. I managed to open it enough to pass through and found a secret staircase on the other side. It was evident it hadn't been used in years but I followed it anyway. It led to a tunnel somewhere under the house. I followed it. One leg of it was caved in. The other led to a door."

"Yeah?"

"It was a room, perhaps originally a wine cellar or something since there were wine racks in it. And shelves. Lots of shelves. Some still had a few dust-covered bottles of wine on them." Rachel took a deep breath. "That was about it, except for the skeletons of five men and the body of one woman."

"Skeletons."

"Yes. The men were just skeletons, mainly. Most of their clothes and flesh had rotted. But the woman hadn't been in there as long as the men. She still had her skin, and most of her clothes were intact, though they were rotting."

"Shit."

"Right."

"Any idea who they are? Could they be tied to the Beaumondiers?"

"The woman is Danielle Toutant, the one I asked you to find out about."

"How do you know?"

"The same brooch that she's wearing in the painting I found in the attic is pinned to the dress that's on the body."

"Maybe it's someone who borrowed the brooch."

"Maybe, but I don't think so."

"Yeah. So what's she doing locked in a room under the house?"

"I don't know."

"And who are the guys?"

"I don't know that either, but they've been there longer than she has, I'd bet you on that."

"Great. Probably clues everywhere, right?"

"Marc, I know I came here to find Steven, but I have a feeling these things are tied in. I don't know how, I just feel it."

"Yeah, well, we always did follow through with your hunches, remember? Why stop now? Besides the fact that you could be sitting in a house whose every member through the ages has been a cold-blooded murderer."

"Maybe she got accidentally locked in there and no one heard her screams."

"And the guys?" Marc retorted. "They were all accidentally locked in there, too?"

Rachel sighed.

"So, you want me to try and find out if five guys disappeared two or three hundred years ago?"

"Yes," Rachel said softly.

"I was afraid you'd say that."

"Steven's been calling me."

Marc remained silent.

"Did you hear me, Marc?"

"Yes."

"He . . . he sounds like he's getting weaker. And he's terrified, Marc. Whatever's happening to him, he's so terrified that my signals to him aren't getting through."

"I'm beginning to understand how he feels."

Rachel smiled. Marc didn't have a ounce of fear in his body, which, she'd told him several times when they'd worked together, wasn't always good.

"I'll call you in the morning." Rachel flipped the transmitter onto the bed.

"Dream of me," Marc said.

Rachel moved to pick up the transmitter and say something back, but it went silent.

Chapter 17

"You're not exactly into this tonight, are you?" Suzanne asked.

Yvette smiled absently. She was watching a young man who had just entered the bar. "No." She sighed. "Not really. My mind's elsewhere tonight."

"Like on Alexandre?"

Yvette turned to look at her daughter. "Yes, on Alexandre. I thought that by getting her to *Sans Souci* . . ." Yvette shook her head and ran a finger lightly around the rim of the glass that sat on the bar before her. She stared down into the untouched whiskey. Only a few slivers of what had, shortly before, been ice cubes remained floating atop the golden liquid. "This has to work, Suzanne. He has to do this, or the Beaumondier line will die."

"Yeah, in about another five hundred years. Give or take." She shrugged. "So what?"

Yvette felt her temper begin to flare as it did every time she had this conversation with Suzanne, which had been several times too many. Especially in the last few years. She was too much like Alexandre on this subject. "Don't you care at all if our name dies? Our line?"

"No." She shook her head, sending waves of dark

hair sliding across her shoulders, and stabbed a toothpick at the olive in her martini. "So the great, illustrious Beaumondiers die out? Would anyone really care? Would the world mourn our passing?" She laughed softly. "I hardly think so."

"The fools would probably celebrate, if they knew the truth."

Suzanne turned on her bar stool and faced her mother. "Why don't you and Grandma tell him the truth, mother?"

"No. That would only make matters worse."

"Then why don't you just leave him alone? It didn't work with Danielle and it's not going to work this time."

"It didn't work with Danielle because she was . . ." Hate, harsh and cold, burned within Yvette's eyes.

"Human?"

"A fool."

Suzanne shook her head. "Did you really think she'd accept him? That she'd embrace the truth? How could she?"

"Others have. Your father, for one."

"Yes, and look what happened to him."

"He tried to leave me."

"Heaven forbid," Suzanne sneered.

Yvette turned an angry eye to Suzanne. "If Danielle had loved him, she could have accepted Alexandre for what he is and everything would have been fine. They would have had a child and the problem would have been solved. Obviously the girl just didn't really love him."

"She was a normal human being, Mother," Suzanne said curtly. "We're not."

"Keep your voice down."

Suzanne chuckled softly. "Why? Afraid someone will hear and try to pound a wooden stake through our hearts? Or throw holy water on us? Or maybe they'll run up and jab a crucifix into your face." Her laugh held a note of derision. "Since when, Mother, have you become afraid of them? They don't even know how to hurt us, let alone destroy us, so why fear them?"

"Because it's not 1593 anymore, Suzanne. The world is a much smaller place. Hard to disappear in. If they knew our secret, believe me, they would destroy us. They'd find a way. They always find a way to destroy what they don't understand."

"Or what they fear?"

"Yes." Yvette pushed the glass of whiskey away. "I want this to work, Suzanne. Do you understand me? I want this to work between Alexandre and Rachel. And I'll do whatever I have to do to see that it does."

Suzanne sighed. "Yes, Mother, I know."

"And stop calling me Mother. I'm supposed to be your sister, remember?"

"Yes, *sister dear.*"

A young policeman entered the bar.

Suzanne caught sight of him out of the corner of her eye and turned slowly on her barstool until she faced him. Her gaze raked over him boldly. Normally her flirtations were directed toward transients. They were the perfect quarry, men whom no one would miss, whom the world had forgotten. But she couldn't deny that the police officer had not only caught her attention, but stirred a desire within her that she hadn't felt for some time. She crossed one long, lithe leg over the other. Maybe she could . . . without . . . She smiled.

Another police officer appeared at the door and approached the first. They talked briefly in hushed whispers and then the two men turned and walked back out the entry door.

Suzanne sighed.

* * *

Steven's eyelids fluttered apart, but only barely, as he heard the soft snap of the door's lock. He was too weak to cry for help, too weak to fight, too weak even to care anymore. Tears blurred his vision. He heard her heels click on the bare plank floor as she walked toward the table where he lay, spread-eagled and tied to its posts like an animal. How long he had lain like this, how many nights she had come to him, laughing and draining him of his life, he didn't know. He'd lost count. And he'd lost hope.

He looked up at her as she stood over him and a stream of tears slipped from the outer corner of each eye to snake down his cheeks. In spite of what she was doing to him, in spite of the evil nightmare she had enveloped him within—a nightmare of childhood horrors come true, of death and terror—he still marveled at her beauty. But it was a beauty, he knew, that masked the coldness within her heart, and disguised the vile, diabolic nature of her very being. He closed his eyes and remembered their first meeting in a bar in the French Quarter, LaliAnn's. Yvette had mesmerized him at first glance, charmed him with laughter, subtle flirtatious caresses, and soft words. There had been no way to resist her, and God help him, he hadn't even tried.

Yvette smiled down at him, then reached out a hand and caressed his pale, gaunt cheek, wiping away the silver trail of tears. "How are you tonight, Steven, my little pet? Sad, *mon ami?* I thought you'd like a visitor." She laughed softly when his lips parted in an attempt to speak, and no sound emitted from his throat.

"Rachel's here, Steven. Did you know that?" She ran the tip of a finger along the line of his parched lips.

"Did that little psychic bond you told me about inform you that she was here?"

He stared up at her, hope filling his chest.

"I guess I should thank you for getting her here, Steven." Yvette's fingers slid down Steven's neck. "Yes, my pet, I should thank you for doing exactly what I wanted you to do." She bent and pressed her lips to his, icy marble against parched flesh. Yvette straightened and laughed. "I had planned on getting rid of you when she came, but . . ." She shrugged and smiled smugly, wickedly, "I've decided to keep you alive a bit longer, just in case she decides to leave."

She began to bend down toward him again. He tried to turn his head, to twist away from her, but there was no strength left in him, and the bindings around his wrists and ankles held his limbs so taut he could barely move.

"Oh, no, Steven, don't try and turn away from me. Relax," Yvette said. "I was just in town." She sighed. "Fools. You're all fools, you know. So easy. A pretty face, a few seductive words, and you're all the same, so ready to follow a woman anywhere." She laughed. "As a matter of fact I think I'm going to go back again tonight." She brushed her lips over his. "So you see, you don't have to worry, my pet, I'm not going to do anything with you now." She let her gaze sweep quickly over the old mill's interior. "Get some of your strength back, darling, and don't be too jealous about the others." Her laugh echoed within the huge cavern of a room. "They didn't mean anywhere near as much to me as you do." She turned to go. "Sleep well, Steven. I'll see you tomorrow night."

* * *

Rachel hurried across the open field. Damn, she'd intended to be back at the house long before darkness fell. She glanced up at the sky, shivered, and as she began to skirt a large outcropping of wild bushes, threw one last look over her shoulder toward the cypress swamp.

"Rachel, what are you doing out here?" Yvette said, stepping into view from the other side of the same bushes.

"Oh, I went out for a walk and lost track of time. I didn't really mean to be wandering about in the dark."

Yvette looped an arm through Rachel's and patted her hand. "Well, we can walk back to the house together. Did you have a pleasant stroll?"

"Uh, yes. I went into the bayou for a while."

"The bayou?" Yvette's eyes narrowed, and her voice took on a slight note of apprehension. She looked at Rachel. "Did you . . . find it interesting?"

"Oh, yes. I used to practically live in the swamps as a youngster. My brother and I used to spend our summer vacations at Shadows Teche with my grandmother."

"Really? How nice. So, how did our little bayou compare? I take it you didn't find any buried treasure," she chuckled.

"No, I'm afraid I didn't find any pirate's gold."

"Umm, too bad."

"Were you out for a walk, too?" Rachel asked.

Yvette smiled and the darkness hid the fact that the gesture failed to warm her eyes any more than it did her lips. "Yes. I try to go for a little walk every night."

Rachel nodded, not knowing what else to say. Yvette wasn't an easy person to converse with. She was pleasant enough, but there was a hardness about her, and despite the pleasantries she issued, she seemed cloaked within an icy shroud, as cold as the hand she had on Rachel's arm.

"You and Alexandre seem to have hit it off rather nicely," Yvette said, breaking into Rachel's thoughts.

"He's a very nice man," Rachel replied with an inner smile.

"Yes, he is, but he keeps much too much to himself. He needs to get out more. Away from *Sans Souci.* He needs to experience more of life. Not stay sequestered here in this horrid old mausoleum." She looked at Rachel and smiled. "He needs someone like you."

"Isn't that up to him?" Rachel felt a tremor of unease. Why was Yvette pushing her brother's cause? What did she care if Alexandre liked her, or she him?

"Oh, he's already decided that."

Rachel gawked at her curiously.

Yvette laughed. "Oh, don't look so surprised, Rachel. I've seen it in his eyes every time he looks at you." She squeezed Rachel's arm intimately. "I think my brother is falling in love with you. And I, for one, hope the feeling is mutual. I like you. So do Marguerite and Catherine."

"Thank you, Yvette," Rachel said noncommitally, wondering again why they were having this conversation. Alexandre Beaumondier was a grown man, and a very intelligent one. If he cared for a woman, Rachel had no doubt, he didn't need his sister, or anyone else, trying to help him. Or did he?

Chapter 18

As Rachel and Yvette approached the front gallery of the house Alexandre suddenly appeared from the shadows. He leaned against a pillar that was badly in need of a few splotches of plaster and a coat of paint and watched them walk toward him arm in arm.

Forgetting herself, Rachel met his gaze and marveled, as she had every time she saw him since coming to *Sans Souci,* at how handsome he was. Most men whose physical attributes were as attractive as Alexandre's did everything in their power to take advantage of them. Yet Alexandre seemed almost unaware of the devastation his appearance had on a woman.

She pulled her eyes from his as she began to feel her senses reel. But then, isn't that exactly what Alexandre had done with her? Used his sexual prowess, his attractiveness, his charm, to seduce her? And now he was acting as if it had never happened. As if there was, and had been, nothing at all between them.

"Good evening, ladies," he said as they paused before him.

He was a master of charm, able to entice, incite, and seduce with merely one suggestive look of his dark gray eyes.

She looked into his eyes and immediately felt that odd, pulling sensation, as if she were about to slip from reality into another world. Rachel tore her gaze from his and felt herself tremble.

"I found Rachel out walking in the fields," Yvette said. She slipped her arm from Rachel's and climbed the shallow stairs to where Alexandre stood, rose up on tiptoe to press her lips to his cheek and then glanced back at Rachel. "She's obviously not afraid of the dark."

"It's her favorite time," Alexandre said softly.

Yvette's thin dark brows arched higher. "Really?" A soft chuckle seemed to waft up from her throat and float on the night air. "Mine, too."

Rachel smiled. "Well, I should get upstairs and freshen up a bit before dinner. I probably reek of the bayou." She climbed the stairs and moved to pass them.

Alexandre's hand on her arm stopped her. "I'd like to talk with you a minute," he said.

Yvette hurried to the door. "I'll just give you two some privacy." She glanced pointedly at Rachel. "Remember what I said, Rachel." The door closed quietly behind her.

Alexandre look down at Rachel, his brow furrowed into a frown, his eyes dark and slightly narrowed. "And just what did she say?"

Rachel stared up at him, her heart pounding rapidly within her breast.

Silence hung heavy between them as he waited for her response, and she wondered what she should say. Finally, she decided on the truth.

"That you should get out more. Not remain so sequestered here. She worries about you. She feels you need to love someone. And . . ."

"And," he urged.

"And that you like me."

He stared at the door through which his mother had disappeared only seconds before. Suspicion and anger clouded his thoughts. He had been right all along. Rachel's coming to *San Souci* had been no accident, no coincidence. He turned back to her, and as his gaze swept over her face, his senses filled with her nearness, the anger left him. Much as he should be, he could not find it within himself to be sorry that she had come.

Rachel watched a smile curve the sensuous lips whose touch she longed to feel again.

"She's right," he drawled, his tone the gentlest she'd ever heard. The words slipped from his mouth and wrapped around her like a warm, seductive cloak of velvet.

Rachel turned toward him and as she did, his hands moved to encircle her waist and draw her to him. His arms tightened about her in an embrace, and crushed her to his length. She looked up and his lips immediately captured hers, taking them prisoner and sending her senses spinning.

This was what she had wanted, what she had prayed for. This was where she belonged. Her arms slid up to encircle his shoulders and she pressed her body to his, wanting to feel the press of him against her, the warmth and strength of him.

Lips ravished lips, tongue dueled with tongue, heart beat against heart.

Behind the lace curtain of the parlor window, Yvette watched Alexandre kiss Rachel. She smiled. This time it would work, she felt certain. This time everything would be all right.

For Rachel time seemed to stand still. Never in her life had a man made her feel so desirable and so complete. Everything she had ever wanted out of life, every goal and ambition, every material possession and dream seemed suddenly to pale and become unimportant. Alexandre was all that mattered, he was all that would ever matter.

For Alexandre, rather than stand still, time seemed to spin out of control and plunge backward, hurtling him back in time, back to a love he wanted to forget, and a heart of anguish that he couldn't. He had loved Danielle, and because of that, of what he was, she had been destroyed. Yet he could not bear to turn away from Rachel. He clung to her, much as a dying man to his last heartbeat, and lost himself within the feelings she stirred in him. He wanted her, wanted to love her and make her a part of him.

"Oh, Alexandre," Rachel breathed against his cheek as he held her to him.

Remember what you did to Danielle, his mind screamed. You don't love Rachel. His arms slipped from around her and his hands clasped about her upper arms. Remember what you did to Danielle. You can't love Rachel. Remember Danielle. He pulled her arms from where they lay on his shoulders, forcing her fingers to retreat from within the curls of hair at his nape. He wanted her more than he wanted anything. He wanted to make her a part of himself, and that's what scared him. He steeled himself against the searing emotions coursing through him. Remember what you did to Danielle, he kept repeating in his mind. Remember Danielle. He drew himself away from Rachel and stepped back, his body suddenly stiff, his eyes cold, masking the pain of his heart.

Yvette's fingers clutched at the lace panel, crushing it within the tight grasp of her fingers. Rage shook her body as she saw regret come over Alexandre's features and watched him pull away from Rachel. They were running out of time, and Alexandre with his damned pious morality was going to ruin everything.

"I shouldn't have done that," he said softly, his voice ragged and deep with emotion.

Rachel stared at him, confused. "Why?"

He shook his head and then looked down at her, his gray eyes suddenly cold, his features as hard as granite. He drew her into him then, into the past that he had tried to forget, into the existence that damned him to hundreds of thousands of endless nights and days.

Rachel felt herself immediately engulfed within a tumultuous squall of emotion, a swirling, rampaging gale that pulled at her and dragged her toward an abyss of infinite, unfathomable blackness.

Suddenly the headlights of a car appeared in the drive, piercing the darkness and illuminating the gallery, the front of the house, Alexandre and Rachel. Its tires cut the silence of the night as they rolled over the slick moss and crunched the oyster shells that lay beneath it.

Alexandre swore silently beneath his breath and turned toward the approaching bright lights. Who could be coming to *Sans Souci?* His eyes narrowed. Who would *dare* come to *Sans Souci?*

The car pulled to a stop before the entry path. It was a blue sedan. New and very plain. Alexandre watched the driver's door open.

Rachel, shocked, watched Marc Dellos slide from the driver's seat, stand, and walk around the rear of the car.

Alexandre felt Rachel stiffen in his arms. He immediately released her and kept his gaze pinioned on the young man emerging from the car.

"Excuse me," Marc said, his gaze purposely averted from Rachel's. "Mr. Beaumondier?" He walked up the entry path toward them, while reaching into the pocket of his jacket and pulling out a billfold. Slapping it open, his badge gleamed in the moonlight.

Alexandre glanced at the i.d. in the plastic slot opposite the badge. "Yes, I'm Alexandre Beaumondier. What can we do for you, Officer . . . Dellos?"

"Well, I need to speak with a Ms. . . ." He flipped a notebook open and stared at one of its pages. "A Ms. Rachel Domecq. The clerk at the hotel she was registered at said she had left and was staying here."

"I . . ." Rachel said.

"What do you want with Ms. Domecq, officer?" Alexandre said, brusquely cutting her off.

"We, uh, well, her brother was reported missing and we think we've found him."

Alexandre nodded.

"We need her to identify the body."

Rachel felt her legs tremble and swayed as the world suddenly began to spin. Steven was dead. The words echoed cruelly in her mind over and over. Steven was dead.

Alexandre saw her waver and reached for her quickly. He wrapped an arm around her waist and pulled her toward him, offering his length as support.

Rachel sank into him.

"He's dead?" she whispered, riveting Marc with a shattered gaze.

"Well, we're not really sure it's him, Ms. Domecq," Marc said. "The man we found in the river is the right height and coloring and all, but . . ." He shrugged. "Since your brother's fingerprints and dental records weren't on file we need you to make the identification."

She nodded as tears filled her eyes and sorrow her throat.

"I'll come with you," Alexandre said.

"I'm sorry, Mr. Beaumondier, but we prefer that Ms. Domecq come alone," Marc said quickly.

Rachel's mind suddenly cleared at the unusual request. She looked sharply at Marc. There was no reason Alexandre could not go with her . . . if this were for real. No police department had a policy against the victim's relatives being accompanied to the morgue. Something was wrong. And then it hit her. If it was Steven, Marc would know. He knew Steven. Knew him well. He'd easily be able to identify the body, if there was a body.

Marc slipped his notebook back into the pocket of his jacket and offered her a hand. "Ms. Domecq?"

She looked up at Alexandre. "I'll be all right," she said softly. "Could you get my purse for me. It's on the bed in my room."

He nodded and entered the house.

Rachel looked back at Marc, her eyes full of questions.

"I lied," he whispered, looking as if he wanted to find a hole and crawl into it.

"Bastard," Rachel whispered harshly. She wiped the tears from her eyes.

"Rae, I'm sorry, but it was the only logical excuse I could think of for coming here. And we've got to talk."

"You couldn't have just radioed me?"

"No, I . . ."

Alexandre's footsteps echoed on the marble foyer floor as he walked toward the door.

"I was just explaining to Ms. Domecq," Marc said, as Alexandre moved to stand beside Rachel, "that we may have to talk with her a while at the station, whether this, uh, whether we have found her brother or not. We have a few more questions."

Alexandre looked down at Rachel. "Are you sure you

don't want me to accompany you? I could drive you in and wait outside? Then drive you back."

She shook her head. "No, thank you, I'll be fine." She slipped the strap of her purse over her shoulder. "If it gets too late I'll just stay at a hotel in the Quarter and come back out in the morning." She smiled, though only faintly, wanting to keep Marc's ploy going, whatever it was for.

Alexandre nodded.

Marc held the door open as Rachel slipped into the passenger seat of his car and fastened the seat belt. He closed the door and hurried around to his own side, then paused and looked over the car's roof at Alexandre, who still stood on the gallery. "If she wants to return tonight, sir, I'll be more than happy to drive her back out."

Alexandre remained silent.

They didn't talk as the car moved down the long, dark drive. Rachel watched as its headlights cut through the blackness of their surroundings, harshly illuminating the trunks of the old trees, the moss that hung from them like curtains of lace, the tall weeds that grew at their bases, and finally the crumbling pillars of the entry gate.

Marc turned the car onto the River Road and accelerated once the tires hit the paved road.

Rachel turned to face him. "All right, dammit, what the hell is so all-fired important that you had to scare me half to death like that?"

"My guys reported back on a couple of those things I had them checking on for you."

"And?"

"And you're just not going to believe what they've come up with."

She stared at him, waiting.

Marc pounded the steering wheel with the heel of his hand. "Hell, Rae, I don't even believe what they've come up with."

Rachel placed her fork on the rim of her plate, drained the final sip of wine from her glass, and leaned slightly forward. "All right, Marc, we're here, we've eaten dinner, and I'm still waiting. Now what did your guys find out?"

Marc drew a napkin from his lap, pressed it to his lips, dropped it to the table and waved a hand for the waiter. The man approached immediately. "Coffee, please, for both of us." The waiter nodded and left.

"Marc," Rachel said, a definite warning note to her tone.

Below the screened balcony where they sat, once the rear gallery of an old French Quarter townhouse now turned into a restaurant, a quaint brick courtyard bustled with sudden activity as a dozen guests were shown to a long, candlelit table that had been reserved for them.

Two sides of the courtyard were enclosed by the old brick walls of adjacent buildings and lit by torches set in wrought iron holders, their flames throwing a dancing reflection of light and shadows onto the ancient bricks. A profusion of luscious ferns surrounded an elegantly designed clay fountain set in the center of the courtyard. Colored lights directed on the spraying water turned it to a glimmering rainbow, and soft music filled the air, along with the fragrance of rich food, but Rachel paid no attention to any of it. She had dined at Brennan's before, and she would dine there again, she was sure. Right now all she wanted, all her attention had room for, was answers from Marc, and she was getting tired of waiting.

She opened her mouth to demand an answer and clamped it shut again as the waiter reappeared with their coffee and asked if they wanted dessert.

Marc looked at Rachel and smiled. "How about *bananas flambé?*"

"Marc," she said again, feeling her temper jump up another notch.

He nodded to the waiter. *"Bananas flambé."*

The waiter nodded his approval and hurried across the room.

Marc turned back to Rachel. "Okay, before you lose your temper and kill me, let me explain why I dragged you away from that plantation."

"Please do," Rachel said curtly.

"My men have been digging through everything they could find to come up with something on this Danielle Toutant woman, but records dating back two hundred years are not exactly complete, as you most likely know."

"So they came up with nothing? That's why you came to get me?" she asked in disbelief.

"On the contrary. What they came up with I wanted to tell you face to face."

"So? Tell me."

"They found out that Danielle was from a very prominent family in France. Evidently back then the Toutants were not only very wealthy, but very well-connected. Her father was some political bigwig."

"So?"

"So, they . . . the family, came here for a visit in 1791. A little less than two years later Danielle returned to marry someone . . ." he hesitated and looked at Rachel.

"Alexandre Beaumondier," she said.

He nodded. "Yes. They met while she was here with her family. A year later the marriage was arranged, but evidently both she and this Beaumondier guy were all for it. Maybe they fell in love or something in '91."

"What else?" Rachel demanded.

"Well, remember, there could be documents missing, but . . ."

"What?" She practically jumped down his throat.

"She disappeared."

"Disappeared? You mean there was no wedding? When did she disappear? How?"

Marc held up both hands. "Whoa, Rae, slow down and let me get a breath, will you?" He took a sip of his coffee. "Evidently she disappeared just before the wedding. None of the papers we found say why. But it was a big scandal back then. Her family came back over here, but no one ever found her. At least, from what we can determine."

"Because she was sitting locked in that room beneath *Sans Souci,*" Rachel said. "Dying."

Marc nodded. "So it would seem."

"Did you find any connection between Danielle and my family?"

"She had a sister."

Rachel stared at him, waiting.

"Actually, a half-sister. Her name was Antoinette Landeneuve."

Rachel frowned. The name sounded oddly familiar, yet she couldn't quite decide why.

Marc sighed and took a sip of his coffee. He set the cup back on its saucer and looked at Rachel. "Antoinette Landeneuve was . . ."

The waiter reappeared pushing a cherrywood cart upon which was a burner and a copper skillet.

Rachel gave him a look that would melt an iceberg but he was too busy spooning a huge dollop of butter, a cup of brown sugar and a bowl of sliced bananas into the skillet to pay her any heed. She looked back at Marc but he seemed hesitant to continue until the waiter was gone. Rachel's foot tapped the floor beneath the table.

The waiter picked up two crystal dessert goblets that had been previously filled with vanilla ice cream, scooped up the now hot bananas and bubbling sauce and ladled them over the ice cream. Then, with a flourish obviously meant to impress, he poured cognac over each mound, held a match to the flame burning beneath the skillet, and touched it to each mountainous concoction. The cognac, dripping over the ice cream and bananas, instantly burst into flame. The waiter set one glass before Rachel, the other in front of Marc, bowed slightly, bid them *bon apetit,* and wheeled the cart away.

Rachel impatiently blew out the flames of her desert. She stared at Marc, her gaze pointed, expectant.

Marc picked up his spoon. "Boy, this looks great."

"Marc."

He raised his hands in a mocking gesture of surrender. "All right, just teasing. There is a connection to your family."

"How?"

"Antoinette Landeneuve was your great, great, great grandmother."

Chapter 19

Rachel stared across the table at Marc in a daze.

Marc waved a hand in front of her face. "Rae, you okay? Rae, hey, are you in there?"

She slapped his hand away and looked him straight in the eye. "Let me get this straight. If I heard you right, you're saying the woman whose body I found in that old wine cellar, Danielle Toutant, was the half-sister of my great, great, great grandmother, Antoinette Landeneuve."

"Bingo. You get the door prize. Evidently, that's why you two, you and this late Danielle, that is, look so much alike. You're related."

"Distantly."

"Maybe, but you're still related. Danielle and Antoinette had the same mother. Who knows, maybe Antoinette looked exactly like Danielle and all those beautiful little physical genes just popped up in you."

Rachel fixed her gaze on the mound of ice cream, too absorbed in trying to figure out why the family connection could be important to the Beaumondiers after all these years, to acknowledge Marc's compliment. Her thoughts spun as she tried to make some sense out of what Marc had said.

"Look, Rae," Marc said, and reached across the table to take her hand in his, "I've made light of it up to now, but I've got to tell you . . ." she looked up at him as his words broke into her musings, "I don't like the path this thing's taking. It's almost as if . . ." He paused and shrugged.

"They want me out there," Rachel said, finishing the sentence for him.

"Yeah, my thought exactly. This whole thing is looking more and more like some kind of engineered plan just to get you to that plantation. Got any idea why?"

She shook her head, and pulled her hand gently from his. "None. I've heard of *Sans Souci* before, of course, through my work. And because of that I've heard of the Beaumondiers, though I never really paid much attention, since we weren't considering the place for a grant."

"Well, let's look at this thing from the beginning. Steven tells you he met this Yvette Beaumondier, right?"

She nodded.

"And that he's fallen in love with her and is going out to her family's plantation the next day?"

She nodded again.

"But he didn't mention the plantation by name."

"Well, no, but it had to be *Sans Souci.* I mean, there aren't any other Yvette Beaumondiers in New Orleans. I checked before I left Baton Rouge. There aren't even any other Beaumondiers in the area, period, so we know we've got the right Yvette, the right family, and the right plantation. Agreed?"

"Yes."

"Okay. So why'd she lie?"

Their eyes met as each tried to determine what possible motive Yvette could have had for telling the police she didn't know Steven Ligere, if what Steven had told Rachel over the telephone was true.

Marc finally shrugged. "Maybe she just didn't want to get involved."

"No." Rachel shook her head. "I don't buy that. The Beaumondiers have enough money and clout to remain uninvolved without lying."

"Has Steven ever lied about ..?"

"No," Rachel said, knowing exactly what Marc had been about to say. "He doesn't brag about his affairs or fantasize himself in love. In fact, I don't think Steven's ever committed to being in love before. You know him." Rachel sighed. "Mr. Footloose and Fancy Free—no strings, no commitments, no promise of a thousand tomorrows."

"Yeah."

"But this was different," Rachel continued. "I mean, Steven thought so. I told him he was moving too fast, that he hadn't known her for very long, but he wouldn't listen. He swore to me that he was in love. Totally. He even said he was going to ask her to marry him."

"Okay, love or not, he said he was going to her place, which we know is *Sans Souci,* right? Now, how did you know to go there when you started looking for him?"

"It was the last place he supposedly went, so it stood to reason I check it out. I sent them a wire from Baton Rouge saying the Preservation Society was interested in sponsoring *Sans Souci* for historic monument status."

He nodded.

"But you know all this. Now, they knew Steven was missing, obviously, since the police went to the house and questioned Yvette. But they didn't say anything when we corresponded, even though I'm fairly certain Steven must have mentioned me to Yvette."

"Which leads me to believe that they wanted you there. That maybe this whole thing was just a ploy to get you down here to that plantation."

"Yes. But why? For what?"

He shrugged. "I don't know, and that's the part I don't like. There are too many threads tying you to them, Rachel, first Steven, and now this Danielle-Antoinette thing, yet we don't have a damned knot to tie them all together with."

"Then I'll just have to find one. Or create one when I go back," she said.

"I was hoping you wouldn't want to go back. Things are getting weird, Rachel. Something funny's going on out there. Let me talk to the captain and see if I can . . ."

"They won't do anything, Marc, and you know it. There's no evidence. Nothing to connect Steven and Yvette except for the phone call he made to me, which isn't much. At least not by police standards."

"You found his wallet in her drawer."

"That really doesn't prove a thing. Not to the authorities."

"It's enough to get a warrant."

Rachel sighed. "Marc, we've already pounded that ground. I don't want to do it that way. We'd come up empty, I know it, and I don't want to jeopardize whatever chance my brother has left. Please, let's just continue to do it my way."

"Maybe she's telling the truth, Rae. Maybe Steven didn't go there."

"He did. I've felt him too many times to believe otherwise. No, Marc, I know my brother went to *Sans Souci,* and I know he's still close by somewhere."

"Unless . . ." He looked squarely into her eyes.

Her hand, resting on the table beside her coffee cup clenched into a fist. "Yes, unless it's too late. But I have to try, Marc. He's my brother. He's in trouble, and I'm obviously the only one who can help him."

He nodded, knowing she was right. The wallet would get them a search warrant, but if the search turned up nothing else the department wouldn't be able to justify doing anything further. Even though the Beaumondiers were, for the most part, reclusive and kept to themselves, they were still one of the oldest and wealthiest families in New Orleans. Not the kind the political maestros of the city took kindly to seeing *harrassed* without a whole hell of a lot of just cause. "Okay, we'll do it your way. Did you find your gun?"

She shook her head. "No."

He pulled a small leather pouch from the pocket of his sportscoat and slid it across the table to her. "Here, take this. It's a twenty-two. Small enough to fit into your pocket. Its clip is loaded with stingers."

Rachel smiled. "Stingers," she repeated, and chuckled. "Are we expecting the Wild Bunch?" With good aim, which she had, one bullet would stop just about anybody—no matter what their size or temper.

"I want you to come back out of there in one piece," Marc said.

"Thanks, I kind of feel that way, too." She slipped the small gun and belt holster into her purse and replaced it beneath her chair.

"So, what's this Alexandre Beaumondier like?" Marc asked. "He didn't exactly fit the physical description I had in mind of a hermit."

Rachel felt a flush of unease. Memory of Alexandre holding her, his hands sliding tenderly over her naked flesh, his lips ravishing hers as his body, his every movement and touch, aroused the most primal desires within her, filled her mind. She had never experienced such passion before. Rachel mentally shook herself. "He's very nice," she said, nearly cringing in embarrassment at hearing the insipid comment slip from her lips.

"Nice," Marc repeated.

"Yes. He lives in the *garconniere.* That's the building that the single men used to reside in back in the 1800s. Very proper and all that, you know. And I believe he reads a lot. The women reside in the main house."

"What are they like?"

Rachel's face screwed into a thoughtful frown. "Pale," she said finally.

"Pale? What is this, Rae, a new game? You give me one word and I figure out the rest?"

She smiled. "Sorry. Alexandre is pretty much an enigma to me. One minute he seems very warm and congenial. The next he's an iceberg. Physically he's not only good-looking, but very tanned. The women, however, though beautiful, look as if they never go out into the sun, which during the short time I've been there, they haven't. Maybe they're following that old tradition of the antebellum period. Women never went out in the sun then either, if they could help it. A tan was a scandal. Anyway, they seem to sleep most of the day and not rise until evening."

"Oh great," Marc laughed. "We've got a family of vampires living in New Orleans and we didn't even know it. Hell, is that a terrific tourist attraction, or what?"

Rachel threw him a sarcastic smile. "Very funny. I figure they must have that sun disease. You know the one, where some people are born with some pigment stuff missing in their skin, so they can't be exposed to the sun or they'll burn to a crisp?"

"Yeah, right, I've heard of it. I think they call it the Vampire Curse." He laughed again. "Christopher Lee, that movie star has it, doesn't it?"

"Marc."

"Okay, okay, just kidding. So all the women Beaumondiers have this disease thing, but not Alexandre?"

"Evidently." She shrugged. "Maybe it only runs on the female side of the family."

Marc's expression said loud and clear that he hadn't accepted the rationalization of a sun disease, though his explanation, if one could call Hollywood horror and fantasy logical, was almost too ridiculous to give a moment's thought to. "Well, do you have any other ideas?" Rachel goaded.

"No. I just don't like this. There's too many—oh, hell, I don't know." He shrugged. "Too many questions. Too much weird stuff." He looked at her pointedly, his eyes narrowed. "You're sure you haven't noticed any voodoo type stuff out there? Heard any drums from the bayou? I mean, maybe that's why they sleep all day. They're in the bayous at night, at their meetings."

She laughed. "No. And I haven't found a *gris gris* under my pillow either."

"You probably wouldn't tell me even if you had."

Rachel smiled. He was right. The last thing she needed was General Custer, aka Marc Dellos, charging to her rescue and sending everything up in smoke, with the possible inclusion of themselves and Steven.

She swept her napkin from her lap and placed it on the table, then bent and retrieved her purse from the floor. "You'd better drive me back now," she said. "It's getting late."

Marc reached across the table and caught one of her hands in his. "No. Stay in the Quarter tonight, Rae. We've got more to talk about."

She looked at him, felt the warmth of his fingers surrounding hers, saw the depth of his feelings for her reflected in his eyes. She didn't want to hurt him. She'd never wanted to hurt him, but she just couldn't feel that way about him. And everytime they were together, she saw the renewed hope in his eyes. "Marc, I really should . . ."

"I think you'd better look at some pictures we found this afternoon," he said. "I'm not really sure they're important, but I want you to see them. Tomorrow?"

"Why not now?"

"They're in the old newspaper tombs of the Picayune. And a few are in the library."

"Can't you just tell me what they are?"

Marc smiled. "No. I think you should see them for yourself."

Rachel nodded.

"Good. Now, let's go for a riverboat ride."

She laughed. "A riverboat ride? Now?" She glanced at her watch. "It's nearly seven-thirty."

"Good. We'll just make the moonlight cruise."

They rose and walked from the restaurant. "So, have you taken a lot of riverboat cruises since you moved to New Orleans?"

Marc shook his head and slipped an arm around her waist. "Haven't taken any."

"Marc, that's almost sacrilegious," Rachel teased. "You should always take your dates on a riverboat cruise. At least the dates you really care about."

"I am," he answered softly.

She had tried to make light of the moment but Marc's words had been too serious, and now she was sorry she'd said anything at all. Rachel walked quietly beside him down the narrow *banquette* toward the docks.

From high up in the sky, almost invisible against the stygian blackness of the night's panorama, Alexandre soared. But this time the surrounding infiniteness, the glimmering brilliance of the stars, the soft glow of the moon and the feel of the clouds against his flesh did not offer him the sense of freedom, it usually did. But then that was not why he had taken to the skies this night, nor why he had come to town, specifically, to the *Vieux Carré*. He had come because that was where Rachel had come.

He had watched them as they'd dined at Brennan's, the historic old restaurant that was a favorite of both locals and tourists.

The police officer had said they'd needed her at the morgue to identify a body as possibly being that of her missing brother, yet instead of the city morgue, he'd taken her to dinner.

Why had he lied? And who was he to Rachel?

The cool air whipping up from the waters of the river streamed over Rachel's face as she stood at the balustrade, her hands lightly wrapped around the mahogony railing. A few yards away the boat's huge red paddle wheel, urged into continuous movement by the burning boilers below deck and filling the air with a soft but steady *whoosh whoosh,* churned through the water and pushed the elegant red and white Natchez downriver.

Marc stood beside her, but both had remained silent since leaving the restaurant, pondering their own thoughts.

The Mississippi sprawled widely on either side of the boat, the twinkling lights of New Orleans and the French Quarter edging the bank on one side, those of the less-polished and less-respectable Algiers on the other. Lacing the black sky like a scattering of precious stones woven casually within an ebony cloak of velvet, stars shone brightly and reflected upon the cimmerian surface of the river.

Rachel sighed deeply. "This really is beautiful," she said, and turned to Marc. "I can understand why you moved to New Orleans."

"I moved here because there wasn't anything for me in Baton Rouge anymore," he said, and looked directly into her eyes.

She turned away. They'd had this conversation before, more than once, but it wouldn't be any different this time. Rachel sighed and turned to face him. "Marc, I shouldn't have asked for your help. It wasn't right, under the circumstances. I should have just . . ."

His hands slipped around her waist and he pulled her to him.

"Marc, please, I . . ."

His lips descended swiftly upon hers, swallowing the sound of her protest. It was a strangely gentle kiss, yet at the same time it conveyed a sense of urgency, a silent but desperate plea from his heart. His tongue darted into her mouth, a caressing lick of flame meant to arouse, to invoke within her the same passion that was driving him, and to make her realize that they belonged together. His hands splayed upon her back, holding her to him, pressing her tighter against his form.

But his kiss, and his touch, both failed in their attempt to awaken within Rachel any desire. She didn't push him away, but she couldn't return his passion. Instead, his kiss only served to remind her of the wanton, almost unearthly rapture she had experienced when Alexandre's lips had claimed hers, and his caresses only made her ache to feel Alexandre's hands on her body again, slipping with featherlight tenderness over the taut planes, massaging with seductive raillery the swells and curves.

She smelled the sweet scent of his cologne, a blend of spices meant to conjure images of ships and open seas.

Instead Rachel thought only of Alexandre and the musky fragrance of rich earth and pine forests.

One man loved her beyond reason, and one man didn't care at all. She had given her body, and a part of her heart, to the man who didn't care, and now she was paying the price. Loneliness gnawed at her every cell.

"Oh, God, Rachel, I've wanted to do that for so long," Marc whispered in her ear.

She pushed gently against his chest and stepped back. "Marc, I'm sorry," she said raggedly, "but . . ."

"I know." His voice was suddenly hard. "You don't feel that way about me."

She looked up at him through the tears that had suddenly filled her eyes. Why couldn't she love him, dammit? Why? She admired him, cared for him, felt comfortable with him. So why couldn't she love him?

Chapter 20

He had felt anger when the police officer had so blatantly rejected Alexandre's accompaniment of Rachel to the morgue. He'd experienced a searing jealousy as he'd watched the man reach across the table at the restaurant and take her hand in his. And he'd felt a mingling of both emotions as he'd watched them saunter through the streets of the *Vieux Carre* and board the riverboat. He had thought about leaving, about terminating his vigil over her, but he couldn't bring himself to do it. So instead, Alexandre tried to steel his emotions against the pain he knew was inevitable.

But denial and hope would not make the scene below disappear, nor change what was happening. He looked down at the slowly moving riverboat with its bright lights, its Dixieland music wafting from its open windows to fill the air, and Rachel standing on its decks. He felt hot, burning fury seize his chest and an agonizing ache of pain fill his heart, as he saw her move into the circle of the police officer's arms, saw her lift her head slightly so that her lips could receive his kiss.

A low moan of torment rumbled in Alexandre's throat. A wave of despair swept over him, pulling him into its infinite chasm and killing the small spark of hope that had, until this moment, refused to be extinguished.

He turned back toward the Quarter. Were all creatures so treacherous? So betraying? He practically laughed aloud. All he had to do was look at his own family to answer that question.

As he neared the docks he looked across the thoroughfare and saw Jackson Square. He remembered when it had still been called the *Place d'Armes*, but that was when the city's soldiers had still used the Square as their marching fields, before the Baroness Pontalba had installed her statue of Andrew Jackson in its center and enclosed the Square with the tall wrought iron fence and gates. Now it was a park; with a well-manicured lawn, rose gardens, curving concrete paths, and ancient, sprawling oak trees that shaded wrought iron benches for weary tourists. Across the way the tall steeple of the St. Louis Cathedral loomed up into the night sky.

The lone figure of a woman walking through the Square caught Alexandre's attention. Tears, glimmering silver in reflection of the night's moon, streamed down her cheeks but she made no effort to wipe them away.

Had he been wrong all of these years? Refusing to follow, to give in to the natural instincts that drove his kind? That enabled them to exist? Was he, like the lion, the snake, the shark, and all the other predators of the world, merely a part of the ecological balance?

He looked back down at the woman.

"Good morning, beautiful," Marc said, walking across the lobby of the Royal Orleans toward her.

Rachel smiled, but remained leery. They'd talked long into the night and when they had finally emerged from the hotel's bar, he to go to his flat on Esplanade, she to her room in the hotel, it was with a kind of sadness between them. Rachel had tried as compassionately as she could to explain her feelings to Marc once more, all the while fearful that this time it would mean the end of their friendship. But she had told him nothing of Alexandre. Of the way he made her feel when he pulled her into his arms and they kissed, when he made love to her. When Marc had finally walked her to the elevator so she could go to her room, he'd kissed her again, but only a light peck on the cheek.

She paused before him. "Is . . . is everything all right?"

He touched his lips to her cheek in a very brotherly kiss. "Everything's fine, beautiful." He took her hand and tucked it into the crook of his arm. "Now, let's get some breakfast and then look at those pictures I was telling you about."

They left the hotel and Rachel fell into step beside him.

"Marc, are you sure everything's okay?" She shouldn't ask, shouldn't push the point, she knew, but she couldn't help it. Marc was important to her, his friendship was important to her, and she didn't want to lose that.

He smiled down at her, but when she didn't return the smile, his face sobered. "No, everything's not okay, but it's the way it has to be. Just don't ever forget, I'll always be there for you, Rae, no matter what."

"I know that," she said softly.

"Good. Then let's eat, I'm starving."

They wove their way through the crowded maze of chrome legged tables that littered the covered patio of the Cafe DuMonde until they found a small empty table.

A waiter placed their coffee before them and returned

momentarily with two plates, each piled high with four fat, powdered sugar-covered squares of pastry. Rachel immediately lifted one in her fingers and, leaning over the table, bit into the fluffy morsel. Powdered sugar puffed into the air as her teeth sank into the *beignet.*

"Oh, Lord, I always swear I'll never eat another one of these calorie-loaded things," she said, "but they're just too delicious to resist."

"You deserve one after the week you've had," Marc responded.

Alexandre stood across the street and to one side of Jackson Square, shielded from sight by the engulfing shadows created by the sprawling, gnarled branches of a live oak. He had been unable to return to *Sans Souci,* unable to leave her here in the Quarter with *him,* and return alone to the desolate rooms of the *garconniere.*

He watched as the police officer laughed and reached across the table to tenderly, intimately, wipe powdered sugar from Rachel's lips. She smiled, and Alexandre nearly groaned in want and despair.

Turning away he walked rapidly from the Square, past the Cathedral, the Cabildo where the Spaniards who had once ruled New Orleans had conducted their government affairs, past the cafes and souvenirs shops. He walked past buildings, people, cars, and all without seeing them, without paying them any mind. All he wanted to do now was to return to *Sans Souci,* to lose himself within the serenity of the bayous, the night, the skies, to forget the hopes his great grandmother had instilled within him, the demands his grandmother and mother still placed on him, but most of all—he wanted to forget Rachel Domecq and what she had made him feel.

* * *

Rachel stared down at the newspaper Marc had spread before her on the scarred and ancient oak table of the Picayune tombs room.

She looked up at him. "It's a picture of Yvette Beaumondier with a man. So what?"

He jabbed a finger to the upper corner of the paper. "This was just last year."

"As I said—so?"

Marc pulled another paper from a rack and spread it atop the one they had been looking at. He opened it to a center page. The society page. Again there was a picture of Yvette Beaumondier with a man. "This one was taken five years ago."

Rachel sighed. "So, she likes men and hasn't settled down. So what?"

He lifted another paper from the huge rack behind them and again, placed it atop the others. "This picture was taken fifteen years ago." He spread another paper out. "This one was taken twenty years ago." Another paper. "This one was thirty years ago." Another paper. "Forty years ago."

Rachel's mouth hung agape as Marc continued.

"Fifty years ago."

"This is impossible," Rachel said.

"Sixty years ago."

"She hasn't aged a day."

"Eighty years ago."

"Are you sure some of these pictures aren't of Marguerite?"

He pointed to the name beneath the picture in the last paper he had set on the table. "Yvette Beaumondier."

"But this can't be, Marc. I mean, Yvette, at least the

one I've been conversing with at *Sans Souci*, can't be more than a few years older than me and I'm certainly not . . ." she glanced back at the paper, "almost one hundred and ten."

"According to this," he said, and jabbed a finger down on the date of the last paper, "that's just about exactly how old she is."

"1914," Rachel said aloud. She shook her head. "No, this is impossible. It has to be Marguerite. No, not even her. It must be Catherine. A woman, a person, can't live for over one hundred years and not age. It's impossible."

"Oh, Marie Laveau."

Marc looked totally confused. "Marie Laveau? The voodoo queen?"

Rachel nodded. "Yes."

"What the hell's a voodoo queen who's been dead more than a hundred years got to do with this?"

"Remember the legend? People swore that Marie lived for over a hundred years."

"So?"

"It was her daughter. Marie lived out her natural life, then when she died her daughter, who looked exactly as Marie had when she'd been young, took over the legend and for all intended purposes, at least to the public, *became* Marie."

"And you think the Beaumondiers have done that?"

Rachel sighed in frustration. "I don't know what to think, but there has to be a logical explanation for this."

"Yeah, like what?"

Then it hit her. "Alexandre."

"Alexandre?" Marc echoed.

She nodded. "It must be the same as with Alexandre."

Marc frowned. "I don't get it. What must be the same

as Alexandre? I thought we were talking about this Yvette thing."

"We are. Remember I mentioned to you that I'd read their family journal, and that all of the men in it were named Alexandre Beaumondier?"

Marc nodded.

"Well, that must be it. The men all receive the name Alexandre, the woman must stick with Yvette. Or at least some of them did."

"Suzanne?" Marc said. "Marguerite? Catherine?"

"Well, I didn't say *all* of them did it."

Marc shook his head. "I don't buy it, Rae. If they were all named Yvette, okay, but they're not."

"Then what's your theory, Sherlock? That Yvette Beaumondier is a hundred and something years old?" She laughed, though what was meant as a merry little chuckle sounded like a nervous cackle even to her own ears. "I need to get back into her bedroom then and find that bottle of youth potion."

"I'm saying I don't buy it. I don't know what's going on, but I don't believe that someone kept naming their daughters Yvette."

"Fine. Well, when you come up with an answer, let me know, will you? I'll be dying to hear it." Though she hoped she didn't mean that literally. She turned and began to walk toward the door. "Now I'd better get back to the plantation."

"There's more, Rae," Marc said.

Rachel stopped dead in her tracks and whirled around. "More?" she echoed.

He nodded. "More."

Rachel walked back to the table. "Okay, let's have it. What's the *more?* You've found a hundred years worth of pictures of Catherine, Marguerite and Suzanne?"

"Every single one of the men in those pictures with Yvette, or whoever it is, turned up missing or dead."

Rachel felt as if her heart had just stopped beating. "Are you sure?" She reached for the table to steady herself, feeling suddenly weak in the knees.

"We checked as far back as we could. The records get a little sketchy before World War I, but there's enough in the archives to give us a pretty damned good picture." He nodded. "Yeah, I'd say we're sure."

"The ones who came up dead, how . . .?"

He shook his head. "Only two were found, one not until he was a skeleton. That was back in the forties. The coroner never could say what killed the guy. There were no identifying marks on the bones, no bullet marks, knife marks. Nothing."

"The others?"

"The other one they found was listed as having his throat slashed. He bled to death, near as the coroner could figure."

"Which means?"

"There wasn't a whole lot left of him when he was found. He'd been in the bayou for a few days."

Rachel's face screwed into an expression of disgust. "And the others?"

"All listed as missing. And never found."

An image of Steven came to her mind and with it, an ache surrounded her heart. "I have to go back, Marc." Rachel rose quickly. "Steven called me. He's still out there somewhere, I know it."

"Rae, it's too . . ."

"I have to go, Marc," Rachel said curtly, her tone cold and hard. "Steven will not remain just a statistic on the police department's missing person's record. He's my brother, and I'm going to find him." She was trembling, but she fought to control it.

He nodded. "I'll be in the car across the road with the transmitter on. You need me, you yell."

"Thank you," she said, the words little more than a whisper.

"But you check in with me at our agreed times, Rae. You miss one, just one call, and I swear I'll come in, guns blazing."

She smiled. "Like the Lone Ranger?"

"No, like the whole damned cavalry."

They left the musty old room where the city's history was stored in decades' old newspapers and walked to Marc's car.

Rachel felt the warmth of the sun on her face and reveled in the feeling. A sudden thought entered her mind. Why didn't the Beaumondier women ever go out into the sun? The question nagged at her much more than she'd wanted to admit to Marc. It was possible, as she'd told him, that they had the pigment disease that made their skin's exposure to the sun hazardous, but she was only guessing. She wasn't a doctor. What if that wasn't true? What if something else was wrong? Something that compelled them to shut themselves up in that house, and only rise after sunset. Only come into town at night.

They passed Madame Zanine's Potions shop. Rachel paused to look at the assemblage of charms strewn about the shelf in the window and saw her reflection look back at her from a small silver-mounted hand mirror. Marc looked over her shoulder. "Forget it. Her voodoo potions don't work. I know, I've tried them." He laughed lightly.

A chill swept up Rachel's spine as she remembered standing before the tall mirror at *Sans Souci.* Alexandre had been the one to peer over her shoulder then but, unlike with Marc, she had not seen Alexandre's reflection in the mirror.

Alexandre stood in the shadow-filled hallway, his dark clothes causing him to blend with the blackness. Marguerite and Yvette's hushed voices drifted toward him from the partially opened door of his grandmother's bedchamber. Their tones, sounding somewhat angry and frantic, and the mere fact that they were speaking in near whispers, had caused him to pause and listen.

"I think Alexandre is suspicious," Marguerite said. "And that worries me. If he finds out . . ."

"He won't," Yvette snapped. "I told you, this will work."

"But if he *does* find out, he might leave. We'd lose him, Yvette."

"He's not going to find out, Marguerite, and we're not going to lose him. Anyway, where would he go? Back to France?" She laughed. "His experience there was so traumatic I doubt he ever wants to go back there."

"I don't know," Marguerite said. "Maybe we should put an end to this. If he does discover that we arranged for Rachel to come here in the hopes he would fall in love with her and mate before it's too late, well . . . I just hate to think what he might do."

"He'll do exactly as we planned, and he won't find out as long as we don't get careless."

Alexandre felt a fury of rage sweep through his body at their words. They had brought her here. They had arranged the entire thing to get him to do exactly what they had wanted him to do for years, and which he'd refused to do—mate.

Chapter 21

Marc pulled the sedan up before the worn slate path that led to the front gallery of *Sans Souci*. "Sorry for the inconvenience, Ms. Domecq," he called out loudly as she climbed from the car.

Rachel waved, turned and walked toward the house. Shadowed by the overhanging portico, the door opened silently and Hanson stood waiting for her.

"Good afternoon, Hanson," she said.

"Good afternoon, Ms. Domecq. Mr. Beaumondier asked me to offer his regrets if you returned today, but he will be unable to join you tonight for dinner."

Rachel felt a sinking sensation in her heart. She knew she'd wanted to see Alexandre but had been unaware of just how much until this moment. "Thank you, Hanson. Are the ladies of the house about?"

"Not yet. They will receive you in the parlor at seven this evening, if you like."

Rachel nodded and hurried up the stairs. She didn't really care about being received by the ladies. She wanted to see Alexandre, but it seemed Alexandre didn't want to see her. A wave of guilt washed over her as the thought of Steven flit through her mind and she remembered the newspaper pictures Marc had shown her. She had to stop thinking about Alexandre and concentrate on Steven.

She forced herself to remember everything she'd learned in town. Every man who had been pictured with Yvette in those old newspapers, or whoever the woman was, had disappeared. Some, if not all, had ended up dead. Was Steven slated to share their fate?

The remainder of the afternoon passed slowly. Rachel perused a few more books in the library, trying to find an answer as to how more than a hundred years' worth of society page pictures could all be of Yvette Beaumondier. Obviously the answer was that there had been other Yvette Beaumondiers through the years. She scanned journal after journal, but came up with nothing. There was no mention of other Yvettes.

"They had to be in this family," Rachel muttered. "So why aren't they in the family journals?"

After several hours, her eyes began to blur from the dim light and the strain of trying to look through the old books and read the fine print. Still seeing no one about, Rachel left the house for some fresh air. She strolled around the grounds, her gaze scanning each shadow, each bush and tree for some hint as to what was going on at *Sans Souci*, but she remained close to the house, reluctant to venture too far from its sight, or too close to the *garconniere*.

Later, when Hanson stepped onto the gallery where she was sitting to announce that her dinner was served, she thought perhaps Alexandre might appear after all.

He didn't.

She picked at her food, not feeling very hungry in spite of the fact she hadn't eaten since having the *beignets* with Marc that morning.

At seven she walked into the parlor and forced a smile to her face and a cheeriness to her voice she didn't feel. They were all there—Suzanne, Yvette, Marguerite, even Catherine. The matriarch of the Beaumondiers sat on an antique ladies' loge, a design meant, in days' past, to accommodate voluminous hoop skirts and petticoats. Catherine sat with her legs stretched out and crossed before her, the pale green silk covering of the loge proving less than complimentary to the pink and burgundy chiffon lounging gown she wore.

"Good evening," Rachel said. Her gaze flicked from one to the other of them.

They all responded cheerfully.

"Rachel, my dear," Catherine said, "where have you been? We were becoming worried. Yvette said you weren't here last night, that some police officer came and took you away."

"Yes, they thought they'd found my brother and wanted me to go to the morgue and identify the body. Thank heavens it wasn't him."

"Your brother?" Catherine said. "Well, my goodness gracious. Is he missing, dear?"

"The police seem to think so." Rachel laughed. "But they don't know my brother. He often just takes off without telling anyone."

"Well, I hope he's all right," Catherine said. "Young people these days can be so irresponsible."

Rachel studied the old lady before answering. Catherine sounded sincere, but then that could be an act. A very good act. "Oh, Steven is the type of person who can get so immersed in his work that he forgets all about the real world and, unfortunately, everyone in it. And that includes paying bills, which is, I suspect, the real reason the hotel reported him missing to the police. He's probably just off tramping about the bayous taking pictures." She laughed. "That's what he does. He's a photographer."

Rachel noticed Marguerite glance quickly toward Yvette, who lounged easily on a velvet-covered settee by the fireplace.

"Well, I'm just sorry you were put through that," Catherine said. "What a horrible, horrible ordeal."

Rachel pulled her gaze from Marguerite and turned it back to Catherine. "Yes, it wasn't very pleasant." She'd seen plenty of dead bodies before in her former profession, but she had never gotten used to it.

"What wasn't very pleasant?" Alexandre asked.

His voice wrapped around Rachel like the enveloping warmth of a fur cloak. She turned to see him walking into the room. Their eyes met and she felt that instant pull he seemed to manifest over her, the swirling unresistible feeling of being dragged into a timeless whirlpool of emotion. She felt suddenly as if she were teetering on the brink of the world or on the edge of a sheer cliff, ready to plunge off and into a vacuous unknown, but she didn't care. She welcomed it, as long as it was with Alexandre.

Her heart began a racing beat as his gaze held hers spellbound, a willing prisoner with no desire to escape. She felt her hands tremble as they lay in her lap, aching to reach out and touch him, to caress the smooth taut line of his cheek, to slip within the silken curls of ebony hair at his nape, to slide over the steel hard muscles of his chest.

"Alexandre," Rachel whispered needlessly.

His face remained stoic, his expression hard and without warmth. He forced it to remain so. If he smiled at her, if he let himself feel anything toward her beside anger, all would be lost, and he couldn't stand that. It had already gone too far. She had touched his heart, just as Danielle had two hundred years before, and left her brand on whatever kind of soul a *Chasseur* had. But this time it would be different. This time it had to be different. He would make it so. He remembered the scenes he had witnessed in the *Vieux Carre* between Rachel and the police officer, Marc Dellos. Rachel had another love, a mortal love, and that was better for her than anything Alexandre could offer.

His gaze swept over her brusquely. This time it would be he that walked away. It was the only way he could protect her from himself, and from the others. He still didn't know for certain why she was here, or what had brought her here, but he would find out. He would find out, and put an end to it.

His gaze moved to rest on Catherine. "So, *Grandmere*, it is good to see you downstairs, but what is it you are all busily discussing that is so unpleasant?"

"Rachel was just telling us that she had to go to the city's morgue yesterday and look at a body. The police thought that it might have been her brother."

Alexandre walked across the room and stood before one of the tall windows that looked out onto the dark landscape of *Sans Souci* and its long entry drive. He turned a pointed gaze on Rachel. "And?"

She started, unnerved at the chill that emanated from his eyes, the hardness she saw etched in the lines of his face, the rigid posture of his broad shoulders. Her mind spun in confusion. What had happened? She searched his features for an answer, and came up with none.

"It wasn't him," Suzanne interjected, her tone laconic and somewhat caustic. She smiled at her brother, though Rachel, catching the brief gesture, considered it more of a sly and knowing sneer than a smile.

Alexandre's gaze moved briefly to Rachel and as quickly away. "That's good," he said softly, and spun on his heel to face the window again, leaving his back turned to the women.

Rachel stared at him as the others continued to talk. Catherine began to relate some story about a person she'd known years before who had been involved in a murder and the dire consequences they'd faced, or some such thing. Rachel wasn't really sure. She wasn't listening.

Her gaze bore into the back of Alexandre's head, willing him to turn around and face her. She hadn't realized until only a few minutes ago, at his cold rejection, how much he had come to mean to her. Her body had ached for him, her passion had reached out to him and gloried in his touch, but now she realized it was much more than that. Never had her feelings for a man taken her to such heights, and plunged her to such low depths, as those she had for Alexandre. And there was only one answer. She was in love with him, in love with a man who, in spite of their night of intimacy, was still a dark, mysterious stranger to her. He was an enigma, a puzzle whose most important pieces were still hidden from her, and which she had no idea how to uncover, or even if he would allow her to do so.

Rachel felt a rending deep within her heart as if it were cracking. Had she found him, tasted his love, his passion, only to lose him? Did he not care for her at all? Once, the thought that a man didn't care for her would have only served to stoke her anger. But not now, not with Alexandre. The thought that she didn't matter to him brought tears to the back of her eyes and a rise of emotion to her throat. She felt the sting of the hot moisture that suddenly swelled at the edge of her eyelids and blinked rapidly. Crying solved nothing, she believed, except to show the world a weakness she would rather it did not see.

Turning in her seat Rachel faced Marguerite and struggled to put a smile on her face and a cheeriness into her tone. "So, Marguerite," she said, "tell me about yourself, about *Sans Souci* and the Beaumondiers. You must have a wealth of stories about your ancestors."

Marguerite laughed. "Oh, dear, I'm afraid I'm not the one to espouse the great Beaumondier legends." She turned toward Alexandre. "My . . . son, Alexandre, is the one who knows all the details of our history, and something of those who came before us. He has," she smiled, "studied it all."

Alexandre turned from the window. "But I'm afraid, *Mother,*" he said, putting a definite and somewhat deriding emphasis on her title, "that I will have to excuse myself from your company tonight. At least for a while." He moved toward the door, making sure to keep his eyes averted from Rachel's. "I'm sorry, Rachel. I have an appointment tonight that I cannot miss."

He walked quickly through the foyer, his steps echoing distinctly upon the marble tiles, and left the house by the front entry, the soft click of its lock falling into place announcing his exit.

Within minutes he was standing in the center of the weed-choked remains of the plantation's formal gardens. What he had said to her wasn't a lie. At least not all of it. He was sorry. Every conscious thought and feeling in him wanted nothing more than to remain in her company, to talk to her, laugh with her, love her. But he couldn't. She had someone else, Marc Dellos, and it was better that way. Memory of Rachel with the police officer, standing on the deck of the riverboat within the circle of his arms, kissing him, holding his hand across the dinner table at Brennan's, laughing lightly with him while breakfasting at the Cafe DuMonde, and walking the dimly lit streets of the *Vieux Carré* with him, filled Alexandre's mind. A low groan of despair emanated softly from his throat, like that of a wounded animal who knows death is not far away. At the same time fury filled his chest; fury at himself for allowing feelings to resurface, to overwhelm him, that he knew could only end in anguish and pain; fury at *them,* for bringing her here, for he had no doubt they, or at least one of them, had somehow lured her to *Sans Souci.* And all because they wanted him to mate. To give them a child. . . . an heir to carry on the Beaumondier name. They had thought, because she looked so much like Danielle, that he would fall in love with her.

A curse slipped from his lips. And they'd been right. He had fallen in love with her, but not only because she looked like Danielle, but because she was strong, independent, and beautiful. Because she was caring and warm.

He walked slowly from the garden and into the open, long fallow, plantation fields.

In the distance, the old cotton mill came into view, its rock, clay and mortar walls a dull brown beneath the moon's glow, the weather beaten slates of its shingled roof little more than a dark slope. The building had only two windows, one on either side of the old plank entry door. The shutters on one were intact and closed over the window, the other was bare of any covering. Moonlight reflected off the one jagged shard of glass remaining in the window.

Once the building had been a bustle of activity, but that had been when Catherine had still taken an interest in her home, and in keeping up appearances. *Sans Souci* had been a thriving plantation in the 1700s and 1800s.

Alexandre stared at the old mill.

Slavery had been a convenient luxury. It had made it easier for them to survive. The Beaumondiers had not been forced to find their prey on the streets of the *Vieux Carré* or the long winding country roads that led into the city, as they usually did. No, during those days they had bought and bred their own.

Scoffing in disgust, Alexandre turned from the old mill and walked on. He had fought in the Confederacy, but not because he believed in slavery, not because his family used the institution for their own, selfish needs, but because he had once again thought to place himself in a situation where his own destruction, the end of his existence, might be possible, might come to him by another's hand.

It hadn't, and he had gone on, unhappily, as he had for so many years before.

"So, when did the Beaumondiers come here from France?" Rachel asked, looking at Marguerite.

Her glance flickered to Catherine, who answered.

"Actually, one of our ancestors was with Bienville when he first stepped foot on Louisiana soil and claimed it in the name of France."

"Oh, yes," Rachel said, as if she'd just been reminded, "I noticed a drawing of such in an old journal I found in the study on some of your family's history. His name was Alexandre, too, wasn't it?"

Catherine smiled patiently. Out of the corner of her eye Rachel noticed Marguerite's hands fidget nervously with one of the cuffs of her blouse sleeve. Yvette's leg, crossed over the other, swung back and forth and Suzanne, standing now by the fireplace kept picking up and replacing a small figurine on the mantel.

"Yes, now that you mention it, I believe it was," Catherine answered. "We have had quite a few Alexandres in the Beaumondier family."

"Yvettes, too, I understand," Rachel said boldly,

though if they questioned her as to how she knew that she hadn't the faintest idea what she was going to say.

Catherine frowned. "Yvettes?"

"What about Marguerites, Catherines, and Suzannes," Rachel persisted, "are those *new* names to the family?"

"Rachel," Suzanne said, interrupting before Catherine could answer, "much as I find this conversation titillating, I'm afraid I must excuse myself." She smiled, though the gesture did nothing to ease the chill in her features. "I have a date for dinner in town."

Yvette rose at Suzanne's words. "Yes, and I am accompanying her." She smiled down at Rachel. "Perhaps we can continue this little talk some other time."

Marguerite had stopped her fidgeting. She stood up, kissed Catherine on the cheek, mumbled something into the old woman's ear, and then turned toward the door. "I'm afraid I also must excuse myself. I have some . . . uh, work to do."

The three women said goodnight and left the room.

Rachel looked at Catherine. "I'm sorry. Did I run them off with my curiosity about your family?" she asked.

Catherine had been staring coldly after the retreating women. At Rachel's question, her eyes warmed and she smiled. "No, dear," she said. "They are always running off here or there, not like in the old days when life was truly enjoyed at a more leisurely pace. But then, it wasn't so hard to find a . . . good meal in the old days."

Chapter 22

Rachel closed the door to her bedroom and slipped the transmitter from her pocket. She flipped its switch and held it close to her mouth. "Marc?"

"Yeah, gorgeous, I'm here," he answered instantly.

She smiled. "Suzanne and Yvette just left the house, and I'm not sure but I think Marguerite did, too. She said she had to work but she doesn't impress me as the type. Most likely it was just an excuse to get away from her mother. Or me. They invited me here, but it seems every time I bring up the subject of their family history everyone scatters."

"Rae, I think you'd better . . ."

She interrupted him, not wanting to hear his words of caution. "I'm going to try and search their rooms again in a little while, Marc. Especially Yvette's. And I didn't get much of a chance last time at Suzanne's. Can you follow them? Yvette and Suzanne are going into town, I think."

"Rae, listen, I was waiting for you to call me. I've got to cut out for a while, but I don't want to leave you in there alone. Let me come in and get you again and I'll bring you back later, when I can return."

"What's wrong?" She felt a sting of trepidation.

"The department just radioed me a few minutes ago. My brother was in a motorcycle accident about a couple of hours ago. He's in surgery now."

"Jeff? Is it serious?"

"Yeah, sounds like it, and since our parents are gone and our sister, Clarice, lives out of state they want me to . . . well, you know." His tone was drawn and sober.

"Go on, Marc. Go to the hospital. And don't worry about me. I can handle myself here."

"No. I'm not leaving you in there with no back-up. I'll get someone else to come out here."

"You know the department won't authorize that."

"Then I'll call in a favor. It's not like there aren't a whole passel of guys out there who owe me." Static buzzed through the transmitter. "Rae, I think I see the two women coming now. I'll follow them as long as I can and call someone else to take over when I have to cut off for the hospital. Check in tomorrow morning. If I'm not back, talk to whoever's at this end of the radio. They'll keep me informed on what's going on here until I do get back. You got that?"

"Okay."

"Check in, Rae," Marc said again, his tone one of harsh demand. "I mean it."

"Yes, all right, I will," Rachel said. "I will." She sighed. "And Marc . . ."

"Yeah?"

"I hope Jeff's okay."

"Yeah me, too."

She slipped the transmitter into her purse, lay it on the settee, and moved to look out the window. Why was it that bad things always happened to the good ones? Jeff was attending college. He wanted to be a doctor, to help people and now he might . . . Rachel forced the unhappy thoughts away and turned her attention back to the matter at hand. But the matter at hand wasn't a much happier one. She had come to *Sans Souci* to find out what had happened to her brother and discover why Yvette had lied to the police about knowing him. So far she had discovered nothing, absolutely nothing, and Steven's cries were coming to her less frequently.

"Hang in there, Stevie," she whispered, using her childhood name for him. "Hang in there." She stared out the window at the overgrown grounds of the old plantation. She had come to find Steven and instead had fallen into the arms of the man who might be responsible for his disappearance. Rachel felt a shiver skip up her spine. Her mind flew to thoughts of Alexandre and her body flushed with warmth as she remembered his hands upon her flesh, caressing, exciting, teasing. No one had ever made her feel the way Alexandre had. Tears filled her eyes. He couldn't be responsible for whatever had happened to Steven. He just couldn't, her heart argued. But her mind had been too well schooled in clues and logic by the Baton Rouge Police Department. Steven had come to *Sans Souci*, and then he'd disappeared. She was convinced that one of the Beaumondiers, or all of them, including Alexandre, knew where Steven was, or what had happened to him, and she had to find out.

She pulled the cool facade of the policewoman over her emotions. It had been a long time, but Rachel found it wasn't as hard to revive as she'd thought. It was time to do what she'd come here to do. Her mind clicked onto a cold, calculating investigative mode.

Rachel listened to the quietness of the house, so intense as to be near oppressive. Catherine was probably asleep, and Marguerite, Rachel suspected, had gone out somewhere. But of course there was still Hanson. An image of the old butler, with his piercing, ever-watchful eyes an unearthly quietness flitted into Rachel's mind and she shivered involuntarily. He was always around somewhere, lurking. She turned and walked to the door, opened it quietly and peeked out, fully expecting to see Hanson emerge from the shadows and shuffle silently down the hallway toward her. He didn't. Silence drummed in her ears as she breathed a sigh of relief and slipped from the room.

A car moved along River Road, passing the overgrown inlet where Marc was parked, hidden from view by the dense overgrowth and the brush and branches he'd thrown across the hood of his car to camouflage it further. He watched the car pass and realized instantly its occupant wasn't either of the Beaumondier women. The driver, and the only person in the vehicle, was a man. A curse slipped from Marc's lips. He got out of the car, walked to stand in front of it and looked toward the entry drive across the road. He had to get to town, to the hospital. Rachel said the women had left before she radioed him. That was a good five minutes ago and the entry drive wasn't *that* long. So where in the hell were they?

A movement off to his right and across the road caught his attention. He looked and saw, several hundred feet away, in the midst of the giant oaks that grew along the boundary of *Sans Souci*, a flowing length of pale color softly reflecting the moon's glow. Marc squinted, strained to see through the inky darkness that surrounded him.

"What the hell?" he mumbled to himself, unable to define what it was he was seeing. He took a few steps toward the road, paused, and reached to his belt to reassure himself his gun was there. His fingers touched the smooth plastic handle with its engraved surface. With his thumb, Marc automatically flipped off the thin leather strap that acted as a safety.

He crossed the road, crouching slightly, and approached the grove of oaks. A woman, dressed in white, moved through the shadows. Marc blinked several times, afraid the night was playing tricks on him, and looked again. She seemed to be wandering aimlessly, sauntering amid the live oaks and overgrown bushes as if in no particular hurry or direction. She didn't seem to notice Marc's approach and he had the definite impression that even if she did, she wouldn't care. He took another halting step forward, careful not to make any noise. Could she be one of the Beaumondier women? He lay the heel of his hand on the butt of his gun, ready, but not quite as tense as seconds before. Rachel had said two of them had left together and were going to town, so they would have been in a car? Could this woman be one of the ones who Rachel thought had retired for the night?

Marc decided to find out. He jogged across the road, his black running shoes making only a momentary whisper of sound on the asphalt strip and his dark clothes leaving him nearly invisible against the black night.

He kept his eyes on the spot of lightness as he moved, but the woman turned and moved away from him. She disappeared within the dark shadows of a cluster of live oaks whose branches grew so thickly entwined that only the barest hint of moonlight pierced their foliage. Marc stepped beneath the sprawling boughs of the old trees and as he did, feeling a self-preservating need for reassurance, he slipped his gun from his holster. The gnarled, wide-spreading limbs of the trees were so heavily laden with dripping strands of gray Spanish moss that passing through them was much like maneuvering through a maze. Many of the curtain-like sheets of growth reached to the ground to form tiny mountains of dried, prickly moss, while others still hung free and swayed gently in the slight breeze that sometimes drifted over the land from the nearby bayous. Marc moved forward cautiously, alert for the slightest sound, the most minute of movements.

The dank odor of the bayous met his nostrils, a musky scent that was a blend of rich marsh earth, lush foliage and sultry air, a smell Marc had, since moving to New Orleans, come to appreciate for its uniqueness. With his next step the gray, wispy wings of a cloud drifted in front of the moon and momentarily cut off its sallow light, plunging the earth, and Marc, into total darkness.

He stopped, his body taut with tension, every fiber, every muscle, every nerve cell, ready, waiting for the unknown to happen, to strike without warning. His eyes scanned the dark shapes around him, trying to make them out, to identify them, but each looked much the same as the other. And then he noticed the distinct and profound absence of sound. The air was deadly quiet, still, mute. Marc looked about quickly, his eyes trying to pierce the blackness that had engulfed him. It was as if he were not only alone in this bayou, but in the world. As if all life, all the plants, animals, and humans had perished, and he was all that was left. His heartbeat began to accelerate. He cocked his head and listened. There was no rustling within the branches of the trees, and no scurrying about of animals skipping through the dried leaves and bramble on the ground.

Marc's thumb pressed down slightly on the hammer of his gun, exerting just enough pressure so that if surprised, his thumb and the finger wrapped securely around the trigger would react automatically, and instantly.

He took several deliberate steps forward and paused again, listening, waiting. Why did he feel such a sense of danger? He had been in dozens of deadly situations on the job, and none had instilled within him the uneasy fear that was threatening to overwhelm him now.

A cloud drifted past the moon and a few pale yellow rays broke through the trees branches above, sending hazy beams of light to the ground that merely caused the shadows to deepen. Marc felt his adrenaline pumping faster, faster. Something rustled in the branches above and to his left. His heartbeat accelerated to a frantic pace. He swung around, arm outstretched, hand and gun acting as one, pointing toward whatever danger, if any, approached. His finger tightened on the thin curve of his gun's metal trigger.

A black cat emerged from beneath the scraggy branches of a bush a few yards away. Its piercing yellow-green eyes pinioned Marc with their unrelenting gaze and a low, growling whisper of sound emanated from the animal's throat. It walked toward him slowly, slinking movements that were at once stealthy, calculating, and gracefully fluid.

Instinct suddenly took over and without knowing how he knew it, and not questioning the feeling, Marc knew that someone was behind him. He whirled around. A woman stood before him, illuminated by a wan stream of moonlight, her porcelain-hued flesh nearly the same shade as the pristine white threads of the silk blouse she wore. Her hair cascaded in voluminous waves over her shoulders, long dark strands that blended with the night. Her eyes, the gray of an early winter's storm, were accentuated with piercing slivers of blue within their depths, and instantly mesmerized him. She smiled as she met his gaze, lusciously full, red lips parting in seductive and blatant invitation.

In spite of being startled at her abrupt appearance, and in spite of the fear that he had felt only moments before, Marc felt himself instantly warm with desire as he stared into her eyes. His fingers relaxed their grip on his gun.

Marc heard the soft rustling of leaves behind him, and the snap of a limb as weight lifted away from it. His mind told him to react, to turn, to take aim with his gun, to ward off the danger his every instinct warned him was imminent. But he remained motionless, his gaze held helplessly captive by the woman who had approached until she stood little more than two feet from him.

Suddenly something struck his shoulder from behind. The blow stole his balance and knocked him forward, propelling the gun from his hand.

The woman before him moved aside, but made no effort to help him.

Teeth sunk deeply into Marc's neck as claws pierced the fabric of his shirt and dug into his shoulders to secure their hold on him.

"Son of a bitch," Marc muttered, and slapped at the thing that had attached itself to him, "get the hell off." He wrenched from side to side and grabbed at the creature. "Get off," he screamed. His breath began to come in gasps as he fought to free himself. "Get off."

The woman in white smiled and took another step back as Marc threw himself to one side, coming near to where she'd stood, in an effort to escape. The animal shrieked loudly and dug its teeth and claws deeper into Marc's flesh. He screamed in agony and slammed a hand down on the creature, but its grip on him was secure. A claw-tipped wing slapped outward to fend off

Marc's hand as he frantically swatted at it. He felt the thing's teeth sink farther into his neck, sucking at the blood that flowed through his veins. His mind reeled. What in the hell was happening? He thrashed, twisted and turned, but the thing remained clasped to him. Small rivers of blood trickled from his neck and shoulder, saturating the front of his dark shirt and streaming down the length of his arm to drop from his fingertips to the ground.

Within minutes he felt an overwhelming weakness come over him. His limbs seemed unusually heavy and his movements became sluggish, each twist of resistance, each slap of defense less powerful and more lethargic than the last. He struggled to keep fighting but it seemed to only intensify the sense of weakness. His trembling legs buckled and he dropped to the ground. His knees sunk into the soft earth and his arms hung limp at his sides. A small pool of blood began to form within the wild grass upon which the fingers of his right hand lay slack.

The woman who had been standing before him as he struggled approached and, smiling, knelt beside him. She stroked a cool palm across his forehead, brushing a lock of hair away and then, placing her hands on his chest, pushed him gently back until he lay sprawled on the cold, dank earth. "So handsome," she crooned softly, her lips only a hair's breath from his own. Her hand moved over his cheek, a featherlight touch that skipped along the line of his jaw and down the curve of his neck. Her fingers wrapped around the open vee of his shirt front and, with a tug, ripped it open. Her hands slid across his chest and her fingers slipped through the thick mat of silken brown hairs that covered the muscular torso. He felt her hands slide downward, move lightly over his ribcage, across the flat plane of his stomach. She released the metal rivet that held his jeans together, pushed down the zipper, and slid her fingers beneath the soft cotton of his jockey shorts. "So big and strong," she whispered, and brushed her lips across his.

The cat rubbed itself against the woman's thigh and meowed. "Not now, Apollyon," she snarled, and shrugged it away.

Marc fought the beckoning of unconsciousness as it swirled around his mind. The thing at his neck gurgled greedily, but he was beyond trying to fight it now. He had no strength left. His eyelids fluttered and he struggled to keep them open. He tried to focus on the woman who hovered over him, whose hands were stroking his body. The touch of her fingers was like a trailing of ice across his skin, the caress of her lips more a winter's breeze than passion's warmth.

Marc felt her fingers wrap around the limp flesh of his sexual organ and heard her chuckle softly.

Through his terror, cold and penetrating as it was, Marc felt a moment of humiliation.

Her fingers squeezed down on him, hard, cruel, filling him with excruciating pain that raced up through his torso to meet that which originated from the side of his neck and shoulder. He was consumed by it, a burning, agonizing series of aches that tore at his insides. He writhed helplessly, weakly, using the last of his strength and willpower, the last of the self-discipline and sense of self-preservation that had seen him through so much. Seconds later, when she knew he could stand no more, and when the small, almost inaudible shrieks that escaped his lips turned to tormented whimpers, the woman who lay atop him released her hold on him. Her hands slid back up over his chest and paused there as she looked down at him, sheer enjoyment sparkling from her gray-blue eyes.

Marc stared up at her, too weak to move, powerless and consumed by stark, near mind-numbing terror. Blackness swirled around the edges of his consciousness, threatening to overtake him, to drag him into its void.

The thing that had clutched at his neck and shoulder also released him and he felt it move away. He wanted to lift a hand to the spot, to assure himself that it was gone, but he didn't have the strength. His mind ordered his arm to move, to raise his hand toward his throat, but it remained lying upon the grass, lifeless.

Another woman suddenly moved into his line of vision, hovering over him from above the same shoulder the creature had just left, staring down at him with that same satisfied smile. She, too, was beautiful, possessing the same long dark hair, porcelain smooth flesh the color of newly fallen snow, and piercing gray blue eyes as the other women.

She would help him, Marc's weary mind reassured. She would help him.

His eyelids fluttered again, yearning to close, and he struggled desperately to keep them open. He had to remain conscious, it was his only chance.

The women smiled and then the one who had spoken, who had kissed him and run her hands over his body, who had wrapped her fingers around his penis, leaned forward. "We need your strength, sweetheart," she whispered softly, and ran her long red fingernails lightly along the side of his face. "All of it." Marc felt her cold lips brush across his again, and then her face disappeared as her lips slid downward, pressing a trail of icy kisses to his throat.

He screamed as he felt a piercing pain stab the flesh at his neck again. Tears of helplessness, despair, and soul-wrenching terror poured from his eyes. His heart beat frantically against his chest, in spite of the fingers of fear that squeezed at it. Over and over he screamed, but the sound that ripped from his throat, that was meant to echo through the still night like the sound of a raging storm, and summon help, was little more than a ragged gasp.

Chapter 23

Rachel wandered through the rooms of the house. She had searched it once and found nothing, but felt compelled to search it again. A wave of self-disgust washed over her. She had been a cop, trained in the rules of deduction, in discovering and identifying clues. She had been a case solver, dammit, a detective, but since coming to *Sans Souci* she felt as if she had discovered little that would lead her to Steven, or help her find out what had happened to him. And if his cries for her were any indication, each weaker and more desperate than the last, she didn't have much time left before it would be too late.

Tears filled her eyes at the thought of losing Steven and she quickly blinked them away. Ever since coming to *Sans Souci* she had been overwhelmed by the frequent, and unusual, desire to cry. "Not now," she said harshly to herself. "Not now."

With her shoulders thrown back in determination, Rachel walked into Alexandre's study. She had planned to search the women's bedrooms, and she still did, but something about Alexandre had begun to bother her. The longer she stayed at the plantation, the more contact she had with the Beaumondiers, the more certain she felt that they were hiding something from her. And that suspicion included Alexandre.

Rachel felt a stab of loss at the thought. She didn't want to think Alexandre was behind whatever it was, she felt unexplainably certain, it was something horrible, something evil, something . . . Rachel shuddered. She didn't want to think of Alexandre in that light. He had made her feel what no other man ever had. She closed her eyes. Oh, God, her mind cried, had she fallen in love with some sort of demon?

Her eyelids fluttered open. She had to forget about herself for now, forget about what she felt, forget about Alexandre and what his kisses aroused within her. She had to find Steven and save him from whatever nightmare had entrapped him.

She looked around the room. The curtains had been drawn and the faint spray of moonlight that shone down on the plantation and filtered through the panes of the tall windows barely illuminated the room. Rachel took a match from a small brass tray that sat on Alexandre's desk and struck it. The tip erupted into flame, throwing an orange gold glow over the immediate area. She touched the flame to a half-burned candle in a brass holder next to the match tray. Its black wick took the fire easily and began to burn. She shook her hand, extinguishing the match and tossed it into the holder's bowled bottom. Inhaling a deep breath, more to give her added courage than air, she moved around the desk and once again began to open its drawers. Her previous search had brought her nothing, but perhaps, just perhaps, she had missed something that would give her a lead to what had happened to Steven, though she hoped not. In Yvette's room, yes. In Marguerite's room, yes. Even in Suzanne's room, yes. But not here. She didn't want to have missed something here, in Alexandre's desk.

The first and second drawers proved just as normal in their contents as they had the first time she'd rummaged through them. She opened the third and pulled out the expense journal she remembered having gone through before. Then an array of ink pens. Pencils. Quills. Paper. And a rabbit's foot keychain. She reached for the journal to replace it in the drawer and paused abruptly. She looked back into the drawer. A rabbit's foot keychain.

A lump of emotion caught in her throat and her heart began a rapid beat. Steven always carried a rabbit's foot keychain. Her fingers wrapped around the small furry paw. He had since grade school, the same one their father had given to him just before his death. Steven had called it his lucky charm, but Rachel had always suspected it was more sentiment than anything else that compelled him to keep it. She opened her fingers and looked down at the rabbit's foot, then lifted it before her to gaze at the silver clasp that attached it to the tiny chain. SL. The initials Steven had scratched into the base so long ago were still there. Faded now. Almost indistinguishable to someone who didn't know what they were looking at, but clear to Rachel.

A sob caught in her throat at what this meant. It was definitely Steven's and it had been in Alexandre's desk drawer. He knew, her mind screamed. He knew where her brother was, what had happened to him. She clutched the furry little paw to her breast, her mind and heart in turmoil and confusion. Her brother was missing, was in trouble, and the man she had fallen in love with, the man she had given herself to only hours before, was most likely the cause. Rachel felt a splintering deep within her heart, as if it were breaking apart, shattering into a million pieces, but whether because of her fear for her brother, or the heartache she suddenly felt at discovering Alexandre's treachery, she wasn't certain.

Suddenly the hairs on the back of her neck seemed to rise and she experienced the definite sensation of being watched. She looked up slowly, her head turning toward the entry door. It was closed securely, just as she'd left it. Her gaze darted around the room, trying to pierce the shadowed corners, pausing to identify each piece of furniture, each lamp, stack of books, and piece of bric-a-brac. But she could see nothing.

From behind the moon-touched leaves of an overgrown banana plant, its huge, curved fronds shimmering emerald and silver against the night and near black within the dusky shadows of the garden, Marguerite watched Rachel. She was fully aware that Rachel had sensed her presence, or at least that she had sensed she was being watched by someone. Marguerite's lips widened slowly into a smile, but warmth was lacking in the gesture as a spark of self-satisfaction, avaricious and savage, lit her eyes.

"You are alone here now, Rachel Domecq," Marguerite whispered. The smile widened. "All alone at *Sans Souci* . . . with us."

As if she'd heard the lightly whispered words, Rachel turned in the large chair Alexandre used at his desk and looked toward the four ceiling windows that led to the gallery.

Marguerite's eyes, their gray as cold as the fog of an English moor, their specks of blue as chilling as winter's mountain morning, raked over Rachel, assessing, scrutinizing, planning. Yvette had been right, the girl looked exactly, uncannily, like Danielle. Unfortunately her temperament was extremely different. Marguerite sighed. Danielle had been an innocent. Easily pliable, gullible, manipulated. At least until that final day. Then they'd made a fatal, stupid, mistake. The truth had been too much for her to accept, and they had been forced to correct their error. Without Alexandre's knowledge, of course.

But Rachel Domecq was no innocent. Neither was she weak. She was strong and independent. Marguerite had sensed that upon their initial meeting. Rachel was not like her brother, whose free spirit and impulsiveness lent him a weakness he could not overcome, but which had fit into their plans perfectly. Steven had mentioned to Yvette that Rachel had been a police officer in Baton Rouge, but that hadn't mattered. What had was that they needed to get her to the plantation. Their plan had succeeded thus far, and Steven, Marguerite smiled smugly, Steven was innocently providing the inducement needed to keep her here.

Now, she thought, Alexandre must do his part.

At Rachel's intent stare, Marguerite took an unconscious step back, putting herself deeper into the shadows of the garden, even while knowing the act was unnecessary. Rachel could not see her, and even if she did, what did it matter? She was theirs now, forever.

Marguerite smiled and shook her head in disbelief at the feebleness of mortals, of their silly fears and ridiculous dreams. When would they ever learn that when *they* wanted them, when the *Chasseurs* decided their fate, there was no escape?

She chuckled softly, remembering the young man who undoubtedly had come to protect Rachel Domecq from the reclusive, suspicious, Beaumondiers. She and Yvette could have allowed him an existence like theirs, but the family had agreed long ago, while still in France, that transmutation was too dangerous. Marguerite had tried it with her husband and Yvette had tried it with hers. Both had been a mistake, and both had been forced eventually to correct their errors, lest the family be destroyed. Converts were unpredictable, temperamental, and careless. They killed without heed to consequence and walked the streets boldly, without caution to exposure or peril. A soft laugh escaped her throat. But none of that was of concern anymore. There were no longer any converts in the Beaumondier family to threaten them.

Marguerite turned and began to walk deeper into the garden and away from the house. It really didn't matter if Rachel searched Alexandre's study, or any of the other rooms in the house for that matter, even their bedchambers. Whatever she would find, and Marguerite had no doubt that Rachel, in the diligent search of a former police officer and worried sister, would find quite a bit, would not help her. Nothing could help her now. The Beaumondiers would do as they agreed; they would continue their line, they had to, but only by birthright, not transmutation, and Rachel Domecq willing or not, would aid them in that task.

Suzanne sat on the dried stump of a long dead cypress tree and looked at her brother. "Why, Alexandre? Why can't you just accept it?"

He stopped his pacing of the small clearing and turned to stare down at her. "Because it's not right, Suzanne, don't you understand that? *We're* not right."

"We are what we are, Alexandre," she said, not for the first time. "And they are what they are. Nothing can change that."

"But I don't have to take advantage of them," Alexandre countered. "I don't have to kill them."

Suzanne sighed. They'd been having this same argument for years, and it always ended the same way, in a stalemate. Each had their viewpoint, their own opinion, and neither seemed willing to change, or accept the others. "We only do what we have to do." She stood and moved to face him, forcing him to again stop his pacing. "Don't you think they'd try and kill us if they knew the truth? Try to destroy us?"

"Yes, and they'd have a right."

"Just as we do," Suzanne said softly. She put a hand on his arm. "Alexandre, the family only wants to see you happy."

He ripped his arm away from her touch. "They only want me to beget them a progeny and keep this damned family going?"

"Is that so bad?" Suzanne snapped, her temper beginning to flare. "We have a right to our existence, too, Alexandre, just as much as *they* do."

He glared down at her, gray-blue eyes piercing eyes identical to his own. Alexandre felt as if his mind and heart were in a battle, a war of wills, and he was about to be his family's hapless victim, torn apart by his own thoughts and feelings. He knew they wanted him to mate, to produce a child to carry on the Beaumondier name, the Beaumondier legend. They had been after him for years, ever since Danielle's rejection of him, ever since he had turned away from their ways. He was their only hope that the Beaumondiers would continue. Yvette was too old to procreate, having passed her five hundredth year long ago.

"Do we have a right to exist?" he said softly. "Are you sure, Suzanne?"

"Would you have rather not been born, Alexandre?" she retorted. "Never to have experienced life at all?"

"Life? Is that what you call our existence, Suzanne?"

he scoffed. "We steal the life force of others in order to continue our existence. We have lived as outcasts of society, unacceptables, for centuries, and always shall. This is not a life, Suzanne," Alexandre sneered. "This is hell."

"And what about Danielle?" Suzanne snapped. "Was she hell, too? Was what you felt for her hell?"

He looked long at his sister. She would have given anything to be in his place, he knew. She wanted to procreate, to give birth to another Beaumondier, but it would never happen. Two hundred years before, a much wilder and impulsive Suzanne had ventured into the primitive swamps of Cajun Louisiana. She had seduced a young boy, Jacques Trudeau, and then, having fallen in love with him, began a transmutation. The villagers had discovered what was happening before Jacques had completely crossed over. They had gathered and, in a frenzy of rage, gone after Suzanne with picks, shovels, guns and knives in hand ready to tear her apart. Jacques stepped in their way, and in their hysteria, the villagers killed him. Suzanne had gone crazy at seeing Jacques killed and had thrown herself at the villagers, screaming, crying and flailing at them.

Alexandre had managed to find her and get her away from the crazed mob, but not before they had nearly destroyed her. It had taken months, long pain filled months of recuperation. She finally regained her strength and her will to live, but the villagers' attack had left its mark. Suzanne's womb had been ripped open by the slash of a scythe. She would never be able to carry a child.

"No," Alexandre whispered finally, feeling as if his insides were being twisted and ripped apart. But not by memory of what he'd felt for Danielle, but for what he knew now that he felt for Rachel. He loved her. More than anything in the world, and that is why he had to reject her, to protect her, from his family and from himself. "No," he said again, "what Danielle allowed me to feel was wonderful, but . . ." he turned away from his sister, not wanting her to see the torment etched on his face, the tears that blurred his eyes. "But it was wrong, Suzanne. It wasn't meant to be for us."

"You're wrong, Alexandre," Suzanne said. "And they're wrong, *Great Grandmere, Grandmere,* and *Mamiere.* Transmutation won't destroy us. It may save us someday. But only if you do what they want now. Take Rachel. You love her. Make her one of us, Alexandre, and fill her with your seed. Have a child, and then they'll leave you alone. You'll have what you want, Rachel, and they'll have the child they want. They'll stop harassing you then, Alexandre. They'll be satisfied."

He whirled around to face her, his features contorted with rage and pain. "No," he thundered, the lone word echoing through the still, dark landscape of the lush bayou. A gator growled a response to being disturbed and a flock of cranes, startled from their slumber, broke from the treetops. "It's too late anyway." The image of Rachel in the arms of Marc Dellos nearly brought a groan to Alexandre's lips as pain, sharp, deep and cutting, tore through him.

"It's not too late, Alexandre. You know that," Suzanne insisted. "She desires you, it's evident in her eyes, in the way she looks at you, talks to you."

"No," he roared again. "I will not condemn another woman to the horrors of my existence, Suzanne. Neither to the ugly realization of it, nor the unearthly experience of it."

"Alexandre . . ."

"Nor will I condemn another soulless," he stumbled

on the last word of his proclamation, ". . . creature to aimlessly roam this earth."

"Say, it, Alexandre," Suzanne demanded, her tone harsh now, "say the stupid, despicable word they have used for centuries to describe us."

His gaze bore into hers, a flaming cauldron of rage that fused with the cool, calm sedate sea of her logic.

"Say it, Alexandre."

His eyes blazed with pain. "Vampire." The word snapped from his tongue and hung between them on the still, sultry swamp air.

"Vampire," Suzanne repeated, her tone one of disgust. "The gods who created us called us *Les Chasseurs*, Alexandre."

He whirled toward her. "The Hunters. They should have called us the killers."

Indignation fired Suzanne's eyes and burned hot in her breast. "We are no different than them, Alexandre, these mortals you feel so sorry for. They hunt for their food, just as we do. They kill to survive, just as we do."

"They kill animals, Suzanne. We kill them, the humans."

"They kill those weaker and less intelligent than themselves, Alexandre," Suzanne said, the words hard with conviction, "just as we do."

Alexandre shook his head in disdain.

"We were given the gift of existing through the centuries. To experience more lifetimes than those poor, weak mortals could ever dream of experiencing. It is not a curse, Alexandre, it's a gift."

"Then I wish to hell they had never given it to me." His voice was a deep rumble of pain as it hung darkly on the night air.

Suzanne once again reached out to him and placed what was meant to be a comforting hand on his arm.

"Alexandre," she said, her tone one of tenderness and caring, "you're my brother, and I love you, but you have a duty to this family. I would take it over for you if I could, you know that, and you also know that's impossible." She sighed. "You have only a few years left until your five hundredth year, Alexandre, then it will be too late, and the decision will be made, like it or not, irreversible. You will no longer be able to procreate. You need a son, Alexandre." She smiled wistfully. "And this family needs an heir, a link to the future beyond our time, a continuance of us." Her fingers squeezed gently down on his arm. "Think of it, Alexandre. It would be good to have a child around."

A child. The words brought forth an image in his mind that nearly tore him apart. His and Rachel's child, a beautiful son with his mother's brilliant green eyes and sun-touched hair. And his father's thirst for blood.

Chapter 24

Rachel pulled open the tall doors of Yvette's armoire and stared in shock at her previous carelessness. She had not searched it before having assumed it was merely a closet. Now she saw her mistake. Only one half of the tall wardrobe was for hanging clothes. The other side had a rack for hanging blouses on the top, with four drawers beneath.

"Stupid, Rachel," she muttered to herself, "stupid, stupid, stupid." She quickly pulled open the first drawer. It was filled with lingerie. Rachel rummaged through the silk and lacey underthings, not caring whether or not she made it obvious that it had been searched. She slammed the drawer shut and opened the next. Hair brushes, hand mirrors, jewelry. She yanked open the third drawer. It was filled with carefully folded sweaters. Very *expensive* carefully folded sweaters. She slipped her hand hastily between the sweaters. Nothing. She yanked out the fourth drawer, feeling desperate now.

A small, inlaid wooden box sat in the drawer. She picked it up and opened its lid.

"Oh, my God." Rachel stared at a small, solid gold scorpion that lay amid a tangle of other jewelry. Lifting it out carefully she held it before her. The scorpion, she and Steven's birth sign, dangling from its serpentine gold chain. It was Steven's. She knew that without question. Her heart raced with both fear and excitement. Their mother had given them each a piece of jewelry for their birthday, the year before she'd passed away. Steven's gift had been the scorpion and chain. Rachel's had been her mother's engagement ring. She glanced down at her right hand where she wore the ring.

Her mind whirled with questions and confusion. What was going on? What had they done with Steven? And why?

Her hands began to shake violently. So much so that she nearly dropped the jewelry box. Rachel placed it back into the drawer where she'd found it and quickly went over each drawer to make sure it was not apparent she had been into them. She was frightened now and suddenly felt it was imperative that the Beaumondiers not realize she was suspicious of them.

Yvette had lied. They'd all lied. Steven was here, on *Sans Souci* plantation somewhere. Somehow Yvette had enticed him here. Rachel nearly groaned. A beautiful woman, especially one as beautiful as Yvette, wouldn't have had to do much enticing to get Steven to follow her to the ends of the earth. But why? What was the purpose of getting him out here, of leaving such a clear path, and allowing Rachel to follow it? Even to the point of inviting her to stay at the plantation?

A sudden shiver, like rippling ice, tripped up her spine. Had that been their purpose all along? To get *her* to *Sans Souci?* Memory of the painting she'd found in the attic, the portrait of the long-deceased Danielle Toutant flashed into her mind. Danielle had been the half-sister of Rachel and Steven's ancestor. But what did that have to do with them today, in 1994? How could a relationship that tied the families together two hundred years ago have any connection, any bearing, on what was happening now?

Inheritance? Was there something about the Beaumondier monies against which the Ligeres posed a threat?

Rachel hurriedly searched the remainder of Yvette's room, all the while her mind buzzing with more and more questions. Had they wanted her here because of who she was, or because she looked so much like Danielle? But why? For what purpose? What did it matter now . . . two hundred years after the woman's death?

She turned from Yvette's writing desk and moved to her dressing table. A box, its lid an intricate design of inlaid lemon, mahogany and cherry woods, sat on the table's surface. Rachel opened it. It was another jewelry box. A cameo brooch lay nestled atop the coiled strands of a pearl necklace. She stared at it, suddenly struck with memory of Danielle's body lying in the long secret cellar room beneath the old house. Or had it been secret? Did they *all* know about the room? About the woman who had been buried there? Obviously alive?

"Damn it," Rachel cursed, "what the hell is going on in this place?"

The center drawer of the dressing table was locked. Rachel smiled. She rummaged in one of the other drawers until she found a hairpin. She straightened it and slipped one end of it into the lock. Several long seconds later she was still jiggling the hair pin and cursing under her breath. It had been a long time since Marc had taught her how to jimmey a lock. She hadn't had any reason to use that particular talent since leaving the police force, and she was rusty. She felt the pin suddenly slip into place. Rachel turned it carefully and pulled the drawer open. She rummaged through it quickly. It was getting late and Yvette and the others could return any time now. She was about to close the drawer again, having found nothing for her trouble, when she paused. Why was the drawer front so deep and the inside of the drawer so shallow. Rachel stood and yanked the drawer from its rails.

"A false bottom," she muttered, as she rapped her knuckle rapped against the thin board.

Emptying the drawer's contents onto the bed Rachel quickly pried the false bottom loose and tossed it beside the array of cosmetics, jewelry and brushes on the bed.

She stared at the drawer's last remaining item—a small book, its leatherbound cover cracked and faded with age. The initials DT were engraved across the cover in a flowing script of inlaid gold to match the edges of the thin, round-cornered pages. Rachel picked it up carefully, almost reverently, knowing immediately that it was Danielle's diary. It could be nothing else.

Having lost all sense of caution now, all sense of haste and heed, Rachel sat down on the red velvet cushion of a nearby ladies' chair and opened the diary. The script was a swirl of flowing lines and curls, the first few pages a description of Danielle's voyage from France to Louisiana.

The end, Rachel thought, turn to the end. She flipped the pages of the diary forward.

I know she'll never let me out of here. This is to be my tomb, shared with these other poor, wretched souls that were put in here before me.

Rachel remembered the skeletons of the men that lay against one wall of the cellar room.

How could I have been so foolish? I recognized the hatred in her eyes that night she came to my room. I heard the contempt in her voice that she held for me, and yet I witlessly drank the warm milk she had brought, and sealed my own fate.

Rachel gasped and her fingers trembled as they

turned the page. Danielle had been drugged. But who had done it? Not Alexandre, her fiancé. She kept referring to a woman.

I should not have let them see my horror, my fear, when confronted with the truth. But I couldn't help it. How could I have thought to love such a . . . thing?

Thing? Rachel's mind buzzed in confusion. What did Danielle mean by "thing?" Was she referring to her fiancé? That long-ago Alexandre Beaumondier? Had he done something in his past that she found so repulsive? Rachel flipped the page and read on.

How could I have been so deceived that I could not have seen the monster of his real self within those gray blue eyes I had once thought so warm and loving? That I did not sense the atrocity, the evil, that he truly is whenever he touched me?

Rachel shuddered. "My God," she whispered, "what had he done?"

I should have pretended to still care for him, if only to escape them. Ah, but there really is no escape from them, and anyway, even if there were, it is too late now. I will die so that their secret will be protected. I can only pray to God that they do not come to me and drain me of my soul as they obviously did to the others who did not recognize them for the monsters they truly are.

Several sentences were blurred by what had obviously been Danielle's tears of despair. Rachel skipped further down on the page until she was able to read the writing again.

I wonder how many other poor wretches the Beaumondiers have preyed upon in the past? And how many will die by their hands in the future? If only I had been brave enough to have tried to find a way to stop them—rather than run away from them. But it is too late now. I can only pray that my dear sister and parents do not come to Sans Souci *in search of me, and that someone, someday, will have the strength and courage to destroy the Beaumondiers, and the Devil who spawned them.*

Rachel stared at the written words, more puzzled now than before she'd read them. What in heaven's name could that Alexandre have done that was so terrible? Had he murdered or raped someone? And then confessed it to his intended bride? She shook her head in confusion. Even if that were the case, why had Danielle condemned all of the Beaumondiers? Written them all off as evil? Were they a family of murderers?

She closed the book and lay it in her lap as she went over and over in her mind what she had read, trying to make some sense of it. Suddenly she became aware of a noise in the room, soft and steady, like the sound of a motor running. Rachel looked around quickly and then, as she began to rise, her foot moved against something warm and furry. She looked down.

"Asmodeus, how did you get in here?"

The cat, curled at her feet, lifted his head and looked up at her.

"Followed me, huh?" she said, and smiled. "Well, as long as it's just you who followed me." She bent quickly and stroked the cat's head several times, then turned back to the dressing table and hastily put the drawer and all of its contents, including the diary, back together and in place.

Rachel paused at the door to the hall and looked back over her shoulder. "Come on, kitty," she said.

Asmodeus immediately rose to his feet and padded across the carpeted floor toward her.

Once she'd closed Yvette's door and moved away from it, Rachel knelt before the cat and scratched beneath his chin with her forefinger.

He immediately began to purr again.

"I'm going out now, handsome," she whispered, "so you go find yourself a corner to curl up in, okay?"

Asmodeus meowed, as if in answer.

"Good." Rachel stood. She had done all she could in the house. Even if there were more clues around that proved Steven was here, she didn't need them. What she needed to do now was find him. She walked rapidly toward her own room. It took only a few seconds to retrieve the gun Marc had given her and check to make sure the clip was securely in place. She slipped it into her pocket. It was a bit bulky, but gave her a better sense of security. She hurried to the main staircase.

Steven had been enticed to *Sans Souci*, and it was obvious now, at least to her, that she had been, too. But why? The question hammered at her brain.

She reached into her pocket to retrieve the transmitter and then remembered that Marc was off following Yvette and Suzanne to town and was then going to the hospital. Even if he'd radioed someone to take his place, they probably wouldn't have arrived yet. She flipped the radio on anyway. "Anyone there?"

Silence met her ears.

She had no backup. A tickle of uneasiness swept over her and she shrugged it away. The women had gone to town. Catherine was asleep, and Hanson was too old and decrepit to be of any real threat. That left only Alexandre.

She felt a tug at her heartstrings. Alexandre. She didn't want to believe that he was a threat. Not to her. He was warm and loving. Sensitive. Caring. Gentle. She remembered the ecstasy that had come over her when he'd held her in his arms, the rapture that had enveloped her as his lips had claimed hers, and the love she'd felt from him when he'd made love to her.

But he had avoided her since that night. Choking back the tears of pain and summoning the fires of rage that would keep them at bay, Rachel grabbed onto the railing and hurriedly descended the wide, curving staircase.

And he had known about Steven. Alexandre had known that Steven was here, on *Sans Souci*, somewhere, and he hadn't told her. He'd pretended innocence, feigned ignorance of what was happening . . . and he had known.

"Damn you, Alexandre," Rachel whispered. "Damn you and your precious family all to Hell."

"Rachel! Rachel, help me!"

Rachel stopped abruptly, one hand on the doorjamb, the other on the edge of the opened entry door. "Steven?"

"Rachel!"

His voice in her mind seemed stronger than the time before, the words more definite. She stepped onto the dark gallery and closed her eyes, centering all of her concentration on her brother. "Steven," she said softly, blocking out the sounds of the night around her, "Steven, can you hear me?"

"Rachel, help me! Please."

"I will, Steven, I will. I promise." She descended the fan-shaped stairs to the entry path and paused again. "Steven? Steven, keep calling to me. Steven?"

She heard him sob, a low, gut-wrenching cry that nearly tore her heart in half.

"Steven?" she cried, suddenly consumed with fear. "Steven?"

"Rachel," he moaned softly, *"Rachel, please help me."*

He sensed she was near, but he couldn't *hear* her. She knew that now by the way he cried to her, but didn't actually answer her. Her psychic abilities had always been stronger. But then she had always been the one to pay attention to them, even attempting to hone them.

Steven had always scoffed, claiming they were more trouble than they were worth.

Watchdog. That's what he'd always called Rachel. His watchdog, because she always seemed to know when he was doing something he shouldn't be doing.

Rachel turned toward the gardens, suddenly sensing that it was the correct direction to take. She pulled the transmitter from her pocket and flipped it on. Maybe he wasn't out of range yet. "Marc? Marc, can you hear me? Is anyone there?"

Static. She dropped the radio back into her pocket and hurried through the garden. Moonlight turned it to a landscape of shining, iridescent surfaces. But even as the overgrown bushes and trees had been transformed by the moon's glow to a scattering of glistening jewels, the draping curtains of Spanish moss that hung from the oaks' gnarled branches now resembled shrouds of funereal crepe, the shadows beneath the big trees alcoves of fathomless blackness, uninviting and unfriendly.

Rachel broke from the garden into the meadow of wild grass that bordered its other boundary. The night's glow had turned the dead, dried wild grass to a blanket of soft saffron, She raised a hand to her pocket and pressured it against the soft linen of her white slacks to reassure herself once again that her gun was safely tucked within her pocket. Taking a deep breath she began to walk across the meadow. She had searched through the outbuildings that were near the house—the old slave cabins, the carriage house, barn, stables and pigeonierre. There had been no sign that Steven had been in any of them, no sense of him there, either present or past. But there were buildings along the far borders of the plantation that she hadn't had time to check yet.

"He has to be in one of those," Rachel muttered to herself. "He has to be."

Her foot struck something hard and it skittered across the grass a few inches. She moved toward it and stared at the object that was half-covered by weeds. Moonlight glistened off of its dark metal barrel. Rachel bent down and picked up the gun, thinking it was the one she had lost days before. Her fingers curled around the handle and she knew immediately that it wasn't her gun. She rose, holding it before her. It was Marc's gun.

"But how?"

She looked around. There was no sign of anyone else in the meadow. A shiver of dread crept over her, invading the tenuous hold she had on her nerves. Fear settled in a tightly coiled knot in the pit of her stomach, ready to explode, to consume her, at the slightest provocation.

Rachel held the .45 Luger up to the moonlight and pulled out its carriage. It was fully-loaded. She slammed back the chamber cover. A bullet was lodged in the barrel, waiting to be fired. She sniffed the end of the barrel. It hadn't been fired recently.

The fear began to creep outward. Rachel felt herself tremble.

Marc was here, somewhere. He hadn't gone to town. Something, someone, had led him away from the car, into this meadow. But why? What had happened? How had he lost his gun? And without even firing it?

She looked around the meadow again, and took several steps in each direction, expecting to see Marc lying hurt somewhere, and seeing nothing but dried, dead grass.

Emotion clogged her throat and she swallowed hard. God, what was happening?

She began to move forward again. The hem of one pantleg caught on a twig. It snapped against her ankle. Rachel paused and reached down to tear it away. Her fingers came away from the small piece of branch covered with smears of blood.

Terror clutched at her heart, its gnarled, cold fingers squeezing cruelly and near robbing her of breath. She stared at the crimson streaks on her fingers.

"Rachel!"

Steven's cry snapped her from her moment of despair. Her eyes darted from her blood-stained fingers to the distant horizon. "Steven?" She ran across the meadow, toward a thick copse of trees at its other end. His cries were coming from there, she felt certain now.

Alexandre felt the coolness of the night caress his face as he let himself become lost within the blackness of its landscape. Nothing could hurt him now. He was invisible against the night, at one with the darkness, and at peace. Only cradled within the night's womb, feeling it envelop him, welcome him, embrace him, did he feel any semblance of peace and freedom.

Alexandre stretched his arms wide and closed his eyes, letting the wind whip past and envelop him. He felt the wispy chill of a cloud on his cheeks and smiled.

If the creators of *Les Chasseurs* had given him merely the ability to just enjoy the naturalness of the earth, if they had given him that, and only that, he would have been satisfied. He might even have been happy. But along with their curse of immortality or at least an existence of fifteen or sixteen times that of normal humans, they had bestowed upon their children, their creations, the need to destroy others in order to survive. For the first few years of his existence, in France, and after moving to Louisiana, Alexandre had given the killing little thought. It had been a natural thing to do, an instinctive thing, and he'd done it. Without conscience or regard for his victims, or their families, if they'd had any. Not until he'd seen the horror in Danielle's eyes that night, heard the terror and disgust in her voice when he'd told her the truth about himself, had he really thought about what he was. And when he had, when he had seen himself through her eyes, he had understood the disdain she'd felt, the horror and revulsion they all felt toward them.

Rachel suddenly stopped. Something was moving along the line of trees in the distance. She squinted, trying to see more clearly through the dark, but it was no use. Whatever or whoever it was had only appeared visible to her because of the light clothing they wore. Rachel crouched instantly, realizing that she too had on light clothing and so must also be visible to whomever she was watching.

She released the safety on Marc's gun and checked the chamber again to reassure herself the weapon was ready to be fired.

The person in the distance seemed to rise above the ground, floating. After a few moments' puzzlement, Rachel concluded they were climbing the stairs of a building. She crept forward, slowly.

"Rachel! Rachel, help me!"

Steven's scream slammed into her mind like the burst of a cannon against her ear. He had been afraid before. Now he was terrorstruck.

Rachel bolted to her feet and began to run.

Chapter 25

Rachel gasped for breath and her heart pounded against her breast, hard thuds that echoed in her ears. She hadn't run for months. Longer. She was out of shape.

Her legs strained to keep moving. She held Marc's gun gripped tightly within the grasp of her right hand, finger on the trigger, ready to pull it without a moment's hesitation. Her eyes stung.

Whoever had been moving about the copse of trees had disappeared.

"Rachel!"

Steven's cries gave her the impetous to continue, even though her body wanted to collapse. She forced herself to ignore the pain of her muscles, the ache of inactivity.

The outline of a building began to take form on the horizon. Steven was in there. She knew it with a certainty that was unexplainable, but absolute. Rachel had no account for why she hadn't known this before and did now, but it didn't matter. Her brother was in there, held prisoner somehow, and he needed her.

"Steven," she screamed, gasping for breath as his name on her lips robbed her of the air in her lungs. "Steven." She pushed her legs for more speed.

* * *

"What do you mean she's not in her room?" Marguerite demanded, her tone one of angry agitation. She stared at Hanson, waiting for him to answer.

"I looked. Thoroughly," the old man said, his own gaze defiantly meeting Marguerite's and challenging her to strike out at him. "She's not there."

For a long, silent minute, gray-blue eyes glared into ancient blue, but neither moved nor gave their ground.

Finally Marguerite tore her gaze from the old butler's. "I swear, Hanson, if Catherine didn't depend on you so much I think I'd destroy you."

He laughed then, the act turning his wizened old face young again. "And if you weren't her daughter, Margie," he sneered, employing the hated nickname, "I might destroy you."

Marguerite turned to glare at him. "Be careful, Hanson. Remember, one of these days my dear mother will be gone."

"One of these days we'll all be gone, Margie." He chuckled again. "You absolutely hate it that Catherine gave me the 'gift', don't you, Margie?"

"Transmutation never works well, Hanson. My husband and Yvette's were proof of that. And the only reason Catherine brought you over was so that you could take care of her. Don't forget that."

"And don't you forget, dear Margie, that I have the same powers as you." His look dared her to challenge him farther.

Marguerite sniffed and turned away. When her mother had first brought Hanson over, against everyone's objections, it was because she'd loved him. Now, the romance, along with their youth, had long since faded away, but not their love. And Catherine needed him now more than ever. She was incapable of hunting for herself. Her limbs were too feeble, her energy level too fleeting. So Hanson did the work for her, and then let her take her nourishment from him.

He also took care of Alexandre, finding and killing the animals whose life force kept him alive.

"If Rachel isn't in her room then she must be somewhere else in the house," she snapped finally, and turned to look around the empty parlor. "Did you look in the other rooms?"

"I looked. Miss Rachel is not in the house."

Marguerite whirled on him. "She has to be," she shrieked. "Where else would she be at this hour." Her eyes darted to the clock on the mantel. "It's nearly midnight. She wouldn't go wandering about the grounds this late. She's in this house somewhere. Probably snooping."

Hanson merely stared at her, offering no comment.

Marguerite huffed and stalked toward the entry door. "That stupid girl," she mumbled. "She's just like the other one. A fool. Why doesn't she just make it easy on all of us and accept the inevitable?"

"She is mortal," Hanson said.

Marguerite whirled around. "Yes, unfortunately she is." A sly smile curved her lips. "But not for long." She chuckled softly. "She will either do as we wish, or she'll die. Just like Danielle."

"You would not make her one of us?"

"No."

"If you kill this one," Hanson said, "there will not be time to find another."

Marguerite's cheeks flared with color as her temper raged out of control. "Don't you think I know that, old man?" she snipped. "But we may not have a choice.

Not if she goes flying into a tizzy like that other one did."

"We don't have to tell her the truth."

"No, we don't. And I for one do not intend to, but that doesn't mean that Alexandre won't, just like he did before. What I do intend, however, is for my handsome grandson to perform his duty and be done with it, whether Rachel knows or not." Marguerite walked toward the stairs and, with a hand on the newell post, looked up to the second floor landing. After several long moments, she glanced back at Hanson. "You're certain she's not in the house?"

"Yes."

"Then she's prowling around on the grounds." Marguerite stormed toward the entry door. "Well, at least I know she's not meeting with her police officer friend." She chuckled softly, an evil, ugly little sound that echoed throughout the empty foyer. "I do know that."

Marguerite stepped out onto the gallery, spread her arms wide, closed her eyes and, allowing her weight to fall forward, let herself meld with the night. Within seconds she felt the freedom of transformation.

The air was a little too cool for her tastes tonight, the sky filled with too many wisps of clouds that left her flesh chilled. She looked down at the meadow and spotted Rachel instantly, her white slacks and pale green blouse a striking contrast to the darkness.

Marguerite swooped downward. Within seconds she was running behind Rachel, the Venetian silk of her own blue gown whipping about her legs in delicate billows, her dark hair falling loose from its neat chignon and flying out behind her in a tangle of black strands. She could have easily struck Rachel down moments ago, without transformation, without giving chase, but she didn't really want to harm the girl, not if she could help it. They needed her . . . for Alexandre. Otherwise, everything would be lost. It would be the end of them.

"Rachel," Marguerite called. "Rachel, wait."

Rachel heard her name and glanced over her shoulder, though she didn't stop running. Marguerite! She tried to hasten her step. Instinct told her to keep running. Not to stop. Not to trust the woman behind her. *"Rachel!"*

She couldn't answer him. She didn't have the strength. All of her concentration now was on her own body. On forcing it to keep moving. It was the only way she could get to him. Could help him. She gasped for breath and shut her mind off to the pain of her muscles.

"Rachel, stop!" Marguerite called. "What's wrong? Let me help you." She moved faster, beginning to wonder if it had been a mistake not attacking the girl before. "Rachel, where are you going?"

Rachel ignored her. She had to get to Steven, and she had no doubt Marguerite knew exactly where she was going, and why. If she slowed, if she faltered, Marguerite would overtake her and Steven would be lost. Perhaps even herself.

She threw a quick glance over her shoulder. Just enough to allow her to see where Marguerite was. Fear, cold, stark and consuming flared within her breast. The woman was gaining on her. She was nearly twice the age of Rachel, and they were both running full out, yet Marguerite was now almost close enough to reach out and grab her.

Rachel tried to run faster, but her legs could not obey the desperate command. Tears stung at her eyes as hopelessness began to fill her heart. She wasn't going to make it. "Alexandre!" she screamed as loud as she could. "Alexandre, help me!"

A sneer of satisfaction curved Marguerite's lips and

sparked from her eyes. The girl thought she was summoning help. Marguerite almost laughed aloud. Alexandre might foolishly loathe what he was, might wish he were mortal, with all their frailties and weaknesses, but he would not desert his family, nor turn against them. He would hate it, condemn it, but she had no doubt that in the end, he would do what was expected of him, what was his duty.

The girl wouldn't accept the truth, Marguerite was certain of that now. No more than Danielle had. But this time they would not make the same mistake. This time they would wait. If she threatened Alexandre, told him she would kill the girl if he didn't cooperate, she had no doubt he would acquiesce. They would mollify her, placate her, lie to her, until the baby came. Then they would be rid of her if she didn't accept the truth. But it would work only if Marguerite could detour her from the old mill. A parade of curses sped through Marguerite's mind. Why hadn't she insisted that Yvette kill Steven earlier? Why had she let Yvette toy with him? If Rachel reached the mill, if she found her brother, all would be lost . . . again.

Alexandre heard the faint echo of his name on the still night air. He grimaced. Even now, when he knew it was impossible, he heard her. His heart twisted in agony. Would his mind always be infused with the sound of her voice? His nostrils filled with the sweet, musky scent of her flesh? Would his arms forever ache to hold her within their embrace? His hands yearn to slide over the subtle curves of her body?

A small, almost inaudible moan escaped Alexandre's throat and his eyes filled with tears. Would he never be able to forget the passion she had aroused within him?

The love that she had awakened in his heart? Was he doomed not only to go through the years bearing the curse of being a *Chasseur,* a hunter, but also the ache of knowing love, and losing it?

He turned away, delving into the midst of a passing cloud, reveling in its chilling fog.

But it was better this way, he told himself. She had allowed him to make love to her, and all the while she'd had someone else, someone she cared for, someone of her own kind. Alexandre felt a great rending deep in his heart. It was better this way, he thought again, trying to convince himself. Marc Dellos was Rachel's kind. He could give her all of the things Alexandre could not; normal life and normal children. She could walk proudly beside him down the streets of the *Vieux Carre,* with their children, beneath a full, blazing sun, and never have to worry about the evil of Alexandre's world, never have to face and endure its ugliness.

Tears slid down his cheeks. Yes, it was better this way. In less than seven years he would face his five hundredth year, and then at least part of it would be over. There would be no more squabbling about his decision not to procreate, no more bickering and nagging from his family. It would be too late. His seed would be useless. They would be disappointed, he knew. Even outraged. But they would get over it. They'd have to. They would have no choice. And eventually, as the centuries passed, the Beaumondiers would come to their end. They would, each in their own time, finally cease to exist.

A sad smile tugged at the corners of his lips. Fifteen hundred years. That's what Catherine had told him. Fifteen hundred years was the longest any of them had ever survived. She was nearing it now.

A soft, barely perceptible sigh slipped from between his lips. If only he could trade places with her.

"Alexandre!" Rachel screamed again. She didn't know why she was calling for him. Hadn't everything she'd discovered pointed to the fact that he was a part of this scheme? Whatever horror his family had devised against the Ligeres? She glanced back over her shoulder at Marguerite. Rachel couldn't believe it, the woman was gaining ground on her. She looked back at the rotting building she was running toward. It was made of stone, and as she neared she could see that mortar had fallen away in large chunks about the building's corners. Its roof sagged, its stairs looked rickety and unsafe. Shutters were closed tightly over all but one window and half of its chimney had crumbled and fallen away long ago. To one side, a huge wheel stood motionless, its water paddles long ago having rotted away.

"Rachel!"

Steven's cry created a surge of energy within her, giving her the impetous for more speed.

"Rachel!" Marguerite shrieked. What she wanted now was nothing more than to stop the other woman from reaching the mill. Marguerite reached out. Her fingers grasped the back of the collar of Rachel's blouse, her fingernails scratching across Rachel's flesh.

Rachel flinched away. "No," she screamed. "No." She jerked free of Marguerite.

Marguerite smiled. "You can't get away, you know. No one can save you now."

Rachel stood defiant, but her insides winced in horror as she saw the malice and pure evil that sparked within the gray-blue eyes. She stood a step back.

Marguerite closed the space.

* * *

Alexandre turned toward the river and the old mill. Tonight the solitude of the sky offered him no real peace of mind.

"Alexandre!" Rachel screamed, as Marguerite reached for her.

His name echoed on the still bayou night, wafting over the cool, glistening waters, weaving in amongst the thickly growing cypress and wide spreading live oaks, and drifting out across the fallow, weed-choked meadows. Alexandre jerked from the reverie of his own self-pity. Her voice. It was no memory, no illusion haunting his thoughts and desires. He scanned the earth below him, searching, feeling a sudden desperation in his heart that was both unexplainable and terrifying. She was in trouble. Rachel was in trouble. Instinct, and the terror in her voice told him that. Rachel was in trouble and she needed him, was calling out to him.

Then he spotted them, arms locked, bodies writhing as they struggled against one another in the center of the meadow that lay between the gardens and the old mill.

"Marguerite." The name of his grandmother slid off his tongue as more a hateful hiss than a word. He didn't know what had provoked her to attack Rachel, any more than he knew how his family had found her, the one woman on the face of the earth who looked like Danielle, but at the moment he didn't care. All that concerned him, all that filled both his mind and his heart, was that the woman he loved, the woman that meant more to him than anyone ever had, was in danger.

* * *

The women felt the shadow soar over them, but both were too caught up in their struggle against the other to pay heed.

Rachel raised one arm to ward off a blow from Marguerite. But rather than a smashing impact, she felt Marguerite's fingers, like bands of steel, cold, and strong, clasp tightly around her wrist. She tried to jerk her arm free, tried to pull away from the older woman, struggled with a frenzy born of desperation, but found the grasp an unbreakable one.

Mindlessly screaming Alexandre's name, the sound rushing from her throat and from her lips with no conscious thought or effort from Rachel, she thrashed out at Marguerite with her other hand, her legs, and her feet.

A malevolent laugh spit from Marguerite's lips as she caught Rachel's other wrist and held both raised high above their heads. "Now it is over, Rachel," Marguerite said, and laughed again. "You won't just accept it, as we'd hoped, so I have no choice now." She began to lower her head toward Rachel's neck.

Rachel twisted and kicked out.

"Marguerite," Alexandre said. "Let her go."

Marguerite, startled at both his command and sudden presence, jerked away from Rachel and spun around to face her grandson. "Alexandre," she said on a rush of breath. She stared at him, a fierce glare in her eyes. "It has to be done, Alexandre. You know that. She won't accept it, and we can't let her leave."

"Like you couldn't let Danielle leave?" he asked quietly.

"Rachel, help me! Help me!"

Steven's cry slammed against her brain, desperate and full of terror and panic. "Steven." Her eyes met Alexandre's. Whatever he was, whatever he had done, he had come to help her. She spun on her heel and ran toward the mill.

"No," Marguerite screamed. She lunged toward Rachel.

Alexandre grabbed Marguerite's arm and spun her back around to face him. "What have you done?" he thundered.

A vicious snarl rumbled deep within Marguerite's throat. "You fool," she said, the words full of loathing and disgust. "You were our only hope of survival, Alexandre, our only hope of this family's continuance, and you ruined it. Twice. They could have given us the child we need to survive."

Before he knew what she intended, her arm swooped upward and then swung down with savage force. Her hand slammed against his cheek with a resounding crack.

Alexandre staggered backward from the blow, reeling more from the shock and unexpectedness of it than the impact. He grabbed Marguerite's arm and yanked her toward him. Holding her against him, he looked down at her, his gaze, hard, cold, and unfathomable. "What did you do, Marguerite?" he demanded again, his tone one of abhorrence and scorn. "Tell me, damn you. What did you do to bring this about?"

She stared up at him defiantly, rancor etched in every line of her once beautiful face. "What you didn't have the courage to do, Alexandre." She tried to jerk away from him and failed. "Danielle would have told the world about us, what we are. And it would have been like France all over again. We would have had to flee. She would have watched us burn in Hell."

"And so you killed her?" He felt his senses reel. Even though he had suspected, had, in his heart known, he still felt shaken by the confirmation. "You killed her so we wouldn't have to leave *Sans Souci?*"

"Yes, I killed her," Marguerite said in smug satisfaction. "So that we could go on without worry. And I'll kill this one, too." She jerked away from Alexandre's hold, weakened as memory of Danielle, of her fragility and beauty, her innocence, swept through and overtook his mind.

Marguerite turned and began to run after Rachel, who was nearly to the old mill.

With a groan of anguish, the sound ripped from deep within his chest, Alexandre swooped down atop Marguerite. She fell to the ground beneath his weight, twisted, and began to thrash at him, writhing savagely, screaming and clawing out at him.

Chapter 26

Rachel slammed against the rock and mortar of the old mill's outer wall, her outstretched hands taking the brunt of the collision. Her body sagged momentarily against the cold, hard surface. She gasped for breath and forced her trembling legs to move again, and staggered up the stairs until she stood only inches from the one window that was not covered by shutters. She dropped a hand into her pocket, her fingers prepared to grip the handle of her gun, but there was nothing there. Her head jerked down, and her gaze focused on the torn material at her hip.

The struggle with Marguerite. She had lost her gun. "No, no, no," she whimpered, feeling suddenly overcome by a wave of utter despair. "Not again. Please God, not again." How could she fight them now? How could she save Steven if she had no way to defend herself? To defend him?

She moved to turn, to look through the grime-covered old window, and as she did, a tiny spark within the meadow weeds caught her eye. Rachel stared at it, afraid to even hope.

"Rachel!"

She froze. Steven's cry was no longer merely within her

mind. This time she had heard it with her ears. Rachel jerked around and stared up at the half-opened door that was only a few steps away. The stairs were rotten, dried, shrunk and splintered by the passing of time. She glanced back at the reflection in the weeds below. Indecision gnawed at her, but only for a split second. Without the gun, without its power, she was nearly helpless. If there was a chance it was the .22, she had to take it. Pushing away from the wall she hurried back down the steps, unmindful now of being quiet or cautious. She stumbled on the last step and fell to one knee. Her hands slammed cruelly down onto the hard, unplowed earth. The breath left her lungs in a rush of air and she gasped painfully in an effort to recapture it. A blinding whir of color swirled within her brain and dizziness blurred her eyes. She shook her head.

"Damn," Rachel cursed. Her mainly sedentary job at the Preservation Society had allowed her to get soft. She didn't work out the way she used to. Rachel took a deep breath and pushed herself hurriedly back to her feet and ran toward the glimmering object in the grass.

She skidded to her knees and groped at the ground. Her fingers rammed into metal, cold, hard, polished metal. It was the gun! Rachel scooped it up. Her hand wrapped naturally around the hard, plastic handle. Her thumb moved instinctively to rest atop the hammer as her forefinger curled from habit around the slender, curved trigger.

She heard a high-pitched scream. Her head jerked up as fear gripped her heart and sent a shiver through her body. But it wasn't Steven who'd screamed this time. It was Marguerite, and it wasn't a scream so much as a shriek of rage. Rachel watched as the older woman strugged against Alexandre, slashing out at him with her nails, kicking, hissing, writhing within his hold. His hands gripped her upper arms as he wrested to hold her away from him, but she keep thrashing, kicking and lunging, twisting her body in a frenzy, even throwing her head forward and attempting to bite him.

Tearing her gaze from them, forcing her mind to turn its attention on Steven and away from the question of why this was happening, Rachel stumbled to her feet and ran toward the mill house. Once again she made her way carefully, but hastily up the half-broken staircase until she reached the window. With the gun in her hand, her finger steady on the trigger, every nerve in her body taut with tension, Rachel moved slowly sideways until she was able to peer around the wooden frame of the mill's old window.

Disbelief suddenly overtook her mind. Terror curled its icy fingers around her heart and began to squeeze unmercifully. Horror gripped the pit of her stomach and turned it upside down, and panic threatened to overwhelm her.

The second story interior of the old mill house was nothing more than one large room. A lone candle, thick, stubby and white, sat wedged within a brass candle holder on a crudely built wooden table that was set to one side of the room. The flame on its wick danced wildly, touched by the faint breeze that slipped through the slats of the rotting shutters. Cobwebs hung from the rafters of the open beamed ceiling, and an array of rusting, rotting, wooden racks, wheel barrows, hand tools and crates littered the floor. But none of these things were what instilled such a dizzying sense of dread within Rachel, and none of these things were what held her attention so spellbound.

Halfway across the room stood a long wooden table, built high off the ground. It was covered by a filthy, stained and yellowed cloth or sheet that had half deteriorated with the passing of years and neglect, and lying atop it was her brother, Steven. His legs and arms were stretched tautly away from his body, spread-eagled, his ankles and wrists encircled by a thickly twined rope that was in turned pulled over the corner ends of the table and tied to the upper part of the table's legs. Impossible for him to move, or escape.

His shirt had been torn open, its front hanging at his sides in near shreds. Covering his chest, a chest that had once been muscular and golden, but was now almost nothing but skin and bone, were open wounds, some of which had dried over with thin, near translucent flesh, others still open and oozing blood.

Hovering over Steven was Yvette, her teeth buried deeply within the vein at his neck.

Rachel's finger tightened on the trigger of her gun. What in God's name had she done to him? She lifted a foot, cautiously, and placed it on the next stair, putting her weight on it slowly. The board creaked beneath the pressure of supporting her step.

Yvette heard the sound and became instantly alert. Her hands, one on Steven's arm, the other clutching at his ribcage, pressed down on his flesh. The long, red-painted nails that curved from the tips of each of her fingers dug into his skin and brought a new cry from his lips. Blood dripped from one corner of her mouth as her head snapped up at the sound and she looked toward the door. Fury at being disturbed blazed within her dark eyes.

"Rachel," Steven sobbed helplessly, the word barely a whimper on his lips. "Rachel, please," he cried again, and sobbed pitifully.

Rachel sucked in a sharp breath. Her heart nearly stopped its slamming beat within her breast at the realization of what she saw. She watched, frozen, both horrified and petrified as Yvette's glance moved slowly from the door to the window and finally fixed on her. Their eyes met and held in a riveting gaze, Yvette refusing to look away, pinning her with those blue gray eyes, and Rachel too afraid to look away, of what would happen if she did.

A low, snarling growl gurgled up from Yvette's throat and she pushed herself away from Steven. Her feet touched the floor as she slid from the table and straightened. She shook her head, causing the long tendrils of coal-colored hair to swish loosely around her shoulders.

Rachel took a step back and felt the stairs rickety wooden railing at her back. She moved a hand to grasp it, needing something, anything, to steady her trembling hands.

Yvette moved toward one end of the table upon which Steven lay. He was quiet now, but whether unconscious or dead, Rachel didn't know. She chanced a quick glance at him and felt her heart contract in alarm. His eyes were closed, and she couldn't tell if his chest moved with the intake of breath or not. Yvette rounded the corner of the table.

Rachel stabbed her with a stare. Instinct told her that she had to keep all of her attention on Yvette, not lower her guard for one second.

Yvette took a step sideways.

Rachel tensed in anticipation and her eyes shot back up to focus on Yvette's face. Her lips were curved in a smile, arrogant, sly, and malicious. She moved around the table slowly, each step one of careful deliberation, each move measured and calculated.

"Stop," Rachel ordered, and swung her arm up, pointing the gun toward the window, and Yvette on its opposite side.

Yvette laughed softly. "You mortals never learn, do

you?" she said smugly and stepped around in front of the table, momentarily blocking Rachel's view of her brother. "There is nothing you can do, Rachel. Can't you understand that? If you had cooperated perhaps things would have been different, in the end."

"Don't come any closer," Rachel said.

Yvette ignored the warning and continued to approach, slowly. "All we wanted, you see, all we've ever wanted, was a child, someone to carry on our line, to continue the Beaumondiers. You could have given us that, you know, and you might even have enjoyed it here at *Sans Souci*, with Alexandre."

Rachel felt her heart skip a beat at mention of Alexandre. Tears stung the back of her eyes as emotion clogged her throat and a painful ache took life within her stomach. She forced the thought of him away, the hurt she knew would come later, if there was a later.

Rachel's grip tightened around the gun handle. "But . . ." the word left her lips as little more than a croak. She struggled to speak. "But why Steven, Yvette?" she asked, her words little more than a whisper. "Why did you do . . ." she glanced toward her brother and felt a churning of nausea in her stomach at what Yvette had done to him. "Why did you do that to him? Hold him prisoner here? Torture him?"

Yvette threw her head back and laughed. "You stupid, stupid child. He was the only way we could get you here."

"But, why me? Why did you want me here?"

A snort of disgust snapped from her lips. "Because, dear Rachel, my spineless son was so . . ."

"Son?" Rachel echoed, confused now.

Amusement sparked in Yvette's eyes. "Of course. Alexandre is my son, Rachel."

"But . . . you're not old enough to have . . ."

Yvette laughed wickedly. "Oh, but I am. How old do you think I am, Rachel? Thirty-three? Thirty-six? Forty?" She tossed her head, sending the long curls of black hair sliding sensuously over her shoulders. "Try seven hundred and sixty, Rachel."

"Hundred?" Rachel repeated, stunned at the women's words. She was insane. Crazy with fantasy. Out of the corner of her eye Rachel caught a movement of Steven's leg. She looked back at Yvette. What she had just witnessed wasn't fantasy. Yvette sucking Steven's blood from his neck, torturing him relentlessly just to get Rachel here, that wasn't fantasy. It was insane, but it wasn't fantasy.

"Yes, Rachel," Yvette continued. "Seven hundred and sixty. Wouldn't you like to live that long, instead of the paltry sixty or so years your God has allotted you?" She laughed cruelly.

Rachel's mind spun in disbelief.

"But you ruined everything, Rachel. Just like Danielle did. I brought Steven here because I knew, after he told me about your little bond with each other, that little psychic link you two have, that his mental cries for help would eventually get through to you. And, good sister that you are, you'd come to help." A chuckle of self-satisfaction spewed from her lips at Rachel's shocked expression. "Oh yes, he told me all about it, and how you always bailed him out of his little troubles, how he could always count on you to hear him."

"But . . . why this?" Rachel croaked. "Why keep him like this once you had me here?"

"Because I needed you to stay here. I didn't want it to be like this Rachel. I needed you to fall in love with Alexandre. and for him to fall in love with you, and that takes time. I needed you to stay here, and the only way to accomplish that was for Steven to keep calling to you."

"But why?" Rachel repeated. "Why me?"

Yvette sighed, tiring of the explanations now. Her temper was rising at the fact that her plan had failed. "Alexandre was besotted with memories of Danielle, and so filled with guilt and grief over her that he wouldn't look at another woman. Do you know how long we've waited for him to get over her and on with things? How long I've waited for him to proliferate? To seed a woman with his child?"

Rachel stared at her, too dumbstruck to answer.

"Over four hundred years, Rachel," Yvette shrieked madly. "Four hundred years."

Rachel felt her mind whirl with the words Yvette had thrown at her. Four hundred years? No, this was impossible. Seven hundred years. Four hundred years. The woman was mad. She had to be. People didn't live that long. Rachel's gaze swept toward Steven again as her mind brought forth the memory of what she had seen only moments before. Unless they weren't . . . people, she thought.

"He was always so headstrong and carefree," Yvette went on. Her voice and words tore at Rachel. "And I loved that in him. My handsome, wonderful son."

"You're crazy," Rachel whispered.

"Crazy?" Yvette's brows soared as her keen hearing picked up the words Rachel had barely muttered. She smiled. "No, my dear, I am not crazy. I am merely a mother who wants to have a grandchild, just like any other mother."

Steven stirred behind Yvette. Rachel heard him moan and glanced toward him again. Impossible. The word echoed within her mind. The woman was mad, that was all. Mad. She was acting out some sort of weird fantasy.

Rachel looked back at Yvette, and as she did, memory of all the other inconsistencies, the other inexplicable and unusual things about *Sans Souci* and its inhabitants whirred in her mind. Was it possible after all? What kind of world had Steven stumbled into? What had she followed him into?

"And then *she* came along," Yvette said. "Danielle." The word was slung from her lips like the discarding of filth from one's hand. "And she ruined everything. First she got him to fall in love with her, and then she denounced him, denounced us, and threatened to reveal our secret to everyone. She should have known once she knew our secret that there was no turning back, that I couldn't allow her to tell anyone, or leave *Sans Souci.* She was a fool."

Yvette took a step toward her. Rachel grasped the railing at her back and lifted her other hand to point the gun at Yvette. "Stay back," she ordered, "or I'll shoot."

Yvette laughed, a deep throated, manical laugh that echoed through the immense interior of the mill house. "Shoot?" She laughed again. "By all means, Rachel, shoot." She took another step forward.

"Rachel, no," Steven croaked weakly. "No."

Rachel heard him, but didn't dare look toward him, could not chance taking her eyes off Yvette, not even for a split second. "I mean it, Yvette," she warned. "Don't come any closer or I'll shoot."

"Oh, I have no doubt you mean it, *chère,*" Yvette said, her lips curved in a malicious and arrogant smile. "And you must have no doubt that I mean to make you one of us. I should have done it before, in spite of what the family agreed. But," she shrugged, "now it's a necessity, and it will solve all of our problems." She took another step toward Rachel.

Rachel's finger pressed down on the trigger, slow,

steady, evenly. She still wasn't sure what Yvette meant by "one of us," and she didn't intend to find out. A blast of sound exploded from the .22 as the gun's hammer slammed against a bullet and propelled it from its chamber and through the short barrel. The weapon's kick vibrated against Rachel's hand and up her arm, but she held her aim steady, ready to fire again if necessary.

The bullet ripped through Yvette's upper left shoulder, just below her collarbone. The impact caused her to pause and stagger. Her shoulder jerked slightly backward, but no blood appeared on the threads of her blouse. Only the jagged, burnt edges of cloth around the bullet hole evidenced that the woman had even been shot.

Rachel stared, ready . . . waiting, and disbelieving. She was using only a .22, yes, but the bullets were hollow point Stingers. They shattered upon impact. Though she hadn't aimed to kill, and the wound wouldn't have been a lethal one, it should have stopped Yvette in her tracks. It would have stopped a man twice as large as Yvette.

"Rachel . . . you . . . can't." Steven gasped.

Yvette straightened and smiled at Rachel, her eyes gleaming with animosity, her smile emanating pure hatred. She took another step toward Rachel, the smile widening, daring, challenging.

"Yvette, don't," Rachel warned.

She began to take another step.

Rachel fired again, and again, and again.

One bullet struck Yvette's arm, another her breast, and yet another her chest. She staggered backward, nearly lost her balance, and then caught it, straightened, and turned back toward Rachel. "Are you through now?" she asked haughtily.

"Rachel . . . you can't . . . kill her," Steven choked weakly. "You can't."

Rachel fired once more, then a second time, a third, a fourth, a . . . The trigger clicked, but nothing happened. She pulled down on it again and again. Only empty clicks met her ears as the hammer slammed down on nothing.

Yvette laughed. "So, now you are finished with this foolishness," she said.

Steven, his eyes fluttered wildly, his chest heaving in deep gasps, summoned what little strength remained within him. "Run, Rachel," he screamed.

Yvette swung around, malice slipping from her tongue in a long hiss, hatred shining from her eyes. She moved toward Steven.

"Run, Rachel!" he yelled again.

Rachel's gaze darted from Yvette to Steven and back to Yvette. She couldn't just leave Steven to this . . . this monster. Yet how could she fight, and save them both, from a woman that wouldn't die?

"I'll get help, Steven," she called, hoping the tactic would cause Yvette to give chase. Maybe she could lose the woman in the swamp and find some help. Or get back here and get Steven away from *Sans Souci.* "I'll find a neighbor." She darted down the stairs and around the house toward the dense, darkness of the bayous.

"No" Yvette screamed. She reeled around and hurried through the door, forgetting about Steven, about caution. In her haste, in her pointed and mindless pursuit of Rachel, she did not notice her son, Alexandre, and her mother, Marguerite, struggling against one another in the center of the meadow.

At the bottom of the stairs she looked around quickly, then, with the keen, almost extreme, sense of hearing only her kind possessed, she heard the rustling, thrash ing sound of frantic footsteps coming from the bayou.

Alexandre threw Marguerite from him and gasped fo breath. The front of his shirt hung open, ripped by he clawing, flailing hands. An ugly trail of deep, jaggec gashes scarred his chest where her fingernails had rakec across the flesh, tearing it apart in her fury at him.

"You're a fool, Alexandre," Marguerite sneered, he voice rasping and weak. She lay on the ground at hi feet, momentarily defeated, her body having spent mor energy than she had consumed that night. "You're de stroying us."

"We should never have existed," Alexandre saic softly.

Marguerite grabbed at his pantleg.

Alexandre jerked it from her grasp. "Live out the res of your existence, Marguerite," he said, "but don't ex pect me to help you prolong this travesty, this abhor rence." He turned toward the old mill and felt his hear contract in panic. It was too still. Too quiet. He brok into a run, fear seizing him in its icy grip. Too late, hi mind screamed. He was too late.

Tears stung his eyes. "No," he moaned, struggling t instill his legs with greater speed. "Not again."

He charged up the stairs of the old mill and crashec through its door, slamming the weak barricade of rot ting planks against the inner wall of rock. The sound re verberated through the mill's interior and startlec Steven back into consciousness. His eyes shot open anc he looked at Alexandre.

"Rachel," he whispered. "Help Rachel."

Alexandre ran across the room and stood ove Steven. "You're her brother?"

Steven nodded.

Rage filled Alexandre's chest. So, this was all their doing after all. "Where's Rachel?" he demanded.

"Yvette . . ." Steven sucked in a much needed gulp of air. "Yvette chased . . . into swamp . . . I think."

Alexandre picked up a rust-covered ax that lay on the floor, its wooden handle having long ago split into two, its end now a jagged piece of splinter, and lifted it high in the air.

Steven looked up at the ax and screamed.

Alexandre brought the rust covered tool down on the rope that held Steven's right wrist prisoner. The rope snapped. He moved to the other side of the table and repeated the gesture, freeing Steven's left hand, and then his feet.

"Get out of here," Alexandre said, and then ran for the door. On the stair landing he paused and looked back at Steven. "Get out of here, Steven," he repeated, "and get your sister some help."

Alexandre turned, closed his eyes, spread his arms wide and, as his weight fell forward, soared into the night.

Chapter 27

Rachel ran into the dark swamp, her arms held out before her, hoping beyond hope that she didn't crash into anything. She tried to stay on the moss-covered strips of soft earth that meandered their way through the densely foliaged slough, curving around cypress trees which sat half-submerged within the murky depths of the swamp. But all too often her running step would slam down not on earth, but into a quagmire of mud and water. Visions of eels wrapping around her ankles, of water moccasins darting forth from the sawgrass to sink their long fangs into her calves, of alligators slipping quickly from the cover of low-growing ferns and banana plants to snap their jaws around her thighs danced sickeningly about the edges of Rachel's mind. But the terror of Yvette somewhere behind her, chasing her, hunting her, seemed to make all the other threats, inconsequential.

She turned left, then right, then left again. She was lost, and she didn't care. All she cared about was finding the other end of the swamp, getting out, getting back to help Steven and losing Yvette within the dank morass of foliage that surrounded them.

Rachel climbed over a fallen tree trunk, the gun still

gripped tightly in her right hand. A soft, invisible veil suddenly covered her face. Something large and black clung to her cheek. She screamed and stumbled forth, swiping a hand at whatever it was that had attached itself to her flesh, clawing at the wispy shroud of nothingness that had draped itself over her. Cobweb clung to the front of her blouse. She hurriedly wiped it off and threw a glance over her shoulder, looking for Yvette. The swamp was quiet. She neither heard nor saw anything . . . including the swamp's inhabitants.

The silence was thunderous. She stood still, listening, breathing deeply, her chest rising and falling rapidly. And then she heard it . . . something moving in the brush a short distance away. She didn't know if it was Yvette, a gator, or some other dreaded creature, and she didn't intend to wait around to find out. Rachel turned and broke into a sprint, forcing her legs to move faster than they had in years. She followed the slice of land she was traversing to the right and, rounding a cypress, fell over a dead tree trunk that lay in her path. Grit-filled water splashed up into her face as her hands slammed down into the black marsh. She jerked them up immediately. Water dripped from every crevice of her gun. Would it fire? Then she remembered she was out of bullets. The weapon was useless. But then, it hadn't helped anyway.

She pushed herself up, climbed over the tree trunk, and ran on. Disorientation took over. It was so dark. Rachel squinted in an effort to better discern her path through the spattering of moonlight that broke through the treetops here and there and checkered the ground. The only thing that helped her define water from land was the water's silvery reflection of the night's sky. She ran on, galvanized by fear and panic. She had to find a way out, a way to help Steven, to help herself.

Alexandre had come to her aid with Marguerite, but could he help her now? Would he help her now? What if he hadn't actually been saving her from Marguerite, but stopping Marguerite from ruining some diabolical plan of his own? What if he was in on whatever Yvette was doing?

Rachel swiped at a long strand of Spanish moss that hung in her path. What if what she saw Yvette doing was real? What if everything Yvette had said was true, and not just the rantings of a mad woman? Rachel groaned. Her heart felt as it if were ready to burst, but from the exhaustion of her physical demands on it, or from the ache of realizing the man she had fallen in love with could very well be as mad as his relatives, she didn't know.

Paying too much attention to her thoughts, and not enough to her direction, Rachel suddenly stumbled off of the path. Her foot sunk into the mud. Ooze immediately sucked at her ankle. Something moved along the surface of the water only a few feet away. She yanked her foot and scurried back up to the path of raised earth. Stumbling, tripping, gasping, she hurried on.

Behind her, sending a stampede of chills racing up her spine, she heard Yvette's fiendish laugh.

Rachel found within herself a new energy. She shot forward, groping blindly, pushing off from the trunks of the trees that grew so close together, weaving in, around and through the narrow passages their trunks provided. She gave no further thoughts to what creatures slunk beneath the still surface of the swamp's black waters, no heed to cobwebs, spiders, snakes or any other type of horror that might loom forth from the bayou. She could think of nothing except getting away from Yvette, breaking free from the swamp and finding her way back to Steven, and to safety.

A thin tree limb, unseen as she thrashed forward, slapped Rachel's cheek. Her flesh stung and her eyes filled with tears at the sharp flash of hot pain. But she didn't stop. She couldn't stop. She ran and ran, trampling over ferns, sawgrass, the huge leaves of banana plants, slipping, falling, and pushing herself up to run some more. Finally, when her lungs burned and her ribs ached at her gasping gulps for air, when her legs trembled so violently they threatened to collapse beneath her, she paused. The swamp was quiet, not a mutter or peep from any direction. The eerie silence sent a shudder of dread through her. It was *too* quiet. She looked about frantically, commanding her eyes to see through the shadows, to pierce the darkness and reveal what was hidden there. The animals, insects and reptiles of the swamp had fled to their lairs to hide and try to avoid whatever danger they sensed lurked within their midst.

Rachel forced her legs to move again, but this time at a steady jog rather than an all out run. She moved around a tree. Her foot rammed into something solid on the ground and she pitched forward, a small shriek of surprise escaping her lips. She threw her hands out to break her fall. Her stomach smacked onto something that was both hard and soft and her fingers tangled with. . . . fingers!

"What . . . ?" Filled with a stark, deep, consuming fear, Rachel jerked away from whatever or whomever it was she had fallen over, scurried across the damp earth and, pausing and gulping for breath, looked back.

A scream filled her lungs and threatened to rip from her throat. Only an instinctive slap of her hand over her lips, a inbred sense for survival that overtook everything else, prevented the sound from leaving her body and filling the quiet bayou. Rachel stared at Marc's body in horror. Emotions of every kind swept over her—sorrow, remorse, anger, fear, rage, loss. Tears filled her eyes and fell from her lids, streaming down her cheeks in tiny silver rivers as a sob nestled within her throat and the pain of loss, deep and cutting settled into her breast.

"Oh, God," she murmured, unable to take her gaze from the pitiful remains of what had once been her best friend. His body looked nearly emaciated, as if it had shriveled up upon itself. Terror filled his still-open eyes as they stared, unseeing, up at the night sky. His lips were still parted in a scream of agony as if beseeching someone, anyone, *her*, to help him, to stop whatever horror had befallen him.

How had this happened? Her gaze darted about the surrounding landscape. How had he come to be out in the swamp? He was supposed to have followed Yvette and Suzanne into town. That's what they'd agreed on. He'd said he had to get to the hospital. Her mind spun with questions. Why had he come here? And who had killed him? Who? Why?

They did, her mind finally answered, when rational thought returned. She shook her head, her eyes refusing to look away from Marc. No, Suzanne and Yvette couldn't have killed him. That wasn't possible. Marc had been strong, very strong. A woman couldn't have overpowered him and done this. Even two women. Her eyes raked the pathetic torso that lay lifeless before her. Or could they? Had they somehow known about him? That he was watching them? Backing her up? Had they seduced him into the bayou, and somehow overtaken him?

Her gaze moved haltingly to his neck. She forced her eyes to focus on the area just below Marc's jawline. His neck wasn't there any longer, not really. Where once veins, muscles, skin and bone had been, there was now only a ragged mesh of fleshy pulp. His throat had been not only slashed, but torn open and mutilated.

Rachel shivered as she stared at Marc. *Sucked the life force from him.* The words echoed in her mind as she remembered how, only a short while ago, Yvette had been lying atop Steven like a predator upon her prey when Rachel had come upon them. Her lips had been on his neck, her teeth sunk deeply into his flesh.

"Oh, God, Marc," Rachel whimpered, trying to deny the truth of the situation. "No." She shook her head vehemently. "No, no, no. This can't be happening." She gulped back a sob. "Vampires don't really exist. This is impossible. It just can't be."

She scooted away from his body, scrambled back to her feet and began to run. Only one thing seemed to matter now, only one thing impressed itself upon her brain. Get out. Get out of the swamp. Get Steven and get them both away from *Sans Souci* and its horrible nightmare. Whether what she had seen was real, or merely the results of a family gone completely and hopelessly insane, she didn't know, and she didn't care.

Her heart struggled against the logic of her mind. Yes, she did care, it argued. She cared about Alexandre. Tears blurred her vision and she frantically blinked and wiped them away.

Slashing through a curtain of Spanish moss, Rachel broke into an open meadow. She paused to catch her breath, and her bearings. She looked up at the moon, nestled within the velvety blanket of a infinite black, peaceful sky, then glanced both right and left. Several hundred yards away, to her right, was the stone mill house. She had somehow run in a circle.

"Thank God," she muttered breathlessly, and dashed toward it. There was no time to think now, no time to wonder where Yvette was, where the others were, where

Alexandre was. There was only she and Steven, and that's all that mattered. Later her heart could mourn having fallen in love with a man who was obviously as utterly insane as his family. He had to be, to live with this . . . this nightmare. No one could live among this atrocity and not know it, not be a part of it. Of that she was convinced.

Rachel stopped at the corner of the mill and listened. No sound met her ears, no movement her gaze.

She crept up the rickety stairs, staying close to the wall, where their structural support was still the strongest, to make as little sound as possible. At reaching the window she turned and peeked in. The candle still glowed, its flickering flame casting a golden light over the old room.

Steven was gone. She stared at the table, its cloth covered with blood stains, the ropes that had been tied around her brother's limbs now dangling loosely. Her eyes focused on the ropes. Even in the dim light she could see that they'd been cut. She moved toward the open door and cautiously slipped into the room, keeping herself flat to one wall as she looked around. Where was he? How could he have freed himself and gotten away?

A sound on the steps alerted her, but it was too late. She spun around.

Yvette's face loomed up before her. A fiendish grin slashed across her face and the red lips spread into a bizarre curve that Rachel suddenly recognized was neither crazy or unbalanced, but purely evil. Her eyes sparkled with satisfaction and her nostrils filled with the scent of her prey's fear. Laughter bubbled up from her throat, deep, diabolical, and hideous. It filled the cavernous room of the mill house and reverberated off of its stone walls, slipped through the cracks of its broken windows and shutters, through the slats of its half caved-in ceiling, and rippled over the bayou and sprawling meadows of *Sans Souci*.

"I told you there was no escape, Rachel," she whispered harshly. "You should have listened to me."

Rachel clung to the wall at her back. She had no weapon, no defense. She inched away from Yvette. Her fingers came into contact with a piece of wood lying up against the wall. They curled around it, holding it tight and she lifted it high over her head into the air. "Stay back, Yvette," she said, her voice little more than a ragged croak. "Stay back."

Yvette laughed again. "Or what, Rachel? You'll kill me?" Her shoulders shook with mirth. "You tried that already, with your gun, remember?"

Rachel gawked, horrified.

"It didn't work then, and it won't work now."

She lifted the beam higher, her fingers gripping it tightly, knuckles white from the pressure.

Yvette laughed, and as she threw her head back in mirth, red lips rose even higher and revealed two long white fangs protruding from each side of her mouth.

Rachel's heart thundered a rumbling beat as fear pulsed in her veins. She felt a moment's frenzy of hysteria, mingled with deep and unbiding incredulity at the sight before her eyes. Nothing in life had prepared her for this. What she was seeing, what she had seen, couldn't be real. Vampires were myths, Hollywood fantasy, and yet now, looking at Yvette, remembering Marc and Steven, she could no longer deny what her eyes had witnessed and her mind had struggled to renounce.

Suddenly, with a lightning speed that shocked Rachel, Yvette struck. Her hands, with their red-painted nails, reached out like grasping claws and clasped onto Rachel's shoulders.

The beam of wood was knocked from Rachel's hand.

She twisted in Yvette's grip, desperate to break it. This was a struggle for her life, she knew, more than any other she'd faced on the police force. If she lost this one, she lost everything. She pushed against Yvette's chest, trying to break the hold the woman had on her.

Yvette twisted Rachel around in an iron grip and pulled her toward her, laughing the entire time, a heinous sound that instilled a deeper sense of panic within Rachel, a more desperate hunger to escape. Lord, help her, she didn't want to die.

"Don't fight me, Rachel," Yvette whispered harshly. "It won't do you any good, you can't win." She chuckled. "And anyway, don't you want to be with Alexandre, to spend endless years being loved by him?"

Rachel's hands held firm to Yvette's arms, keeping the woman at a distance, but as they did, her mind, at Yvette's words, conjured up an image of the man she had come to love. He couldn't be like Yvette, her heart argued. He couldn't. Alexandre was warm, sensitive, and gentle. He was a caring man. He loved her.

She struggled against Yvette. Alexandre was not like her. He wasn't.

"He loves you," Yvette cooed, smiling. She jerked Rachel's arms out to the side and, teeth bared, thrust her head toward Rachel's neck.

Suddenly a shadow moved between the two women and the candle across the room, cutting off its feeble light.

Chapter 28

"That's right, mother," Alexandre said. "I do love her, and that's exactly why I will not allow you to hurt her."

Yvette instantly released Rachel and spun around to face her son. "Alexandre."

One black-winged brow rose at her acknowledgement.

"You fool," she snarled. "You're ruining everything. Don't you see that. Everything. Just like you did the last time."

"Danielle had a right to know the truth."

"The truth? Hah! She had a right to nothing. *We* are all that matters, Alexandre. This family. Our kind. *Les Chasseurs*. Don't you understand that? Us! We're all that matters. Us!"

"No, you're wrong."

Rachel tried to inch away from them but a table, pressed up again the wall, prevented her escape. She stared at Alexandre. How could he have been the Alexandre who loved Danielle? Her eyes shot back to Yvette. The woman was insane, filled with delusions.

"Danielle could have given us the child we need, Alexandre. And you loved her. She would have done it. There was no need to tell her anything."

"And what would you have done when it was finally impossible to hide what we are from her, Mother? Kill her? The woman I loved? Kill the woman who gave birth to my child?"

"Yes."

His eyes narrowed in loathing. "You brought Rachel's brother here. You knew about their psychic bond, and used it, used him, to get her here. All because she looks like Danielle." Disgust laced each word that passed his lips. "You brought her here to mate with me, didn't you Mother? You want a child so badly, you'd do anything, wouldn't you?"

"Yes," Yvette hissed. "No one can save us now but you, Alexandre. I'm too old and Suzanne is incapable. Only you can do it. And you must, Alexandre. It's not too late." She threw a glance over her shoulder at Rachel. "She loves you, and you love her. I've seen it in your eyes. Take her." Yvette's voice had begun to rise until it was almost a shriek. "Take her to the *garconniere* and mate with her until you are sure she carries the seed of your child."

"And then what, Mother?" he asked, his tone one of deadly calm.

Yvette shrugged. "Then she'll deliver to us what we need."

"And then?"

She shrugged again and chuckled. "Then it is up to you, my dear. Make her one of us, or kill her. I really don't care which."

"Why not just let her go?" He smiled, but there was no warmth, no familial respect or feeling in the gesture.

Yvette's temper flared. "Because she would betray us, damn it. You know that. She'd denounce us to the world, just like that silly fool you fell in love with years ago was going to do. She'd tell our secret."

"And then they'd come to destroy us?"

"Yes," she shrieked.

Alexandre smiled, a sad, but satisfied smile. "I think I'd welcome that," he said softly.

Rachel stared, unable to believe what he was saying. He was one of them, he was some kind of blood-sucking, murdering . . . *vampire,* her mind shrieked finally. They were vampires. Alexandre was like Yvette, physically the same as her . . . but not emotionally, her heart argued, not emotionally.

A snarling growl emanated from Yvette's throat. It rose in tempo until it was a wail of fury. "You fool!" she screeched, finally. "You'll destroy us all!" She launched herself at her son, claw-like hands spread wide to slash at him, rage shaking her body and spewing from her lips like fire.

He had not been prepared. Regardless of whatever else she was, Yvette was also his mother. It had been difficult enough to bring himself to fight with Marguerite, his own grandmother, but to fight his mother, even in self-defense, was almost more than Alexandre could bring himself to do. He lifted his arms to ward off her attack and tried to take a step back, to take himself out of her line of assault.

"I will not allow you to destroy us, Alexandre," Yvette snarled. "And I will not allow her to bring you down."

Alexandre grabbed Yvette's wrist as she slammed herself against him. Fury brought a crimson glow to her pale skin and a stygian darkness to her eyes. Alexandre wrestled her arms back, trying not to hurt her.

"Do as I say, Alexandre," Yvette groused, "or I swear, I'll kill her."

Rachel climbed over the table that blocked her path

and darted for the other side of the room, stepping into its shadows. But Alexandre and Yvette, struggling against one another, still blocked her only means of real escape, the entry door. She pressed herself against the cold stone wall, trying to become invisible, to lose herself within the inkiness the candle's glow failed to reach.

"You'd do that, Mother?" Alexandre said. He stared down at Yvette, his fingers closed around her wrists like steel bindings. "You'd kill Rachel, even knowing how I feel about her? Even knowing that I love her beyond all reason?"

She writhed in his grasp. "Yes," she snapped. "Why should I care about your feelings for her? Do you care about ours? About this family's right to continue?"

Rachel saw the shadow of anguish that momentarily etched itself on Alexandre's handsome features, saw it darken his eyes and pull at his lips.

"I do care, Mother," he said quietly, "I just can't do anything about it."

"You can," Yvette roiled. "And only you can. But you won't." She jerked one of her hands free and, swinging her arm upward, brought it down on his face, raking her nails across his cheek and snagging the skin.

Alexandre yanked back in both surprise and pain. He reached out to grab her arm again, but was too quick. She whirled around to face Rachel, her eyes glaring madly into the shadows where Rachel stood. "She has to die now, Alexandre. If you won't use her to do your duty to this family, then she has to die." She snapped her other arm free of his clasp.

"No," Alexandre groaned, torn between his love for Rachel and that for his mother. To protect the woman he loved, and whom he knew would turn away from him once he had saved her, he knew he had to destroy his own mother. Rage at the situation he'd been forced into burned hot and bright within his heart. But the decision had already been made. Yvette had made it the moment she devised the plan to lure Rachel to *Sans Souci.* She had left him no choice. With tears in his eyes, and more hurt in his heart than he had ever felt, he lunged toward her, his arms outstretched.

Suddenly, the soiled cloth that draped the long table Steven had lain upon for so many days while the very blood that kept his body alive was slowly drained from his veins, was thrown back. A figure loomed up from the table's shadowy shelter, his dirty, blood stained shirt hanging in little more than ragged shreds around his emaciated torso, his face so pale and gaunt to be almost unrecognizable.

Rachel gasped and slapped a hand over her mouth, afraid to move, afraid to call out to him.

With a strength, speed and agility she would never have thought possible from him at the moment, Steven dashed toward Alexandre and Yvette.

A low scream, primal and piercing, emanated from his throat.

Rachel watched Steven lunge across the room. His arms swung upward, lifting a thick, long, rod of metal he held in both hands. One end hovered over Steven's back.

Horror filled her racing heart as everything seemed to be happening in slow motion.

A low wail spilled from Steven's lips as he ran toward the struggling Beaumondiers.

Rachel stared at the rod.

Steven's arm swung downward.

Alexandre looked up just as Steven paused behind Yvette. His eyes filled with horror, and the helplessness of knowing there was nothing he could do to prevent what was happening.

Yvette, seeing the look that came over her son's face, jerked one arm away from him and spun around.

Steven brought the old baling rod down with every ounce of strength he could summon. Its pointed end plunged into Yvette's body, ripping through the thin veil of her silk blouse and puncturing the pale sheath of skin beneath to pierce her heart.

She fell backward into Alexandre's arms and a scream, like that of a mortally wounded animal, spewed from her lips. Her hands clutched at the rod as her eyes met Steven's and she began to sag to the floor, the pointed sphere of metal protruding from her back.

Alexandre caught her and as the weight of the baling bar pulled her body downward, he lowered her to the floor and knelt beside her, grasping one of her hands in his and holding her head cradled in the crook of his arm.

Rachel stepped hesitantly from the shadows, her body trembling violently.

Steven staggered to the door and out onto the stairs.

"Alexandre?" Rachel said softly.

He looked up at her. Tears filled his eyes. He shook his head and, releasing Yvette's hand, grasped the rod and pulled it from her chest. It clattered noisily to the plank floor. "Go, Rachel," he said quietly, his deep drawl edged with sorrow. "Get your brother and go before the others come."

She looked down at him for several long seconds. In all the years of her life, in everything she'd done, seen, felt, Rachel had never wanted anything as much as she wanted to stay with Alexandre. She loved him, there was no denying that, but they were from two different worlds. She felt her own tears begin to fill her eyes, felt the ache of loss spark to life within her breast. She and Alexandre were like night and day, fire and ice, sunrise and sunset—so different, and yet feeling the same things for one another. But he could never be accepted into her world, and she could not belong to his.

Rachel turned from him, her heart breaking into a million pieces that she knew would never fit back together again. Her heart would never be whole again for a part of it would always belong to Alexandre.

"You killed her," Marguerite screeched.

Rachel's head jerked up and she looked toward the door. Marguerite stood within its opening, profiled against the night, her hands clasped to the doorjamb, feet spread wide. Hatred flared from her eyes as she looked from Rachel to Alexandre and back to Rachel again. "You killed her," she repeated. "You killed my Yvette."

"No," Rachel said softly. "It was . . ." she looked at Alexandre, ". . . an accident."

Marguerite released her hold on the door and stepped back. "Liars!" She spun around and ran down the rickety stairs.

Rachel ran to the door.

Marguerite was already halfway across the meadow, little more than a flowing spectre of pale chiffon against the dark night.

"Go Rachel," Alexandre said again. He stood, lifting Yvette's lifeless body in his arms, and carried her to the table. "Hurry."

Looking back at him through her tears, wanting nothing more than to run to him, to feel his arms around her again, Rachel whispered for what she knew would be the first and last time, "I love you, Alexandre." She stepped from the mill house, and taking a deep breath, hurried down the steps. "Steven?" She looked around for him and finally spotted him sitting beneath an old oak tree several yards away.

"It's over," she said as she paused beside him. "I don't know if I'll ever truly understand what happened, but it's over."

Steven looked up at her then and let his head fall back to rest against the tree. "She wanted you," he whispered, his voice raspy with weakness. "That was the whole thing. She wanted you here."

Rachel nodded. "I know."

"I told her about our bond, about the way we can communicate with our minds, how we always could, since we were children. She seemed so wonderful, Rae, like everything I'd ever wanted in a woman, you know?"

Rachel nodded again. She glanced back at the mill house. "Yes, I know," she answered softly. A tear slipped from the corner of her eye. "I know."

"After I came here she . . . I was photographing the carriage house and she knocked me out, I guess. I don't know. I mean, everything suddenly went black and I woke up here, tied to that table and every night she'd . . . she'd . . . His voice broke and he shook his head.

"I know, Steven," Rachel said. "It's all right." She bent down, clasped his arm and gave a tug.

"I loved her, Rae, and then she turned into that *thing.*"

"Come on, we have to get you to town. You need a doctor."

"What do we tell them?" Steven asked as he struggled to his feet. "The doctor? The police?" He inhaled deeply, the sound a ragged gasp of weakness. "What do we tell them, Rae?"

She didn't answer.

"They'll never believe this."

"Then we'll figure out something to tell them that

they will believe," she said finally. "I was a cop, remember? I'll think of something."

Suddenly, off in the distance, the sound of several shots being fired echoed on the still night air and shattered the silence.

Steven jerked around to look at Rachel. "What was that?" he asked, panic lacing his words.

She stared toward the old plantation house, in the direction the sound had originated. "Gun shots," she said needlessly.

"The others," Steven moaned, "they're coming after us."

She felt him tense and felt his panic.

"No," Rachel said. "They don't need guns for that. Something else has happened."

He calmed enough to remain still, though he was trembling violently. "What?"

She shook her head. "I don't know."

As the sound of the last shot echoed on the night, Alexandre burst from the doorway of the mill house. He charged down the stairs and ran toward Rachel and Steven.

"Get him out of here," he shouted and bolted past them, the tails of his black jacket flapping behind him.

"Alexandre, what's wrong?" Rachel cried after him. Panic, unreasonable and uncertain, swept over her.

He didn't answer, didn't pause, but merely continued running toward the house.

"Steven, stay here," Rachel said. She helped her brother back to a sitting position beneath the tree. "I'll be right back. I've got to find out what happened."

"Rae, no, it's a trick," Steven croaked.

"Stay here." She turned and ran after Alexandre. Somehow, and she didn't know how, she sensed that he knew what the shots meant, that he knew what was happening, and whatever it was, it wasn't good. She wouldn't let him face that alone.

He had disappeared into the shadows that surrounded the main house.

"Alexandre."

She ran across the open meadow toward the line of giant live oaks that bordered the once formal gardens. The sky above the old trees suddenly seemed incredibly bright and tinged with an orange cast. Rachel ran on, afraid of what she was going to find, but more afraid for Alexandre, without knowing why.

She saw him reach the line of oaks, slow and then pause. He stood beneath one of the ancient trees, the black of his slacks and jacket, the wavy strands of hair that covered his head, fused with the darkness from behind, tinged golden at the forefront from the brilliant light he faced.

He stood still, looking across the tangled brush of the garden, toward the house.

Rachel approached slowly, suspicion of what held him so mesmerized, of what he was watching, forming in her mind. As she moved to stand at his side the house came into view, and she gasped softly. It was engulfed in flame, the entire structure little more than a ball of raging fire. She moved to stand beside him and though she wanted to reach out to him, ached to hold him in her arms and feel his body, his warmth, his strength wrap around her as it had that night in the *garconniere,* she remained still, her hands cold and limp at her sides.

"What happened?" she asked in a whisper.

"Catherine."

She turned to look at him, her brow nettled in a frown of confusion. "Catherine?" She looked back at the house. "What do you mean?"

Alexandre continued to stare at the house that had

been his home for over three hundred years. An endless vista of ugly, vicious, yet radiantly beautiful tongues of flame, orange, yellow and blue were, in their insatiable hunger, rapidly devouring *Sans Souci.*

Rachel looked at his profile, committing each curve and plane to memory, carving his face, each line and feature, into her mind's eye. It was the only way, she knew, to retain a small part of him so that in the long nights of her life that lay ahead she could recall him, could bring him back to life in the secret darkness of her mind, this man she loved, and could not have.

"She knew they would never give me any peace," he said suddenly.

"She killed them?"

"Yes."

"And herself?"

"Yes."

"But why?"

"It was her way of releasing me. Long ago my great grandmother told me that the only way a . . ." he turned and looked down at Rachel, ". . . a *Chasseur* life. . . ."

Rachel frowned. Her French had never been that good. *"Chasseur?* A hunter?"

"I believe your kind call us vampires."

She stared at him. It sounded ridiculous, but she knew it was true. She had seen it with her own eyes. And Steven had nearly been its victim.

"The only way a vampire's life," Alexandre continued, "can be ended, other than by its own natural termination of aging, was by a piercing of the heart with a shaft of steel." He inhaled deeply and released a long sigh. "I've tried for years to bring that about on myself," he avoided looking into her eyes, "but it always eluded me."

He turned to her. "But I didn't kill to exist," he said

quietly. "I used to, I admit, years ago. So long ago now that I barely remember."

"What happened?" Rachel whispered, almost afraid to ask.

A sad smile of remembrance pulled at one corner of his lips. "I met Danielle."

"Danielle Toutant?" Rachel said, shocked.

He nodded. "Yes. How did you know her last name?"

"I . . . I found her portrait in the attic and . . ." She didn't want to say it, didn't want to be the one to tell him, but she had to. He had a right to know. "And her body locked in the cellar."

A cloud of anguish swept its way across his face. "In the cellar," he repeated, and shook his head. "I didn't even know *Sans Souci* had a cellar."

"It has a secret entrance. Behind the fireplace in the bedroom I was staying in."

"Danielle's room." He nodded. "That explains how she disappeared so thoroughly. Without my ever seeing her leave the house. I'd always thought I'd just missed her."

"But Danielle disappeared over two hundred years ago."

"That's right. I was two hundred and ninety six then."

"That's impossible."

"Only for humans," Alexandre said, "not for *Chasseurs.*"

He inhaled deeply, though the gesture was more a sigh than an intaking of breath. "Danielle allowed me to feel love, Rachel, but with it I also felt guilt, both at continuing to kill, and for not telling her the truth about myself."

Rachel waited, needing to hear more, but afraid to

ask, afraid to speak aloud and break the spell between them.

"I told her, and she left me." He sighed again. "But then, how could she not? After that, I couldn't kill anymore. Each time I went out, each time I hunted, I would remember Danielle and the horror and disgust I'd seen that night in her eyes when she discovered the truth. I couldn't kill, and yet I couldn't survive without blood."

"Then how . . . ?"

"Hanson. Catherine made him one of us long ago. He brought me what I needed. The rabbits, remember?" he said, reminding her of the cook house where she'd seen the rabbits, their blood draining into the drysink.

She nodded.

"Even that appalled me, but I had no choice."

Rachel remained quiet.

"When I was younger, that same evening Catherine told me of our . . . weakness, she showed me a gun she kept hidden in her room. Its bullets had been specially made of steel. If anything ever went wrong she'd said, if there was ever a need to . . ." his voice cracked slightly, "to end the existence of one of us, there was the gun, with its steel bullets."

"But . . . why now? What was the threat?"

He looked deep into her eyes.

The swirling started almost immediately. The castle with its rock walls, its turrets and peaked roofs loomed out of the gray mist that had invaded her mind's eye. The blue sea, endless, glistening, rolling with waves swept over the scene, only to be instantly overtaken by sprawling green forests, the ancient streets of the *Vieux Carre,* battlefields and prairies.

Alexandre tore his gaze from hers then, and the memories she had witnessed, disappeared.

Rachel felt a rush of weakness but struggled to maintain her balance and composure.

"You were the threat, Rachel," he said gently.

"Me? But how?"

"I love you. Catherine knew that, and she also knew that, as with Danielle, it couldn't work. If they allowed you to live, they knew you'd reveal our secret to the world . . ."

"But I wouldn't," Rachel said. "I could never hurt you . . ."

He shook his head. "They wouldn't take that chance."

"But why this?" She glanced back at the burning house.

"Rachel, I have four years left in which to father a child. After that, on my five hundredth year, my seed will no longer carry life." He laughed bitterly. "Or at least life as my kind knows it."

"But I thought . . ."

He smiled then. "Contrary to the many myths your kind have propagated about us, *Les Chasseurs* are born. There are some transmutations, yes, but they are not considered true *Chasseurs*. We call them changelings."

"But a changeling is . . ."

"Yes, a child secretly exchanged for another."

"As your transmutation changes a human's life from one essence to another."

"Yes."

"But I don't understand this?" Rachel motioned toward the still burning house.

"Catherine knew Yvette and Marguerite would never give up. They would never stop haranguing me to give them the child they so desperately thought they needed to carry on the Beaumondier line."

"But Suzanne?"

"Suzanne could not have children. She was injured long ago."

"So Catherine destroyed them for you?"

He nodded and looked back at the raging flames devouring *Sans Souci.*

"She must have loved you very much," Rachel whispered.

"Your brother needs you, Rachel," Alexandre said, terminating the reflections on his family. "You'd best go."

A tear slipped from the corner of her eye and streaked down her cheek.

It was over, both for the Beaumondier women, and for her and Alexandre. Rachel turned away and began to walk back toward the mill.

Chapter 29

Rachel managed to get Steven to the end of the drive, then left him there while she hiked her way to Marc's car and used his radio to summon help. Within half an hour several police cars, fire trucks, and an ambulance were parked on both the road and the drive to *Sans Souci,* their red and blue lights illuminating the landscape in a grotesque display of eerie color.

Rachel looked around at the aftermath. Both police car and hand-held radios squawked loudly and continuously. The coroner and the fingerprint team were busy going over Marc's car and the Captain of Detectives had assaulted her with so many questions she felt as if her mind were whirling out of control.

The firemen had found little to do by they time they arrived at the old plantation. The house had burned quickly, the centuries' old wood and furnishings fueling the flames like dried kindling.

Rachel looked down the drive toward the house. All that remained was a black skeleton of beams, rafters and brick columns. The old brick chimneys that had been positioned on either end of the mansion and the pillars that had lined the galleries and supported the portico remained standing like silent sentinels guarding their once regal realm.

She thought of the secret cellar room that had been Danielle Toutant's tomb, as well as that of several others, and wondered if the fire and police officials would discover it. Or had the earth above it caved in when the house burned and its clayed inner walls collapsed? Had the long, dark tunnel that led to that secret room been filled in? To remain a secret forever?

Her gaze swept the area around the house. There was no sign of Alexandre, nor had she mentioned him, or what had happened to Yvette in the millhouse, to the police. They would find that out soon enough she assumed, as they would discover the remains of those that had perished within *Sans Souci,* and perhaps wonder at the steel bullets and the motive behind the old woman's killing spree.

Rachel forced her thoughts back to the present. "Captain," she said finally, trying to sound somewhat authoritative and determined, "my brother is being taken to the hospital, and I'm going with him."

"We still have questions for you, Ms. Domecq," he answered stiffly, throwing her a quick, cold glance from beneath bushy gray eyebrows as he scribbled something hastily into the little writing pad he held in one stubby hand. "Like exactly what did happen to your brother out here? And by whom? I will also need you to lead me to Marc Dellos's body."

She felt herself cringe involuntarily at the thought of having to view Marc's remains again. Emotion formed a painful lump in her breast. She had lost a good friend, an irreplaceable friend, and one she knew she'd miss for a long, long time. Rachel sighed and pushed the memory of Marc's horrible death, of what he had looked like when she'd discovered him, from her mind. She'd rather remember him as he had been, healthy, strong, and alive. Her hand clenched at her side. She had also lost the man she loved.

Pain, a terrible aching, gnawing pain, swelled to life within her breast. "Tomorrow," she said curtly to the police officer.

"Ms. Domecq," Captain Jack Moreau bellowed, his tone meant to invoke fear and compliance in her. "I need you here now." His wide brow burrowed into a deep frown of disapproval.

Rachel stiffened. She was used to dealing with that tone, and Captain Moreau's type, or at least she had been used to it in Baton Rouge, when she'd still been *one of them*. But she wasn't one of them any longer, and she didn't have to be intimidated by his brusqueness. Finding the dead could wait until tomorrow. Tonight she was more concerned with the condition of the living. "Tomorrow, Captain," she said, invoking a stern edge to her own voice. "I'll show you tomorrow and answer your other questions."

The police captain glared after her as she followed her brother, who had just been lifted into the ambulance on a gurney. Rachel climbed in and sat beside him.

"Eight o'clock, sharp," Moreau called after her.

She looked up just as the attendant slammed the doors of the ambulance closed.

Rachel stood in the waiting room of the New Orleans hospital. She had been there for over an hour, and she hadn't been able to sit down for more than two minutes at a time. Her mind was a blur of worry—over Steven and over Alexandre. What if the police tried to approach Alexandre? What would he do? Was he still at the plantation? Had he left? Where would he go?

The doctors had clucked their tongues and shaken their heads continuously at Steven's condition, telling her after only a few minutes of tests it appeared he had about only one quarter the amount of blood in his system that a person needed to function normally. Transfusions were immediately set up. Then they'd bombarded her with questions. The same questions the police had asked. How had he lost the blood? What had caused the puncture wounds all over his body? What had bitten his neck and left those two deep fang-like holes?

She hadn't been able to answer any of their questions to their satisfaction. How could she? It was impossible to answer without endangering Alexandre, and she wouldn't do that, no matter what.

So she'd lied. He'd had an accident while scouting a location to take photographs for his books. He had been reported missing, but the old place he'd gone to had been well-hidden, obscure, and he'd told no one about it, so they'd had a hard time finding him. He had fallen into some old mill contraption, that's what had cut him. The marks on his neck weren't bites, they'd been made by pieces of metal sticking up from an old machine he'd fallen on, as had the other marks.

The doctors had looked at her with blatant skepticism. Some had shaken their heads in disbelief. A few questioned her story, just as the police had and most likely would continue to do, but Rachel had insisted that was all she knew.

"Ms. Domecq?"

Rachel whirled around. A nurse stood at the doorway of the waiting room.

"Yes? Is he . . ."

"Your brother is fine. He's resting comfortably,

asleep." She smiled. "Why don't you go on home or back to your hotel room, and get some rest yourself. You look quite done in."

Rachel nodded. "Yes," she murmured, "I will."

But that's not what she intended to do. She could rest later. She could sleep later. Right now there was something much more important she had to do. Hurrying from the hospital's entrance doors Rachel stepped out into the cool night. A taxi was just preparing to pull away from the curb.

"Wait! Taxi!" she yelled, and waved.

The cabbie slammed down on the brake and looked back at her. "Yeah?" he grumbled, slipping a stub of cigar from one side of his mouth to the other.

Rachel ran toward his car.

The cabbie pushed a baseball cap back off of his forehead and, leaning over the seat, snapped open the passenger side rear door and pushed it out for her. He looked at her over pudgy cheeks, sizing her up and then, seemingly satisfied, said, "So, where you wanna go, lady?"

"Take the River Road south," Rachel said. Remembering the reaction of the last cab driver who'd taken her to *Sans Souci* she had determined that it was best not to tell him her destination just yet.

The taxi pulled away from the curb and out of the hospital's driveway to the street. "Yeah, and then where?" he asked.

"I'll show you."

He glanced at her in the rearview mirror. "Don't know the address? Could be kinda hard to find a place in the dark if you ain't got the address."

"I can find it," she said.

It took nearly forty minutes to get back to *Sans Souci,* the cab hitting almost every red light in town.

"Here," she said finally, and pointed over his seat toward the tall brick pillars that stood on either side of the entry drive to *Sans Souci.*

The man shook his head. "Uh-uh, I ain't going in there, no sirree, bob."

Rachel felt a momentary flare of anger, and then shrugged it away. What did it matter? She wasn't even sure Alexandre was still here, and if he was, a cab lumbering down the drive might cause him to leave. She pulled a twenty from her pocket, grateful that the pockets of Steven's jeans had not proven entirely empty, and handed it to the cab driver. She'd lost her purse, and her luggage, when *Sans Souci* had gone up in flames. Which meant, at the moment, she had no cash and no credit cards. She'd fix that later, right now she had to find Alexandre.

If nothing else she had to make certain he was all right.

"You sure this is where you want to be let off, lady?" the cabbie asked. "This place belongs to the Beaumondiers, and most people don't think they're exactly normal. Besides it looks like there's been a pretty bad fire recently."

"I'll be fine," Rachel said, and climbed from the car.

"Suit yourself, lady, it's your funeral."

She slammed the door and stepped back as the cabbie gunned the motor and the car shot forward. The tires squealed as he jerked the steering wheel and turned the car back in the direction they'd come, rocks and gravel spewing up everywhere. She watched him drive away, not moving until he was out of sight, then she turned and began to walk down the drive.

Everything was dark now, lit only by the faint glow of the moon. The fire was completely out and, as she rounded a curve in the drive, she saw that the *garconniere* was also completely dark. Rachel felt her heart contract. Was he gone? A flash of panic swept over her. Had he decided to leave *Sans Souci?* Louisiana? Possibly the country, before the authorities came back in the morning? Before the truth of what had happened finally came out and he was exposed to the world?

Tears stung Rachel's eyes and her hands began to tremble as an ache of loss and loneliness formed, like a lump of coal, in her breast. No, he couldn't have left. He couldn't have.

She walked to the wide fanning entry steps that had once led to the old plantation house. With carefully slow steps she mounted them and then, standing on the uppermost one, looked down into the rubble of what had once been a great old plantation mansion. Wisps of smoke drifted up into the night air from the piles of debris, in spite of the fact that the firetrucks had hosed it down with hundreds of gallons of water, which glistened here and there beneath the moon's light.

Suddenly something rubbed against her leg. Rachel stiffened, afraid to look down.

"Meow."

Relief flooded through her. "Asmodeus?" she cried softly, and looked down at the black cat.

He rubbed lovingly against her leg again, his long tail wrapping around her calf as he pressed himself to her.

Laughing, she bent down and scooped the animal up and into her arms, cradling him securely against her chest. She nuzzled his forehead with her own. "I'm happy to see you, too, friend," she whispered.

The cat snuggled deeper into her embrace, closed his big green eyes and began to purr loudly and contentedly.

Rachel turned and descended the small staircase, then stopped and looked around. Where was he? She fixed her gaze on the *garconniere.* Could he be there? Sitting in the dark? Alone? She walked toward the old guest house.

At its door she paused, uncertain. Should she knock? Or just enter? She decided on the latter. Shifting Asmodeus's weight to one arm, she wrapped a hand around the doorknob and, turning it, pushed the door open. It squeaked faintly on its old hinges but swung open easily enough. Rachel stepped into the foyer. Moonlight followed her through the open doorway, lighting a path for her but unable to completely obliterate the shadows that clung to the far corners and the elegant stairwell that curved its way to the second floor.

Invasion of the night's light glistened a reflection on the polished mahogany of the stair's banister and lent the faded white paint of the foyer's walls the facade of gracefully aged ivory. The crystal teardrop prisms of the chandelier that hung overhead, its many tapers sitting cold and unlit within their delicate sconces, glimmered a rainbow of color as moonlight touched each plane of cut glass. Silence filled Rachel's ears and seemed to hammer at her as she strained to hear a sound, any sound, that would tell her that the *garconniere* was not empty, that Alexandre was somewhere within its confines.

"Alexandre?" Rachel called softly. She walked toward the parlor on her right and peered in. "Alexandre?" Her eyes scanned the various shapes and shadows that filled the room. She turned and moved to the door of his study. The swelling sense of emptiness, of being alone, built within her, but she wouldn't give up, not until she was sure he wasn't here somewhere. She turned toward the staircase and looked up at the inky blackness into which it disappeared.

"There's nothing to fear at *Sans Souci* anymore," she told herself in a mumbled voice. "Nothing." She took several halting steps up the stairs, cringing inwardly, hesitating momentarily as each movement brought forth a creak from the mahogany planks upon which she placed her weight. On the landing she paused and looked toward each bedchamber wing. There were two rooms on each side of the landing. His, she remembered, had been the first door to her right. Memory of their night together, of the urgency of their lovemaking as they surrendered to the feelings that burned hot between them, swept over her and Rachel felt a knot of longing coil tight and achingly deep inside of her.

She closed her eyes to prevent the scorching tide of tears that threatened to fill her eyes and stream down her cheeks. Nothing in life had prepared her for the pain of such a loss, for the piercing, gnawing ache of loving someone so deeply, so desperately, that losing him was like enduring a slow, neverending death.

She moved toward the door that led to his room. Her fingers trembled slightly as they clasped the old silver doorknob. She turned it and pushed the door open. Rachel stepped across the threshold, unaware until that very moment, when the breath rushed from her lips in disappointment at seeing the room empty, that she had even been holding it within her lungs. Unable to help herself she walked toward the large poster bed that dominated the room and bent to run her hand lightly across its coverlet. Her fingers moved slowly over the dark burgundy satin threads, their silkiness beneath her touch like a cool caress.

A hushed groan slipped from her lips as an image of Alexandre, his naked body entwined with her, muscle-honed arms and legs holding her close, their flesh pressed together, filled her mind. She could almost feel the circle of his arms around her, smell his musky fragrance of earth and forest, taste the sweet flavor of his lips upon hers, and hear his voice, that deeply rumbling, softly drawling voice that had whispered such tender words of love to her that night.

Yearning tore at her. She had to find him. She had to. Forcing herself to straighten, to turn away from the bed, Rachel walked back to the open doorway and into the hall. She quickly checked each of the other bedchambers, even though she knew, if he hadn't been in his own, the hope of discovering him in any of the others was next to nothing.

Finally, finding no trace of him, she descended the wide staircase to the main floor and walked back out into the moonlit night still holding the cat in her arms. "Where are you, Alexandre?" she asked the night. A sob caught in her throat. "Where are you?"

On the path leading away from the *garconniere,* a patch of wildflowers hugged the edge of the walkway, their blossoms squeezed tightly closed against the night. Rachel stared down at the white buds as another memory assailed her. How had she known about the music box?

She bent down to touch the flower. It had been a psychic impression. Nothing more. She refused to believe Danielle had come back to haunt her body. A shiver rippled up Rachel's spine. Could Danielle have led her to the portrait in the attic? To the cellar?

Her flesh suddenly chilled. "Impressions," she mumbled again. "Psychic impressions, that's all it was." She'd had them in the past, about other things, just not as strong. But that was all it had been. Nothing else. Danielle had not come to her, had not taken over her mind or her body. Psychic impressions. That was all.

She began to wander the grounds aimlessly, not knowing where else to look for him, where he would have gone. The ache of loss grew with each passing moment. What if he had left New Orleans? Left Louisiana? What if she never found him?

She found herself suddenly standing in the middle of the meadow of weed-choked grass which she had run across only hours before, first seeking her brother, then fleeing for her life.

In the distance, at the opposite end of the meadow, silhouetted by the first faint rays of the coming day's dawn, she saw the old mill house, and shuddered. She turned away.

Asmodeus jumped from her arms and promptly took off at a lope back toward the house.

"Asmodeus, come back," Rachel called.

The cat meowed but didn't stop or turn back.

Alexandre sat quietly on a small knoll that had once overlooked the main house of *Sans Souci.* The gnarled, sprawling branches of the lone live oak that grew almost directly from the center of the knoll, spread widely over him, creating a ceiling of living foliage that blocked out all vestiges of the waning moon and the steadily approaching dawn. Long, draping strands of Spanish moss hung from the tree's age old branches, thick sheets of prickly gray growth that acted as curtains against the night. Alexandre stared past the netlike moss toward the still smouldering embers of *Sans Souci,* of the house he had called home for so many years. A long sigh of resignation left his lips. He was alone now. The only Beaumondier left.

The irony of it would have made him laugh if it didn't stab at his heart so fiercely. He was the one who had always wanted his existence to end. He was the one who had never wanted to go on, who had tried, so many times, to destroy himself, and failed. He closed his eyes. And now they were gone. The ones who had wanted to go on. His family. The ones who had enjoyed and accepted their existence for what it was. No more, no less. And now they were gone, and he was left here alone. Why?

A deep sigh rushed from his lips. He opened his eyes and looked back at what little was left of the once grand house. Because of him, because of his idyllic morals and dreams, because of his refusal to look, so long ago, at reality, he had destroyed them all.

His heart ached with loneliness and grief.

And yet, much as he had loved them, a part of him was glad they were gone. They could rest in peace now, as could the world, and the humans they had preyed upon. Perhaps, if he was lucky, his existence would also be cut short.

A faint whiff of lilac drifted to him on the cool morning air and stirred within him other memories he didn't want to think of, yet couldn't deny. Rachel had worn lilac perfume the night they had made love, the night that he'd known, more so than any other time in his long existence, that he could no longer stand his life the way it was.

Suzanne had believed that being a *Chasseur*, a hunter, was a gift because it enabled them to live for centuries. Like him, it had bothered her to kill the mortals, so she had soothed her guilt by preying on what she considered the dregs of society, the unwanted, the humans who preyed on their own kind.

Alexandre had always believed "the gift" was actually a curse. A sad smile curved his lips. Perhaps they had both been right, in their own ways. The gift of long-lasting existence had allowed him to experience Rachel's love, and though he would carry with him forever the ache of losing her, of wanting nothing more than to be with her, he had at least been granted the privilege of being touched by her love. And along with the curse of what he was came the added penalty that he would go on, for more years than he cared to contemplate, without her.

A burning tide of desire tore at him as her memory filled his mind. And this was part of the curse, too, he thought woefully. That he could love her, so desperately, so completely, and could not have her, did not dare go to her again.

Memory of her pliant body pressed to his, of her breasts crushed up against his chest, of her arms encircling his shoulders, pulling him down to meet her lips, filled his every thought.

He rose to his feet, tearing his mind away from the painful recollections of Rachel Domecq, and forced himself to face the hard, cold fact of his reality. He was alone now. More alone than he had ever been in almost five hundred years. His family, the ones who had brought him into this world, raised him, and cared for him were gone. Hanson, the old man who was one of them, and served them faithfully all the years of his existence, who had felt compassion for Alexandre's emotional and physical struggle and tried to help him through it, was gone. And Rachel, the one and the only woman he had ever truly loved, was lost to him, as completely, as thoroughly, as if she had never existed.

Throwing his head back, eyes closed, Alexandre spread his arms wide and let himself sway forward, wanting nothing more than to become one with the sky, to soar freely and forget, if just for a little while, the horrors the night had brought to his life.

But, as he let the weight of his body fall onto the night air, as he felt the first tinglings of transformation begin to assail his limbs, something rubbed up against the calf of his left leg and pushed against him.

Chapter 30

"Meow."

Alexandre looked down at the animal who was twisting itself round and round his legs, its long silky tail curling itself about his knee.

Asmodeus paused, rubbed his forehead against Alexandre's calf, and then glanced up at him with sparkling green eyes.

"Meow."

Alexandre smiled and hunkered down beside the cat. "So, old man, I'm not the only one left here after all, huh?" he said softly. "I'm stuck with you." The words were harsh, but his tone was one of caring gentleness. He stroked a hand tenderly over the cat's head and back. A surge of emotion came to his throat as Suzanne's pet began to purr loudly.

"Asmodeus?" Rachel called. Concern was etched clearly in her tone. "Asmodeus?" she called again.

Alexandre jerked around and stared in the direction from which her voice had come. He saw her immediately. She was standing near the fanning stairs that had once led up to the front gallery of the house. He looked at her across the blackened debris. Behind Rachel the sun was slowly rising into view, its pinkish gold rays pushing their way upward to invade the last hanging shrouds of the night's gray sky. Brilliant beams of sunlight streamed from the boughs of the bayou's trees, pierced the shadows, and settled a golden haze over the sprawling entry drive and fallow fields behind and off to one side of her. The radiance of the new day touched the tendrils of her auburn hair and lent them highlights of gold, silver and red, turning the wavy dark tangles to a shimmering, etheral mane about her face. Morning light fairly glowed off the smudged and torn white linen of her slacks, accentuating the subtle curve of her hips and long length of her legs, and transformed the sheer threads of her pale mint silk blouse into a diaphanous veil of near nothingness that made him ache with want of her.

"Asmodeus?" Rachel called again, louder.

The cat meowed in answer and, swishing away from Alexandre's legs, pranced daintily toward where Rachel stood.

But Rachel's attention was no longer focused on Asmodeus. The moment the cat answered her call and she turned toward the sound, her heart had lurched crazily and skipped a beat. The breath she had been about to inhale caught momentarily in her throat. Through the shimmering silver of tears that, for the past few minutes had filled her eyes, she caught sight of Alexandre.

His name left her lips in a whispered hush of joy. She stared at him, wanting to run to him, to throw her arms around him and press her lips to his, but she remained still, apprehensive.

For several long seconds, an eternity of time in which each faced their own fears, their dreads and uncertainties, and their secret hopes, they stared at one another, gray-blue eyes fusing with green. In hers, Alexandre saw the hopelessness of all the tomorrows he knew he was destined to endure, saw the love he knew he could never hope to possess, and the pain he knew their love would bring to her when he finally left.

Rachel welcomed the pull of his gaze. As she had the first time she'd looked deep into his eyes, she saw all that Alexandre Beaumondier had ever been—the young man who, because of his impulsiveness and love for life, had been forced to flee his home in France with his family. She saw him some years later as he stood beside Bienville on the swampy shores of what was to become New Orleans, and the two claimed it as a possession of France. With a blinding whirl of color the scene changed to that of a swashbuckling privateer standing on the decks of an old schooner, the blasts of cannon sounding all around him, the smell of canister and gunfire permeating the air. Like the flip of a television channel the scene changed again, to a montage of men in blue uniforms struggling against men in gray, and Alexandre, clad in resplendent gray, in their midst, a sword held high over his head. For long moments she let his life pass before her eyes, absorbing each scene, her heart near frozen in fear for his safety even though he now stood before her, unscathed.

And then suddenly, as if the curtain in a theatre had been abruptly drawn closed before its performers had finished their last act, the scenes disappeared, and only darkness was revealed to her, a cold, blank, infathomable darkness.

Rachel closed her eyes and shook her head, and then looked back at Alexandre, confused, uncertain as to what had just happened.

He walked toward her slowly, knowing what he must do, what he must say, and dreading it, wishing there were some way he could turn back the hands of time.

Both her gods and his had proven crueler than he

had ever believed possible. They had given them life, given them love, but had made them so different—her a creature of the day, him a creature of the night—that their two worlds could never meld. They had no alternative but to turn their backs on the love they felt for one another.

"I had to come back," she whispered as he paused before her. "I had to know that you were all right."

He smiled down at her, but there was no joy in the gesture, merely sadness. "Rachel," he said softly. "My beautiful Rachel. What pain we have caused you." He reached up and stroked her cheek, a touch that was so gentle, so light in its caress that it brought a fresh wave of tears to her eyes.

She tore her gaze away from his, afraid now that she would turn into a simpering, wailing idiot if he said another caring word to her. "Are they . . . ?" She looked at the skeletal remains of the house. "Are they really . . . . ?"

He nodded. "They're gone."

"'I'm sorry, Alexandre." Tears fell from her eyes. "I'm so sorry."

He shook his head. "No, it's better this way. Now they can rest in peace." He took her hands in both of his, lifting them to his chest and holding them secure there. "I'm glad you came back," he said, his voice husky with the emotion that was coursing through him at her nearness. "I shouldn't be, and you shouldn't have come back, but I'm glad you did, so that we could say goodbye."

"Alexandre, no, I want . . ."

He pressed a finger gently to her lips to quiet her words. "I have to leave New Orleans now, *chère,*" he said. "There are others like me, like my family, and though I might loathe our ways and wish they were different, I have no right to jeopardize their existence by allowing my family's secret to be revealed. That would happen if I stayed."

Tears fell from her eyes and streamed down her cheeks, rivers of moisture turned golden by the glow of the morning sun as its newborn warmth touched her skin. She couldn't argue with him, couldn't plead with him to stay with her, because she knew he was right. If the authorities, the public, found out what he was, they would lock him away in some experimental laboratory. They would see him not as a man with feelings, with emotions and sensitivities, but as a specimen of something they didn't understand. He would be deemed nothing more than something that could give them, if they could discover his secret, the ability to lengthen their lives.

"I know," she whispered, finally.

He released her hands then and, knowing what he was doing was wrong, that it would only deepen the pain and anguish that already dwelt within their hearts, Alexandre slipped his arms around Rachel's waist and pulled her to him.

The tangy fragrance of freshly turned earth, of pine trees spreading their boughs in embrace of a new spring, of the lush blades of an emerald meadow waking to a new summer's dawn, and wild flowers and bayou ferns opening lazily to the warmth of a sultry southern sun, suddenly enveloped Rachel.

His lips claimed hers, as his love had claimed her heart. The ecstasy of his touch brought a moan from her throat, only to sweep faintly toward his lips and be swallowed beyond their sweet curves. The fire of loneliness, anguish and mutual need burned between them, turning what Alexandre had intended as merely a gentle goodbye into a hungry, soul-wrenching embrace. His mouth ravished hers as his heart cried out against the cruelties of their fate and his arms held her locked against him, like bands of steel, strong, powerful and unrelenting.

This was what had always been missing from Rachel's life, this man, with his strangely gentle yet savage love, his mysterious and forbidden existence. This man who was of her world, and yet apart from it. Nothing had prepared her for Alexandre, for what he was, for the complexities she would have to face to remain with him. Yet as his kiss deepened, branding her soul forever his, entwining their spirits, she knew, with a certainty beyond question, that to be apart from him would be more agony than she could stand. All the complexities in the world, all the hardships, the hiding, the running, would be nothing compared to spending the rest of her life without him, missing him, yearning to feel his touch, to hear his voice.

Her fingers slipped within the curls of hair at his nape, disappearing within the silken black strands as she held him to her, savoring his kiss and wanting it never to end.

Alexandre felt as if his heart were shattering into a million pieces, pulling inward and then self-destructing, like the implosion of a star. Nothing, not one thing in nearly five hundred years, had touched him the way Rachel's love did, and nothing had ever meant more to him.

Suddenly, knowing if he didn't break their embrace, if he didn't pull away from her now and say goodbye he never would, Alexandre forced his arms from around her. He clasped her shoulders and, dragging his lips from hers, held her firmly in place and stepped back from her.

Rachel stared up at him, passion still moist upon her

lips, her heart pounding a thunderous beat within her breast.

"I have to go, Rachel," Alexandre said, his voice nearly breaking on her name. He fought to remain strong, to remain in control. His hands released their hold on her arms and dropped to his sides. A sad smile tugged at the corners of his mouth. "I'll never forget you, Rachel." Once again he reached out and caressed her cheek with the tips of his fingers. He wanted to tell her he loved her, that she was his life, the only thing that mattered to him now, but he couldn't, because that would only cause her more pain. "No matter how long I live," he said instead, "I'll never forget you."

He turned to go.

"Alexandre," Rachel said, fighting to hold back the tears that threatened to burst from her eyes and run like a raging torrent down her cheeks. "Please . . ."

He paused and looked back at her. "It's no good, *chère,*" he said, his deep voice like a roll of velvet on the still morning air. "It can never be for us."

"Yes, it can."

He stared at her long and hard, knowing instinctively what she was saying, and struggling against himself to accept it. His heart said yes, but his mind screamed no. He could take her, he could make her like himself, but how long would it be before she hated him for it? Before she loathed the existence she was forced to lead, as he had loathed it for over four hundred years? He shook his head and began to turn away again.

"I love you, Alexandre," Rachel said. "I know what you are, I know what you have to do, what you need to survive, and I don't care. I love you."

He stopped again, but did not look back at her. He couldn't. He wanted so desperately to drag her once again into his arms, to taste her lips beneath his, to hold her to him forever, and if he looked back, if he looked into her eyes again, he would not be able to deny himself, or her, what they both wanted.

"Alexandre." Rachel closed the distance between them and then stepped around him so that she stood facing him, forcing him to once again look down at her. "I love you," she whispered again. "I love you more than anything. More than life. If you leave me, I . . ." her voice broke and she fought to regain her composure, tenuous as it was. "I can't face tomorrow without you, Alexandre." She blinked back her tears. "Take me," she said softly. "Make me like you, so that we can be together, in your world."

Alexandre stared at her, struggling to deny her. The fury of battle raged within him as he fought to keep his hands at his sides and not reach out for her.

"No," he groaned finally, and shook his head. "No."

Slipping her arms around his neck, Rachel pulled his head down toward hers and pressed her body to his long, hard length. Her lips captured his in a kiss that was gentle and giving, a kiss that promised him sunshine and laughter, and hundreds of tomorrows filled with love.

"I love you, Alexandre," she whispered into his mouth.

He was unable to resist her. His arms wrapped once again around her waist and pulled her to him, crushing her against his form. He reveled in the sweetness of her lips. And I love you, he said silently, afraid to say the words aloud, afraid that if he did, he would lose all self-control and do as she'd asked.

Suddenly he felt a searing pain deep within his loins. It was not the gnawing, delicious ache of passion that he would expect at having her in his arms. Instead, it hit him savagely, a burning, tearing pain that ripped at his insides, tore him from her arms and sent him to his knees in writhing agony. A low wail split from his lips, its tempo rising with each second that passed as Alexandre, arms wrapped tightly about his chest, doubled over on the ground in an effort to fight the torment that had suddenly erupted within his body.

"Alexandre," Rachel screamed, dropping to her knees beside him and clutching at his shoulder. "What's wrong?"

He rocked back and forth, his entire body shaking with violent tremors, and continued to groan in pain, every muscle held whiplash tight, his eyes blazing dark with disbelief at what was happening to him.

Rachel's heart thudded frantically as fear gripped her. She didn't know what to do to help him, or if there was anything she could do. "Alexandre," she cried again, terrified, "what's happening? What's wrong?"

He shook his head as he continued to rock back and forth in an effort to deal with the pain slashing at his insides, tearing at his limbs and burning his flesh. Every cell, every muscle, fiber and length of bone within him felt as if it were splintering, exploding or erupting in a burst of flame. He felt his features contort first in one direction and then another. His hands, clasped under his armpits, clenched and unclenched as their length snapped long, short, and long again.

Then, as suddenly as it had started, the attack was over. Alexandre sat, exhausted, on the ground.

"Alexandre," Rachel said, her tone hushed, "are you all right? What was that? What happened?" She brushed a lock of hair from his forehead and ran a caressing hand down his cheek. "Alexandre, talk to me, please. What happened?"

He inhaled deeply, exhaled, and then struggled to his feet, pulling her with him. Turning, he looked directly at the sun as it rose higher in the sky, breaking over the jagged tips of the trees on the horizon and filling the sky with the light of a new day. Alexandre reached out and, wrapping an arm around Rachel's shoulders, pulled her to his side.

"I didn't believe her," he said, a note of awe in his voice.

"Believe who?" Rachel echoed, watching him.

He turned toward her and pulled her once again into his embrace. "Catherine. I always thought the stories she told me were just that, stories, to make me feel better."

Rachel frowned. "What stories? Alexandre, what are you talking about? What just happened to you?"

He shook his head. "I have to make sure, Rachel. I have to be sure it's true before I tell you."

"Tell me what?"

He looked at the small scratch on her neck that Yvette had caused that first night when she'd attacked Rachel. He reached up and ran a fingernail over it, reopening the wound.

Rachel jerked back as a sting of pain burned her skin. "What's going on?"

Pulling her back into his arms, Alexandre pressed his lips to Rachel's neck and sucked softly. A droplet of blood slid onto his tongue. He drew back then, tasting the tangy flavor of her life force, letting it settle over his tongue and slip down his throat. His eyes closed and he waited, but nothing happened. The hunger didn't come.

He opened his eyes and looked down at her. "It's over," he said, and smiled.

"Over?"

Alexandre laughed then, a deep, rumbling sound filled with joy and happiness, and drew her tighter into his embrace, savoring the feel of her in his arms, her body pressed against his.

"Alexandre?" Rachel said. "What's happened?"

He stopped laughing and brushed his lips across hers. "It's over, *chère.*"

"What . . . ?"

"After Danielle disappeared Catherine called me to her room one night. I was despondent, and I think she was afraid for me. I had come to hate what I was, and for some reason, my great grandmother understood my feelings. Maybe," he shrugged, "maybe in her own way she felt that way, too. I don't know." He hugged Rachel to him. "That evening she told me that, if I truly wanted not to be a *Chasseur,* there was a way."

"Then why haven't you . . . ?"

"Love," he said simply. "She said that only the love of a human could change me." He tightened his arms around Rachel. "But the woman who loved me had to know what I was. She had to accept me for what I was, a *Chasseur* . . . a vampire, and still love me. That's why, Catherine said, it hadn't happened with Danielle. When Danielle discovered the truth, or rather, suspected it, and I insisted on confirming it, she was horrified. She couldn't accept it and turned away from me."

Rachel stared up at him. "She didn't truly love you."

"No, but I thought she did, so when Catherine called me to her room and told me about the 'cure,' I didn't believe her. I thought she was only trying to ease the guilt I felt and feed my hope. That's why I felt I had to leave you. I didn't believe her, and I couldn't subject you to the same horrors of life that my kind endure."

She was afraid to hope. Rachel looked into his eyes, but there was no swirling pull, no other worlds reaching out to draw her into their realms. "You mean, because

I love you and don't care what you are, that you're no longer a . . . that you're . . ."

"Free," he said, and covered her mouth once more with his.

Dear Readers,

If you enjoyed *Night's Immortal Kiss* then be prepared, because we're not done.

NIGHT'S IMMORTAL TOUCH
is a July 1995 release.

You think Alexandre is the only Beaumondier left, but perhaps, just perhaps, you are wrong . . .

Physically injured, confused, and fearing for her very existence, Suzanne Beaumondier fled Sans Souci as it burned to the ground. Now a year later, her strength renewed, her courage revived, she returns to New Orleans to confront her brother, Alexandre, and discover if her suspicions are right: he is the one responsible for the destruction of their family.

But with Suzanne's return, a series of murders begin in the old French Quarter of New Orleans, murders which remind Alexandre of the way Le Chasseurs kill. Brother against sister, the hunter and the hunted. It's a battle that must be fought to the death . . .

Happy Reading!

Cheryln Jac
Aka Cheryl Biggs

Biography

Cheryln Jac lives at the foot of Mt. Diablo in California, with her husband and five cats. She is the author of several other Zebra/Pinnacle titles including: *Shadows in Time,* and her upcoming sister book to *Night's Immortal Kiss, Night's Immortal Touch,* and another time travel, *TimeSwept.*

Writing as Cheryl Biggs, her titles include: *Mississippi Flame, Across a Rebel Sea,* and an upcoming series, *Hearts Deceived, Hearts Denied, Hearts Defiant,* and *Hearts Divided.* Readers may write to Cheryl for bookmarks or promos at: P. O. Box 6557, Concord, CA 94520

**IF ROMANCE BE THE FRUIT OF LIFE—
READ ON—
BREATH-QUICKENING HISTORICALS FROM PINNACLE**

WILDCAT (772, $4.99)
by Rochelle Wayne
No man alive could break Diana Preston's fiery spirit . . . until seductive Vince Gannon galloped onto Diana's sprawling family ranch. Vince, a man with dark secrets, would sweep her into his world of danger and desire. And Diana couldn't deny the powerful yearnings that branded her as his own, for all time!

THE HIGHWAY MAN (765, $4.50)
by Nadine Crenshaw
When a trumped-up murder charge forced beautiful Jane Fitzpatrick to flee her home, she was found and sheltered by the highwayman—a man as dark and dangerous as the secrets that haunted him. As their hiding place became a place of shared dreams—and soaring desires—Jane knew she'd found the love she'd been yearning for!

SILKEN SPURS (756, $4.99)
by Jane Archer
Beautiful Harmony Harper, leader of a notorious outlaw gang, rode the desert plains of New Mexico in search of justice and vengeance. Now she has captured powerful and privileged Thor Clarke-Jargon, who is everything Harmony has ever hated—and all she will ever want. And after Harmony has taken the handsome adventurer hostage, she herself has become a captive—of her own desires!

WYOMING ECSTASY (740, $4.50)
by Gina Robins
Feisty criminal investigator, July MacKenzie, solicits the partnership of the legendary half-breed gunslinger-detective Nacona Blue. After being turned down, July—never one to accept the meaning of the word no—finds a way to convince Nacona to be her partner . . . first in business—then in passion. Across the wilds of Wyoming, and always one step ahead of trouble, July surrenders to passion's searing demands!

Available wherever paperbacks are sold, or order direct from the Publisher. Send cover price plus 50¢ per copy for mailing and handling to Penguin USA, P.O. Box 999, c/o Dept. 17109, Bergenfield, NJ 07621. Residents of New York and Tennessee must include sales tax. DO NOT SEND CASH.

GOT AN INSATIABLE THIRST FOR VAMPIRES?
LET PINNACLE QUENCH IT!

BLOOD FEUD (705, $4.50)
by Sam Siciliano
SHE is a mistress of darkness—coldly sensual and dangerously seductive. HE is a master of manipulation with the power to take life and grant *unlife.* THEY are two ancient vampires who have sworn to eliminate each other. Now, after centuries, the time has come for a face-to-face confrontation—and neither will rest until one of them is destroyed!

DARKNESS ON THE ICE (687, $4.50)
by Lois Tilton
It was World War II, and the Nazis had found the perfect weapon. Wolff, an SS officer, with an innate talent—and thirst—for killing, was actually a vampire. His strength and stealth allowed him to drain and drink the blood of enemy sentries. Wolff stalked his prey for the Nazi cause—but killed them to satisfy his own insatiable hunger!

THIRST OF THE VAMPIRE (649, $4.50)
by T. Lucien Wright
Phillipe Brissot is no ordinary killer—he is a creature of the night—a vampire. Through the centuries he has satisfied his thirst for blood while carrying out his quest of vengeance against his ancient enemies, the Marat Family. Now journalist, Mike Marat is investigating his cousin's horrible "murder" unaware that Phillipe is watching him and preparing to strike against the Marats one final time . . .

BLIND HUNGER (714, $4.50)
by Darke Parke
Widowed and blind, pretty Patty Hunsacker doesn't feel like going on with her life . . . until the day a man arrives at her door, claiming to be the twin brother of her late husband. Patty welcomes Mark into her life but soon finds herself living in a world of terror as well as darkness! For she makes the shocking discovery that "Mark" is really Matt—and he isn't dead—he's a vampire. And he plans on showing his wife that loving a vampire can be quite a bloody affair!

Available wherever paperbacks are sold, or order direct from the Publisher. Send cover price plus 50¢ per copy for mailing and handling to Zebra Books, Dept. 000, 475 Park Avenue South, New York, N.Y. 10016. Residents of New York and Tennessee must include sales tax. DO NOT SEND CASH. For a free Zebra/Pinnacle catalog please write to the above address.

D0001347

Come talk to your favorite authors and get the inside scoop on everything that's going on in the world of romance publishing, from the only online service that's designed exclusively for the publishing industry.

With Z-Talk Online Information Service, the most innovative and exciting computer bulletin board around, you can:

- ♥ CHAT "LIVE" WITH AUTHORS, FELLOW ROMANCE READERS, AND OTHER MEMBERS OF THE ROMANCE PUBLISHING COMMUNITY.
- ♥ FIND OUT ABOUT UPCOMING TITLES BEFORE THEY'RE RELEASED.
- ♥ COPY THOUSANDS OF FILES AND GAMES TO YOUR OWN COMPUTER.
- ♥ READ REVIEWS OF ROMANCE TITLES.
- ♥ HAVE UNLIMITED USE OF ELECTRONIC MAIL.
- ♥ POST MESSAGES ON OUR DOZENS OF TOPIC BOARDS.

All it takes is a computer and a modem to get online with Z-Talk. Set your modem to 8/N/1, and dial 212-935-0270. If you need help, call the System Operator, at 212-407-1533. There's a two week free trial period. After that, annual membership is only $ 60.00.

See you online!

brought to you by Zebra Books

KENSINGTON PUBLISHING CORP.